Concerto

CONCERTO

Paul Myers

CENTURY
LONDON SYDNEY AUCKLAND JOHANNESBURG

First published in Great Britain in 1993
by Century, Random Century House,
20 Vauxhall Bridge Road, London SW1V 2SA

Copyright © Paul Myers 1993

A catalogue record for this book is available from the British Library

ISBN 0 7126 3954 3

Typeset by Pure Tech Corporation, Pondicherry, India

Printed and bound in Great Britain by
Mackays of Chatham PLC, Chatham, Kent

For Nicholas and John

Author's note

Authors sometimes find themselves in the embarrassing position of being accused of reproducing the truth in a thinly veiled novel form. On several occasions, I have been confronted by people claiming that I have depicted them as characters in my books. One even assured me that I had used the same 'speech patterns' and, despite my protestations, could not be persuaded otherwise, insisting that, if it was not deliberate, I must have done it subconsciously!

This book is entirely a work of fiction, and although a number of famous musicians and locations are identified, none of the characters or situations is based upon any real person or event.

P.M.

1

The auditorium of the Musikverein was hushed. On the stage, the Vienna Philharmonic had finished tuning, and conversation in the hall was reduced to a whisper in anticipation of the conductor's arrival. One could sense the undercurrent of excitement, for although music was a way of life and Viennese concertgoers usually affected a blasé attitude towards all performers, an appearance by the legendary Karl Henrik Vonheim had to be acknowledged as a special occasion. The audience waited restlessly.

The Arts correspondent from the *International Herald-Tribune* nudged her companion and muttered, 'Jesus, if he doesn't show soon, I'm going to wet my pants!' She was a petite, angular woman in her late thirties, wearing a two-piece black suit with the sort of perfect bow at the neck of her silk blouse that only an American woman knows how to tie. She was also doing her best to sound hard-boiled.

The Englishman at her side chuckled. 'I'd hold that until you hear what he does with the Mahler Ninth.'

'The suspense is killing me.' She glanced at the orchestra, which was sitting as stiffly as a parade of soldiers awaiting inspection. 'Are you sure he's going to make it?'

'Positive. He never cancels. It's a matter of timing.'

'I hope you're right. This place feels like it's going to blow its top.'

'That's the way Vonheim likes it. He'll wait until the last second before he comes out. Vladimir Horowitz used the same trick, holding everything to the final moment. You could almost touch the electricity. Is this the first time you've seen him?'

She nodded. 'I only started this job a few months ago. It's a hell of an introduction!' Her gaze took in the golden auditorium, with its heavy Austro-Hungarian Empire decorations. Full-breasted caryatids hovered over them. 'I feel as though I'm witnessing some kind of religious experience. He's only a conductor, for God's sake! How about you? I guess you've seen him before?'

Peter Meredith shrugged. 'Most of my life, whenever I've had the chance. Besides, he's not just a conductor; he's Karl Vonheim, in a class of his own.'

'I hear you.' She was eager to appear well-informed. 'Who'd have thought a Norwegian would end up on top of the heap? I mean, it's not a country you'd normally associate with heavyweight music-makers.' She eyed Peter severely, and he suspected that myopia was the cause of her intense stare. 'Did your magazine send you all the way from London for this one concert?'

'Lord, no. They won't usually cover the cost of a taxi to the Festival Hall! I'm reporting on the entire *Festwochen*, as well as tomorrow's conference. That's the biggest event of the week.'

'You think so?'

'Of course. It's the first time Vonheim's met the press in twenty years.'

'You're kidding!'

He shook his head. 'We're usually out of bounds. He never gives interviews, and nobody's allowed to attend his rehearsals. You've either got to be a member of his inner sanctum or play in an orchestra if you want to hear him talk.'

'Why all the secrecy?'

'Who knows? It's not so much secrecy as a sort of mystique. Conductors are somewhat aloof at the best of times. I suppose it comes from having absolute control of all those musicians. Vonheim's totally removed from the ordinary world. He certainly doesn't talk to us mere press mortals. He's up on Mount Olympus, communing with Beethoven and the gods.'

'That's crazy!' She seemed outraged. 'The man's a superstar already. He's made more movies than Sly Stallone! People have a right . . .'

'Not according to Vonheim. As far as he's concerned, his life's dedicated to music, and he's not interested in talking about it. The last time someone tried to interview him, he told them to listen to the music. He claimed it was more interesting than anything he had to say and would tell them more about him than any words could.'

'That's a load of crap! A great artist is public property. Who does he think he is?'

She was about to continue, but a man in the row in front turned in his seat and glared at them, hissing slightly. The gesture was so vehement that she was silent.

There was a movement on the left side of the stage, and all attention was directed towards the point where the conductor would appear. The orchestra rose. Someone started to clap, and a wave of applause surged through the hall, gathering momentum. The dramatic build-up was released by physical energy, and the sound increased in volume. Several men stood, their hands level with their shoulders as their arms swung in exaggerated arcs.

The maestro had arrived.

Karl Vonheim walked slowly towards the podium, seeming to ignore the thunderous reception and occasionally pausing to smile and place a hand on the arm of the musician he was passing, as if sharing a private joke. A man of medium height, his impeccably tailored suit emphasized broad shoulders that tapered to a narrow waist and, although in his late sixties, he moved with the grace of an athlete. He greeted the leader of the orchestra with a brief handshake, then stepped lightly onto the podium, his face expressionless. He waited a moment, then raised his arms, the palms of his hands open, as though accepting the public's adulation, and smiled. The cheering increased.

The woman from the *Herald-Tribune* placed her mouth close to Peter's ear to make herself audible. 'I didn't realise he was so beautiful!' Her voice was awe-filled. 'I take it all back. Anyone who looks like that can do what he likes!'

'He usually does.' She was wearing too much perfume, and he found himself enveloped in Diorella. Watching Vonheim, it struck Peter that the conductor was indeed an exceptionally handsome man. He had never thought about it before, having always been absorbed in the music. The maestro had aged since those early years when he had first seen him. Silver at his temples framed the finely chiselled features and sensitive face, and heavier lines permanently furrowed the corners of his eyes and mouth. But his appearance remained youthful and, even at a distance, the blue-grey eyes were penetratingly alert. It was the face of an actor, mobile and expressive, who would be equally at home playing Lear or Falstaff.

3

The conductor turned to face the orchestra, and the auditorium was immediately hushed again. After the ovation that had greeted his arrival, the silence was almost shocking. His head was bowed, his arms at his sides, like a supplicant before a high altar.

Vonheim's hand moved, and the baton, barely visible, directed the orchestra. Low strings, horn and harp exchanged calls, there was the sound of muted trumpets, and the violins introduced the melody of the great *andante* that opens the symphony. Around him, Peter could feel the audience settling comfortably into their seats, like travellers embarking on a long voyage. The work would last nearly an hour and a half, during which it would pass through a vast panorama of changing emotions.

Peter watched Vonheim. He stood very erect, his torso rigid, his right hand moving gently to give the slightest indication of the rhythm. His left hand, graceful as a ballet dancer's, hovered delicately, clearly indicating gradations of dynamics and expression. He felt as though he could see the sounds that the maestro was drawing from the orchestra, and the players responded immediately to each gesture. When he was in his nineties, Leopold Stokowski claimed that conducting was easy: he could teach anyone to do it in ten minutes. It was all a matter of the hands and the eyes. But he had left out the vital ingredients: a lifetime of study and experience, coupled with that rare power of communication that only a great conductor possesses. Was it arrogance or deep conviction or a kind of metaphysical magnetism that gave Vonheim the power to mould and shape the music from more than a hundred individual musicians? The invisible link between conductor and players was uncanny, and he could only marvel at the strength and plasticity with which he directed the orchestra.

He glanced at the woman from the *Herald-Tribune*, who stared at Vonheim, her eyes wide, as though hypnotised. Apparently, she was not as hard-boiled as she pretended. Between the movements, she did not look round. Her gaze remained fixed on the conductor's back, awaiting his next command.

The symphony ends with a long and deeply moving *adagio*, representing for many the composer's final leave-taking from a world that had neither understood nor appreciated his music. How ironic that Mahler, aware that death was near, had gone 'home' to Vienna, the city whose musical politics and anti-semitism had driven him out a decade earlier. But he had prophesied that his time would come and, that evening in the Musikverein, his words were fulfilled. As the sound of the final chord slowly died, seemingly suspended in time, the maestro remained motionless, his head again bowed, and the hall was absolutely still. No-one dared to break the spell. Then the applause began, starting tentatively and building to a great roar. Despite himself, Peter found that he was caught up in the drama of the moment.

Vonheim turned towards the audience and lowered his head, then stepped from the podium to shake hands with the first violinist. He faced the auditorium again, nodding and half smiling, and the cheering increased. After a momentary hesitation, he walked briskly off the stage.

Standing at Peter's side, the woman from the *Herald-Tribune* seemed slightly dazed, her hands clapping automatically. She noticed that he had stopped. 'What's the matter? Didn't you like it?'

'Yes, of course, but there's no point in continuing. Vonheim never returns for a second bow.' He smiled. 'I think most of the people here know it, but they'll go on applauding anyway.'

'That's arrogant! Why can't he come out again, like anyone else?'

'Because he's Karl Vonheim. That makes him different from anyone else.'

The maestro had not reappeared, and the audience started to leave. A few stalwarts continued to clap, but their enthusiasm was diminishing. When the orchestra began moving off the stage, the applause petered out.

The American shook her head in wonder. 'What an incredible experience. I don't believe what I just heard!' She grinned. 'And what a beautiful man! Those concert movies don't do him justice. Instead of taking pictures of a bunch of players, they should leave the cameras focused on his face.'

'I don't think he'd approve.'

'I sure as hell would! He should have come out again, for one last look.'

'He doesn't need to. Besides, you'll anticipate his next concert all the more.'

'I guess so.' She sighed. 'At the last Bernstein concert I went to, Lenny insisted on kissing every goddam player in the orchestra before he left, and we just had to stand there, clapping our hands and watching him. By the time he'd finished with the back row, my palms were sore!'

A small, portly figure awaited the maestro outside his dressing-room. Zoltán Teleki's close-cropped white curls looked as though they had been pasted to his scalp. They did not match his pink, cherubic face, which had hardly aged over the many years they had worked together. Nor had his taste in clothes varied. He always wore a black and white herring-bone suit whose colour and cut were inappropriately youthful and, Vonheim thought, styled for a used-car salesman.

As the maestro's international manager, Teleki wielded great power in the music world, which he manipulated zealously, bullying and cajoling clients, managers, entrepreneurs, orchestras, television producers, travel agents, head waiters, hotel staff and anyone else who came into contact with Karl Vonheim. He smiled readily, exuding old-world Hungarian charm, but his eyes, beneath rolls of fat, watched coldly and without compassion. He had few friends but fewer overt enemies, because nobody wanted to cross swords with the maestro's manager. In Vonheim's presence, Teleki was ill at ease, nervously shifting his considerable weight from one foot to the other. His geniality was tempered by a deeply rooted magyar instinct for survival.

As Vonheim drew close, he noted that Teleki was breathing heavily. There was a thin film of perspiration on his forehead. Presumably, he had run from his seat to reach the dressing-room first.

'Bravo, maestro! An unforgettable performance – historic!'

'Thank you, Zoltán. I think it went well.' He smiled gently. 'The orchestra lived up to its magnificent reputation for a change.'

'How could they do otherwise?'

'Is everything arranged for tomorrow morning?'

'Everything.' He hesitated. 'I think I should mention that ORF is sending a television crew. I hope that's acceptable?' Seeing Vonheim frown slightly, he continued quickly, 'You see, they're from the News department. I had already turned down the Music department. I told them they couldn't have an interview.'

'Very well. In fact, in view of what we're doing, I think it's a good idea.' Teleki looked relieved. 'Will everyone be there?'

'Naturally. They're all desperate to be included! I think I counted journalists from eleven countries. Believe me, maestro, the place will be packed! The BBC from London wanted a camera crew as well, but I told them to share a line with the ORF.'

'Good.' As if anticipating Teleki's next inquiry, he said, 'No visitors, please. I shall be leaving immediately.' He sighed. 'It's an exhausting piece.'

The Hungarian looked disappointed. He had promised two record producers and a prominent local politician brief audiences with the maestro. 'As you wish.'

'Thank you. Is Erich waiting outside for me?'

'Yes, maestro.' Teleki cleared his throat uneasily. 'I'm glad you mentioned him.' The manager paused, uncertain whether to continue.

'Is there a problem?'

'Well, not exactly.' Teleki paused again, but the maestro nodded, as if to encourage him. 'You see, Erich was involved in a rather embarrassing incident last night. It seems he was being very indiscreet. I think perhaps he'd drunk a little more than he should have. There's a nightclub called The Hussar. It's just off the Graben. Fortunately, the owner's a friend of mine, so he managed to keep the whole thing quiet. It's a respectable place.'

'Yes?' The maestro seemed puzzled.

Teleki was clearly embarrassed. 'Erich was pestering one of the young men sitting at the bar. Apparently, he wouldn't leave him alone and, when my friend interceded, he became extremely ... offensive.'

'I see.'

The manager spoke quickly. 'They tried to explain to him that it wasn't that sort of bar. Vienna has plenty of places that cater to the ...' He left the sentence unfinished, but continued, 'Heaven knows, I've got nothing against the gay community ...'

Vonheim smiled. 'Some of your best friends ... ?'

'Exactly.' He was relieved that the maestro was in a relaxed mood. 'Nevertheless, it's not the sort of thing one wants publicised, especially in a city like Vienna. You know how people here love to gossip.' He lowered his voice. 'I wouldn't want your name involved. The young man Erich ... approached comes from a very good family, and ...' He decided to leave the rest of the story untold. 'Anyway, they bundled Erich into a taxi and got him out of the way before he attracted any more attention. I told my friend you would appreciate his help.'

'Yes, of course.' Vonheim placed a hand on the man's shoulder. 'It sounds as though everything was handled very competently, Zoltán. You know, Erich may work for me, but I can't be responsible for him when he's away from the house.'

'No, of course not.' Teleki was visibly relieved by the conductor's reaction. 'I thought I should mention it to you.'

'I'm glad you did.' Vonheim was silent for a moment. 'I'll have a quiet word with Erich. As you say, there are plenty of bars that offer the sort of entertainment he wants.' He smiled. 'Thank you for telling me. I'll rely on you to look after anything that needs to be done.' His voice softened. 'You always do.'

'I'll make sure it goes no farther.'

'Good.' Vonheim opened the door to his dressing-room. 'I'd better make my exit before we're besieged.' He grinned charmingly. 'Will you stand guard?'

'Don't worry, they won't get past me!'

'And we'll see each other in the morning?'

'Yes. The conference begins at eleven.'

'I hadn't forgotten. We'll be there just after. You can start things.' His confidence restored, Teleki beamed. 'With great pleasure!'

'Thank you again for looking after the situation with Erich. Let me know if you run into any further problems.'

Before the manager could reply, the door to the dressing-room had closed.

Vonheim sank into a chair at his dressing-table and, taking a towel, buried his face in it. He was physically tired, but his mind still relived the music. For a moment, he wondered idly whether he had held on too long to the final chord of the symphony. The silence that had preceded the first burst of applause had seemed endless. What was it his old master had said? 'Good taste is the ability to gauge the length of a pause. Too little makes it superficial; too much, and it's bathos.' He removed the towel and stared at his reflection. What a long time since he had heard those words!

Almost impersonally, he examined the features brightly illuminated by the lights surrounding the mirror. He smiled. Was that what a conductor was supposed to look like?

He glanced down at the open concert programme that Zoltán had carefully placed on the table. The photograph was an old one, taken some years earlier, subtly lit and retouched to remove all but the gentlest indications of age. Under it, the text began, 'Born in Norway,' [the date conveniently omitted!] 'Karl Henrik Vonheim has become one of the world's . . .'

Norway. His eyes returned to the mirror, and he nodded almost imperceptibly. A survivor. He was staring at the face of a survivor.

2

The two soldiers, shapeless in bulky overcoats, their faces swathed in woollen scarves, tramped along a narrow path bordering the railway line. Deep snow was frozen solid in the sub-zero temperature, and its surface crackled under the weight of their boots. The slighter of the two slipped, losing his balance and dropping his rifle.

His companion reached out to break his fall. 'Watch yourself!' He spoke gruffly. He was a big, heavy man, and his gloved fingers almost encircled the other's forearm. 'Dig your heels in, or you'll end up on your arse!' The boy bent cautiously to retrieve the gun. Christ! Was this all the Wehrmacht could supply? 'Get the snow out of that muzzle!'

The young soldier looked round helplessly, then snapped a twig from a nearby sapling and scraped at the end of the barrel. 'Do you think we'll need guns?'

'I hope to God not!' He glanced down the sloping track through narrowed eyes, wincing from the icy wind that cut into the exposed skin of his face and blurred his vision. 'All we're supposed to do is check this stretch of line.'

'What for?' The boy was shivering violently.

'Explosives.' He walked on slowly, limping slightly. The field hospital had done a bad job on his leg wound, but it had earned him the reprieve of being posted to the relative safety of Norway. 'Bastard saboteurs are always trying to blow it up. It's the link between Bergen and Oslo, and the stretch between here and Finse is the most exposed. Derail a train, and it ends up at the bottom of that gorge. How long have you been here?'

'A few days. I was posted here last week.'

'I thought I hadn't seen you before. These mountains lead up to what they call the Hardanga Vidda: that's the plateau that separates one side of the country from the other. To get across, you have to go over the top.' He glanced across the track towards the precipitous drop beyond. 'It's a good thing you weren't walking on the other side, or you'd have said goodbye to more than that rifle!'

'Yes.' The boy was shaking. 'I don't like heights.'

'You'll get used to them. No point walking on the outside in this wind. Stay next to the hillside. Shit, it's cold! What have you got under that coat?'

'Just my uniform.'

'No wonder you're freezing. Find yourself some old newspapers, and stuff them under your shirt. They'll help to keep you warm. I learned that on the Russian front. Didn't you ever see tramps sleeping under them in the park?'

The boy shook his head. 'I'm from a village near Augsburg. We let tramps sleep in the barn.'

'A farm boy, are you? I thought you were Bavarian, from your accent. I'm from Berlin. There's a railway hut just down the line. When we get there, I'll give you a couple of sheets of paper to stick under your jacket.'

The boy moved slightly faster, but his boots slid precariously on the frozen surface, forcing him to slow down. 'D'you think we'll find . . . anything?'

'It wouldn't surprise me.' Explaining, he added, 'Troop trains. We're pulling everyone out of here.'

'Why?'

'Because it's all but finished. We're done for.'

'You mean the war?'

He nodded. 'They're already across the Rhine. It can't last much longer.'

'How do you know?' The boy's voice trembled.

'I keep my ears open. They're shipping everyone out for a last-ditch stand. The idea is to get them to Berlin before they're cut off, but I wouldn't fancy their chances. You should thank your lucky stars you're up here, freezing your balls off. You've got a better chance than those poor bastards! He was silent, letting the information sink in, and hesitated before asking, 'What's your name?' In the normal way, he did not like to know names or personal details. Over the past two years, too many of them had ended up as corpses, but this kid was little older than his own son.

11

'Werner.'

'Well, Werner, keep your eyes and your wits about you, and you'll get through. In a few months from now, you'll be back on the farm.' The boy appeared to relax, reassured. They were approaching a corner of the steep mountainside, where tall pines offered additional shelter from the wind. 'I seem to remember that hut is just round the next bend. We can stand inside for a few minutes, and get our circulation back.'

Werner nodded. 'What should we look for?'

'Anything unusual along the track. Watch out for snow that's uneven. There hasn't been a fall for twenty-four hours. D'you know dynamite when you see it?'

'No.'

'Well I do. If you notice anything at all, for Christ's sake tell me!'

The boy's voice was tremulous again. 'What do we do if we find any?'

'Disconnect it and get it away from the rails, then get back up to the field telephone and report it. You won't want to hang round, I can tell you!'

'Why not?'

Taut nerves made him angry. 'Because the stuff's wired to a detonator, and the chances are there'll be a Norwegian at the other end, waiting to push the bloody plunger down! If he sees us dismantling the dynamite, we're in trouble!'

'What should we do?'

'Run like the bloody clappers! I don't know about you, but I'm not planning to die like a hero.' The boy nodded without speaking, his eyes on the ground, and he took pity. The gesture reminded him of his son. 'Don't worry.' His voice was gentler. 'It's not likely to happen.' He pulled back the end of his glove to look at his watch. 'There's a train due any minute. If they were going to attack it, they would have done so by now.'

'You think so?'

'I'm sure. Once the train passes, there won't be another for about three hours, so we can relax. There's a little village – Fjordby, I think it's called – just on the other side of this hill. I've been there before. It shouldn't take us more than about half an hour to get there. We'll see if we can find something to eat.'

'Is there a café?'

12

'Christ, no! There isn't even a shop. It's only about ten houses and a church. It's a funny little place, cut off from the world, but the people are quite friendly, for Norwegians. The last time I was there, I knocked on one of the doors, and the woman inside gave me some bread and bowl of soup. I think she realised I didn't like the idea of being there any more than she did.'

The boy was uncertain. 'Is it all right for us to go there? I thought we were supposed to stay close to the railway line.'

He shrugged. 'Who's going to miss us? Once the train's gone through, we've done our job. There's no harm in showing a little initiative. That's something you'd better learn if you're going to play soldiers.'

They rounded the corner, and a long valley, cut into the mountains, came into view. Fir trees covered the upper slopes on either side, giving way to grass-covered meadows and farmland. A thin ribbon of river glistened in the basin. A mile away, a passenger train was beginning the slow ascent up the narrow shelf of land cut into the hillside. It was still too distant to be heard, but he sensed a slight vibration in the track at his feet.

'There's the train.' Despite his discomfort, he smiled. 'It looks like a toy from here, doesn't it?' Quickening his pace, he gazed across the tranquil valley. Apart from the train, slowly approaching, nothing moved. In the far distance, at the foot of the valley, he could make out some brightly painted farm buildings. The sun was breaking through the clouds, its light brilliantly reflected by the snow. 'It's a beautiful place. I'll come back here one day, when this lot's over.' He grunted. 'But not at this bloody time of the year! Come on, there's the hut. We can stand inside and watch the train go past from there. Poor buggers! I don't envy them.'

They were already inside the shelter when the explosion shook the ground. The wooden structure trembled and swayed. Its single window shattered, and a gust of cold air blew in their faces. For a moment, it felt as though the flimsy building would collapse. He heard the sound rumble across the distant hills.

Swearing unintelligibly, the man flung the door open, his rifle at the ready. The train was less than a quarter of a mile away, its front enveloped in smoke and a shower of snow and earth, but it continued to move forward as though unaffected. As the smoke cleared, he could see a gaping crater under the lines, which were bent out of shape. The engine was pointed slightly sideways, bumping across the track towards the outside rim of the ledge on which it was travelling. Then, almost in slow motion, it tipped lazily over the side of the hill. The huge machine gathered momentum as it rolled down the steep slope, pulling carriages with it, and the whole train was dragged down by its weight. There was the piercing squeal of grinding, crushed metal, the explosion of smashing glass and escaping steam, and thousands of tons of steel plunged downward, like a grotesque iron snake, twisting and writhing in agonised death throes. The few trees and boulders in its path could not halt it, and caused carriages to fly in the air, wrenching themselves free of their neighbours, before crashing many feet lower. Some bounced on impact, to become shapeless, dented tubes. Wheels were thrown free, rolling and leaping and, within moments, the last of the carriages crashed into the river, where plumes of spray and steam bubbled and shrouded the white-hot metal.

He stared in disbelief at the wreckage-strewn landscape. He had been too distant to hear the screams of the hundreds of men trapped inside the train. None of them could have lived. At his side, the boy whimpered, his face ashen, and he placed an arm around his narrow shoulders. 'Bastards! Murdering bloody bastards!' The last of the steam drifted away, revealing the scattered carriages, battered into unrecognisable masses, half-submerged beneath the water. The silence and stillness were eerie.

'The phone!' He started back up the hill, slithering and slipping in his haste. The boy kept level, using the butt of his rifle to steady himself. Breathing heavily, he said, 'You'd better go ahead. Your legs are younger than mine. Call Headquarters. D'you know how to work the machine?'

'Yes.'

'Tell them what's happened. Tell them what the bastards have done!' The boy was already some distance ahead, rounding the corner, and he shouted, 'Warn them to stop the next train. The line's gone!'

When the boy was out of sight, he slowed, limping heavily. His leg ached, and there was a pain in his side from a fall. 'Bastards! Shit! Someone's going to pay for this!'

The little hamlet of Fjordby, so small that it was frequently left off all but the most detailed ordnance maps, appeared uninhabited.

Nobody could be seen on the single street that ran between the houses, and the square outside the church was deserted. News of the destruction of the troop train had spread rapidly, and the villagers remained behind closed doors to avoid confrontation with any German soldiers in the vicinity.

Towards noon, a covered army truck arrived, its low gears grinding. It crawled to the end of the street and parked in the square outside the church. A platoon of soldiers clambered out of the back and formed two lines, stamping their feet and swinging their arms against the cold. A sergeant descended from the cabin and faced them.

'All right, settle down! The weather won't kill you. Böttcher, put that bloody cigarette out!' The men responded, coming sloppily to attention.

Lutz, one of the old hands, asked, 'What are we supposed to do here?'

'I'll tell you in a minute.' He reached into his greatcoat pocket for some documents. 'Stand still, for Christ's sake!'

In the house closest to the square, Lis Halvorsen joined her husband by the window. 'What do they want, Per?' Even behind thick glass, she kept her voice low.

'I don't know.' He was a tall man, now stooped with age. 'They could be after the men who bombed the train.'

'What will they do to us?'

He shrugged. 'Search the houses; ask a few questions.' Seeing his wife's reaction, he took her hand. 'Don't worry. We can't tell them anything. When they realise they're getting nothing out of us, they'll leave.'

'What about your gun? They'll see it!'

He laughed. 'They're not interested in a 1912 shotgun. Let it stay where it is.' The gun had been his father's, and it hung on a wooden beam in the living-room. When he was younger, Per had hunted rabbits with it. 'It's just a routine check.' He stared at the soldiers, who had returned to stamping their feet and swinging their arms. 'Look at them. That's your master race!'

'I wish they'd leave us alone. Why don't they just go away?'

The sergeant looked up from his reading. 'I said stand still, for God's sake! You're like a bunch of school kids!' He waited for them to show a semblance of military discipline. 'I want all the inhabitants rounded up and put in that church. There's nine houses and ten of you, so you can take a house each. Edel, you wait in the church, and when they're all inside, lock the door and report back to me. I'll want all their identity papers, too. Bring them with you.' The soldiers had not moved, and he looked irritated. 'Come on, what are you waiting for? Get to it!'

'What do we do if they refuse?' Böttcher would have continued, but the sergeant silenced him with a grim stare.

It took twenty minutes to round up the villagers, most of whom were elderly. One old woman walked with difficulty, leaning on Lutz's arm for support. No resistance was offered, and the twenty-two inhabitants of Fjordby walked in dignified silence. Occasionally, the soldiers shouted at them to hurry, and the Norwegians obeyed them in silence. The sergeant noted that there were no children.

When the search was complete, Edel handed a small pack of identity cards to the sergeant. 'Quite a haul!' He grinned in the direction of a pile of articles taken from the houses: several radios, two shotguns and a rusty old revolver dating from the First World War. 'What do we do now?'

'We wait. Someone from HQ in Bergen is on the way.'

'Do we have to stand out here? It's bloody freezing!' Böttcher was stamping his feet again. The clouds had dispersed, and sunshine illuminated the snow-clad village, but the temperature remained well below zero.

'You can take cover inside one of the houses.' He pointed to Per Halvorsen's. 'Use that. Someone had better stand guard outside the church. Riedel, take the first watch. I'll be in the truck. If anyone shows up, I want you all out here on the double. Understand?'

Lutz stared moodily out of the window, watching the street for any arrivals. Another soldier joined him. 'It's better than freezing out there, I suppose. Not much of a place, is it?' His gaze took in the church. 'What d'you reckon we're supposed to do with them?'

'Question them, I suppose.' He was a heavily-built man in his forties, taciturn by nature. 'I hope that's all.'

'What d'you mean?'

Lutz nodded towards the square. 'That truck. It's loaded with explosives at the back. There's enough in there to blow up half the countryside. I was shit-scared all the way here. If someone had taken a pot-shot at us, we would have been blown to kingdom come!'

16

'Jesus! They should have said!' The man took it as a personal affront.

Lutz did not comment. A black Mercedes staff car was approaching slowly. Its tyres, armed with snow chains, bumped over the icy surface of the road. 'Someone's coming. Tell the others.' He picked up his rifle and moved to the front door.

The soldiers ran across the street and formed two lines by the truck. Accompanied by the sergeant, they watched the Mercedes enter the square and stop. At a word from the sergeant they came to attention as two men stepped from the car.

Lutz watched the first man walk towards them. He was dressed in a long black leather overcoat, its collar turned up to cover his cheeks. Dark sunglasses protected his eyes from the glare of the sunlight on the snow, and his hat identified him as an SS officer. His knee-length boots were newly polished. The second man, bundled into a brown cloth overcoat and with a fur hat covering his head, was a civilian.

'Shit!' Lutz swore under his breath.

The young man standing next to him muttered, 'What's wrong?'

'It's the Horseman.'

'Who?'

'The Horseman. He's from SS Headquarters in Bergen. He got here last week, but he's already well-known. Don't you fools ever find out what's happening?'

Hearing them, the sergeant turned towards the platoon and glared. The SS officer and the civilian had halted twenty paces away. 'For Christ's sake, keep quiet! You're supposed to be at attention!' He wheeled and marched smartly across the square to greet the new arrivals.

When he was out of earshot, the soldier asked Lutz, 'So who is he?'

'One of the coldest bastards you're ever likely to meet. He's young, too. Maybe that's what makes him so hard.' He was thoughtful for a moment. 'That one's a real sadist. They brought him in to sort out the resistance. I should have guessed he'd show up here.'

'What's all the crap about horses?' The man chuckled. 'He came in a car.'

'It's what they call him. Haven't you read your Bible?' He answered his own question. 'The Four Horsemen of the Apocalypse.

17

They named him after the fourth: the one who rides a pale horse and brings death and destruction.' Lutz was silent. When he spoke again, it was as though he was talking to himself. 'Poor bastards!'

'Why d'you say that?'

'Nothing. Wait and see.'

The officer and the sergeant were speaking in low voices. Lutz strained his ears, but could not hear what they were saying. At their side, the civilian appeared to be remonstrating.

'Who's the other one?'

'Looks like Olav Hanssen. He's the local quisling. Little shit!'

'What's wrong with him? He's on our side.'

'Against his own people. What sort of a man does that?'

'The sort that knows which side his bread is buttered. I'd rather have him than some Norwegian sticking a grenade up my arse.'

'Maybe. How would you feel if one of your neighbours turned you in?'

The man's voice was derisory. 'You're getting soft in your old age, Lutz! A traitor's a traitor. I reported my father for disloyalty when I was in the Hitler Youth.' He spoke with pride. 'He was against the cause.'

'Well, good for you, shithead. That's something to tell your grandchildren!'

The sergeant saluted, and marched back to the platoon. The SS officer remained behind. Hanssen was speaking animatedly, his hands mobile, but the Horseman ignored him.

'Pay attention.' The sergeant was ill at ease. 'At the back of the truck you'll find explosives and detonators.' He turned for a moment towards the officer, who watched silently. The dark sunglasses covering his eyes and the upturned collar of his coat made it impossible to discern his expression.

The sergeant returned to his men. 'Explosives are to be laid in each of the houses in the village.' He paused. 'They are to be destroyed.' Some of the soldiers reacted, and he barked, 'Stand still! You're still at attention!' The shuffling ceased. 'Which of you knows how to set charges?'

After a long pause, Lutz spoke quietly. 'I do.'

'Very well. How long will you need?'

Lutz hesitated, glancing at the houses. 'I'm not sure. A couple of hours.'

18

The SS officer had approached them, and the sergeant turned towards him. Hearing Lutz's words, he nodded curtly. At his side, Hanssen started to speak, but the Horseman raised his hand, commanding silence.

The sergeant addressed Lutz: 'Right. Take the others with you, and show them what to do. After that, you can supervise their work.' His voice hardened. 'Move! We haven't got all day. The quicker we get this finished, the sooner you can go back to base.'

Inside the church, the inhabitants of Fjordby spoke in whispers.

'What's happening?'

'I can't see.' Asbjørn Haugland was standing on a chair, peering through a window. 'The glass is frosted on the outside.'

'Be careful!' His wife Vessa spoke. 'If they see you watching them, they might fire at you. Is the door locked?'

'Yes.' Per Halvorsen rattled the handle.

'What should we do?' There was a general murmur of anxious voices.

Per held up his hands. 'There's nothing we can do except keep calm. Maybe we should pray.' He smiled. 'We're in the right place! They're probably searching our houses, but they won't find anything. We know nothing, and we'll tell them nothing, so don't panic. I suggest we all sit quietly and wait for them.'

Karl Vonheim spoke. 'There's a window at the back. It looks over the graveyard. I'll open it and see if I can spot anything.'

'Take care! There could be a soldier out there.'

He returned almost immediately. 'There's no-one. They didn't think about it, seeing there's only one door.' His voice was excited. 'If I put a chair against the wall, it would be easy to climb out. It's only a few yards to the trees.'

'What of it?'

'We could make a break for it. Once we're into the trees, they'd have a hell of a job catching us. Let's get out of here!'

'No!' Per spoke sharply. 'What good would it do?'

'We'd escape.' Karl laughed. 'There aren't enough of them to stop us.'

'There are, and they've got guns. They could pick us off one at a time.'

'It's worth a try.'

19

Per became angry. 'This is nonsense! Running away suggests guilt. Anyway, they've taken our papers. We'd be rounded up in a few hours. What then?'

'I'm prepared to try. I'll take my chances.' Karl turned away.

His father placed a hand on his arm. 'Wait! Be sensible, Karl. Per's right. We haven't done anything. Half the people here are too old to start running through the woods with the Germans after them. I doubt whether your mother could climb through that window.' His voice softened. 'Look, you're young. Maybe you could get away, but the rest of us wouldn't stand a chance. Do what Per suggests, and keep calm.' Karl tried to pull himself loose, but his father's grip was strong. 'Be sensible. This is no time for schoolboy heroics.'

'Let me try.'

'No. When they find you're missing, they'll assume you were involved with the train, and that could mean the rest of us will suffer. You'll have to sit it out with us.' He paused. 'I'm sorry Karl. You'd be endangering all of us.'

It was not yet four, but the sun was already moving towards the horizon, and the buildings cast long, slanting shadows across the street. A light snow had started to fall, and gathering clouds threatened the last of the golden light.

Lutz watched the sergeant approach the Mercedes. The officer stepped out. He saluted casually as the NCO came to attention.

'Everything is ready, sir.'

The Horseman nodded, and spoke in a low voice. Lutz was too far away to hear what he was saying. Then the officer pointed, indicating a corner of the church, next to the graveyard, where the land sloped suddenly down until it met the edge of the forest.

'Yes, sir.' The sergeant spoke crisply, his voice displaying no emotion. He stepped back, and was about to return to the platoon, when the Horseman spoke again. His head was lowered, and he appeared almost to be whispering in the sergeant's ear. For a moment, the junior man looked startled, but his face became expressionless as he saluted and turned away. He marched back to the platoon with parade-ground discipline. The quisling Hanssen watched them nervously from across the square.

When the door of the church was unlocked, the villagers emerged cautiously. The sun had vanished behind clouds, and the snow was

20

falling steadily. A freezing wind blew flurries into their faces. Soldiers, their rifles at the ready, herded them towards the edge of the graveyard, motioning them to stand together in a tight group.

The Horseman approached them until he was standing a few feet away. He stationed himself next to the sergeant. Despite the fading light, he had not removed his dark glasses. Silence descended on the group, and he nodded to the sergeant to begin.

The man spoke in halting Norwegian. 'You all know what happened this morning. Hundreds of men died because of your saboteurs.'

Per Halvorsen stepped forward. He would have advanced farther, but a soldier forced him back with the butt of his rifle. 'We know what happened, but it had nothing to do with us. We were in our homes at the time.'

The sergeant glanced at the Horseman before continuing, 'You have all helped the resistance in one way or another: offering food and shelter, hiding them from patrols. Don't try to deny it.' The villagers were silent, and his voice hardened. 'An example has to be made, as a warning to others. Because this village is closest to the derailment, it has been selected.'

'But we have done nothing!'

Several other villagers spoke out, their voices mingling in growing anger. The soldiers surrounding them pointed their rifles menacingly. One of the women, fearing she was about to be shot, cried out.

The sergeant faced them. His voice was unsteady. 'An example must be made.' He turned again to the Horseman, who gave a slight nod, then shouted a command.

Suddenly, before their eyes, the village erupted in a series of deafening explosions, and each house was blown apart by the dynamite. A blast of hot air swept down the street towards them, its force so great that many of the onlookers fell to the ground. Huge splinters of metal and burning timber, thrown high, crashed about them, and the street was a blaze of brilliant red light. As the explosions ended, the sounds echoing and rumbling, fire engulfed the shattered remains of the buildings. Timber and broken floorboards crackled and twisted in the conflagration, and there were further small explosions as cannisters of cooking gas burst into flames. Farther down the street, a ruptured water main threw a fountain into the air. The shells of the houses burned like ghostly funeral pyres, spewing flaming debris around them.

21

The Horseman had not moved. A few feet away from him, Hanssen had fallen to his knees, his head buried in his hands. The soldiers stood with their rifles at the ready, forbidding anyone to leave the close group into which they had been pressed. Then, at a further command from the sergeant, they stepped back several paces, their guns still aimed at the Norwegians.

Per Halvorsen stared at the SS officer. 'My God! What have you done? You're mad!' Around him, many of the villagers still lay on the ground. Watching the blazing remains of Fjordby, their faces horrified, they rose slowly to their feet, as though unable to comprehend what had happened in those few, brief minutes.

'Animal!' Halvorsen took a step forward, and the SS officer produced a heavy pistol, pointing it at the man's heart. Quite deliberately, he unfastened the safety catch, and the Norwegian stopped.

The Horseman spoke in fluent Norwegian. His voice was low. 'You will learn what it means to challenge the German army. Fjordby is an example for all your countrymen. Let them remember what happened here today!' He turned his back and walked away.

'Wait!' Over the roar of the flames and the crash of broken beams, Asbjørn Haugland shouted to make himself heard. 'What about us? Where will we live? You've destroyed our homes!'

Ignoring him, The Horseman nodded to the sergeant again, and the man barked a short command. At his signal, the rear canvas of the truck was pulled back. A machine-gunner, his weapon mounted on a tripod, faced the villagers. At his side, a white-faced soldier held a bandeau of rounds, ready to feed through the gun.

The Norwegians stumbled back. Women screamed, raising their hands before their faces, and the men threw themselves in front of them. They were too late. The man opened fire, and a shower of bullets cut them down, its force so great that it seemed to sweep the entire group back until they toppled down the steep slope bordering the graveyard. Their bodies sprawled and scattered, falling and rolling down the hillside. Within a few moments, they were immobile: a lifeless heap of human debris. Large snowflakes settled gently on their clothing.

What remained of Fjordby blazed steadily. The houses had collapsed, and their broken wooden skeletons burned brightly in the fading light.

The Horseman stared at the fires for a moment before looking at the sergeant. 'Take the men back to base.'

The sergeant's glance took in the bodies at the edge of the forest. 'What about them? Should someone stay behind to . . .'

'No. We'll be moving out shortly.' He looked at the sky. 'There's more snow on the way. It will cover them sufficiently. Get your men out of here.'

Olav Hanssen was waiting by the Mercedes. He shook his head in horror. 'My God! What have you done?'

'What I said I would do: taught them a lesson.'

'But this was murder!' The events of the previous minutes had given him unexpected courage. 'You shot them down in cold blood! You didn't say anything about killing them!'

'What the hell do you think happened to the men on the train?'

'They were soldiers, fighting a war. These were innocent civilians!'

'I don't care whether they were civilians or soldiers. You're right, Hanssen. This is a war. They were our enemies, and they died for it.'

'What about me? This is my district. I have to answer for it.'

'You failed. You were responsible to the occupying forces for the peaceful collaboration of the local community. Collaboration!'

'They won't understand. Nobody will believe me!'

'In that case, I'll save you the trouble.' The Horseman was still holding his pistol and, without speaking further, he raised the gun, pointing it at the quisling. Hanssen screamed as the SS man fired, and the bullet passed between the man's eyes, making a neat red hole in the bridge of his nose. He fell back, the scream cut off by the sound of the shot. He was dead before his body had settled into the snow.

The Horseman stared down at him, then stepped over his body to enter the Mercedes. He started the engine and turned on the wind-screen wipers, then drove slowly down the remains of the street, occasionally pulling at the steering-wheel to avoid burning wreckage in the road.

Heavy snow continued to fall. After an hour, the last of the timber beams ceased to burn, and the wood steamed and charred as gusts of freezing wind piled flakes against them. Ice clogged the burst water main, and the stricken village moaned and shifted in the storm.

Under the weight of several bodies, their torn and bullet-ridden clothing providing slight protection from the elements, Karl Vonheim stirred. A searing pain in his right shoulder, where a bullet had passed through, made him gasp, and his right thigh, in which a bullet had lodged, was numb. He had lost blood and, when he had first fallen with the others, the physical shock of his wounds had left him unconscious.

The biting wind revived him, and he moved cautiously, edging himself sideways to test his strength. The body covering him slipped away, and a shaft of pain drove through his shoulder. He fought against dizzying nausea, determined to remain conscious. To his right, he was aware of the dark form of the church, about ten yards away. The building was undamaged and, if he could drag himself inside, there was a chance of survival.

He moved again, crying out as the pain returned, and pulled himself free of the dead-weight that had pinned him down. He felt his senses returning and, concentrating his power, slid his body, inch by inch, towards the church. He knew he must reach it before the cold and the snow took his life.

Using his weight, he turned so that his left shoulder and leg were against the ground. Snow covering his face revived him, and he edged forward again, pushing with his undamaged leg and using his arm to lift his body over the rough surface. After three such manoeuvres, he fell back, dragging icy air into his lungs and waiting for the agony to diminish. For a moment, he felt a sort of heady triumph. He had not fainted!

He had already progressed several feet from the bodies that had covered him and was fully exposed to the wind and snow, but within a few yards he would be in the shelter of the church. He was close enough to see its dark shape looming over him, and the snow had lessened. The thought kept him alive, and he raised his body again, digging his foot deep into the snow and slithering forward. The pain had diminished slightly, and he attacked the ground with new strength, throwing caution aside. He was almost there!

He craned his head round, looking upward. Against a velvet night sky, the outline of the church was clearly discernible, and he breathed deeply, preparing for his next effort. At first, his leg would

not move, and he felt a momentary panic. Then the muscles con-
tracted, and he slid forward, moving under the protective overhang
of the building. It was within reach, and he pressed onward with
renewed urgency, determined to survive.

3

The hammering of pneumatic drills outside his window awoke Otto Thomas, and he lay on his back, staring at the cracked and discoloured ceiling, trying to focus his thoughts. He had been dreaming, or perhaps remembering; he was not sure which. There had been a concert, many years earlier, but the details eluded him. It had been a success, and a woman in a dark red silk dress had been waiting for him in his dressing-room. She had been holding a glass of champagne. He could not recall her name, but he felt again, for an instant, the surge of pleasure that had filled him when he had seen her standing there, her smile provocative but slightly uncertain. He shook his head slowly. That must have been thirty years ago!

The vision faded, erased by the insistent noise of the drills. Everything in Munich was being rebuilt, replacing the substantial old houses he loved with hideous utilitarian concrete blocks. It was hateful! He could not take a walk without having to pick his way past building sites, and there was a constant film of sandy dust that clung to his clothes and stung his eyes. Only yesterday, a workman shouldering a load of planks had shouted, 'Watch your back, Grandad!' and forced him to step into the street. A few years earlier, the man would have stood aside, addressing him as *Herr Doktor* or, if he had any education, *maestro*. Instead, he had grinned contemptuously at his dark overcoat with its faded Astrakhan collar. 'On our way to a fancy dress party, are we?' Lout! He closed his eyes, longing for sleep and, with it, the image of that woman. What was her name? He could still see the wine-coloured dress, cut low across her sensuous breasts . . .

A loud rap on the bedroom door awoke him again. 'Who is it?' His voice sounded thin and reedy. When he was younger, it had been a deep baritone.

26

Frau Häusler opened the door and looked in. Her face registered disapproval. 'It's only me, Herr Doktor. Aren't you up yet?'

'What time is it?'

'Nearly ten.' She glared at the large, untidy room with its heavy, old-fashioned furnishings. 'Aren't you feeling well?' She was a small, dumpy woman in her sixties. Her old brown dress was protected, as ever, by a flowered apron.

'I was tired. The damned drilling woke me early.'

'Some people have to work for a living. Do you want coffee?'

He grimaced. 'That instant muck?'

'Take it or leave it. There's nothing else, unless you want to pay under-the-counter prices. I have to get on with the living-room. I'll be using the vacuum-cleaner.' The latter statement sounded like a threat.

'I'm sorry if it's a little untidy . . .'

'I'll manage. The whole place needs a coat of paint, if you ask me. Not that it's worth bothering. You'll be wasting your money.'

He put on an ancient quilted silk dressing-gown, frayed around the cuffs. He had bought it in Paris in the early 1930s for what had been an outrageous sum even then, but it had impressed the woman who had shared his hotel suite. Little items of luxury had always stimulated her sexual appetite. 'What are you talking about?'

Frau Häusler was rearranging books on the shelf by the fireplace. It was a high-ceilinged, airy room, and the wall was covered by a bookcase for his library of scores. 'They're talking about pulling the building down. A couple of men were looking round yesterday afternoon. One of them said he was an architect, or maybe a surveyor; I don't remember which. He said the foundations were cracked during the bombing, and the building is subsiding. If you ask me, they're probably looking to pull it down and sell it for a fat profit. Land round here is worth a fortune.'

'What about me and the other tenants?'

'Who knows?' She lifted a battered copy of the score of *Don Juan* and wiped it with a cloth. If she had looked inside, she would have seen the inscription from Richard Strauss. 'They'll probably offer to buy you out or relocate you to one of those new apartment buildings in the suburbs. I'm told they're very comfortable . . .'

'I don't want to move to some suburban matchbox! I've lived here most of my life.' She shrugged indifferently. 'Is there any post for me?'

'A couple of bills. I left them with all the others by the front door.'

'I'll deal with them later.' He was disappointed. He had written to Strauss, begging for an interview, but had received no reply. He had also tried telephoning, but had been told the composer could not be disturbed. He was still convinced that his old teacher would not forsake him as everyone else seemed to have.

Thomas walked slowly to the kitchen, stretching cramped limbs. At seventy, one had to expect some stiffness, despite regular exercise. What he needed were the physical demands and concentration of an orchestra to regain his fitness. Frau Häusler had left a spoonful of powdered coffee in a cup, and he poured boiling water over it. There were also two fresh rolls, but he had no appetite for them.

He stared out of the rain-spattered window. The news about the building was worrying. He was not sure that he could afford to move. There was a little money in the bank, but he had no guarantee of future income and no immediate prospects. The money would not last forever, and everything had become so expensive.

One thing was certain: he had no intention of being installed in some concrete beehive in the back of beyond, to spend the rest of his life in obscurity. For God's sake! He was Doctor Otto Thomas, one of Germany's foremost conductors . . . until eighteen months ago. He had been internationally known and admired. On the piano in the living-room there was a 1720 Stradivarius. It had been a present from Joseph Goebbels, 'for services to music', (though God knew where the little man had got it from!) It was probably worth a fortune, if his savings were dwindling. But why should he sell it? It had been a present from the State!

He sighed. That was long ago, before the thousand-year Reich had suddenly collapsed, before those ridiculous show trials in Nuremberg, before the telephone stopped ringing, before his former colleagues and friends ceased to acknowledge him. How quickly they had all vanished. It was as though he no longer existed!

His music world had disappeared. The Bavarian Symphony Orchestra was under new management, and the Director, a man of whom he had never heard, refused his calls. And all the others – orchestras, managers, performers – avoided him, pretending urgent appointments or previous engagements.

It wasn't his age. For a conductor, he was in the prime of life, and he had enjoyed a brilliant career, travelling between all the great concert halls and opera houses of Europe. Perhaps he should have visited the United States too, but he had never liked Americans. They were brash and coarse, like Australians, lacking any real understanding of Europe's musical heritage. All they wanted was virtuosity and kitsch! Besides, it was a country owned and dominated by Jews, and there was no way he could be persuaded to perform for them.

A familiar wave of anger filled him. The Jews were behind it! The Party had gone, the leaders were dead, the army destroyed, and the jewboys were already back, sidling into power behind the forces of occupation, infiltrating their way into every walk of life, bringing their old Mosaic law of an eye for an eye. It was all part of some vengeful Jewish conspiracy! No wonder his yellow-bellied former colleagues and friends would have nothing to do with him! He banged the coffee cup on the table, spilling brown liquid across the white surface.

Frau Häusler appeared in the doorway. 'What's the matter?'

'Nothing.' He glared at her testily. 'What do you want?'

'You've got a visitor. A young man. He says it's very important.'

'For him or for me?'

'He won't say; only that he has to talk to you. He won't go. He says he's a musician, and must see you.'

Thomas looked up. 'A musician? What sort of musician?'

'How should I know? I said you were busy, but he pushed his way into the living-room and wouldn't leave. He's quite polite. Shall I send for help?'

'Don't be stupid!' He rose to his feet. 'Very well, I'll see him.'

'Dressed like that?'

'It's a perfectly respectable housecoat.' He ran a hand through close-cropped silver hair. 'He's probably just an autograph-hunter.'

A bearded young man was standing by the bookcase, staring at the rows of leather-bound scores. He was reaching for one as Thomas entered the room.

'Well?'

The man turned to face him. He was wearing a tan trenchcoat whose shoulders were soaked with rain. 'Forgive me for intruding, maestro. I would have telephoned for an appointment, but your name isn't listed.' He spoke gravely.

'What do you want?'

'A few minutes of your time. I would have called first . . .'

'Yes, yes, you already explained! Why do you want to see me?'

The young man hesitated momentarily. Then he seemed to straighten. He spoke slowly and firmly. 'I intend to become a conductor.'

Thomas gave a gruff laugh. 'Why bother me? Go to a music school . . .'

'No!' The young man's voice had hardened, and Thomas stared at him. 'Music schools can't teach me what I need to know.' His blue-grey eyes were fixed on the older man's face. 'Maestro, I don't think you realise what this meeting means to me. I've travelled halfway across Europe to find you . . .'

'For God's sake, why?'

'Because you are the greatest living conductor of our time! I have admired you all my life. I grew up with your records, and I have learned your interpretations by heart. I can tell you every pause, every rubato, every phrase you recorded! I only saw you conduct once. It was in Oslo in 1938, and it was the most important and moving experience of my life! That concert has lived with me ever since.'

Otto Thomas paused before speaking. He was touched by the speech, and the young man's intensity was disquieting. 'Who are you? What is your name?'

'My name is Karl Henrik Vonheim. I am from Norway.'

'You speak very good German.'

Vonheim nodded. 'I also speak fluent English, French and Italian, and I intend to learn Russian. It is all part of my preparation.'

He was puzzled. 'Preparation?'

'To become a conductor.'

'There's more to conducting than being a linguist!' He hesitated. 'You'd better take off your coat. It's dripping on my carpet. Would you like some coffee?'

'Thank you.'

'Frau Häusler!' As soon as he called her name, she appeared in the doorway. 'Would you be kind enough to bring another coffee.' He looked at Vonheim, who was sitting on the edge of the sofa. 'And those rolls.'

Thomas seated himself in an armchair, and studied the young man. He had a handsome face: high forehead, clean-cut features, and those intelligent eyes that seemed to concentrate attention. The beard made him look older, which was probably why he had grown it. 'So, you think you would like to become a conductor?'

'It's not a matter of conjecture. I know I will become one.'

'Why come to me? I can do nothing for you.' For a moment, anger and self-pity filled him. 'Nobody's interested in me. I am persona non grata in the new Germany. I have not conducted an orchestra for more than a year.'

'I don't understand.'

'Neither do I, Mr Vonheim. It appears that my . . . past affiliations disqualify me from continuing my work.'

'But others . . .'

'Others? You mean Fürtwangler, or Knappertsbusch, or the dreary Mr Böhm and the arrogant young Mr von Karajan? You will have to ask them about it. Ask them what they didn't do that makes them so different from me!' He stared into space. 'I served my country, Mr Vonheim, as any good German should. I was too old to carry a rifle, so I made my contribution in the only way I knew, with a baton. However, it appears that I am to be punished for it. Perhaps I should be grateful that I wasn't put on trial!' He paused. 'But I am forgetting that you are not a German. You speak my language so well. As a Norwegian, you are a conquering hero!'

The young man spoke quietly. 'The war is over, Maestro. I'm a musician first, and a Norwegian second. I am here because you are a great conductor.'

'That's very flattering, but there's nothing I can do for you. How can I help you when my own career appears to have come to an end?'

'You can teach me.'

'Teach you?' He was shocked. 'I am a conductor, not a professor!'

'That's my point!' Vonheim's words tumbled out. 'I don't want to study with some dusty academic in a conservatory! Conducting is a living, active profession, based on knowledge and experience. You can't learn it from books and lectures. You have actually done it, maestro! You were a colleague of Weingartner and Mengelberg. You knew Toscanini and Walter. You studied with Nikisch and Strauss. My God, you watched them and talked to them and learned from them! You know! You've worked with the finest composers and artists of this century, and you have a greater understanding and

31

experience than any other living musician. It's all stored there, in your head and memory! Let me study with you, learn it all from you!' In his excitement, the young man had risen, and now stood facing the conductor. 'Give me that knowledge and experience and training, and let me pass it on to the next generation. I won't fail you, I swear!'

Thomas was silent, affected by the intensity of the young man's words. 'But I don't know you. I don't know anything about you.'

'Let me prove myself. Let me show you what I've learned so far. At least listen to me, hear what I have to say, before you turn me down. I've dedicated myself to my studies, prepared myself as far as I can go alone. That's why I waited until now.' He became calmer. 'You cannot waste what you know, maestro. You owe it to future generations. If they won't let you conduct at the moment, which is a situation that can change, then let me do it for you. Teach me what you know!'

Thomas was thoughtful. 'You believe things will get better for me?'

'They must. Everything is upside-down at the moment, because of the war, but that's temporary. The music world can't ignore you forever.'

Frau Häusler appeared, bringing two cups of coffee on a small silver tray, accompanied by the rolls. 'I'm leaving now. May I speak to you for a moment?'

'Can it wait?'

'I'd be grateful if you'd spare me a moment in the kitchen.'

'Oh, very well.' He followed her out of the room. 'What is it?'

She was embarrassed. 'You haven't paid me for over a month, Herr Doktor.'

'You should have told me. Where's my wallet?'

She handed it to him. 'I brought it from the bedroom.'

He counted out her wages, noting that it left little remaining. Another trip to the bank! There were also the unpaid bills on the hall table.

She put on an old cloth coat. 'I'll be back on Friday. If you learn anything about the building, please let me know. I'll need to find other work.'

'Do you think there's any truth to the rumours?'

She shrugged. 'I'd like adequate notice. Work isn't easy to find.'

32

'So I understand!'

Vonheim was standing by the bookcase, a score in his hand.

'What instrument do you play?'

'The piano, maestro, but I also studied the violin at home.'

'Good. One must have a knowledge of bowing a stringed instrument. What are you looking at?'

'Mozart; the G Minor Symphony.'

'Could you play it on the piano?'

'I think so.'

'You think? If you want to conduct, you should be able to play a reduction, reading from the full score, at sight. The score is all you will ever have to work with, and it should be as familiar to you as the fingers on your hands.'

'I believe it is. Would you like me to show you?'

'Not yet.' An idea was formulating. 'How old are you?'

'Twenty-four; nearly twenty-five.'

'That's young. Tell me, how do you plan to live if you study with me? I haven't said this will happen, but I'm curious to know.'

'I can support myself. I would also expect to pay for my instruction.'

'We have not yet reached that point. How will you support yourself?'

Vonheim's expression was closed. 'I do a little buying and selling.'

'Really?' He glanced at the young man's shabby outfit.

'I assure you I can manage.' He reached into a pocket and produced a thick roll of notes. 'I have more than a thousand dollars here.'

'That's a lot of cash to be carrying. What do you buy and sell?'

Vonheim shrugged. 'It depends what is in demand. I have contacts in the occupying forces – mostly Americans – which is why I happen to have dollars at the moment. There are many shortages in the shops . . .' He left the sentence unfinished.

The conductor smiled faintly. 'In other words, the black market.'

'Not really. My contacts have various items for sale. Acting as an interpreter, I find buyers for them. I receive a commission.'

'They must be substantial.' He stared hard at the young man. 'Are you dealing in drugs?'

'No. I would not even consider them, but certain new medicines are in great demand. Have you heard of Penicillin?'

'No.'

'It's highly valued by doctors and hospitals at the moment, but supplies are limited. I can sometimes put them in touch with ... sources of supply.'

'How very convenient!'

His eyes held the conductor's. 'It is only a means to an end.'

Thomas was thoughtful. 'You're very determined.'

'I have no other interest in the world.'

'And you'll continue your ... business dealings here in Munich?'

'Yes. I have a number of associates. If there are certain items you need, maestro, I'll be happy to find them for you. The shops here are poorly stocked.'

'Yes.' He stared out of the window. 'I miss good coffee.'

'I'll bring some on my next visit, if you'll permit me to come here again.'

'We'll see.' He became brisk. 'Now, tell me what you have studied so far.'

When Otto Thomas opened the door, he did not at first recognise the man standing before him. Karl Vonheim had shaved his beard, and his hair was cut short, giving him a youthful, clean-cut appearance. His clothes were new. Before speaking, he inclined his head and presented a small paper bag of freshly ground coffee whose seductive aroma seemed to fill the foyer of the apartment.

'I hope you will enjoy this, maestro.'

Thomas hesitated before taking it, but the perfume was irresistible. 'Thank you.' He led the way to the kitchen. 'Shall we have some now? I think I can remember how to make it!' He busied himself with a kettle. 'Did you study the Brahms?'

'Yes.' The young man placed the leather-bound copy of the Second Symphony on the table. 'I think I followed your additional markings.' He opened the book at random, glancing at the printed page on which Thomas had scrawled innumerable hieroglyphics in thick black pencil. 'You made many alterations.'

'Naturally. You must understand that, to interpret a work, the score is only the route map of the journey. You must know it by heart, but after that, when every detail is clearly imprinted on your mind, you may stretch and squeeze the music as you see fit.' He looked at Vonheim. 'That's something nobody can teach you. The notes are your guide, but it's the holes between the notes that contain the essence of the music. It lives and breathes, and you can't reproduce it mechanically. That's your job as a conductor, and you have to find a way to convey your ideas to the orchestra.' He wagged a finger. 'But if you're going to deviate from the written instructions – a longer pause or a change in tempo where no change is marked – you must have a valid reason. Don't meddle with it for the sake of change, and don't fool yourself into believing you have to place your special stamp on the piece with some eccentric invention. The players will see through you, and you'll lose their trust. If that happens, the audience won't believe you either.'

Vonheim nodded slowly. 'I've listened to your recordings, and . . .'

Thomas pointed a teaspoon at him accusingly. 'That's my next instruction: don't listen to any more records! Music must have spontaneity, depending on the time and the moment. Records freeze that moment. They never change! Besides, if you're going to conduct a Brahms symphony, the interpretation must be your own; not some rehashed version of what you heard me do.'

'But if I don't listen to records, how will I learn?'

'By reading the original and making your own decisions. All I can do is guide you; maybe offer a few suggestions. You have to make up your own mind. When you have, you can listen to someone else's performance: see how they solved certain problems; got round the difficult corners. If I ever hear you conduct, I don't want to listen to what I might have done. I want to hear what you have to say.'

When Vonheim smiled, he looked very vulnerable. 'That's frightening!'

'You're the one who wants to be a conductor. What did you think you had to do: wave your arms and expect the music to make itself? Listen, an orchestra is a musical instrument, and you have to learn how to play it. The difficult part is that it's made up of individual, living people, and you have to tell them what to do. You're the dictator of a small, subservient nation. It's an arrogant sort of profession, when you think about it.'

'But how will I know?'

'By using your instincts and your training. Take command!' His manner softened. 'You won't know all the answers, and you'll make mistakes like everyone else, but if you perform every work with

35

knowledge and with conviction, with a clear understanding of what you want to say, you've got a reasonable chance of becoming a conductor.' He poured steaming liquid into two cups and, closing his eyes, inhaled the rich, dark bouquet before taking a sip. 'God, that's good! I'd almost forgotten what real coffee tasted like!'

'I'm very glad. When you need more, please tell me. There's a man . . .'

Thomas raised a hand. 'I don't want to know. Come, let's go next door. I want to see you conduct the first movement of the Brahms.'

'Without an orchestra?'

He scowled. 'Do you think I've got the Berlin Philharmonic in there?'

'Should we play a record?'

'Of course not! Don't tell me you've been wasting your time, waving your arms like an idiot at a gramophone!' Vonheim blushed, and Thomas shook his head pityingly. 'Don't you even realise that the conductor gives the indications first, and the orchestra follows him? You're always fractionally ahead.'

In the living-room, he handed the young man a baton. 'Very well. Begin.' A moment later, he interrupted angrily. 'Don't wave your arms like a maniac, and for God's sake, stand still! A conductor doesn't have to leap about like a dancer. It's unnecessary, distracting and self-indulgent. If you want to give a dramatic interpretation of the music with your body, go to ballet school!'

'I'm sorry.'

'Try to remember what I tell you. I'm not a teacher, and I hate to waste time. Start again. Now, you use that stick to give a small, clear beat. The less you give them, the more the players will concentrate on what you're doing. Once you get going, you don't have to beat out every bar like a drum-major. Orchestral players can count just as well as you – better, probably – but they'll be watching for any changes in tempo.' Vonheim began again, and he called irritably, 'Don't wave your left hand like that! You're duplicating what your right hand's doing. You have to learn to use them independently. Start again!' As the young man, red-faced, paused before a further attempt, Otto Thomas permitted himself a brief smile. 'Look on the bright side, Vonheim. If you fail as a conductor, you could still get a job as a traffic policeman!'

36

After thirty minutes, during which the interruptions became less frequent, the conductor raised his hand. 'Stop! That's enough.'

Karl Vonheim laid the baton across the open score. 'Was I that bad?'

Thomas spoke quietly. 'No, Mr Vonheim. On the contrary, you were remarkably good. Either you were misleading me at the beginning, or you have a natural aptitude and an instinctive understanding. I'm inclined to think it's the latter. I've never seen a young, untrained conductor do what you have just done.' His tone became gentler. 'You needn't look so astonished. One of your future responsibilities will be to identify real talent in other musicians and develop it. Don't ever forget that!' He paused, his eyes never leaving Vonheim's face. 'You asked me to evaluate your potential. I would say you have the necessary ingredients to become a good conductor, provided that you're prepared to learn and study and dedicate yourself to your work. With your sort of determination, you could even become a great conductor.'

The young man looked as though he might burst into tears. 'I don't know how to begin to thank you. I . . .'

'We'll think of a way. Perhaps it will be mutually beneficial.' He scanned the bookshelves. 'I will select some scores for you to study. I'm not sure where to start. Not with Brahms. He comes later. You have many other works to learn, and we have a lot of talking to do. I've already explained that I'm not a teacher. I can show you how to use a baton, and I can try to pass on whatever I have acquired over the past fifty years. When you're ready, you'll have to find an orchestra.'

'How will I do that?'

He shrugged. 'That's the hardest problem, but everyone has to start somewhere. As you know, my own future is somewhat undecided for the moment. However, I still know a number of influential people. If they're not interested in employing me, they may at least take note if I contact them on your behalf. I still have something of a reputation.' He was silent for a moment. 'That's still in the future. As we get to know each other, I'll tell you what I know of the other side of the music world: the intendants and the managers and the agents and the promoters. You have to understand that this is a business as well as an art-form.' His voice was bitter. 'Now that the jewboys are back in control, you have to learn to be both cautious and astute, or they'll pick your bones clean!'

'I will appreciate your advice on all matters.'

'Good. Would you like another coffee?'

The young man glanced at his watch. 'I have an appointment that I ought to keep.'

Thomas smiled. 'A business meeting?' Vonheim nodded. 'I won't delay you.' He took several scores from the bookcase, including a heavy volume. 'Have a look at these. One of them is Bizet's *Carmen*. Did you know that Strauss, who was my teacher, always made his students study it? He gave them *Carmen* because he believed it was the perfect score: not a note out of place, not a bar too many.'

'What about his own scores?'

'No. Believe it or not, he always seemed rather embarrassed by them, and when he conducted his own music, he was very cool, pulling away from the overtly romantic aspects. He found them excessive! On the other hand, I've never heard a nobler *Fidelio* or a more inspired *Così*.'

'Have you spoken to him recently?'

Thomas was daydreaming, lost in memories. 'What? Oh, no. He's very busy at the moment. I'm sure he'll get in touch with me when he has a minute to spare.' He noticed the young man glance towards the clock. 'You'd better keep your appointment. I'm going to have some more of that delicious coffee.' He walked towards the kitchen. 'I'll expect you tomorrow, and we'll plan a serious schedule of work.'

When he returned to the empty living-room, Otto Thomas noticed a white envelope that had been left on the mantelpiece. It contained dollars, and he was surprised by the generous amount.

The secretary at the record company in London took several minutes of valuable long-distance time to locate Lancelot Gordon, and Otto Thomas waited impatiently.

'He's on another line. Would you like him to phone you back?'

'I would prefer to wait.' He was all too familiar with promises to call.

'I don't know how long he'll be. What was the name again?'

'Please tell him it is Doctor Thomas.'

After another long wait, Lancelot Gordon was connected. 'Hello?'

'Mr Gordon? This is Doctor Otto Thomas.'

There was a momentary pause. 'Good Lord! My dear fellow, what an extraordinary surprise! When the girl said Thomas I was thinking of somebody else.' His voice boomed in the earpiece, making it rattle. 'My dear Otto, is it really you?'

Thomas winced slightly at the use of his first name. He had forgotten the record producer's tendency towards over-familiarity. 'I hope I do not disturb you?'

'Of course not! I had no idea you were still ... As a matter of fact, I was talking to Tommy Beecham about you the other day. You know, that was a quite wonderful Dvořák D Minor we made in Prague back in ... when was it?'

'I am not sure. I think it was 1937.'

'That must have been our last meeting. Where are you?'

'I live in Munich, as ever.'

'Really? That's odd! I was talking to Herr what's-his-name last week, and he didn't ...' He changed course. 'Are you keeping busy?'

'Not exactly. This is a matter I would be most anxious to discuss on another occasion.' He glanced at the clock, wondering how much the call had cost so far. 'My reason for contacting you is to tell you about a young protégé of mine: a conductor.'

When Gordon laughed, the plastic receiver vibrated even more violently. 'I can't imagine you as a teacher, Otto. You'd never have the patience!'

'In the normal way, I do not teach, but this young man, Mr Gordon, is quite ... exceptional. His name is Karl Vonheim, and he has been working with me for nearly a year. I have never encountered anyone quite as talented. He is what you used to call "a natural", and he displays a surprisingly deep understanding of music.'

'Really? You intrigue me, Tell him to drop me a line.'

'I will, of course. However, I wondered whether you could come and hear him for yourself. He is giving a concert here next month.' He spoke with pride. 'I was able to recommend him to ...'

'Next month? When?'

'The tenth.'

'Just a moment, Otto.' After a pause he returned. 'You know, I could fit that in. I'm due in Vienna on the twelfth, and I could break the journey. Tell me a little more about him.'

They spoke for a further five minutes and, in his enthusiasm, Thomas forgot about the cost of the call. Finally, Gordon brought the conversation to an end.

39

'I must run, Otto. There's a room full of visitors waiting to see me. I will come to Munich. If you're prepared to recommend the fellow so glowingly, there must be something to him! Tell me, is he *malleable*?' He emphasised the word.

'I do not know what that means.'

Gordon searched for an appropriate definition. 'Is he open to suggestions? Can he take criticism, even to the point of re-thinking a reading? Does he have very fixed ideas about repertoire?'

Thomas paused to think. 'No, I do not think so. He is a very fine young musician, with a deep and thorough understanding, but also eager to learn. Why do you ask?'

'No special reason. I have something in mind for London.'

'Ah. If I can be of service . . .'

'Not for this sort of thing, Otto. You see, I'm thinking of forming a new orchestra, and I want to find a young, talented conductor for it. I need someone who would collaborate very closely with me. I'm sure it'll work, but I need someone flexible enough to go along with my programmes, if you see what I mean. We're desperately short of real talent. The war ended a number of very promising careers.'

'Karl Vonheim might be very suitable, but you must hear him for yourself.'

'Of course. Otto, I am delighted to hear from you!'

'And I. I would like to discuss some plans of my own. You see, I . . .'

'Yes, yes. We'll talk about it when I see you. It will be lovely to reminisce about the old days. Goodbye, my dear fellow, goodbye!'

Gordon wagged a yellow, nicotine-stained finger. 'I like what I heard. You have a real talent. Listen, Karl, keep studying with Otto. Don't do anything else for the moment.' He paused to light a new cigarette from the smouldering stub of the last. 'Stay in Munich and go on learning. I'll send for you as soon as I'm ready.'

They had taken an early lunch, but the Englishman had scarcely touched his food, preferring to chain-smoke through the meal. Vonheim was dutifully silent.

Otto Thomas nodded in agreement. 'I will see what I can do. There are a number of people I have not yet managed to reach.' He watched Gordon carefully, hoping for a moment to offer his own services. The producer had hardly changed in the decade that had passed. A large man with a powerful, commanding voice, he had grown a little more corpulent, and his well-tailored tweed suit was tightly stretched across his waistline. His sandy hair was tinged with grey, but his face remained baby-pink, with slightly protuberant eyes that suggested an excess of thyroid. It probably accounted for his seemingly boundless energy.

'Good man!' Gordon beamed at Thomas and swallowed a mouthful of coffee. He addressed Vonheim. 'Now, you're going to need a manager to look after your business affairs. I can set you up with one of the better people in London when you get there. On the other hand, I could probably look after you myself, which would save us all a lot of trouble. I must congratulate you, Otto. This is a very able young man, and just the sort of person I'm looking for.'

'I'm very happy to hear it. He has been a dedicated student, and . . .'

'It's time for him to go out into the real world and prove himself. That's different.' He turned to Vonheim again. 'Appearances count for a lot. The first thing we must do when you get to London is visit a tailor and get yourself a decent suit of clothes. I'll take you to see my man. Good Lord, look at the time! If I don't leave now, I'll never make Vienna!'

As they walked to the hotel foyer, Otto Thomas drew the Englishman aside. 'I hoped we would have time to discuss other matters, Mr Gordon. Your new orchestra, for example. Before Mr Vonheim appears with them, they might enjoy the benefit and the discipline of an older, more experienced conductor; someone who knows how to train and prepare them. I would be pleased to offer my . . .'

'Well, that's not such a bad idea, Otto. I'll give it some thought.' Gordon's pace increased. 'We don't have time to discuss it now, but I'll come back to you when I'm ready.' He offered his hand. 'It's been lovely seeing you again. What a shame we didn't have the opportunity to talk about you, but we'll make up for it next time. Do keep in touch.' He turned to Vonheim. 'Goodbye, Karl. I'll be calling you when I get back to London. Keep at it!'

Before picking up the telephone, Otto Thomas walked slowly across the living-room of his new apartment and closed the window. It was

41

on the ground floor of the multi-storey suburban building, and the noise of children in the playground was distracting.

Lancelot Gordon's secretary recognised him immediately. 'Hello, Doctor Thomas. You again!' She was cheerfully offhand. 'I'm afraid you've missed Mr Gordon. He's at a recording session, and can't be disturbed.'

'Did you tell him that I had called?'

'Yes.' He had the impression that she was suppressing a giggle. 'Every time. He's a very busy man, you know.'

'It is most important that we speak. He never returns my calls!'

'Well, I don't know what I can do about it. I'll leave a message on his desk. I always do. Have you thought of writing to him?'

'I have written several times. I am still awaiting a reply.'

The testiness in his voice brought about a more subdued reply. 'I'm very sorry. I'm sure he'll be writing to you shortly, as soon as he finds some time.'

'Well, please be sure to tell him that I called again. I am also very anxious to speak to Karl Vonheim.'

'Yes, I know. I passed the message to Mr Gordon the last time you called.'

'Can you tell me where I can reach him?'

'I'm afraid we're not allowed to give out artists' telephone numbers or addresses, Doctor Thomas. You could always write to him care of this office.'

'But he's an old friend! I introduced him to Mr Gordon.'

'Yes, you mentioned that before. I expect he'll be in touch with you, in that case. Of course, he's very busy too.'

Otto Thomas sighed audibly. 'Yes, everybody's very busy!'

There was a muffled sound, as though she had covered the mouthpiece with her hand. 'Is there anything else I can do for you?'

'No, thank you. Just tell them that I called.'

He replaced the receiver and shuffled back to the window. Bright sunlight made the small room warm and stuffy, and he edged the window open again. The sounds of the children greeted him. Then he seated himself at his desk and, taking an old-fashioned pen from the silver tray and inkwell, began composing another letter to London.

After a few sentences, he set the correspondence aside. He could not concentrate properly, and the words on the page looked blurred

42

and indistinct. The letter would have to wait until another time. A growing doubt inside him questioned whether it would ever receive a reply.

4

MAY, 1989

Sunshine had brought the morning crowds out on the Kärntner-strasse. The length of the great pedestrian show street, window-shoppers sauntered past brightly decorated displays, and the tables at the open-air cafés were already busy. Under coloured umbrellas, tourists in sports shirts and jeans rubbed shoulders with formally dressed Viennese businessmen, and even the grim-faced *hausfrauen* in traditional tweed suits and walking boots had been seduced by the warm air to throw off their heavy capes and woollen coats. Golden light dispelled the overcast that had enveloped Vienna all winter, persuading them that such a grey city really was the home of sparkling wine and Strauss waltzes.

Ignoring the festive atmosphere, and dressed in his usual black three-piece suit, Alexander Leitner scowled at some distant horizon and dared anyone to cross his path. The senior music critic of one of Vienna's most important newspapers, he was a well-known local figure, and it irritated him when the streets were littered with for-eigners. They clogged the pavements, took all the best seats in restaurants, and caused prices to soar. Despite the city's size and international history, it remained an overgrown provincial town, and Leitner shared its xenophobic mistrust of outsiders. He wished it would rain.

Leitner was disappointed. The damned Karl Vonheim press con-ference interrupted the routine of his day. Why did it have to be at eleven o'clock? All Vienna knew that, at that particular hour, he occupied his special table at Demel's café, where he read the day's articles, critiques and music news, occasionally invited guests, and frequently listened to musicians, dancers, composers, singers (whom he rarely included with musicians,) set-designers, directors, choreographers, writers and any other young hopefuls eager to draw

44

attention to themselves. A word in the right quarter or a comment in his daily column could make or break a career. It was his personal court, and he had been holding it for more than twenty years. Vonheim's army of minions should have taken it into account when they planned the conference.

He had considered ignoring the gold-embossed invitation (pretentious!) that had been hand-delivered to his apartment, but an opportunity to meet the elusive Karl Vonheim was too important. It might even justify a front-page story.

His mood darkened. It was that odious little Hungarian, Teleki, who was behind the conspiracy. Which of his artists had been in *Der Rosenkavalier* at the State Opera two nights ago? Leitner had written a particularly vitriolic article about the production, looking forward to the reaction it would cause at Demel's. The Hungarian had probably been forewarned, and arranged the conference accordingly, selecting The Imperial (more pretention!) at eleven just to steal his thunder. Leitner understood enough about politics in a city where every statement had a secondary meaning for those in the know.

It had to be Teleki! Karl Vonheim was above local intrigues. Irritating though his aloofness might be, he was unquestionably a great conductor. Still smarting at the loss of his moment of glory, the critic had spent longer than usual searching for the right balance between respectful praise and patronising encouragement in his review of Vonheim's Mahler Ninth. In the end, he had opted for a long dissertation on the symphony itself, adding that the conductor had given an almost-perfect reading.

He did not like to admit to it, but Leitner was curious to know the reason for the conference. In a city where gossip and rumour were life's blood, it was frustrating not to know in advance what Vonheim was going to say, and it had been infuriating not to learn anything from his usual sources of information.

When he was only two blocks away, he hailed a taxi. 'The Imperial Hotel.'

The driver looked round in surprise. 'But it's just around the corner!'

'Do you want the fare or not?'

The man shrugged. 'It's your money!'

He settled back, pulling ineffectually at the waistcoat that did little to conceal his spreading paunch. He had no intention of arriving on foot, but there was no need to waste money. Pop music blared from the radio, and he tried to ignore it. Viennese cab-drivers weren't what they used to be; so much for their famed *Gemütlichkeit*! Anyway, from the man's swarthy appearance, he was probably a Turk.

At the entrance to the hotel, Franz Gulick, a critic from one of the less influential papers, watched Leitner's disembarkation. He was accompanied by a severe-looking woman in a dark suit. 'Good morning, Herr Professor.' Gulick addressed his senior colleague deferentially. 'I expected to meet you here.'

Leitner grunted, shrugging. 'The gold-embossed "imperial" command? Naturally, my paper is interested.' He stared at the woman.

Switching to English, Gulick said, 'May I introduce Miss di Bonaventura. She is the Arts correspondent for the *Herald-Tribune*.' He turned to her. 'This is Professor Leitner.' His voice was suitably respectful.

The woman displayed expensively capped teeth and grasped Leitner's hand firmly. 'Hi!' It was evident that she had not heard of him.

Leitner retrieved his fingers. 'You are Italian?'

'Several generations back. I was born in Brooklyn.'

'Ah.' He smiled thinly, feigning Viennese charm. He disapproved of women in the music world. Anyway, what sort of person was an Arts correspondent? No doubt, she prepared glossy little reports for English-speaking tourists. In Vienna, music alone was a full-time occupation. His readers expected four full serious music pages daily.

They entered the elegant foyer of the hotel, and she abandoned Gulick. 'This is my first visit, so I'm hoping to do a little sightseeing.' She gazed at the pale décor and gleaming polished wood of the foyer. 'This is very fancy. The problem with the Hilton is that you could be anywhere in the world. I mean, this looks like the real old Vienna.'

'You might not have thought so in 1945, when the hotel was commandeered by the Russians.'

'Russians?' She looked nervous.

'Certainly. The city was divided, if you recall. They used this building as their headquarters. I remember that the foyer was a very gloomy place, with a single light bulb hanging from the ceiling, and a grim-faced Russian soldier behind the desk.' He paused, lost in thought. 'It was not a good place to be brought for questioning.'

The American had produced a note-pad and pencil. 'I understand Vonheim flew into Vienna this week, piloting his own jet.'

'Probably.' Leitner wondered whether he was about to be interviewed. 'He likes to fly himself round Europe when he travels. Otherwise, he prefers to drive his Ferrari.'

She was unaware of the disapproval in his voice. 'He's a character.'

Leitner smiled. 'On the contrary, my dear young lady, he is our greatest living conductor, which is why we ignore such little self-indulgences.'

'I don't understand.' She stared at him intently.

Leitner smiled patronisingly. Americans were always impressed by the trappings of success. 'It is not very dignified for an artist of his stature to fly aeroplanes and drive Italian sports cars.'

'It's no big deal as far as I'm concerned. Michel Legrand flies himself everywhere between concerts.'

'Really? And who is he?'

She was astonished by the question. 'Legrand? He's a composer and pianist. He writes all those terrific movie scores.'

'Ah yes, of course.' Leitner caught the eye of the music critic from *Le Monde*. Normally, he would not have bothered, for although he respected the newspaper, he had yet to be convinced that the French knew anything about music. Bowing slightly, he took his leave.

The American turned on Gulick, her voice accusing. 'I thought you said he was your top music man!' She spotted Peter Meredith and, without waiting for Gulick's reply, bore down on the Englishman. 'Hi, Peter.' She lowered her voice. 'With so many Herr Professors and Herr Doktors around, it's a relief to run into a plain old Mister!'

The Imperial's handsome dining-room had been transformed for the conference, its tables removed and the plush red armchairs arranged in rows facing a raised platform. Microphones were clustered before a wooden lectern, and the subdued lighting had been replaced by bright spotlights. A television crew had set up a camera. The lights made the room uncomfortably warm.

47

When about thirty journalists, self-conscious in the presence of the camera, had seated themselves, Zoltán Teleki appeared, leading three men to the platform. Smiling radiantly, he approached the microphones.

'Good morning, ladies and gentlemen.' His voice, amplified through speakers at the back of the room, boomed. 'My name is Zoltán Teleki, and I am very pleased to welcome you. I thought it would be best to speak in English, for the benefit of guests from other countries.' He glanced towards two empty chairs on the platform. 'The maestro and his guest will be here shortly, so I'll take this opportunity to introduce some very distinguished members of our organization.' He turned to the elegantly dressed man closest to him. 'First, may I present Mr Gregory Richmond, President of U.S. Artists Management Corporation in New York. Mr Richmond is Chief Executive Officer of Telmusik, our international television and film company, and he also looks after all the maestro's musical activities in North America.'

There was scattered applause as the American uncrossed a well-groomed leg to stand, briefly nodding acknowledgement. Richmond looked like a mature fashion model. Beneath the razor-edge crease of his trousers, his Gucci shoes glinted in the spotlights. His Ferragamo tie was perfectly knotted between the vee of an immaculately white custom shirt, and his Savile Row suit looked as though it had been freshly delivered that morning. Tiny lines were etched in the skin of a face that combined a deep tan with the smoothness of regularly applied hot barbershop towels.

While Richmond was thanking the journalists, Miss di Bonaventura stuck her elbow in Peter's ribs and whispered, 'The Romanian.'

'Who?'

'Richmond. His real name's Gregorio Romanescu, and he's known as the Romanian in New York music circles, but don't let him hear you say it!'

'I know who he is.'

'I should hope so. That man controls the American music world, and probably most of Europe, too. He's almost as exclusive as Vonheim. Just don't cross him, and don't let the suave charm fool you. That guy's got the instincts of a street fighter and the moral fibre of a rattlesnake!'

Peter grinned. 'I know quite a lot about him already, but I hadn't come across the nickname before. I'm rather interested in some of his dealings.'

'Tread lightly!'

Richmond had seated himself again, and Teleki indicated the heavy-set man at his side. 'My next colleague has appeared on your television screens many times, so he requires few introductions. Simon Ravenscroft started directing music films for the BBC in London many years ago and, since 1973, when our organisation was formed, he has been both the producer and director of all the maestro's Telmusik productions. I hope he'll have time to tell you about several major new projects.'

In contrast with Richmond, Simon was dressed in a cream-coloured safari jacket and matching slacks. His flowered shirt had a maroon cravat at the neck, and he gave the impression of a man in his late forties fighting the inevitability of age. His hair was cut short to disguise its rapid thinning, and his broad-rimmed glasses partially covered thickening jowls. Remaining seated, he waved a casual, self-effacing hand.

'Know him?' She bore into Peter with her myopic stare.

'Yes. We often run into one another.'

'I've seen his name on all those Vonheim movies. What's he like?'

'Very pleasant. Good at his job. He was one of the bright young men of the television industry. A whole bunch of them started in the BBC's Music and Arts Department and went on to bigger and better things: people like Ken Russell. Music films were relatively new then, and Simon was one of the directors who developed the technique of shooting them.'

She made a note. 'I guess I should try to talk to him while I'm here.'

Teleki moved towards the third man, who had chosen a seat at the far end of the platform. 'Finally, may I present Herr Wolpert, who's in charge of maestro Vonheim's secretariat in Hamburg.' Hans Wolpert, in a neat grey business suit, looked up in embarrassment, adjusting his rimless glasses, as though he had not expected to be included in the introductions. 'We rely absolutely on Hans to keep us advised of all the maestro's commitments and movements, especially when we need to talk to him.'

The reporter from *Der Spiegel* said 'Fat chance!' and there was a ripple of laughter.

Teleki simulated good-natured surprise at the comment, and pointedly ignored it. 'The maestro will be here shortly. Perhaps I can answer some questions?'

Pleased with the reaction he had achieved, the man from *Der Spiegel* asked, 'Will you tell us what maestro Vonheim earns. Is it true that he makes even more than Luciano Pavarotti?'

'I couldn't tell you.' Teleki smiled happily. 'I don't know what Signor Pavarotti earns.'

'You could give us a rough estimate.' There were more smiles.

'Please, ladies and gentlemen, we're not here to talk about money, although it always seems to fascinate the press. I remember when Isaac Stern gave a news conference at the Savoy in London, and all the reporters wanted to know was how much his Stradivarius was worth!'

'That was what interested their readers.' The reporter from the *Züricher Nachrichten* spoke earnestly. 'Most people want something more down-to-earth than a lot of high-flown talk about art and music.'

Alexander Leitner turned in his seat and glared at the man. Trust a Swiss to think like that! In the brief pause that followed, he surveyed the room, taking in his colleagues and appointing himself their spokesman. 'Perhaps you would be kind enough to tell us why we are all here today, Herr Teleki. You will appreciate that this is a very busy time for all of us.'

'Of course. That's why I'm so delighted to see you all here.'

'Rubbish!' *Der Spiegel* was hoping for another laugh. 'The mountain has finally come to Mohammed, or vice versa, and that's big news for all of us. Mind you, I'd better not print that, in case I have to move in with Salman Rushdie!' He was rewarded with a chuckle. 'You could at least give us a hint. The man has been avoiding us for twenty years.'

Teleki turned to Richmond for support, but the American said nothing, smiling encouragement. He faced the audience again. 'I don't want to spoil the effect. All I can promise is that the maestro has some very interesting news.'

'Will he answer questions?' Miss di Bonaventura did not want to be left out.

'If they are appropriate, yes.'

'Ah!' There was a note of triumph in Leitner's voice, and he again looked round to include his colleagues. 'Who is to say what is appropriate? What sort of questions will we be permitted to ask?'

A voice from the side of the room replied, 'Why don't you ask me, and I'll tell you.'

Karl Vonheim was standing in the doorway, watching him. He appeared to find the inquiry vaguely amusing.

5

The maestro entered the room and, in the buzz of excitement that his presence created, strolled casually to the platform. Under the lights, it had become oppressively warm, but he seemed unaware of it. His pearl-grey tropical suit bore no creases, and a pale eau-de-Nil shirt perfectly balanced a dark blue tie. When he faced the press, he nodded genially and, despite themselves, several journalists applauded enthusiastically.

At Peter's side, Miss di Bonaventura whispered, 'I see what you mean about his timing!'

Peter nodded. He wondered whether the conductor had been standing outside, waiting for the right cue to enter.

Vonheim faced the journalists. 'Please accept my apologies for being a little late.' His English was perfect. 'I knew I could rely on Zoltán to entertain you. I hope you weren't trying to make him reveal too many secrets.' The man from *Der Spiegel* nudged his neighbour and winked. 'Thank you for coming today. Your interest is flattering, and I hope you won't feel I've wasted your time.' For a moment, his gaze rested on Leitner, who shifted uncomfortably in his seat.

'Herr Teleki may have told you that I have prepared a statement.' A charmingly boyish grin appeared. 'I'm afraid that I am not a very accomplished public speaker, so I hope you'll forgive me if I read it.' He reached into his breast pocket.

Leitner rose to his feet. 'Maestro, before you read this statement, would you be kind enough to answer a few questions?'

The smile left Vonheim's face, and the room was still. 'What do you want to know?' His voice was cool.

The critic faltered momentarily. 'I think we all have questions we would like to put to you. You have never given us this opportunity before.'

For a moment, Vonheim did not reply, and his silence intensified the brittle atmosphere. Then he shrugged. 'I'll try to answer you.

By now, I would have thought my career was a matter of record.'
He smiled again, and the audience relaxed.

Gaining confidence, Leitner said, 'I think you underestimate
people's interest. You must be aware of the public's admiration for
you as a conductor. You heard that last night.'

Miss di Bonaventura whispered, 'Good for you! Ask him why he
didn't come out for a second bow!'

Leitner treated her to an irritated frown before addressing the
conductor again. 'From such a response, you must realise that
people want to know more about you as a person: your background,
your tastes, your interests.'

'Not necessarily, Professor Leitner.' He spoke mildly, and the critic
reacted at the sound of his name. He had not expected the conductor
to recognise him. 'I'm not a film star. My work involves the study and
interpretation of music, and I hope that last night's applause simply
reflected public approval of that work. I don't have many other interests and, as to my background and tastes, why should anyone really
care whether I prefer my steak rare or which is my favourite piece of
music? Is that the sort of thing they want to know?'

'No, not exactly.'

'That's a relief!' His smile broadened. 'I promise not to hide
anything from you. I confess that I like steak rare, but not blue. I
believe the French call it *saignant*, which is rather callous of them,
and I have no favourite work. There are too many!'

Leitner sat down abruptly, but Gulick came to his aid. 'Maestro,
my colleague was speaking for all of us when he said the public
would like to know more about you. Your opinions are valued.
There's a whole generation of younger musicians who'd like to
learn from you, and it's only natural that audiences are curious. As
journalists, we would like to tell them.'

'That's very kind of you.' Vonheim turned again to Leitner, and
Peter was conscious of his power to focus his attention. 'Forgive
me, Professor, I didn't mean to belittle your interest, nor to ridicule
serious questions. I suppose I've side-stepped flippant inquiries for
such a long time that I've come to assume that every question would
concern the most trivial aspects of my private life. Please ask your
questions.'

Encouraged, Gulick spoke firmly. 'Can we look forward to your
autobiography? We know so little about your early life and career.'

Vonheim considered the question before nodding slowly. 'I suppose so. One of these days, I'll put it all down on paper. I'm sure you know the old saying about some people enjoying their lives and others keeping diaries.' The quicksilver smile returned. 'I've never kept a diary! I hope you'll find my life interesting. Otherwise, I'll have to make it up as I go along.'

'That would hardly be necessary.'

Vonheim shrugged. 'What's so interesting about years of studying and learning scores, or reading biographies and correspondence from another age? That's what I do. Are you really fascinated by the amount of time I spent learning to master my baton technique? I haven't kept a scrapbook of reviews, and I've no intention of writing memoirs sprinkled with little bits of gossip about the people with whom I've worked, so it seems to me the book's going to be rather boring!' He paused, becoming more serious. 'My life has been dedicated to making music for the past forty years. There hasn't been time for anything else.'

'But people would like to know how you did it.'

'My friend, I'm still doing it – every day! I know it's been said many times before, but the joy and fascination of music, of any art form, is that the more you learn, the more you become aware of your ignorance. When I was twenty, I knew all the answers. By the time I was thirty, I was not so sure. Today, thank God, I realise how very little I know! So, as far as memoirs are concerned, I will write them when I retire. That, I hope, will be at some distant, future date. I simply don't have the time now.' Many of the journalists were making notes, and a Japanese reporter was holding up a tiny tape-recorder to catch every word. Vonheim shook his head slowly. 'I'm not as colourful a character as some of your articles suggest.'

'You read them?'

'From time to time.' He glanced towards Wolpert. 'I'm just as human as anyone else. My secretariat saves the more outlandish speculations about me. Who can resist the temptation to read such fascinating and imaginative stories about himself?'

Several questioners spoke at once, but Miss di Bonaventura raised her hand, and Vonheim singled her out with a friendly nod. 'Why didn't you take a second bow last night?'

Vonheim was silent, and Peter groaned inwardly. That sort of question belonged to the secretariat collection in Hamburg!

The maestro smiled at her. 'Do you think I should have?' His voice was almost intimate.

She looked confused. 'I guess most other conductors would have.'

'Perhaps.' He spoke gently. 'Don't you think we have allowed concerts to follow a certain ritualistic form?' Before she could reply, he continued, 'I'd prefer to think they're about music-making. You came last night to hear Mahler's Ninth symphony and, when it was over, you thanked me very generously. It didn't seem necessary to come back and ask for more thanks. If Mahler had been in the hall, I would have been delighted to see him take a bow, but I saw no reason to prolong the evening with an unnecessary ceremony. I understand that Sviatoslav Richter only plays an encore at the end of a recital if he feels he hasn't given his best during the concert itself.' He watched her face. 'Does that answer your question?'

'Yes. Thank you.' Her cheeks had coloured.

Peter raised his hand. 'Maestro, it seems to me that you spend most of your life travelling.'

'Musicians do. We're the last true nomads.'

'But as a Norwegian, you spend very little time in your homeland. You hardly ever conduct in Oslo. I would have thought that, as a war hero . . .'

The conductor frowned. 'I am not from Oslo. The hall there has a very dry, unflattering acoustic. The Grieghalle in Bergen is much better. Unfortunately, the orchestra leaves something to be desired.' Peter's question seemed to have touched a nerve, and the conductor's voice hardened. 'There is nothing left of my early life in Norway – nothing. It was all destroyed in the war. I have no reason to return. Those early years have only bad memories for me, and many regrets.' He was silent for a long time. 'I must also contradict you about my wartime experiences. I was not a hero. I was a survivor.'

Vonheim started into space, as though remembering. Taking advantage of his silence, Leitner cleared his throat noisily. 'Will you tell us how your career began? The details are very sketchy.' The maestro did not reply, and he continued, 'There is little information about your early years, and the first review I can find comes from London. Did you study there?'

'No.' He focused his attention again. 'When the war ended, I made my way to Germany, and lived in Munich. You see, since the age of ten, I have only ever had one ambition: to conduct. I studied the piano and, as a teenager, I taught myself languages because I knew they would be essential.' He shrugged. 'After all, I depend on language and gesture for my work. Living in a small village, cut off from the world, was an advantage, because I knew nothing about the distractions of urban life. I was in my early twenties at the time . . . at the time that the war ended.' He spoke hesitantly. 'When I escaped from Fjordby, I was given refuge by an old couple in the mountains. It was a wonderful place, even smaller and more remote than my own. I wasn't there for so very long, but it gave me time to recuperate. I was young and strong, and they took good care of me.' He smiled. 'I've tried to remain fit all my life. The calisthenics of conducting is good for the circulation. That's why we conductors keep going long after most other professions have retired!'

'You had no formal musical education?'

'It depends what you mean by formal. Not all of us need that sort of routine. Look at the Canadian pianist Glenn Gould. He studied with his mother, then a local teacher and, somewhat unwillingly, at the conservatory in Toronto, where he paid little more than lip-service to the formal academic syllabus. Not the sort of education you'd expect from an artist whose readings of Bach have influenced a whole generation of younger pianists. I suspect that very little of what he learned at school had anything to do with the way he played the piano.'

'You went from Norway to Germany. When was that?'

'In 1946.'

Miss di Bonaventura looked up from her notes. 'You didn't resent the Germans, after what they'd done?'

Vonheim's face was expressionless. His moods changed swiftly. 'That's a complicated question, and I think we'd need another time and place to discuss it. Yes, of course I resented the German army – particularly the SS – for what they had done to my home and family, but music and politics are separate issues. Even the communists finally had to concede that! The political life of a country should be divorced from its artistic activities, even though artists may reflect their world. Perhaps the downfall of Germany caused Strauss to write *Metamorphosen*; perhaps not. When I perform it, and when others play it fifty years from now, it will stand or fall simply as a work of art. In the same way, I must confess that I don't understand why the Israel Philharmonic, half a century after the end of the war, is not permitted to perform Wagner.' People were writing, and he smiled. 'As I said, it's a complicated issue. We should leave it to another occasion.'

Leitner was thoughtful. 'You said you went to Munich.'

The maestro laughed. 'So I did. We seem to have got side-tracked!' He glanced at the paper-thin Vacheron watch on his wrist. 'I had a burning ambition: to conduct. As a European, I felt that only two countries could offer me the musical background that I needed, and they were Germany or Austria. I chose Munich.' He spoke with an air of finality, as though closing the subject.

Professor Leitner was puzzled. 'But you first appeared in London.'

'No, my debut was in Munich, but it was attended by few people. You see, I was very lucky; very lucky and extremely ambitious. Nothing was going to stand in my way! My career began because I was discovered by an extraordinary musical personality who happened to be looking for someone like me at that moment: Lancelot Gordon.'

Leitner nodded, but Miss di Bonaventura, who was writing furiously, asked, 'Could you tell us a little about him?'

It was Vonheim's turn to look surprised. 'What can I tell you that is not already known? Gordon was one of the first great classical record producers, among many other things.' He glanced again at his watch, as though irritated by the diversion. 'Lancelot was a brilliant, self-educated, domineering and determined man of enormous foresight and talent. He was much more than a record producer: an entrepreneur and a showman who created the right circumstances. He had a sparkling wit and, when he needed it, great charm. He was innovative, charismatic, imaginative and totally dedicated to his work. The sort of plastic young men who call

57

themselves record producers these days could have learned a great deal from him!'

'How did you meet him?'

'Through a friend. In post-war London, the musical situation was an interesting one, ripe for exploitation, and Lancelot recognised it. The orchestras were in a sad state of disrepair, crippled by conservative, outmoded attitudes and strangled by overbearing unions. So he created a new one of his own: The British Symphony Orchestra. It was made up of the best players from all over the country, handpicked by Lancelot. And, as producer-in-chief of a powerful record company, he was in a position to use them, making sure they would become internationally famous. There were new technical developments too: tape recording and long-playing records, and Lancelot and his engineers were there to take advantage of the situation. All he needed was a young, malleable – that was one of his favourite words! – conductor through whom he could realise his plans.' He smiled broadly. 'He chose me!'

There was a long silence when Vonheim finished speaking. Professor Leitner could not hide his surprise. 'You attribute your career to good luck?'

'No.' The maestro seemed to relax, his concern with wasting time apparently set aside. 'I think recognition will eventually come to those who have the talent. Forgive me if this sounds conceited. I don't mean it that way. I was thinking of all those pianists and violinists, not to mention conductors and piccolo players, who tell you they *could* have been major names in the music world if only they'd been given the right opportunity. Of course, being in the right place at the right time is helpful but, sooner or later, if you have the ability, it will be recognised. The only element of chance is how long it takes to happen.'

Miss di Bonaventura whispered, 'Gee, I'm glad he warned me he wasn't conceited!' Raising her voice, 'Did Mr Gordon come specially to Munich to hear you?'

'He was on his way to recording sessions, and stopped in Munich.' Vonheim smiled. 'I told you I was lucky! I was still young and, to be honest, very green. Lancelot saw in me the opportunity to realise his own aspirations, and I was so grateful that I was prepared to do whatever he wanted.'

58

Leitner's bushy eyebrows were raised. 'Musically?'

'For a while, yes. Lancelot may have been self-taught, and he was certainly strongly opinionated, but he was also a man of taste, discrimination and musical insight. The fact that he was also a showman and a shrewd businessman taught me a lot, too. Above all, he had the ability to find talent. That was why his orchestra was so good.' He hesitated, looking again at his watch, and his glance travelled towards the door of the conference room. 'To recognise talent when you hear it is an important responsibility . . .'

Leitner interrupted. 'You said "For a while", maestro.' He was aware that the blue-grey eyes were watching him. 'I seem to remember a certain amount of publicity surrounding your separation from Mr Gordon and the orchestra.'

Vonheim was silent, and the journalist sensed a sudden coolness. Then the conductor shrugged. 'It was inevitable. We worked together for five or six years, and it was a wonderful experience. I owed much to Lancelot, but like many brilliant men, he was arrogant, egocentric, demanding, obstinate and tyrannical, and he never let me forget that I was his creation.' He smiled ruefully. 'It was true, but I wanted to show him that I had something to say for myself.'

'Did you resign?'

'We reached a compromise. I had little experience of the opera house, which was an area of music that didn't interest Lancelot as much. I think he found singers too independent and, unfortunately, less intellectually challenging! So, after much discussion, he agreed to release me to accept a position with the Colón in Buenos Aires. As to the comments in the press at the time, they were as usual grossly exaggerated.' He grinned. 'You journalists love to build up a drama! We were all raised on the apocryphal stories of the rivalry between Heifetz and Elman, and even today, music columns are full of reports about the supposed antagonism between two leading tenors who are, I'm told, on perfectly amicable terms.' His smile broadened. 'I'm sure you know all about such things, Professor Leitner!' There was a chuckle from one of the back rows, but Leitner's expression was stony.

Miss di Bonaventura asked, 'Did you enjoy your years in Argentina?'

The conductor's mood remained light. 'Very much. In some ways, opera is the most challenging of all musical disciplines, because it involves so many different forces. In others, it is the most frustrating, because the conductor cannot have absolute control. There are constant compromises with directors and set-designers, with chorus masters and, above all, with singers.' He shrugged. 'The music is not always of the highest standard, either. It's designed to show off the singers, but there are other compensations.'

'I understand you met your wife Dorothea there.'

'Yes.' He answered quickly, looking away.

'Is she an Argentinian?'

'Not really. Her family settled there.' The coolness returned, and Peter had the impression that part of the conductor had suddenly closed shut.

Miss di Bonaventura, unaware of his change of mood, gushed, 'Do you think she would give me a few minutes of her time? I'm sure readers would be interested to know about your life from the woman's angle.'

Vonheim's voice was cold. 'I don't believe my family or my private life are subjects for today's discussion.'

A devilish impulse made Peter ask, 'Is she a musician?'

'No.' He stared at the Englishman for a moment. 'I think we've met before haven't we?' Peter nodded. 'Aren't you the young man who came to see me in Salzburg?'

'Yes. It was in 1980.' He wondered why he was blushing slightly.

'I thought so. I seem to remember that you were proposing to write a biography, and wanted my official blessing.' The blue-grey eyes were very cold.

'Yes.'

'And I told you that I wasn't interested.'

'I'm afraid you did.'

Vonheim's expression was contemptuous, but he spoke mildly. 'I haven't changed my mind.' He turned away.

'I had hoped you would tell me why.'

The conductor had been about to speak, and glanced again in Peter's direction. 'Because, as I said earlier, I will write my own story, when I have the time.' His voice hardened. 'In addition, if I were to choose a biographer, I would hardly select a British journalist. That country's tabloid press is the ugliest and least informed

60

in the world. As my colleague George Szell used to say, you can't give good taste to people who don't have any!' He looked away again, and a murmur of conversation greeted the sharpness of his sudden attack. Professor Leitner looked delighted.

6

Leaning back in his chair, a relaxed smile frozen on his face, Simon Ravenscroft tried to concentrate on the conference. Karl was explaining why he had settled in Lausanne and had spent nearly twenty years building a great symphony orchestra in Switzerland. It was one of his favourite hobby-horses, and he disapproved of the new breed of young whiz-kids who spent their time guest-conducting around the world. The maestro was right – as usual! – but it was unrealistic to assume that every young musician must have the same kind of monastic dedication to his art. There was only one Karl Vonheim. Simon was tired and anxious from a sleepless night, and his attention wandered. Where the hell was Rachel?

She had promised to join him in Vienna the day before, but had not arrived. Long after the last plane from London, he spent the rest of the evening calling her flat in Putney, to be frustrated by her answering-machine announcing that she was unavailable but please leave a message. Where was she and, even worse, with whom? And why did a natural emotion like love have to be such a bloody possessive affliction? He glanced at his watch. The first flight from London wasn't due for another hour, so there was no point in fretting. Pay attention to the Great Man!

It was all so painfully humiliating. Simon Ravenscroft, age forty-eight, internationally known television producer, director and presenter, a leading figure in the medium, cannot think straight because his bloody twenty-six-year-old assistant secretary, aide, companion and bedfellow is giving him the runaround! What was the expression his teenage children used? Naff! What the hell was the matter with him? He should have spent the previous evening preparing the score of the Bruckner Seventh, planning camera shots for the maestro's Salzburg concert. Instead, he had sat by the phone, willing it to ring and, when it didn't, dialling London to hear that stupid machine with its impersonal message. Why was he so upset? There had been several young women in his life before Rachel, so what made her so different?

She was different. He was convinced of it. When she had first come to work for him at Telmusik, three years earlier, he had immediately found her physically attractive. He liked women with big breasts and narrow waists. It was probably a throw-back to his teenage years at boarding school, when pin-ups in smuggled copies of *Playboy* had inspired his sexual fantasies. But he had been more impressed by her intelligence. Rachel revealed a knowledge and sophistication beyond her years and, when he questioned her about it, had shrugged it off.

'Oh, one of my lovers was an older man. I learned a lot from him.'

The comment had intrigued him. What else had she learned? From casual remarks, her life seemed to have included a wide variety of men. Simon has been amused when she had used the old-fashioned term 'lover' instead of 'boyfriend'. Later, after they became involved, the images of those others returned to taunt him. Christ, she had once confessed that she couldn't remember all their names!

They had become lovers within a year. It had happened, romantically enough, in Venice, when they were there for a shoot, selecting background material for the maestro's programme about Vivaldi. Too much wine, a sultry evening, and he had stumbled into her bedroom, to find her waiting for him, laughing.

'What took you so long?'

He had been astonished and thrilled by her passionate responses and uninhibited love-making. It was different from anything he had experienced before, and the memory of her elated cries as she climaxed still excited him. They had made a joke about keeping a pillow handy to stifle the noise.

It should have ended there, but it hadn't. Whenever they were together, he wanted to recapture the clumsy, breathless frenzy of that first time, and his senses were constantly aroused by the taste and perfume of her body, the firmness of her flesh. It had never happened again in quite the same way. The intensity of that night in Venice eluded him, no matter how desperately he tried to evoke it. A familiar gesture or a moment of physical contact took on a disproportionate significance, and their clandestine meetings for a few stolen hours in her flat became the most important moments in his life.

At first, she would not permit the word 'love' in their whispered conversations. Their relationship was to be light-hearted. It was all supposed to be a temporary situation, but as weeks drifted into months and inconsequential events became secret anniversaries to be celebrated, their attachment became more emotional than physical. On a trip to Paris, when Vonheim was conducting *Pelléas et Mélisande* at the Opera, Simon had spoken of divorce, but she had silenced him.

'I don't want to be the cause of your break-up. If you want to leave your wife, that's up to you, but you've got to do it for yourself; not for me.'

He had been hurt. His offer to give up everything – home, family, security – was a sacrifice: a token of his love, but she had rejected it, unwilling to share the responsibility.

In the past six months, the situation between them had changed subtly. She had become a passive, almost docile partner. If they made love, it was because he initiated it, and she seemed indifferent to his efforts to arouse her. Excitement and anticipation had been replaced by routine foreplay.

'Christ! Why do you leave all the work to me?'

'I'm sorry, darling, but I'm not really in the mood.'

'That's patently apparent!'

'Well, you can't expect me to switch on at the drop of a hat.'

'If you didn't want to, why didn't you say so?'

'I didn't want to hurt your feelings. You're so uptight about sex.'

The words stung, and he had left her flat early, angry and frustrated, but wanting her more than ever.

Lately, she had become critical. At the beginning, Rachel had admired everything he did, confessing in a small voice that she was slightly in awe of him and secretly astonished that he should waste his time on her. He had been touched by her naïvety. More recently, she had discovered flaws.

'Why do you wear that awful suit? It's so old-fashioned. If you're going to appear on camera, you should try something by Armani.'

'I hate his stuff. It looks as though it's been slept in!'

'It's better than what you're wearing. That one looks as though it smells of moth-balls!'

He had ordered a new suit, but she hadn't like the style or colour.

'You know, you should try contact lenses. You'll soon get used to them.'

'I'd rather not. I hate having anything put into my eyes. Anyway, what's wrong with my glasses? They're almost a trademark.'

'Maybe. I think you should change them. If you won't try contacts, order new frames.'

'What's wrong with these?'

'They make you look old.'

Who the hell did she think she was? He was Simon Ravenscroft. He had interviewed leading figures in the world of music and the arts, and they hadn't criticised his taste in clothes. He had produced and directed award-winning programmes, and appeared before an audience of millions. Nobody had mentioned his 'old-fashioned' glasses. Was he really supposed to worry about what Rachel thought? Simon hesitated. He cared more about her opinion than anyone else's.

Perhaps it was just the disparity in their ages. He wasn't old but, for God's sake, Rachel was only nine years older than his daughter Sarah! For all her experience and worldliness, it had to make a difference. Her generation had grown up with other standards, which explained the long succession of lovers who had shared her before him. And, if that had been her previous life-style, what was to prevent her from returning to it? Which brought him back to last night. Where had she been? Had she met someone new and, with the same casual abandon that had once been reserved for him, invited a stranger to occupy her narrow little bed in Putney? The thought tortured him.

It was time to leave her. Perhaps that was what she was waiting for him to do. She had joked about those louses going back to their spouses, in the words of the song, but maybe it had been wishful thinking. What about his spouse? If Ann suspected anything, she gave no indication of it. She rarely told him what she was thinking. They were still friends, but they shared little. They rarely made love any more, and he suspected that she was secretly relieved. Ann had never enjoyed the physical side of their marriage.

Perhaps it was time to find a way out of his relationship with Rachel, but it was not going to be easy. His body still ached for her, and the memory of Venice still haunted him. Maybe he could find her new responsibilities at Telmusik that would bring them less into daily contact with one another. Enforced separation might draw them together again.

Or perhaps it was time for him to leave Telmusik. Everyone at the Beeb had been surprised when he had resigned to become a freelance. It paid better, covering the mortgage on the house in Richmond, but they had all assumed that he, as the bright young man of serious television, would eventually head the department. He had been in his late twenties when he had first met Vonheim, and was flattered that the maestro should have singled him out to develop the new film company. The early period had been exhilarating and when, after five years, Gregory Richmond had proposed a full-time association, there had been no reason to refuse.

Simon frowned. The possibilities were more limited than he had first anticipated. Telmusik was supposed to diversify, making programmes that did not necessarily involve Karl Vonheim. They had never materialised, and Richmond was always too busy to discuss other aspects of the company's operations. There had been occasions when Simon hated Telmusik and the demands it made on his life. Bloody Hamburg! It had been the cause of too many problems.

He glanced at his watch again, and tried to concentrate on what the maestro was saying. Question Time was coming to an end, and it was the moment to get down to the real business of the conference.

But where the hell was Rachel?

7

A number of journalists, still eager to question the maestro, spoke at once, but Vonheim raised his hands to silence them.

'I'm sorry, but I've said all I want to say about myself. If you need additional information, I'm sure the press departments of the various companies who produce my records will be only too happy to supply you with biographies and illustrated brochures.' He grinned. 'Despite the somewhat florid prose, they usually manage to print the facts right! We've wasted the last quarter of an hour going through an encapsulated biography of my early years and, as I warned you, there is nothing exceptionally revealing about them. Besides, I don't enjoy talking about myself. I asked you to join me here because I wanted to tell you about somebody else.'

He withdrew his prepared statement from an inner pocket and, after a slight hesitation, tore it in half. The gesture was dramatic enough to command absolute silence. 'I don't think I'll read this after all. A carefully written press-release won't communicate the sort of personal excitement I feel.'

There was a stir of interest in the room, and the audience leaned forward intently.

'As you know, a conductor performs with many soloists. Over the years, I must have worked with hundreds, if not thousands, ranging from the legendary, like Artur Rubinstein, to the immediately forgettable, like . . .' He stopped himself, smiling. 'That wouldn't be kind, would it?' He was silent, but nobody interrupted him. When he spoke again, his voice was soft, but the words were very clear. 'I hope you will understand my astonishment and my exhilaration when I chanced – quite by accident – to encounter playing by a young pianist of such extraordinary quality that I can say without exaggeration that I was completely transfixed. It was the sort of playing you hope to hear all your life, if you're lucky: in the great tradition, yet with something new and imaginative to say; with virtuoso brilliance, but always serving a musical purpose; spontaneous, but at the same time deeply considered. This was music-making at the highest possible level.' He was silent again, allowing his words to sink in.

Despite his interest, Peter Meredith was forced to admire the theatrical way in which the maestro stage-managed his presentation. So much for his self-effacing modesty! He would have been willing to wager that Vonheim had never intended to read that statement.

The maestro looked at his audience, and his gaze seemed to rest on each person in the room. 'Having made this rare discovery, I decided on an unusual course of action: to make myself totally responsible for the development of the career. It is a talent too precious to slip through one's fingers. It needs to be nurtured, encouraged, trained and protected until it blossoms into full maturity. That, in itself, is a very serious responsibility, but I am prepared to take it on.' He stopped, and the audience remained silent.

'However, before I say anything further, let me introduce you.' He turned towards the open doorway and, with the briefest nod, invited his unseen guest to enter.

There was a gasp of surprise. A young woman appeared. She was tall and slim, and the dark hair falling to her shoulders framed pale skin and classic features. Except for a trace of red on her lips, she did not appear to be wearing make-up. It was the sort of face that needed no artificial enhancement. Despite her slender frame, her body had a suggestion of voluptuousness, disguised beneath a simple black dress on which there was no jewellery. She moved gracefully towards the platform, her deep blue eyes never leaving the maestro's face. Karl Vonheim took her hand, bowing over it with old-world courtesy before turning again to the audience.

'Ladies and gentlemen, may I present Miss Francesca Noble.'

In the scattered applause which followed, Miss di Bonaventura leaned against Peter. 'Jesus Christ! He's picked up a showgirl!'

'She's very beautiful.' He would not have chosen the same description. Beneath the high cheekbones and the serene, perfectly moulded features, there was a suggestion of passionate intensity which he found intriguing.

The American laughed. 'You noticed! I was beginning to wonder about you! Jesus, I'd kill for a body like that! She's fantastic! I'd also bet my last traveller's cheque that little item she's wearing is a Pucci. I saw it in last month's *Vogue*. D'you think she's for real?'

'She must be. Vonheim wouldn't talk about any musician that way if he didn't mean it.'

'Well, you know more about him than I do. Someone told me that our Karl was something of a lady's man. Maybe he felt like a last fling before he traded in his baton for a walking-stick. It's been known to happen.'

'Not with a conductor like Vonheim. You don't know what makes him tick.'

She chuckled. 'With a broad like that around, he'll vibrate!'

Professor Leitner was astonished. He mistrusted all women in the concert world, believing them incapable of real musical understanding. For him, it had always been a male domain, and women could never comprehend the depth and philosophy of the great masters. This one looked like a model or a chorus-girl! Karl Vonheim must have taken leave of his senses!

The maestro nodded, acknowledging the applause. 'Miss Noble comes from the United States of America. She is from Roxbury, Connecticut.'

The Viennese critic was horrified. An American! The conductor was adding a further insult!

'However, her family was originally German.' There was a gentle smile on Vonheim's face. 'I'm sure you would approve of that, Professor Leitner!' He turned towards the young woman, whose hand he still held. 'I understand your grandfather's name was Edel.'

When she spoke, her voice was pleasantly low-pitched but with a detectable hint of nervousness. 'That's right. When he became an American citizen, he decided to translate it into English, so we became Noble. I'm not sure where the Francesca comes from. I guess my mother just liked the name!' She shrugged uneasily, seemingly at a loss to add further explanations.

Professor Leitner stood. Inside, he was trembling with rage, but his voice remained calm. 'May we learn, sir, where this . . . unusual audition took place?'

The maestro was very relaxed. 'Certainly. It happened, purely by accident, a few months ago in Switzerland. Miss Noble did not realise at the time that she was auditioning for me. I suppose you could say that I eavesdropped on her, and took upon myself the discourtesy of interrupting her. You see, what I heard was a musician of very special and unique talent: someone who understands the meaning as well as the language of music. As a conductor, I have spent my life searching for qualities such as these. That is why I have undertaken, with Miss Noble's consent, to sponsor her career and, wherever I can, to further her musical education. I hope that my own knowledge and experience over the past forty years will bring something to it.'

'I see. Will Miss Noble play for us today?' The conductor's smile vanished, and Professor Leitner pointed to a piano in a rear corner of the dining-room. 'There is an instrument here. I do not know whether it is very good.' His voice had a hard edge. 'It is usually used to entertain hotel guests at dinner.'

Vonheim's voice was cold. 'You surprise me, Professor. A hotel press reception is hardly the place for a piano recital, would you say? I have taken this opportunity to present a very important young musician; not a circus act!'

Almost under her breath, Miss di Bonaventura muttered, 'Whoops! Here comes trouble!' Peter did not reply. He found himself still gazing at the young woman standing next to the maestro, fascinated by her beauty.

Leitner's complexion darkened, but his voice remained even. 'It would seem like a reasonable opportunity.' He turned to face the audience. 'I am sure we would all want to hear her play.' He was gratified to hear a murmur of assent. Even the Swiss reporter smiled encouragingly.

After a moment, the maestro shrugged. 'Perhaps you are right, Professor, although I'm not certain whether she is ready to play for you yet. She must decide that. After all, she finds herself standing before a very distinguished panel of critics and journalists; rather an awesome ordeal! She has already auditioned for me. I would have thought that was sufficient.'

'Quite so.' Leitner was subdued. 'If Miss Noble does not intend to play, I was curious to know why you chose this particular time to introduce her.' He stared at Zoltán Teleki.

Vonheim's glance took in the room. 'That's easy enough to explain. This is Vienna's *Festwochen*, when the city, which is the heart – if no longer the centre – of the music world, plays host to the international music press. It seemed like an excellent time for you to meet her. I am sure that, in time, you will hear her play – frequently.'

Peter smiled. That fat old Viennese windbag had puffed up like a pouter when the conductor had described his city as the heart of the music world, and winced when he had added that it was no longer in the middle. Vonheim one, Leitner nil! Despite a life preoccupied with music and contemptuous of 'showbiz' excesses, the maestro was no mean showman himself.

The critic was about to reply, but Vonheim continued, 'If Miss Noble would like to play for you, I'm sure she will. Why don't you ask her?' He faced the young American, who shook her head briefly, and he nodded sympathetically. 'We'll have to wait for a more suitable occasion. Now, you asked how we met. It was in Geneva . . .'

Listening to Karl coping with the press so easily, Francesca wondered whether she would ever have the same confidence. He made it all sound so simple! 'We met in Geneva!'

Her money had been running out, which meant that the long-awaited Grand Tour was over. She had hoped it would last at least a month longer. There were still so many places to see, but everything had been twice as expensive as anticipated, even though her carefully planned budget had been allocated to cheap *pensions* and the ubiquitous fast food houses. Imagine sampling the glories of Europe on a diet of Big Macs and french fries! She had vowed, several times, that she would never eat another.

And then, out of the blue, Mike had materialised. They had known each other as fellow students at the Peabody Institute in Baltimore, but had never been close friends. At the time, she had been suffering the agonies of puppy love for a violist who had wooed her, bedded her and abandoned her three months later. After the break-up, she had been distraught, burying herself in her studies, until a kindly bassoon student who told jokes had made her laugh all the way into his bedroom, where he taught her that sex could be

71

exciting, innovative and entertaining, but did not necessarily have to be taken seriously all the time. She had recuperated from her unhappy affair with such rapidity that it still made her blush. Meanwhile, Mike had been going steady with a skinny blonde pianist who had also been his accompanist.

She had been window-shopping on Geneva's Rue du Rhône, looking at shoes and watches and dresses she could not afford, and delaying the visit to the airline office to confirm her return flight. A voice had hailed her.

'Hey, Fran! Where the hell did you spring from?'

'Mike, is it really you?' In her delight, she had thrown her arms around his neck and kissed him on the mouth. 'What are you doing here?'

'Subbing in the Suisse Romande orchestra. They're short of violinists, so I got the job for six weeks. They won't let me stay longer. How about you?'

'Vacation. I've been doing Europe: London, Paris, Rome, Florence. It's all so beautiful!'

'Then why so sad?'

'I'm leaving tomorrow.'

'D'you have to go? Why?'

'No more money. It just ran out. As a matter of fact, I'm on my way to the ticket office now.'

'Don't do that.' His arm was still about her waist, and he had hugged her. 'We only just met. It's so good to see you again! Listen, I rented a little apartment in the old town, just up the hill. Why don't you stay? It's pretty cramped, but there are two rooms and a hot water system I don't understand. You could sleep on the settee. It wouldn't cost anything. Do you need to get back?'

'Not yet, I guess, but . . .'

'Then stay for a while. To be honest, this is a nice town, but it's not much fun doing everything on your own. Do you speak French?'

'Some.'

'Mine's terrible. I can't even ask for the bathroom without making people laugh! You could be my interpreter. Listen, it would be great to have you around!'

'I don't think I . . .'

72

'Oh, come on! Why not? We've got a lot of catching up to do. Christ! It's been nearly four years!'

'As long as that?'

'Sure. Are you still going round with that funny bassoon player?'

'Jake? No, we split up years ago, before I finished at Peabody. How about you and . . .'

'Alice? She's teaching in Omaha, or Wounded Knee, or some place like that. She settled down and married the boy next door. Well, what do you say? Will you stay on for a few days?'

'I suppose I could.'

'Listen, Karl Henrik Vonheim's conducting the orchestra next week.'

'Really?'

'In person! I tell you, the whole goddam place is going crazy, with extra rehearsals scheduled, and all. It's going to be the biggest event of the season. I might even be able to get you a ticket. I know a guy who knows a guy.'

'I've always wanted to hear him, but I don't think I can . . .'

'Tell you what, let's talk about it over a cup of coffee. There's a little brasserie called La Cave, opposite Victoria Hall. All the boys in the band hang out there. I might even stand you a fondue.'

'Anything, as long as it's not a hamburger!'

She had stayed and, of course, she had not slept on the sofa. Mike had been generous and thoughtful, both in and out of bed. On the first morning, he had woken her gently.

'Listen, this is great, and I'm glad you're here, but let's keep it cool. OK?'

'OK.'

'I mean, we can have a terrific time, exploring Switzerland together. Maybe I'll rent a car. But let's not do something dumb like fall in love. It's not on my agenda.'

'Nor mine.' Momentary disappointment had given way to a sense of relief.

'I'm glad. Jesus! I'd forgotten how incredibly beautiful you are! His fingers, delicately tracing the contours of her body, had raised goose-flesh on her skin and, with it, a renewed surge of passion.

For an instant, Francesca remembered the open window of his bedroom, and hot sunlight streaming across them.

73

It must have been a week later. The orchestra had been rehearsing, and Mike had gone to see the personnel manager about something. While waiting for him, she had wandered onto the deserted stage of Victoria Hall. A piano had been left in place, and she had sat before it, letting her hands idle on the keyboard. It seemed as though an age had passed since she had last played, and her fingers felt clumsy and out of practice. Concentrating her attention and feeling impatient with herself, she had been absorbed in the music. Gradually, as discipline and control returned, the slow movement of the Schumann Concerto had taken shape.

A voice, somewhere behind her, had asked, 'Why did you make a *ritardando* there? It isn't marked in the score.'

'It felt right. Anyway, I have to slow down, or the next sequence would rush.'

'Good. As long as you have a valid reason, any alteration is justified, with or without the composer's consent!'

She had continued to play, ignoring the intruder. He was obviously trying to be a smart-ass! The next passage was difficult to bring off, and she had leaned forward, willing her fingers to respond.

'That was excellent, but you should allow a longer pause at the end, or the orchestra will never catch you.'

Francesca had looked round, irritated by her self-appointed advisor. Then she had recognised him.

'Oh my God!'

'Am I that frightening?' The maestro's smile had been disarming. He was slightly shorter than she had imagined.

'Yes . . . at least, no. I mean, I guess so.'

'I'm sorry. I didn't intend to disturb you, but I was impressed by . . . Please don't go.'

'I shouldn't really be here.'

'I promise not to report you. What is your name?'

'Francesca. Francesca Noble.'

'I don't think I've heard of you. Do you live here in Geneva?'

'No, I'm just . . . visiting.'

'But you are a pianist?' He had continued to smile, and his gaze was hypnotic, making her feel trapped.

'Well, yes, I guess. I hope so.'

74

'Then why don't you finish the concerto? Let's do it together. Shall I conduct for you?'

'Conduct?' The stage was empty.

'Certainly. I'd like to hear what you do with the third movement.' Karl Vonheim had stepped onto the podium. 'Start with the big theme after the transition. I'll follow your tempo.' She had hesitated, unable to move. 'Don't think about me.'

'I haven't practised!' It was almost a plea.

'That's not important. Don't worry about wrong notes. They're not what I'm listening for. Now, play!'

It had been an unreal, dreamlike experience. For a few seconds, she could not see the keyboard of the piano, was convinced that she could not remember the music. Then, she had begun to play, closing her eyes and trusting her memory. The triumphant theme seemed to play itself, and after several more bars, she had forgotten the name and the awesome reputation of the man who faced her, his hands indicating a subtle tempo change or an instrumental entry. Everything had been concentrated on her performance and, as her confidence grew, the music had emerged effortlessly. When it was over, she had sat in silence, staring at the piano, afraid to look at him.

His voice had been very soft. 'You're a fine young pianist, Miss Noble. I hadn't expected you to play like that. Remarkable! I'd like to know more about you. Tell me, is that young man over there waiting for you?'

Mike had been standing at the side of the stage, half-hidden. 'Yes, we're supposed to . . .'

'Tell him to go home. I want to talk to you.'

They had spoken for more than an hour, at the end of which Karl Vonheim had instructed her to return the next morning at eleven.

'I'll be in my dressing-room. Please try to be prompt.'

'Yes. Thank you. I'll be there, and . . .' She had called her farewell, but he was already walking away.

The events of the following morning had been even more extraordinary. The maestro, seated behind his desk, had handed her a typewritten document.

'Good morning, Miss Noble. May I call you Francesca?'

'Yes, of course.'

'Very well. I have written a letter to your parents, which is self-explanatory. You'd better read it for yourself, however. You'll also need to add the correct names and the address.

'I'm proposing to sponsor your career. You are an excellent young musician, but you still have a great deal to learn. What I have heard so far are only the basic ingredients, but those qualities are extremely rare and possessed by very few artists. They have to be carefully developed.'

She had been too astonished to reply, and his voice became coolly impersonal. 'What I suggest, therefore, is that you move immediately to my house in Lausanne, where you will start to work with me. You have much studying and practising alone ahead of you, but whenever I am in Switzerland, I am prepared to supervise your preparation personally. When I am away, I will arrange for a piano tutor from the Conservatoire in Lausanne, who can help you with your technique but, as you probably know, that's something that only you can develop.

'When I think you're ready, I will supervise your European and American debuts, including the concerts I'll conduct for you, but that won't happen for a while. Right?'

'Yes.' She could not have managed a longer sentence!

'Good. Now, when it's appropriate, I'll expect you to accompany me to other cities when I'm giving concerts. It would be helpful for you to become acquainted with them and to meet the influential figures who will play a part in your public career. You'll need to come to terms with the sort of life you'll be expected to lead. I assume you already realise it's an entire way of life; not just some sort of everyday profession?'

'I guess so.'

'The sooner you adapt yourself to it, the better. From now on, you have to consider how you live, how you dress, where you stay, with whom you associate; how you eat, even. They're all going to be part of your future persona.'

She would have spoken, but he continued, 'For the moment, I don't think it's advisable for you to give more than a handful of concerts and recitals. Apart from the experience of playing before the public, they'd be a waste of time that could be better applied to study and preparation. Of course, I realise this will give you little financial independence, so I'll include a modest monthly allowance. Your food and accommodation will be looked after, so it amounts to little more than pocket-money. I hope you don't smoke.'

'No.'

'Then everything seems to be settled. How soon can you move?'

She had hesitated. 'I'm not sure. I mean, it's all so unexpected! I don't know what to say. What exactly do you expect from me?'

He had been puzzled, then impatient. 'I've just spent the last few minutes telling you. Listen, Francesca, you have a real and very special talent, one that few musicians of your age or experience will ever possess. By a happy coincidence, I was there to recognise it. But it's still a raw, undeveloped talent that will only surface if you're prepared to work, practise and dedicate yourself to developing it twenty-four hours a day, every day! If you don't think you can do that, we have nothing further to discuss. Well?'

'I didn't mean to sound ungrateful. It's just that . . . well, moving into your house and . . . .'

He had been amused. 'My dear child, what on earth are you suggesting? I'm old enough to be your father. I live in a huge house with my wife and, the last time I counted them, five servants. I have absolutely no interest in anything but the talent you displayed yesterday!'

'I'm sorry. I didn't mean to . . .'

'Listen, Francesca. When you played, I heard enough to convince me that you have the potential to be not just a good musician but a great artist. Do you understand what that means? I'm offering you the opportunity of a lifetime!'

For a moment, his expression was sad. 'I'm not sure whether I should be pleased or sorry for you. Greatness carries with it a loneliness and a dedication that will separate you from the rest of the world. If you come to me, it won't be easy. It will require hard work, of course, and self-discipline, but it will also call for self-denial, including any emotional attachments. That young man who was waiting for you yesterday, is he your lover?'

She had blushed. 'Well, yes, I guess so. We're just friends, really.'

'He'll have to go. You won't have time for attachments like that.'

'Well, I . . .'

Mike was already dismissed. 'Shall I send your parents this letter? I know you're old enough to make up your own mind, but I'm old-fashioned enough to believe they should know what sort of decision you're making.' His smile was charming. 'Besides, I would hate them to think you were in the clutches of a white-slaver!'

It seemed to Francesca that there never really had been a choice.

8

'Now, if you will forgive me, I must go.' Karl Vonheim faced the journalists. 'I will leave the stage to Miss Noble and my colleagues. I believe they have some announcements regarding future plans. I hope you find them interesting.' He stepped back from the microphone, shaking his head to a chorus of further questions, and walked to the door. 'Good-bye, and thank you.'

The man from *Der Spiegel* called, 'See you again in twenty years!', but if the conductor heard him, he gave no indication.

The maestro's departure caused an uneasy hiatus. The television crew at the back of the room started to dismantle their equipment noisily, and the bright lighting was turned off. There was a murmur of conversation.

Zoltán Teleki took over, planting himself next to Francesca. 'I expect you would like to ask Miss Noble a few questions.' He smiled expectantly, looking from face to face, but nobody responded. Karl Vonheim had been the star attraction of the conference.

Sensing that a fellow American was in distress, Miss di Bonaventura came to the rescue. 'Would you like to give us a few details of your background? Where did you study?'

'Mostly at home in Connecticut. I started in Roxbury with a local teacher, then went to a music school in Danbury. After that I won a scholarship to the Peabody Institute in Baltimore.'

She would have liked to add much more: the years of practice, and the long hours of sweating it out over a phrase that her fingers could not manage; the times when she had nearly given up in desperation, convinced that she would never master the instrument; the moments of elation, when she finally achieved a passable performance. In retrospect, they seemed trite. Every pianist went through the same apprenticeship, and the international press was not interested in hearing about it.

79

'Did you enter any competitions?'

'A few. I never made the finals, I'm afraid.' Should she describe the long, unnerving periods of waiting in musty dressing-rooms, the chilling shafts of uncertainty; the fear that, when the moment came, she would freeze onstage; the brief moment before the jurors, when the piano itself had seemed to resist her? On two occasions, she had sworn never to compete again. How could they compare a Beethoven Sonata with a Debussy Prelude? Were you first past the post if you played Mozart rather than Rachmaninov? She wished the maestro were still there.

'How about concerts?' Miss di Bonaventura was reaching.

'I played a number of community concerts and recitals.'

Her teacher had organised them through colleagues in other cities, and she had sent tapes to various orchestras around the country. Few had bothered to reply.

She had also done the rounds of New York managements, begging for interviews, typing biographies and saving good reviews from local newspapers. No-one had displayed more than a passing interest, promising at best to come to her next New York performance, if she found an engagement. But how, without a manager could she do that? As one elderly agent, close to retirement, had explained, the world was full of pianists. She would need something special. A young man working for one of the bigger groups had taken her phone number and made a pass at her, suggesting that a 'warmer relationship' might inspire interest. In one of the smaller agencies, a middle-aged woman with hair like wire wool had made a similar proposition. She had turned down both. Reaction to her had varied from total disinterest to patronising encouragement. It was too bad she hadn't won a competition.

But Karl Vonheim believed she had something special, and his opinion meant more than all the others. Then again, he had actually heard her play.

Peter Meredith asked, 'How did you actually meet maestro Vonheim?'

She smiled at him gratefully. 'Like he said, by accident. He heard me playing, and came over to talk to me. Actually, he apologised for interrupting me!'

'What happened next?'

'We talked for a while. He said some encouraging things about my playing, and then he offered to sponsor my career. I've been working with him ever since.' She hoped he would not ask her about living in the Vonheim household. Journalists had a talent for making embarrassing assumptions.

Alexander Leitner fixed her with a glassy stare. She wondered why he was so hostile. 'When will you make your debut with Mr Vonheim?'

'I . . . I'm not sure.'

'Why is that?'

'He said he would tell me when he feels I'm ready. I have to work on my keyboard technique, and I need to prepare a repertoire. After playing for him, and discussing the music, I have to re-think a lot of my interpretations.'

The Austrian's eyes narrowed. 'How about you, Miss Noble? When do you think you will be ready?'

She hesitated. 'I'd sooner trust in maestro Vonheim's judgement.'

Teleki came to her aid. 'I will be looking after Miss Noble's future concert plans. Several are awaiting confirmation. It hasn't been necessary to bother her with the details. We want her to feel free of the pressures of the concert world.' He brushed aside a further question from Leitner. 'We'll be offering you some refreshments shortly, so perhaps you'll prefer to talk to Miss Noble in person at that time.'

He signalled to the girl to sit in one of the vacant chairs. 'I thought we might talk about some of the maestro's future plans. I am particularly pleased that Mr Richmond is here, because there are interesting developments in our Telmusik Corporation. We established Telmusik in 1973 and, over the past sixteen years, we've built a library of great performances on film that have been seen all over the world. These films are of enormous educational value to musicians, and will be historically important documents for future generations.'

The man from *Der Spiegel* grunted, 'Not to mention the cash they earn!'

Teleki ignored him. 'Telmusik will be embarking on an ambitious educational series using the video medium. We will be able to teach young musicians by showing them the interpretations of the great artists of their time. We have therefore established The Vonheim Trust, a non-profit institution devoted to education via audio-visual aids. This will be supervised by Mr Richmond.'

Peter raised his hand. 'What form will the audio-visual aids take?'

'First, we'll distribute our existing library to music schools and academies around the world. There will be video-cassettes and discs, but we're also hoping to develop material of a more technical nature to supplement the training syllabus.' He smiled. 'There must be few conservatories that would turn down the chance of having maestro Vonheim on their teaching staff!'

The reporter from Zurich asked, 'How will the Trust be funded?'

'A number of sources. Obviously, there will be hire fees, to cover production and administration costs, but we'll also discuss the underwriting of new productions with the educational authorities of those countries wishing to benefit from the scheme. Perhaps Gregory should explain how this will work.'

He turned to the American, who seemed disinclined to leave his chair. 'You've covered the overall approach very well, Zoltán. I have a committee preparing the full programme. We'll send out details when they're ready.'

Peter addressed his next question to Richmond. 'Will all this be on a strictly non-profit basis?'

'Of course.'

'But the material won't be free of charge?'

Richmond shrugged. 'That's not possible. The escalating costs of video production are so horrendous that we'll need funds for an on-going programme. A one-hour documentary used to be budgeted for a few hundred thousand dollars. Today, the same movie runs over a million. Musicians and technicians have to be paid, you know.' He smiled condescendingly. 'You're confusing non-profit with charity.'

'Not really. I always understood that Telmusik was a successful operation. The films have been shown around the world in every major market.'

'Yes.' Richmond appeared slightly irritated. 'What's your question?'

'Why would the Vonheim Trust need funds from national education budgets? Television usually makes its investments back

82

from showings in each country, plus the sales from commercial releases on home video. Mass circulation gives you pretty generous returns.'

'Not as generous as you think. I don't see why government authorities would object to contributing towards such valuable films.'

'Well, speaking for my country, the education budget's pitifully inadequate as it is, and the government's constantly under fire for failing to meet basic requirements. I can't imagine them setting aside the taxpayer's money to pay for music films, much as I would enjoy seeing them.'

Richmond's vulpine features creased contemptuously. 'Oh, you English! You're always crying poor and asking for something for nothing! Nobody's forced to take part in our programme. The project is still in the planning stages. We'll let you know more when we've done all the arithmetic. The only thing I'd like to add for now is that Telmusik was never really envisaged as a profit centre. The films were made to preserve a living record of the maestro's achievements.'

Peter was irritated by the American's dismissive manner. 'Then I assume there's no truth to the suggestion that some of the maestro's films have been used as a bargaining point to guarantee his personal appearances?'

Richmond stared at him coldly. 'I don't think I understand you.'

Peter was conscious that attention was focused on him. At his side, Miss di Bonaventura whispered, 'Take it easy, kid. You're getting into deep water!'

Ignoring her, he continued, 'I heard that, in a recent tour of the Far East by maestro Vonheim, one of the conditions you imposed was that the local national television station should buy and broadcast some of his older films; otherwise, he would not appear. Would you care to comment?'

Despite the Caribbean tan, Gregory Richmond's face had paled. He forced a smile. 'What a ridiculous idea! When Karl Vonheim made his last tour, I negotiated with entrepreneurs who were falling over themselves to present him. They were lining up to bid!'

'Despite fees far in excess of his European rates?' Peter spoke calmly.

There was a subdued murmur of conversation. The other journalists were enjoying themselves. Richmond continued to smile uneasily. 'We asked for fees that reflected the maestro's name and reputation. The gentlemen I met didn't find them unreasonable; otherwise, we wouldn't have reached an agreement.'

'Nevertheless, the films were paid for with government funds?'

'I wouldn't know how the local stations were funded. When the news spread that Karl Vonheim was coming, the programme directors were anxious to show his movies. It was a big event.' Richmond shook his head. 'I don't know where you reporters get hold of this gossip. Everything gets blown up into a "shock-horror" story! It sounds to me as though the maestro's observations about British journalism are running true to form! Anyway, none of this has anything to do with the Vonheim Trust.'

'I was interested in how Telmusik operates.'

Richmond settled back in his chair, pausing to brush a speck of dust from his impeccably pressed trousers. 'Our work is recognised around the world for its standards of excellence. The Hamburg office has a whole room set aside for all the awards and trophies. When the maestro invited me to join him, along with Mr Teleki, Mr Wolpert and Mr Ravenscroft, it was to make sure his musical integrity was preserved. The whole operation was never that concerned with profit.'

'But it is a commercial success.'

'There's nothing shameful about making money in the arts, although I guess you Britishers are inclined to turn your noses up at the idea. We've been around for a long time, you know. You must have been in short pants when Telmusik was founded.' He winked and looked away, and there were several chuckles.

Peter felt his temper rising. 'On the contrary, I was in Hamburg in the summer of 1973, putting an article together about the seamier side of some of the major cities of Europe.'

His statement was true but not entirely accurate. That year, he had been a first-year student at London University and, hoping to establish himself as a journalist, had spent a few days in Hamburg gathering information for what he hoped would be a provocative article about the city's notorious red light district.

Richmond smiled coolly. 'That must have been fascinating for you.'

'It was. I seem to remember an unpleasant incident involving a bar girl from the Reeperbahn while I was there. It was in all the newspapers at the time. Perhaps the Vonheim Trust would consider making an educational documentary about it!'

'Perhaps. I don't recall the incident.' Sarcasm was lost on Gregory Richmond. Why was the young man bringing up an obscure incident like that? 'Anyway, for the moment, we're concentrating on musical subjects.'

9

It was a quiet evening in the Club Acapulco. Willi, the bartender and proprieter, passed the time by polishing glasses on the formica-topped counter. He was worried. If business didn't pick up soon, he would be even further in arrears with the rent. He had received a letter that morning, pointing out that he had not paid the previous month in full, and ownership of the nightclub was under serious consideration. Nightclub! The place was a flea-pit!

The trouble was that it badly needed renovating, and that meant investing capital he didn't have. 'Hamburg's Most Exotic Rendez-vous' required several coats of paint, some glitzy furnishings and a new neon sign to pull the customers in. He could never compete with the big clubs on the main strip of the Reeperbahn, round the corner, with their uniformed doormen to entice passers-by and their windows filled with colour pictures of sexy girls in suggestive poses. Those places looked like the old cinemas he remembered from his youth: all gold paint and plate glass. They were ridiculous-ly expensive, but they had real bands, and featured live sex shows for their customers.

He glanced at the young Englishman sitting at the end of the bar, nursing a beer. The kid was trying to play it cool, a bored expression on his face, but Willi noticed that he sneaked surreptitious glances at the soft porn film projected on a torn screen behind the bar. He had looked like a frightened rabbit when Maisie, one of the girls, had asked him to buy her a drink. He had nearly fallen off the bar stool when she'd stroked his thigh, letting her hand rest firmly on his crotch.

He moved towards the young man. 'You here on holiday?'

Peter Meredith nodded. 'Sort of. I'm doing some research.'

'What's that?' Willi's English was limited.

'I'm a reporter.' Willi looked blank, and Peter pretended to write. 'A journalist . . . newspapers . . . *Zeitung.*'

'Ah.' He did not believe it. 'What do you report?'

'I'm doing a piece about Hamburg: the night life.'

'Yes? You should have talked to Maisie. She would tell you good stories.'

'I suppose I should have.' He looked round nervously, in case Maisie reappeared, but she had vanished into the shadows with another customer.

'You want another beer?'

'Not yet.' Peter placed his hand over the glass. 'I'll finish this first.'

Willi returned to his glasses. The kid was a waste of time, and the problems facing the Club Acapulco preoccupied him. Bits of plastic were crumbling off the artificial straw roof of his imitation beachside cantina. He wiped the counter with a discoloured cloth. If he didn't do something about it soon, the bloody thing would cave in on him! It was a warm, humid evening, and there weren't enough patrons to warrant putting on his broad-brimmed Mexican hat. It was too tight anyway, and made his head sweat. He had long since replaced the record of Rosita Serrano singing *Cielito Lindo* with some equally worn tapes of heavy rock. He had chosen the Latin music because it gave the place a bit of atmosphere, but nobody remembered Serrano any more, and people preferred the new stuff, which was louder and, to his way of thinking, less erotic.

It was also time to replace the porno film, but that meant more money. The print was fuzzy and scratched. It had broken so many times that, with re-splicing, the couples fornicating in endless variations jerked and leapt about in a way that was more humorous than sexy. Sometimes, he wondered whether his patrons came in for a laugh. Not that it mattered. His three hostesses kept the drinks flowing, so why should he care what they thought?

Sitting across the bar, his friend Max sipped slowly from a tall beer glass. Max was a regular, although he never bought drinks for the girls. They had been at school together and, ever since the car crash and the death of his wife, Max had taken to stopping by. Willi supposed the man was lonely.

Max finished his drink and glanced across the dimly-lit room, its worn-out décor occasionally illuminated by a flash of light from the porno screen. 'A bit slow this evening?'

'Warm weather's always bad for business. The tourists go to Eros, or do a bit of window-shopping for their kicks. Saves paying for a lousy drink!'

Max nodded. Eros was an officially designated pick-up place, where the street-girls and boys stood against inner walls, waiting for clients. It looked more like the entrance to a subway, and he and Max had shared a familiar story several times, about an unwary tourist who had walked in thinking it was a U-bahn stop. To amuse one another they had concocted imaginary conversations, rich with double-entendres, between the unsuspecting visitor and the professionals. It reminded Willi of their schooldays. Window-shopping referred to the famous Reeperbahn street, forbidden to minors, where women of every colour, size and shape sat naked or semi-clothed in the windows, displaying their well-used bodies and encouraging spectators to buy their services. It was one of Hamburg's favourite tourist attractions.

'Want another beer?'

'May as well. Where's everybody?'

Willi jerked his head in the direction of two curtained booths at the rear. The lighting was so dim that they were not visible. 'Maisie and Lisl have got a couple of boys back there. Looked like Dutch sailors. Must be a ship in port.'

'Then you're not doing so badly. That's at least two bottles of champagne.'

Max scowled. 'They ordered beer.'

'The girls too?'

'No. They get champagne. I tell them to drink it faster, but they bitch about it; say they can't drink so much fizz. It blows them up.'

'It's a hard life!' Max was silent, watching Willi refill his glass. 'Where's Gisela?' He asked the question casually.

'She'll be along. Said she had an errand.' Willi suspected that Max was attracted to Gisela, the liveliest of his girls, but said nothing. She was probably the reason for Max's regular visits.

'I miss her cheerful back-chat. It brightens the place up.' He swivelled on his bar-stool and stared into the shadows. 'You could do with brightening up around here, Willi. I hate to think what this place looks like in the daylight.'

Willi shrugged, and returned to polishing glasses. He was a laconic man, gloomy by nature, with broad shoulders and a hard body.

As a youngster, he had been a bouncer in one of the clubs down the road. 'About the same as it looks now.'

'Gisela was saying it was worse than that.'

'I didn't invite her to work here.'

'Keep your shirt on. She was joking.' He drank. 'She's a good sort.'

'Gisela?'

'Yes. She's nice.'

Willi did not reply. As far as he was concerned, she was no better or worse than she should be. Bar girls like Gisela drifted in and out, working for a few months before moving on. He had lost count of all the 'nice' women who had worked at the Acapulco over the years.

The moth-eaten velvet curtain covering the doorway was pulled aside, momentarily allowing daylight into the dingy room. It was June, and would not be dark for another hour. Customers, if there were any, would start to drift in later.

'*Buenas noches, amigos!*' Gisela, dressed in a light summer frock, made a mock theatrical entrance. 'How's the world of show business?' She was a good-looking woman in her early thirties – handsome rather than pretty – with a well-proportioned body that was beginning to thicken at the waist and hips. 'Is the joint jumping?' She used the archaic term to tease Willi because he had once confessed that he liked Fats Waller.

'How does it look?' Willi was always gruff with his employees. Secretly, he felt rather protective. 'Where's your costume?'

'At the back. You don't expect me to walk around dressed like a Mexican peasant, do you?' She ran a hand through hair that had been teased into curls, and treated Peter Meredith to a winning come-on smile. He looked away, pretending not to notice her.

Max grunted. 'The way people dress around here, nobody would bother. Go and change.'

'In a minute. I'm all hot and sticky at the moment.' She smiled again at Peter, but the Englishman had placed some money on the bar and was heading towards the exit. She made a *moue*. 'I must be losing my touch!' Placing herself on the stool next to Max, she took out a cigarette. 'Give us a light, love.'

Max reached hurriedly into his pocket for a lighter, and Gisela watched him. She knew that he fancied her, She placed her hand

89

over his, ostensibly to guide the flame, her fingers remaining there after the cigarette was lit. 'Thanks. Are you going to buy me a drink?'

Max laughed. 'I can't afford that watered-down ginger ale Willi calls champagne!'

'Skinflint! D'you think you could manage a coke, then? I'm thirsty.'

Willi produced a bottle from under the counter. 'Drink it, and go and change. You look like a customer.' His voice registered disapproval.

'What's wrong with that?'

'I don't pay you to sit around enjoying yourself.'

She grinned. 'I thought you did.'

'You know what I mean.' For a moment, he was tempted to tell them both about his financial worries, but decided against it. 'You're here to work.'

'Yes, O Lord and Master!'

Max smiled. 'Let her have her drink in peace, Willi. Nobody's watching.'

A bell behind the bar rang, and Willi took a bottle of champagne from the refrigerator, placed it on a plastic tray, and walked over to one of the booths.

Gisela looked at Max. 'Are the others working?'

He nodded. 'A couple of Dutch sailors. Willi says there's a boat in.'

She raised her glass, saluting him. 'Here's to the navy!'

Taking advantage of Willi's absence, Max lowered his voice until it was barely audible over the music. 'Did you give some thought to our last talk, Gisela?'

She laughed. 'Oh, come on, Maxie! You're not going to go into that what's-a-nice-girl-like-you routine again, are you? I've heard it all before!'

'I'm serious. I was talking to an associate yesterday. He's looking for a receptionist, and . . .'

She squeezed his hand. 'I appreciate the thought, Max, but I'm not interested.'

'Why not?'

'Because I like it here. I'd be no good in an office. I'm not qualified.'

'You don't need to be. All you'd have to do is answer the telephone, and . . .'

'No, thanks. Look, this isn't such a bad old place. I enjoy myself, and it pays better than I used to earn at the factory. It's harmless enough. All the customers want is a bit of a chat, a sympathetic companion and, if I'm in the mood, a cheap thrill. You're such a prude!'

Willi reappeared out of the gloom. 'Are you still here?'

'I'm just leaving. I was entertaining your friend while you were away.' She leaned against Max. 'What about another beer?'

'No, I've had my quota for today.'

She smiled seductively under her false eyelashes. 'What's the matter, Maxie? Afraid you might get carried away?'

The bell behind the bar rang again and Willi departed with more champagne. Max watched him. 'It looks like the girls are doing their stuff.'

'That's because the bottles are only half-filled. Willi's crafty!'

'What do they get up to in those booths?'

'Not what you think, Maxie. Lisl probably gave her one a quick flash of her tits. She's very proud of them, you know. That's about as far as it goes, unless he wants to pay a little extra for a quick feel!'

'You shouldn't be doing that sort of thing, Gisela. It's no life for a decent young woman.'

She laughed, throwing her head back and clasping his knee to prevent herself from toppling from her stool. 'Who said I was decent? Don't be such a prick!' She was crude to shock him. 'It's just good fun.'

'Well, it's not my idea of fun. Where does it lead to?' He looked at her earnestly. 'Why won't you let me help you?'

Gisela leaned forward and kissed him quickly on the mouth. The gesture startled him. 'You're a good man, Maxie, and I like you, but you're too bloody pi! Don't worry about me. Listen, one of these days, the man of my dreams could walk through that door, take one look at me, and whisk me away from all this, just like in the movies!'

'You really believe that?'

'No, but I can daydream. Don't give me a hard time, Max. All right?'

When Willi returned, Max put money on the counter. 'See you tomorrow.'

Gisela smiled. 'Keep it warm!' When he had gone, she leaned her elbows on the counter, looking thoughtful 'Poor old Maxie!'

'He's not so old.' Willi wiped the counter. 'He's the same age as I am. We were at school together.'

'Really? He could be your father.'

'That's only because he's losing his hair and putting on a bit of weight. He's not yet forty.'

'Christ! He shouldn't let himself go like that.'

Willi shrugged. 'He's had a hard time. He lost his wife in a car crash.'

'I know. He told me all about it.' She chuckled. 'He's got the hots for me, but he's still too shy to come out and say so. I've never asked him what he does for a living. Did he say?'

'I don't know. Some sort of import business. He brings in cheap plastic stuff from Hong Kong or Taiwan or somewhere, and sells it to the distributors. Does quite well, as far as I know.' He wondered whether he should invite Max to invest some capital in the Club Acapulco; offer him a partnership, maybe. He probably didn't have that sort of money. 'I noticed he's been paying you a lot of attention.'

She grinned. 'He wants to make a decent woman of me!'

'You could do worse for yourself.'

'No thanks! I'd be bored stupid. He's nice enough, but not much of a prospect.'

'Your prospects are going nowhere if you don't change. Get a move on!'

The rest of the evening passed slowly. A few customers came and went, mostly sitting at the bar and ignoring Gisela's efforts to draw them into conversation. Maisie and Lisl remained closeted with their sailors until quite late. When they left, very drunk, the younger of the two seamen complained about the cost of the drinks, but Willi was an old hand at handling difficult customers, and the men paid without further argument. Towards eleven, two more young sailors arrived, apparently from the same ship, and the girls immediately led them to the private booths. The main room was empty again.

Gisela smiled. 'Their friends must have recommended us. What're you putting in their beer, Willi?'

92

The barman grunted contemptuously. 'Kids! I'll go broke on crap like that!'

Towards midnight, a man entered and made his way to a corner table at the back of the room. His conservative jacket and slacks were out of place in a bar whose clientèle usually went no further than shirtsleeves and jeans. Willi jerked his head towards the darkened recess where the visitor, barely visible, had seated himself.

'Do your, stuff, Gisela. You haven't earned your keep all evening.'

She approached the table, her smile automatic. 'Can I get you something?'

'Thank you. I'd like a schnapps.' He spoke in English.

'Oh, are you English? American?' She sat at the table for a moment. 'I speak English, but not very good. I didn't study; just picked it up.' Her accent was marked.

'Where?'

She winked, laughing. 'In bed. Isn't that the best way to learn things?'

The man nodded. 'So I'm told. Would you like to join me?'

'Thanks.' She looked him over. Although casually dressed, his clothes were well cut, and he was wearing an expensive watch. 'I'll have champagne.'

'Not tonight.'

'Why not?'

'Because I don't like being taken for a ride. I know what places like this call champagne, and it makes me feel like a country bumpkin. So, no champagne, if you don't mind, but I'll make a deal. I'll be delighted if you keep me company, provided you drink whatever I'm having. How's that?'

'Well,' she wavered between curiosity and professional duty, 'I'm not sure.'

'I don't care if the bartender charges his usual prices. It's just pride on my part. I hate to feel I'm being made a fool of. Why don't you ask him?'

'I suppose I could. It's a funny request . . .'

'Not really. Tell him it's a matter of principle, and you'd better warn him that I'll take a sip from your glass too, to make sure he isn't cheating. I hope you don't mind.' He smiled. 'I like your dress. It's pretty. What's your name?'

93

'Gisela.' She did not ask his name. It was a house rule at the Club Acapulco that visitors remained anonymous.

'All right, Gisela. Ask the barman for two large schnapps. Do I pay for them as we go along?' He handed her a fifty-mark note. 'Will this cover it?'

She laughed. 'We're not that expensive!'

'Good. Tell him to hold onto it, and we'll order more later.' As she stood, he half-rose from his chair, nodding courteously.

When she conveyed the request, Willi shrugged. 'Why not? We get all sorts of fools in here. You're the one who's going to have to drink it.'

'This one's no fool. He's quite a gentleman.' She glanced towards the shadows. 'He's very attractive.'

Willi filled two glasses. 'Prince Charming?' He sneered, knowing her secret aspiration.

'Better than the usual crap that falls into this shit-hole!' She turned away angrily, and carried the glasses to the table.

'Willi says it's OK with him if you want to waste your money.' She let her hand rest on the visitor's wrist and leaned closer with a conspiratorial whisper, her cheek almost touching his. They were already like intimate friends. 'He thinks you're crazy!'

'I don't care.' He held her hand gently for an instant, then raised his glass. 'Here's to us! You must tell me about yourself, Gisela. I promise not to ask what a beautiful young woman like you is doing in a place like this.'

'Thank Christ for that!' She drank quickly, enjoying the burning sensation at the back of her throat.

An hour and a half passed, during which they refilled their glasses many times. Unaccustomed to the hard liquor, Gisela found herself becoming mellow. Her companion was charming and witty, subtly flattering her and responding smoothly to her increasingly overt amorous advances. Feeling slightly muzzy, she moved her chair closer, so that she could lean against his shoulder. He inclined his head towards her, their mouths brushed, and her tongue darted out, teasing his lips.

'I like you.' Her hand massaged his thigh. 'Do you want another drink?'

His cheek was against hers, and she was hazily aware of a pleasantly cool after-shave. 'Not really. How about you?'

'No, but for God's sake don't tell Willi!' She thought this was funny, and giggled. 'He's probably watching us.'

'Then let's get out of here and go somewhere else.'

'I'm supposed to be working.' She guided his hand so that it traced the swell of her breast.

'When do you finish?'

'Around two.'

'It's almost that now. Why don't we go?'

She hesitated, but his mouth was temptingly close, and she felt a vague stirring in her loins. It had been a long time since a customer had turned her on. And he treated her so well: it was just as she had always dreamed it would be. 'I'll have to tell Willi.'

'Don't worry, I'll take care of him.' He hesitated. 'I'll also . . . compensate you for any loss of income from leaving early.'

'Would you?' This was a real gentleman!

'Of course. Otherwise it wouldn't be fair. Do you live round here?'

'Yes. I've got a place nearby.' Their lips met again. 'It's not much.'

'It will be better than here. That music's giving me a headache. I can't hear myself think.'

'Silly! You don't make a noise doing that!' She giggled again.

He smiled, his features silhouetted against the flickering lights of the porno film. 'I try not to make a noise whatever I do.'

She drew closer. 'I sometimes can't help myself!'

When they reached the door to her apartment, he kissed her, and she held herself against him, her hips gyrating slowly. 'You'll have to look for the key. It's somewhere in my bag.' She leaned against the wall. 'I'll never find it.'

'It's the night air. You'll feel better if you lie down.' He found the key and inserted it.

'I'll pass out if I'm not careful.' Placing her arms around his neck, and pressing her cheek against his, she whispered, 'I want to stay awake, or I'll miss all the fun!' The door opened, and she walked backwards, drawing him into the room. 'Don't look at the place. It's a mess!' She led him to the bed. 'Leave the lights off. I'll turn on the one in the bathroom.' She kissed him briefly. 'Make yourself comfortable.'

A wave of dizziness hit her as she entered the bathroom, and Gisela splashed cold water on her face until her balance returned.

She undressed quickly, throwing an old dressing-gown round her shoulders. When she returned to the other room, she left the door ajar, so that it threw a gentle shaft of light across the carpet.

He was sitting on the edge of the bed, dressed only in a pair of white shorts, which seemed to gleam in the pale light. Seeing her, he stood, and she walked slowly towards him, letting the dressing-gown fall to the floor. She laughed breathlessly. 'Here I am!'

The man siezed her roughly, throwing her face down on the bed. Before she could cry out, he stuffed a handkerchief into her mouth, tying it in place with a second one. Her senses reeling, she thought she would suffocate. Her hands were forced behind her back and tied with a pair of tights. She struggled wildly, her body thrashing, but he held her ankles in a powerful grip and bound them together with a stocking. He was very strong. A moment later, he lifted her from the bed and sat her in a wooden, hard-backed chair, strapping her in place with the belt from his trousers.

Gisela stared at the man, terrified, dragging air into her lungs through her nostrils. Fear sobered her quickly, and she tried desperately to control her heaving body, lest rising vomit would choke her.

The man stood before her, illuminated by the thin shaft of light from the bathroom. He spoke in a low voice. 'Bitch! Do you think I'd touch a cheap whore like you? Look at you! Slut!' He paused, breathing hard from the exertion of overpowering her. When she tried to make a sound, it emerged as a muffled whimper. 'You filth! There's only one way to deal with a pig like you!'

His jacket was lying on the bed and he reached into a pocket. She saw the glint of metal as he slipped a knuckle-duster over the fingers of his right hand. 'Whore!' He moved closer, his eyes never leaving her face, then swung his arm in a vicious blow that struck her left side, shattering the bone of her elbow. 'Filthy, bloody whore!' He hit her again, smashing into her ribs, the metal gauntlet tearing her naked flesh.

Agonizing pain seared her body and Gisela writhed and twisted, unable to avoid the rain of blows. 'Oh God! Oh Christ! Oh Jesus Christ! He's going to kill me!' A third punch, carefully aimed, broke her jaw, and she fainted. She did not know for how long she was insensible. It was probably a few seconds, because she was restored by the shock of cold water thrown across her face and body. Her arm ached savagely, white-hot spasms shot through her broken ribs, forcing her to take shallow breaths, and her jaw felt as though it was on fire. He must have struck her while she was unconscious, because her left eye was throbbing and swollen. She could feel blood dribbling down her sides and buttocks, and the chair on which she sat was warm and wet with her urine.

She was lolling forward, held in place by the belt, and the man grabbed her by the hair to drag her head back, sending needle-sharp convulsions through her broken jaw. His face was close to hers, and she could see a thin stream of saliva crawling from the corner of his mouth to the line of his chin.

'You filthy, stinking slut!'

He stepped back and, through half-closed eyes, she saw that he was sexually aroused. He must have been aware of the direction of her gaze, and his face distorted with fury. 'Whore! Bitch! Slut!' He rained blows on her head and body, striking her again and again. He continued to beat her long after she had sunk into senseless oblivion.

White light, painfully bright against her eyelids, awoke her and Gisela allowed her eyes to flicker open. The pain had receded and she seemed to be floating. Her face and body felt curiously numb and, with concentrated effort, she summoned her muscles to react but they would not respond. The effort drained her and she closed her eyes again waiting for strength to return. After a pause she made a second attempt and the hospital room in which she was lying came into focus. A young man in a white coat entered her line of vision. He was engrossed in a file that he was reading.

Eventually, he looked up, and their eyes met. 'Oh, you're awake.' He did not smile. Then he leaned over her, his hand moving down to pull back an eyelid. 'Don't try to talk. Your jaw's wired up, and you'll find it painful to move. Are you feeling a little better?' She blinked in response. 'Good.' He reached down and felt her pulse, checking it against his wristwatch.

Gisela tried to speak, but her mouth would not obey her. Strange sounds came from her throat.

The young man looked severe. 'I told you not to talk.' He stepped back. 'You've had a pretty bad beating. In fact, you're lucky to have pulled through. You were in intensive care for two days.' He seemed to sense her question. 'One of your . . . colleagues, a Fräulein Lisl, stopped by your apartment, and found you . . .' He left the sentence unfinished, but could not hide the disapproval in his voice. 'It's lucky for you that she did. Otherwise . . .' He picked up the file, and wrote in it. When he spoke again, there was a look of reproof on his face. 'The police will want to talk to you when you're feeling better, and there's a reporter from the newspaper, but you don't have to see him if you don't want to.' She tried to nod, but her head would not move. For a moment, the young man looked frustrated. 'I can't understand what makes people like you . . .' He checked himself and was silent.

Gisela stared at the ceiling. 'I'm alive!' She felt no particular pain, and an overwhelming drowsiness made it difficult to concentrate her thoughts. When she closed her eyes she had a sudden image of the man who had beaten her, standing in the shaft of light from her bathroom. Her body began to tremble.

The young doctor's voice calmed her. 'You should be back on your feet in a week or two. We'll have to make a series of tests but, apart from the fractures, there doesn't appear to be any permanent damage. We'll try therapy, but I doubt whether you'll recover full use of your left arm. It was badly broken at the elbow, and there weren't enough bone particles left to repair it completely. It's a delicate mechanism. I'll show you the X-rays. With luck, you should regain partial use.' His voice was coolly impersonal. Her first thought was, 'Oh God, I'm crippled!' Then she wondered, 'What do I look like?' She opened her eyes again.

The young man was standing by the bed, looking down at her. 'There's a Mr Weidlich waiting outside to see you.' For the first time, his severe attitude softened slightly. 'He's been here for the past twenty-four hours or so, waiting for news of your recovery. In fact, he's paying for you to have this private room. Do you want to see him for a moment?' When Gisela looked puzzled, the doctor repeated the name. 'Mr Weidlich — Mr Max Weidlich.'

Max! She blinked her eyes in acknowledgement.

The doctor appeared to understand. 'I'll let him in, but only for a minute or two. You shouldn't have visitors, but he's been waiting for a long time.'

When Max entered, he was carrying a large bouquet of flowers. He looked tired and unshaven. He walked over to the bed, smiling shyly, and it occurred to Gisela that they had only ever seen one

98

another in the half-light of the Club Acapulco. 'Well, you've got yourself into a fine old mess! How are you feeling?'

Gisela could not reply. She was suddenly ashamed, and felt tears running from the corners of her eyes and across her temples.

Max was embarrassed. 'It's not as bad as all that. You'll be up and about in no time, once they take off all that gift-wrapping!' She realised, from his glance, that she must be swathed in bandages. 'I hope they're looking after you properly. The doctor said you were in a bad way when they brought you in.' He busied himself with the flowers, placing them on a table next to the bed. 'Willi sends his love; so do the girls. They all miss you. I expect they'll be round to see you later.' Then he looked at her again. 'I'm glad you're back among the living, and you're not to worry about anything except getting better. I'm taking care of everything.' He hesitated. 'I'll look after you.'

She closed her eyes again, and sank into a dreamless sleep.

10

Miss di Bonaventura snapped her notebook shut. 'I guess that's that. Considering the big build-up, there weren't any fantastic revelations. Frankly, I'm positively underwhelmed!' They were still sitting, but many of the journalists had lost interest, and were chatting among themselves.

Peter shook his head. 'I found it fascinating. You forget we've never had the chance to speak to Vonheim before, or hear his thoughts on anything.'

'Maybe, but I didn't hear him say anything world-shattering, and I sure as hell won't be ringing my editor in Paris to tell him to hold the front page. The background stuff was interesting, but it didn't make for banner headlines. I was hoping for hard news.'

'What about the girl?'

She cocked her head on one side, squinting towards Francesca. 'She's cute enough – not much to say for herself – but she didn't play the goddam piano, so what the hell? It's a non-event.'

'Except that the great Karl Vonheim has singled her out, and broken his lifelong vow of press silence to do it. If you'd followed him round for as long as I have, you'd appreciate what that means.'

She emphasized her New York accent. 'I appreciate, awreddy, but a scoop it ain't!' She glanced at the television crew. 'It won't make the six o'clock news!'

Teleki took control of the microphone again. 'This concludes the formal part of our conference, ladies and gentlemen, but I hope you'll stay on for some refreshments and meet Miss Noble and my colleagues in person. Mr Ravenscroft and Mr Richmond can tell you about our next big film: Verdi's *Un Ballo in Maschera*, which the maestro will be conducting at the Salzburg Festival next year.' There was a mild stir of interest. 'Following the performances, the

100

entire production will move to Drottningholm Palace in Stockholm for filming. You'll find a press kit on the table by the door, with details of the cast, as well as photographs and a biography of Miss Noble. In the meantime, I wish you *bon appétit*!' He bowed dramatically, and a small army of waiters entered, bearing trays of champagne and canapés. It was done with such old-world exaggeration that Peter was reminded of the second act of *Arabella*. One could always trust the Viennese to put on a show like that!

'Are you staying?' The American journalist was consulting a tourist guide-book to Vienna.

'Of course. Who ever heard of a reporter missing out on free food and drink?'

'Suit yourself.' She inspected a tray laden with delicacies. 'This food's covered with so much gunk it makes me nauseous to look at it!' She lowered her voice slightly. 'Listen, if you'd like a piece of advice, I wouldn't mix it any further with Greg Richmond. He bruised you a couple of times back there. The Romanian doesn't like people stepping on his toes.'

'He doesn't bother me.'

'Maybe, but he carries a lot of weight in all sorts of quarters. There's no need to go looking for trouble.'

Peter smiled. 'I'll leave him alone. Anyway, I'm more interested in talking to the girl. She intrigues me.'

'I noticed. You haven't taken your eyes off her since she walked into the room! Not that I blame you. She's a good-looking kid.'

'It's not just that. I want to find out what it's like to work with Karl Vonheim. He's never sponsored anyone before.'

She stared at Peter. 'That guy really gets under your skin, doesn't he?'

'He's a great conductor. There's no-one quite like him. You were at the concert last night. I seem to remember you were pretty spellbound yourself.'

'I'm not putting him down. He's fantastic, but let's face it, he's not here any more. I'd sooner use the time looking around the town. I can pick up all the background stuff from the press kit. Listen, do me a favour before you sweep Cinderella off her feet. Introduce me to Simon Ravenscroft. He's pretty famous, and I could use some copy on him.'

Peter led her to the director, who was edging his way towards the door. 'Hello, Simon.'

'Peter!' Simon Ravenscroft greeted him effusively with both hands. 'I didn't expect to see you here. What do you think of our discovery?'

'She's very lovely. Have you heard her play?'

'Not yet. She's due to give a concert in Bern in a few months. I'll be shooting some sequences for a documentary about her.'

'She'll certainly look good.'

'Yes.' Ravenscroft frowned. 'That could be a problem, I suppose.'

Miss di Bonaventura asked, 'Why a problem?'

'Well, to be honest, the public is always a little suspicious of beautiful women musicians. I don't know why, but I have a theory. They only take them seriously when they look like Wanda Landowska.'

'What's the theory?' There was a gleam in her eye.

'The ugly ones are the best musicians because they stayed home and practised while the pretty ones were out having a good time.'

Miss di Bonaventura bristled slightly. 'That sounds like a sexist remark!'

'It probably is.' Simon beamed at her. 'I'm the last of the male chauvinist pigs.'

'That's nothing to be proud of!'

'I was only joking. What I said about the public suspecting beautiful women is still true.' He looked towards Peter for help.

'Miss di Bonaventura is the Arts correspondent for the *Trib*.'

'Oh Lord! Please don't quote me.' He continued towards the exit.

Her notebook was already open. 'I won't if you'll answer one or two questions. Can you spare me a couple of minutes?'

'I'd love to, but I'm a little tied up at the moment.' He glanced at his watch. The first flight from London should have arrived. Rachel had to have taken it. 'I have an appointment at the Hilton, and . . .'

She was undeterred. 'Great! I'm going there myself. Why don't we walk together, and I'll talk to you on the way?'

'If you like.' Simon shot Peter an unfriendly glare.

'Aren't you going to talk to Miss Noble?'

She grinned. 'I'll leave that to you, Pete. You might check out whether that dress is a Pucci. I'll call you later. OK?' Placing a small, firm hand in the small of Simon Ravenscroft's back, she propelled him towards the door. 'Ciao!'

Peter waited until the small group surrounding Francesca had temporarily dwindled to two Japanese reporters holding tape-recorders under her nose and smiling energetically. She seemed relieved when they completed their inquiries and departed. He introduced himself.

'That was quite an ordeal Maestro Vonheim subjected you to.'

'I guess everybody has to go through it once. It would have been easier to play the Liszt Sonata!'

'I wish you had.'

She looked at him curiously. 'Do you?'

He nodded. 'I'm looking forward to hearing you play.' She was silent. 'Simon was saying you'll be in Bern in a couple of months. I'll try to come. Will Vonheim conduct?'

'No. It's supposed to be a kind of warm-up, to give me some practice in front of the public.'

'I'll try to be there, all the same.'

'That's kind of you.' Her manner was cool and poised, but he sensed that she was ill at ease, unsure of herself.

'By the way, I'm supposed to ask if that dress is by Emilio Pucci.'

She looked uncertain, unprepared for the question. 'I'm not sure. Yes, I guess it is. It was chosen for me, and . . .' She checked herself, as if worried that she had said too much. 'Who wants to know?'

'The lady from the *Herald-Tribune*. She was the one who asked you about your background. She had to leave.'

'Oh. She doesn't want to print that, does she?'

'Possibly. Do you mind?'

'I don't know. It doesn't sound like a very musical observation.'

'To be honest, you didn't give her much to work with.'

'I know.' She lowered her voice confidentially. 'I felt horribly tongue-tied up there. I couldn't think of anything interesting to say.'

She seemed very vulnerable. Her serene features disguised her insecurity. Peter smiled. 'I thought you did very well. The vultures couldn't find much to pick over.'

'Vultures?'

'My distinguished colleagues from the musical press. They love to gossip and, given half the chance, they'll pick your bones clean!'

'Oh.' She was thoughtful. 'Aren't you one of them?'

'I hope not.'

'How do I know that?' Her eyes were an extraordinary shade of dark blue.

He spoke quietly. 'Because anyone who inspires Karl Vonheim to speak like that must have something very special to offer.'

She seemed suddenly to relax. 'I hope so. Sometimes it feels like a frightening responsibility.'

'I wouldn't worry about it. He wouldn't have chosen you if he hadn't been sure.'

She looked at him. 'You admire Karl?'

'All my life. He's been a hero since I was a teenager. As a matter of fact, he was giving me a hard time before he brought you in.'

'Why?'

Peter smiled ruefully. 'It happened quite a long time ago, in 1980. I went to the Festspielhaus, managed to talk my way backstage, and got to his dressing-room. That may not sound much to you, but when Vonheim's in Salzburg, it's probably easier to break into Fort Knox!'

'Why did you?'

'I wanted to write his official biography. I'd admired him most of my life and, after all, I was a veteran journalist, all of twenty-five years old. How could he refuse me?'

She laughed. 'What did he say?'

'No! He sent me packing with a few short, sharp sentences. I still blush at the memory.'

'What happened today?'

'Unfortunately, he remembered me. I should have let it go at that but, when I didn't, he fired a couple of broadsides at the British tabloid press, and sank me without a trace. Professor Leitner was delighted!'

'I'm sorry.' She put her hand on his arm, then quickly withdrew it.

'It was my own fault. I should have known better. As a matter of fact, I was afraid he might remember another time, years ago.'

'Really?' Her self-consciousness was forgotten.

'Promise you'll keep it secret?'

She raised her hand. 'Hope to die!'

He took a deep breath. 'Well, when I was about sixteen, a friend and I got into the old Kingsway Hall in London, which was a great recording studio for many years. It's got a balcony overlooking the studio floor, and we hid up there for about two hours, long before the orchestra or the recording engineers arrived.'

'Why?'

104

'Because Vonheim's recording sessions are closed to all outsiders. Nobody's allowed near. The janitor told us he was going to be there, and we bribed him to let us in.'

'What happened?' Francesca giggled. Peter had almost forgotten that she was only in her early twenties. Her clothes and demeanour made her seem older.

'We watched the whole session. It was marvellous! He conducted a Sibelius Fifth, and we heard every note of it. It was one of the most exciting experiences I've ever had, especially as we shouldn't have been there. We only dared peer out from behind the seats every now and then, but we heard it all. Luckily, Vonheim was facing in the other direction on the floor of the hall, so there was no danger of him looking up and seeing us. I think one or two members of the orchestra spotted us, but they didn't let on. We also heard all the talk with the control room. Lancelot Gordon was producing the record, and he was incredibly dictatorial, telling Vonheim to change this or that, or to re-make a part where the ensemble was bad. I remember being amazed that the great Karl Vonheim did what he said. I don't think anyone would dare to talk to him like that today. It was extraordinary!'

'I wish I'd been there. What went wrong?'

'Everything was perfect, right up to the end of the session. The orchestra packed up and left, and we waited, hugging ourselves because we'd actually got away with it. Then Gordon and Vonheim came back into the hall and stood there, talking. They were discussing the next session. The maestro wanted to reposition the brass, but Gordon insisted they couldn't be moved. As they were leaving, my friend – like an idiot! – couldn't resist the temptation to take a photograph. He had one of those Kodak Instamatic cameras, and he popped up from behind his seat and took a picture. I don't know why he tried. We were much too far away and the light was all wrong, so nothing would have come out.'

Francesca did not speak but nodded for him to continue the story.

'Vonheim heard the tell-tale click of the shutter, and glanced up at the gallery. He didn't say anything, and went back to the control room. A couple of minutes later, two large German "heavies" arrived upstairs. They grabbed us both by the scruffs of our necks, and hauled us down to face the maestro.'

'Jesus! What did he say?'

'Well, he was sitting behind a table, with his score laid out before him. I can still picture it as though it happened yesterday! Then he snapped his fingers, and held out his hand for the camera. He hadn't said a word, but we were both petrified. He ripped the film out of the camera, handed it back, and said, "Don't ever let me catch you trying something like that again!" God! His voice was like ice!' Peter smiled. 'Then he took two five-pound notes out of his pocket, threw them on the table, and said, "Buy yourself another film with that!" I don't think he realised it, but in those days we could have bought another camera for that sort of money!'

Francesca laughed. 'Did you say anything?'

'I think I said, "Thank you, maestro", which seemed to amuse him. Anyway, he signalled to his heavies, who frog-marched us to the back door of the hall and sent us on our way with a well-aimed boot to our behinds! I suppose the funny part is that we both thought it was the most wonderful experience of our lives, despite a definite tenderness in our rear quarters when we sat down!'

She laughed again. 'I understand why you're glad he didn't remember. I nearly died when he walked in on me playing the piano.'

'It must have been a traumatic experience.'

'Yes, and yet within a few minutes I'd forgotten all about who he was, and just played. I guess one of the things that shook me was that he treated me like an equal; well, sort of like an equal!'

'A working colleague?'

'Right!' She smiled at Peter, grateful that he was not cornering her with searching official questions about her career, making her conscious of every word she chose. The isolation of life in the Vonheim household, no matter how luxurious, was depressingly lonely at times.

'I'd love to ask you more about Karl Vonheim.' Peter lowered his voice slightly, and she was immediately wary. 'But I won't. Much as I admire the maestro, it wouldn't be fair to pry on him through you. Besides, I'd like to know more about you. Will Bern really be the first chance I'll have to hear you play?'

'I guess so. Karl chose the date.'

'Will he make all your decisions?' When she reacted to his question, Peter said, 'I'm sorry. That came out the wrong way. I simply wondered whether you might feel frustrated at having to wait so long. You must know inside whether you're ready.'

'I suppose, but I'd sooner be guided by Karl. I owe everything to him.'

It was a puzzling reply, but before Peter could question her further, Zoltán Teleki appeared. 'Francesca, my dear, you have other guests waiting to speak to you.' He beamed at Peter. 'You'll forgive us?'

'Of course. I didn't mean to monopolise Miss Noble. I was asking her whether her plans include London.' He noted that she seemed relieved by the white lie.

'Yes, yes. London will be an important engagement.' He bustled away, taking Francesca with him.

'Well, my friend, you seem very taken with our young discovery.' Gregory Richmond's expression was slightly sardonic. 'I think you'll find she's more than just a pretty face.'

'I hope so. I can't imagine maestro Vonheim would let that colour his judgement.'

'Quite.' The American was silent for a moment, rocking on his well-shod heels. 'I'm curious as to where you got hold of those stories about the television films. They're quite untrue, you know. Karl's films are in constant demand.' He laughed thinly. 'We don't have to blackmail people into taking them! It's amazing how people come up with such rumours. I suspect the maestro has too many jealous colleagues!' Peter did not comment, and he continued, 'Television sales are handled by my Vice-President, Howard Erlich. You should have a talk with him about them.'

'I'd like to.'

'Good. He's always at the office, except when he's out of the country. Have you ever been to New York?'

'A few times. I wrote a piece about American orchestras for one of the British sundays last year, and I covered the Metropolitan Opera season in 1987.'

His eyebrows raised. 'You're quite a high flier, Mr Meredith. I thought you were a London music critic.'

'Not really. I'm more of a reporter.'

Richmond's expression was cynical. 'Including investigative journalism? It's a very fashionable profession.'

'No, I just try to cover whatever's going on in the music world.'

'That's very interesting. I think I could use a man like you in my own organization, Mr Meredith. We're diversifying so many of our

107

activities these days that it's hard to keep up with the latest developments. It used to be a relatively simple business of setting up concerts and booking artists, but now, with the growth of satellite communications, home video, stadium concerts, multi-media entertainment, we're putting together some very complicated packages. You should consider having a look at the other side of the picture.'

'It must be fascinating.'

Richmond reached into a pocket of his waistcoat and produced a heavily embossed card. 'You must come and see us. Why don't you give me a call the next time you're planning to be in New York, and we can have a talk. I'm always interested in fresh ideas.'

'Thank you.'

He winked. 'You never know, I might even be able to help you persuade Karl to agree to a biography. We're constantly pestered to produce one. I had someone do some background work for me a few years ago. It should make an instant best-seller.'

'Yes, I think it would.'

'Good. We'll stay in touch, and I'll tell Howard to look out for a call from you.'

Richmond seemed to glide away, and Peter watched him hail the critic from *Le Monde* with a warm handshake. The American had been unexpectedly charming, but why would he offer him a job?

The room was emptying steadily, and the waiters were already removing plates and glasses. He found himself standing next to Francesca again, and she seemed pleased to see him.

'I thought you'd probably be gone by now.' She sipped her drink. 'I was just cross-examined by Professor Leitner. He's very fierce! I don't think he approves.'

'Probably not. The Viennese have fixed ideas.'

'Karl warned me. They're so conservative!'

Peter smiled. 'Console yourself with the thought that things are better than they used to be. They're marching steadily into the 1960's!'

She laughed, 'Listen, I'm serious, too. Doesn't he realise that?'

'I don't think the good Professor believes women should be included in musical circles. To make matters worse, you're an American and, if you don't mind my saying so, beautiful.'

'Thank you.' She spoke softly

'Qualifications like that are bound to make him highly suspicious. Just keep remembering that this is Vienna! How long will you be staying?'

'Until the day after tomorrow. Karl has meetings with the Phil-harmonic. It will give me a chance to look at the city. I've never been here before. Did you go to the concert?'

'I wouldn't have missed it for anything. And you? I didn't see you there.'

She nodded. 'I was in a box with Mrs Vonheim.'

'What's she like?'

'Dorothea? OK, I guess. A little vague. We don't see a lot of each other. She's usually somewhere around the house or the garden, but I'm tucked away in the music room with my piano. We meet at meals.'

'Is she a musician?'

'I don't think so.' She became guarded. 'Are you . . . ?'

'No, I was just curious. Honestly! I've been fascinated by Karl Vonheim for such a long time that I can't help being inquisitive about anyone or anything involving him.' When she looked doubt-ful, he added, 'I promise I'm not making notes for future use. You don't realise how lucky you are to know him.'

'I don't know him very well.'

'Certainly better than I do. I told you, he's inspired me for years. Now that the conference is over, would you like to have some lunch? If you're not busy, I'd be pleased to give you a quick tour of the city.'

Francesca hesitated. 'I'm not sure. They may be expecting me back at the house.'

'You could give them a call. I'll return you safe and sound.'

'I guess I could. I know I have to go to a dinner party this evening: some people from the Opera.' She looked towards Teleki and Rich-mond, but they were engaged in conversation. 'It would be fun to take a walk. I've read so much about Vienna . . .'

'Then why don't we? It's a lovely day. We could have a quick bite of something, and I'll show you round.'

She smiled. 'I'd like that.' Her expression changed. 'Oh no! Here comes the creep!' She indicated a middle-aged man, slightly bal-ding, who was watching her from the doorway. He was dressed in a black jacket and grey trousers, with a white shirt and silver tie.

Peter followed the direction of her gaze. 'Who's that?'

'Erich.' She gave a small, involuntary shudder. 'He's always slink-ing around the place. I get the feeling he's constantly watching me.'

'Who is he? What does he do?'

109

'He works for Karl. He's a sort of chauffeur, handyman. I guess you'd call him a manservant. In America, he'd be described as a gofer.'

'You call him the Creep?'

'Not to his face.' She looked round guiltily. 'I shouldn't have said that.'

'I won't tell.'

'Thanks. I . . . just get a funny feeling whenever he's there. It's not that he does anything wrong. He hardly ever talks to me, but I guess he doesn't like women . . .' She lowered her voice. 'I shouldn't have said that, either!'

'I wouldn't let him bother you. Shall we go?'

Erich approached them. When he drew close, he barred their way. 'The car's outside.'

'Oh?' Francesca made to pass him, but he changed position slightly, blocking her path.

'The maestro's expecting you.'

'I may not be coming.' She paused uncertainly. 'This is Mr Meredith, from London.'

Erich ignored Peter. 'Did you bring a coat?'

'No.' She looked at Peter nervously.

'Then we should leave now. The maestro's waiting to eat.'

'Well, I . . .'

Peter stepped forward. 'Miss Noble's having lunch with me.'

Erich glanced at him, his face expressionless. 'I'm afraid that won't be possible. The maestro has invited several guests to meet Miss Noble.' He spoke deferentially, but with scarcely concealed disdain. Turning back to Francesca, he asked, 'Are you ready to leave?'

She was about to say something, but lowered her head. 'I guess so.' Turning to Peter, she spoke in a low voice. 'I'm sorry. I think I have to go.'

'Couldn't you join them later?'

Once again, Erich ignored him. 'We really should leave now, if we're to be there on time.'

'Yes.' Her voice was subdued.

Peter held her arm for a moment. 'Can I get in touch with you? Where are you staying?'

'At a house in Himmelstrasse. It's near a place called Grinzing.'

110

He nodded. It was one of Vienna's most exclusive suburbs. 'I'll call you. Do you know the telephone number?'

'No.' She looked at Erich, but he remained silent, staring into space with a vaguely bored expression.

'Well, perhaps you could call me. I'll be at the Ambassador Hotel all week. If I'm not there, you could always leave a message.'

'Yes, I'll try.' She hesitated, seemingly at a loss for words, then shook his hand formally. 'Good-bye, and thank you.' Erich stood aside, leaving her enough room to pass. He did not look at Peter.

'Good-bye.' Peter watched her leave, a thoughtful expression on his face.

11

Simon, lying on his back, had fallen asleep and was snoring lightly. The room felt warm, and Rachel edged towards her side of the bed, pulling back the duvet very gently, for fear of awakening him. It was still quite early, and she was not tired.

She leaned on her elbow, watching his face. He was a big, heavily built man with a large and, she used to think, leonine head. It was a pity that he insisted on cropping his hair so short, but he was self-conscious about the spreading bald patch, and had reduced everything above his eyebrows to little more than a fuzz. Without glasses, his face in repose looked flaccid and slack, and his mouth, partially open, was like an old man's. He looked as though he was coming apart at the seams! A wave of tenderness filled her, until she remembered their conversation.

'Where the hell were you?'

'I told you. I worked too late, and by the time I reached the M4, it was jammed. I missed the plane by minutes.' Why didn't he believe her? It was the truth.

Well, almost the truth. She hadn't wanted to come to Vienna. Things hadn't been right between them for a long time, and when Vienna came up, she'd been relieved at the thought of not seeing Simon for a few days. She had worked in the office longer than necessary, half hoping that she would miss the flight, but she'd still driven all the way to Heathrow out of a sense of guilt.

'Why didn't you call? I waited in all evening.'

'I meant to, but I'd left my phone card in my other bag, and I didn't have change for a call-box. I thought you'd guess what happened.'

'I'm not a mind-reader! Anyway, if you missed the direct flight, you might have taken a different one and changed. You could have found a connection through Frankfurt or Zurich. How was I supposed to know?'

'I'm sorry. I didn't think.'

'You could have called me when you got back home.'

'I tried to, but there was no reply from your room.'

That was partially true, too. She had telephoned the hotel, but had hung up while the operator was connecting her to Simon's room. She hadn't wanted to go through the explanations, the unspoken recriminations, the hurt silences. Maybe she'd feel better about the trip in the morning. Simon had been talking about it for weeks, as though its had some special significance. For God's sake, it was just a dirty weekend in Vienna! It would have been easier to go to Brighton, but he always insisted on doing things in style. Anyway, he was afraid of being recognised in England, so it meant dragging halfway across Europe.

'I called the flat several times.' The accusation was unspoken.

'We must have missed each other. Betty rang just after I got back, and I spent the evening at her place.'

'Why didn't you call me from there?'

'I didn't like to. Anyway, I thought you'd realise.'

She hadn't lied about that. She had spent the evening with her friend. Once back in Putney, Rachel had phoned Betty. She hated spending time alone, and despised the idea of wasting an evening in front of a television set. Her friend disapproved of her relationship with Simon, conceding that he was amusing and attractive, but never failing to point out that he was married. She was constantly inviting Rachel to meet other, younger men, closer to her own age. So they had gone to Betty's new tennis club in Richmond, where they'd met two 'eligibles'. One of them, John, had driven Rachel home in the small hours of the morning, and she had been tempted to invite him in, but changed her mind at the last moment, telling herself that the chemistry wasn't right. She knew that it had been conscience that had made her hesitate. They had exchanged telephone numbers and agreed to stay in touch.

'I rang quite late, but all I got was that damned answering-machine!' Why did Simon spy on all her movements?

'You should have left a message. I didn't get home until after one, and flaked out. You know I always leave the answering thing on when I'm asleep. Look, I'm sorry, darling. Yesterday was a bit of a write-off, but I'm here now. Let's go and look at Vienna.'

'Wouldn't you rather stay here?'

God, he was looking hurt again! 'We've got so little time, and it took hours to get here. Won't you show me round?'

Rachel stared out of the window. They had left the curtains open, making love by the rosy glow of light reflected from the evening sky. Sleep evaded her, and a familiar catalogue of problems disturbed her thoughts. If only they could go back to being good friends! She enjoyed being with Simon. He was debonair and sophisticated and, when he wanted to be, quite witty, although lately she had noticed that he tended to repeat the same stories. God, it was as though they were already married! She frowned. It was no use thinking about that. He was never going to leave Ann and the children. For her own safety, Rachel couldn't allow herself to fall in love with him.

When they were first involved, it had been a happy, uncomplicated affair, filled with intimate jokes, cryptic messages, secret revelations and adventurous sexual discoveries. They had laughed at everything. Before Simon, she had offered her bed to various partners, who had stayed anything from a single night to several months. None of those liaisons had been serious, except perhaps for Abel, who had moved in for almost a year, and even he hadn't been a problem. They'd tired of one another.

Simon didn't understand. Perhaps it was because he was so much older. Her friends, except for Betty, had been impressed by her glamorous boss, and Rachel had revelled in his world of television studios, concert halls and opera houses. Simon knew absolutely everybody, and everybody knew him, and she loved being part of his cosmopolitan life. He was kind and generous, frequently bringing her little presents and souvenirs. Sometimes, she'd felt he'd treated her more like a spoiled child.

More recently, the glamour had begun to wear thin. Of course, it was still fun to jet in and out of various cities, to stroll through the stage door of a hall, barging past the civilians who waited patiently on the pavement, but after a while one concert hall was like another, and the Duty Free shop in Frankfurt was not very different from the one in Paris. Rachel sighed. When you came down to it, the scrambled eggs at the Savoy Grill had not been any different from the ones they served at the little café round the corner from her flat, except for the price. It was fun to meet the rich and famous, but many of the artists they entertained, on Simon's Telmusik expense account, had been dull and self-absorbed, preoccupied with their own careers. They laughed politely at Simon's well-worn jokes and talked about themselves. As Simon's assistant, they accepted her presence but ignored her, assuming she was there to run errands. She was little more than a note-taking spectator, and often wondered how many of them assumed that her chief function was to provide physical comforts for the director. It was a humiliating thought.

To make matters worse, Simon had become increasingly 'heavy', insisting that he was in love. At first, she had been flattered, but her feelings had changed to panic when he'd suggested a divorce. Not that she should have worried. He hadn't shown any inclination to change his way of life, and no longer talked about leaving home, which was a relief. She had deliberately withdrawn from him, making herself less obviously available. She knew he resented her minor criticisms or that she made jokes of his mannerisms and habits of speech, but she couldn't decide whether they were genuine irritations or whether she was looking for faults. Her indifference seemed to make him more ardent than before, as though determined to prove his love. It made her feel guiltier than ever.

Several times, she had resolved to stop going to bed with him. Their pleasure together was too infrequent, and she hated the inevitable moment when it was time for him to leave. It seemed to hover over them, spoiling the few precious hours they could steal away from the office. Anyway, sex had stopped being fun. Simon was always watching her, waiting for each Pavlovian reaction, timing his movements with hers until she felt distracted and self-conscious. Twenty minutes earlier, she had faked an orgasm to please him. It made her feel cheap.

Sooner or later, they would have to make a clean break. There was no sensible alternative. People seldom just drifted apart, unless the disenchantment was mutual. But she would miss him.

She thought about John, who had driven her home the night before. He was pleasant and amusing, even if he hadn't circled the globe several times and met every famous artist in the bloody music world! Rachel frowned. Why hadn't she invited him to stay? Maybe that was what she really needed to get things back into perspective. She had never been unfaithful to Simon, but she felt that he constantly suspected her. Whenever they met, he wanted to know where she'd been, what she'd done and with whom, and although his questions were mild inquiries, they were more like a cross-examination. So why should she feel so damned guilty?

Letting her leg trail to the floor, Rachel slipped quietly from the bed, moving cautiously. She walked slowly, inching forward like a sleepwalker, and felt her way to the bathroom, closing the door behind her. Simon disliked the smell of cigarettes in the bedroom. She smoked sitting on the toilet, but the small room was stuffy and humid, and the cigarette tasted musty. After a few puffs, she flushed it away. Tomorrow, they would have a long, quiet talk.

'I wondered where you'd gone.' He was awake, still lying on his back, his head turned towards her.

'I couldn't sleep. It's too warm in here.' She stood by the window, conscious that her naked body was silhouetted against the pale light.

'There's a thermostat on the wall. Turn it down a little.'

'I will in a minute. Go back to sleep.'

'I was just dozing. I thought you'd be tired.'

'I'm still wide awake.'

'Why?'

'I don't know. My mind's churning. I was thinking.'

He hesitated. 'About something or someone?'

'Neither – just thinking.' She remembered John again, and felt guilty.

'Like the couple making love? After a long silence, he says to her: "What's the matter: can't you think of anyone either?"'

'That's horrid!'

'Not really. People lose the urge. It happens to the best of us.'

She felt defensive. 'Well, it doesn't happen to me!'

He spoke quietly. 'You could have fooled me.'

'Damn you!' She ran to the bed and, pulling back the duvet, threw herself on top of Simon, clinging to him and kissing him greedily. For a moment, he resisted, but she forced her tongue into his mouth and writhed against him sensuously, using her breasts and hips to excite him. Then she pulled her mouth free, and let her tongue slide across his chest and stomach. She felt her own excitement mounting as he became aroused and, quickly straddling him, used her hands to guide him into her body. Leaning backwards, she placed his hands on her breasts and rode him, urgently thrusting her pelvis against him. Her head back and her eyes closed, Rachel increased the tempo of her movements, heaving and rocking wildly until she climaxed with an anguished shout. Her body convulsed, oblivious to his reactions. Then she slumped forward, breathless and sticky with sweat, until she lay full-length against him.

After a while her trembling ceased and Simon lifted her off his body so that she was cradled in his arms.

'My God! What brought that on?'

Rachel did not reply, and he held her tightly, pressing her head to his shoulder. His hand reached round to stroke her cheek, and he was surprised to find that her face was wet with tears.

12

The helicopter rose thirty feet into the air and hovered, nose tilted down, waiting for an Air France jet to cross its path on the landing strip of Nice airport. Then it swooped forward over the sea and headed across the wide bay towards Monaco.

Seated next to Karl behind the pilot, Francesca looked at the banks of dials and meters. She had not ridden in a helicopter before, and had feared that the sensation might make her queasy. Apart from a certain amount of vibration and louder background noise, it was reassuringly similar to the flight from Lausanne that they had just made in the conductor's Learjet. For that leg of the journey, she had travelled alone in the luxuriously fitted compartment. Karl had been in the cockpit behind closed doors, and when she asked him whether he had piloted the aircraft, he had smiled secretively.

'You're not supposed to know. Were you comfortable?' He was cheerful.

'Very. I've spent most of my life in tourist class, packed in like a sardine. Why shouldn't I ask?'

'Because I forgot to renew my licence. There aren't enough hours in the day to look after every detail.'

'Which means, I suppose, that you did?'

A youthful grin. 'I held the controls for a while. Conductors always want to be in charge!' His arm was round her shoulders, and he hugged her gently.

She stared out of the perspex bubble of the cabin. Beneath her, afternoon sunlight glittered on the tranquil waters of the Mediterranean. Sailing boats and cabin cruisers looked like superbly detailed miniature models. The landscape was disappointing. It was

118

pale and sunbaked, a combination of browns and yellows, and the inland hills were lost in a misty haze. It reminded her of the California coastline around Los Angeles. She had expected the French Riviera to be lush and tropical.

Vonheim's face was close to hers. She was conscious of his proximity. His after-shave was cool with a trace of spice. 'Have you been here before?' When she shook her head, their cheeks touched. 'It's much too crowded. They've built over every available space. There's not much left from the old days. You should have seen it in the 1940s, when it was a lovely sleepy little place. Now, it's one great stretch of suburbs strung together. At this time of the year, the corniche drive to Monte Carlo takes anything up to an hour, in bumper-to-bumper traffic. This way takes seven minutes!'

Francesca wondered whether it might have been more interesting to spend the additional hour on the road, and see everything at close quarters. There were times when she felt removed from the real world. 'Why are we here?'

The conductor did not hear her question, and his arm around her shoulders tightened, drawing her closer. She enjoyed the sensation, and wondered for a moment whether he had used the gesture as an excuse to hold her. She repeated her question.

He smiled. 'I'm not entirely sure. Gregory Richmond asked us to join him. He's anxious to introduce some business associates, but he wouldn't go into details on the phone. He was being rather mysterious about it.' She was again conscious of his perfume. 'I thought you'd like to come along for the ride. You've been working very hard.' Another gentle hug. 'I'm pleased.'

'Thank you.'

'You need to relax occasionally. To be honest, I don't usually make myself available to Richmond like this, but it was a good excuse to use the plane. I hope we're not wasting our time. You may find it amusing to watch Gregory in action. He's quite an operator. He made a point of including you in the invitation.'

'A year ago, I never dreamed I'd meet him, let alone be invited to join him in Monte Carlo.'

'Why not?'

'Because U.S. Artists is the biggest management group in America.

They just about run the music world. The only time I went to their offices, I couldn't get past the receptionist.'

'Did you try?'

'Of course. I arrived with a handful of reviews and a freshly typed resumé, but she wouldn't let me near the lowliest member of the staff. I didn't have an appointment.'

'What did you do?'

'Panicked! I asked her if she would at least show my home-made brochure to someone, and scuttled out of there like a frightened rabbit! She probably gave it to the janitor!'

The maestro stroked her cheek. 'Poor Francesca. You must have been very green!' His face was very close, and she wondered whether he might kiss her.

She laughed. 'I think I can tell you about every waiting-room on West 57th Street. I'm personally acquainted with all of them!'

He nodded. 'New Yorkers love to put all their eggs in one basket, don't they? The garment district in one area, lampshades and lighting on the lower East Side, jewellery on Sixth Avenue in the forties, and theatres crushed together round Times Square. I suppose it's only natural that they put all the leeches in one place too.'

'Are they as bad as that? Greg Richmond gives me the impression that he's more like a patron of the arts.'

'He tries to. It adds dignity to his machinations.' His hand held hers. 'You have to understand that men like Richmond, for all their grand talk, are parasites, living off you. Their interest in your musical career is purely financial. Believe me, Francesca, if Richmond didn't regard you as a potential investment, he wouldn't give you the time of day. He knows very little about music. There are underlings for such mundane matters.' His voice was bitter. 'His preoccupations are money and power, each of which feeds the other. Unfortunately, such men are necessary. If they're good – and Richmond is one of the best – they can place you in the position where you will have the artistic freedom to do what you believe in. You have to learn to use them while they think they're exploiting you. The real, old-fashioned managers, who advised you what to play and where to play it, and who weren't afraid to turn down a concert rather than take the money and run, are an almost extinct breed. They've been replaced by these smooth-talking salesmen who can calculate their percentages faster than a computer!' For a moment, the pressure of his hand increased. 'That's why I've placed myself personally in charge of your career. We'll talk more about it later.'

Richmond, looking impeccably cool in a pale grey lightweight suit, was waiting for them at the heliport. Heavy sunglasses protecting him from the brilliant light gave him a slightly sinister appearance. He was accompanied by an equally smart younger man dressed in a cotton seersucker suit of narrow blue and white vertical stripes. Both men looked as though they had just arrived from Wall Street.

'Greetings, maestro! Have you met my colleague Howard Erlich?' Richmond made a point of calling employees colleagues. The younger man was in his early forties and slightly overweight. His shock of ginger hair had been carefully blow-dried into shape. He gestured towards an outsized Lincoln Continental limousine with darkened windows. 'I thought we might go directly to our meeting, if that's all right with you. The chauffeur will check your things into the hotel.'

The interior was chilly with air-conditioning, and Francesca sank into the deep leather seat. She had hoped she would have a few minutes alone at the hotel, if only to look at Monte Carlo from the window of her room.

Richmond glanced at his watch to make sure they were on time. 'The young man we're going to see is Alexander Kostiras. His family owns the Kostiras shipping line, which you've probably heard of, but he's not interested in following in his father's footsteps. He graduated from the Harvard Business School a few years ago, and spends most of his time in New York.' He winked. 'It's a little livelier than Athens.'

Vonheim nodded. 'What is his connection with our meeting?'

The American smiled. 'I'll let Howard do the talking when we get there. This is really his party.' Erlich looked confident, but said nothing.

The chauffeur manoeuvred the car through narrow streets to the harbour of Monte Carlo, parking on the quayside next to a gleaming white ocean-going cruiser that occupied twice the space allocated to its not inconsiderable neighbours. Francesca, whose parents kept a sailing dinghy on Lake Waramaug in Connecticut, had never seen a private vessel quite as large. Its streamlined, avant-garde super-structure made it look like a grotesquely overgrown Italian sports car.

Two deck-hands in quasi-naval uniforms accompanied them up a ramp at the stern, and ushered them into an airy, walnut-panelled stateroom large enough to accommodate thirty or forty guests. The carpeting was white, and clusters of cream-coloured armchairs and sofas gave the impression of the foyer of a luxury hotel. There was a low hum of air-conditioning, and Francesca shivered slightly as a draft of cold air cut through her thin summer clothes.

Vonheim glanced in her direction, and spoke to one of the men. 'I wonder if you would increase the temperature, please. My companion is in danger of developing pneumonia!' The deck-hand almost jumped to attention, and adjusted a wall-setting.

Howard Erlich glanced around the room, addressing no-one in particular. 'Nice. Very nice! This must have set him back a couple of million!'

Richmond shrugged. 'I shouldn't imagine that was of any great consequence. Hello Alex.'

The person he addressed had just entered the room. The heir to the Kostiras empire was a handsome young man in his late twenties. He was bare to the waist, wearing only a pair of white linen Bermuda shorts. His sunglasses had been lodged in his curly dark hair, and a heavy gold medallion hung from his neck. As he came forward, two young women, dressed in the scantiest of sun-suits, followed him into the room. All three were tanned a rich golden brown.

'Hi, everyone! It's good to see you. Is someone getting you a drink?' He spoke with an American accent.

'Not yet.' Richmond acted as spokesman. 'I hope we haven't kept you waiting.'

Alex winked. 'We were playing upstairs on the sun-deck.' The girls giggled, and he added, 'Trivial Pursuit. I have my own special set of rules!' His companions found this even more amusing.

Introductions were made, and their host welcomed the maestro and his guest with exaggerated deference. The girls were identified only as Suzie and Colette. Choosing a group of furniture surround-

122

ing a large coffee table, the young man sprawled on a sofa and gestured to his visitors to seat themselves. His two companions, still giggling, retired to a corner of the room and absorbed themselves in a pile of magazines.

'Who's going to get this show on the road?' Kostiras lit a cigarette.

Howard Erlich left the room for a moment and returned carrying a leather document-case of the type favoured by art directors. He remained on his feet, and his speech was addressed directly towards Karl Vonheim.

'I'm sure you're aware that our industry is in danger of stagnating.' When the conductor looked puzzled, he continued, 'You may be surprised if I call it an industry, but that is, in effect, what it is. I know we call it management, but U.S. Artists, if you look at it realistically, is in the packaging business. The only difference between us and, say, a big manufacturer like Nabisco, is that we're selling talent: unique talent by artists of the highest calibre, whose proven qualities place them in tremendous demand.' He smiled smugly. 'Not a bad set-up!'

His face became grave. 'The danger our industry faces is that we're using the same old methods of selling and the same worn-out techniques to attract the public that have been tried for the past hundred years. We tell people we represent the world's greatest artists, and they should come and hear them. In my book, that's stagnation! What we're failing to do is to develop greater public awareness of the talent we represent, nor are we taking advantage of it to the full benefit of all concerned.'

Gregory Richmond nodded. 'He's right, you know. When you think about the success of performers in other walks of life, it's shameful that many of our artists are unknown to the bulk of the public. My God! When you consider that the man in the street can tell you the names of the world's top golfers and tennis players, whether or not he's interested in sport, it's pitiful that he's unable to name the great classical artists of our time! And that's our fault!'

Erlich resumed his theme. 'The answer, of course, lies in advertising and marketing, but advertising alone isn't enough. It's essential to have a product with which the public can identify, and which represents the style and good taste of the artists.' As he spoke, he

123

unzipped the leather case. 'I'm sure you're aware that a number of organisations have already taken advantage of public acclaim for certain performers in order to sell themselves. We've all seen the American Express promos on TV and read the Rolex ads in the glossies. I looked at them, and it suddenly occurred to me: why should we let them use us? They're exploiting our great names to sell their product! What we should be doing is creating our own markets, using our own top artists, so that we control the results. Why give away our most precious commodity – our talent – to a bunch of outsiders?' He paused somewhat dramatically. 'In other words, we should be doing our own merchandising.'

Opening the leather portfolio fully, Erlich took out a number of cardboard posters portraying artists' impressions of various items: perfume and toiletries, men's clothing and jewellery, leather accessories and luggage. 'For the past few months, I've been working with a couple of the top agencies on Madison Avenue, developing a series of campaigns. I've also been talking to top designers on both sides of the Atlantic: people like Gil Travis in New York . . .'

'Who is he?' Vonheim spoke for the first time.

'Travis?' Erlich seemed astonished that the maestro had not recognised the name immediately. 'He's the world's greatest designer of casual clothes and sportswear. Then there's Reginald Davidson of Savile Row for formal clothes, and Armando Graziello of Milan and Guy Bergerac in Paris for contemporary styles. These guys are the best in the business! At the same time, I've been in touch with Wirtz Laboratories in Basle, who develop new perfumes for all the leading names; the watch-makers Planchet in Geneva, and the jewellery designer, Anton Scheppler. Every person I've approached is a recognised master-craftsman in his own field.' He smiled expansively. 'The list gets longer daily, but I can tell you without exaggeration that each man I've approached is incredibly excited with the whole concept!'

Richmond leaned towards the maestro confidentially. 'Howard's been doing his homework pretty thoroughly, Karl. I think I already told you he's something of a genius at this sort of thing.'

'Apparently, but I'm not sure that I understand the purpose of this meeting.'

Erlich moved towards the young man sprawled across the couch.

'This is where Alex comes into the picture. As you may well imagine, the scheme we have in mind is going to cost millions, even if we inaugurate it on a modest basis. I've drawn up estimates for the initial advertising campaign, and the product development costs are enormous. All the items we're considering are of the highest luxury level and will carry a very expensive retail tag, but that's the point. Each item will be the Rolls-Royce of its genre, with a quality that no competitor can challenge, but to set up a scheme like this will take considerable investment.' He looked expectantly at their host.

'I don't see any problems.' The young man stubbed out his cigarette. 'I'm prepared to undertake a considerable part of the outlay, and I have a number of friends who are eager to invest. My financial advisors have already drafted very optimistic forecasts. Initially, they proposed going public on this, but it may not prove necessary. My own inclination is to keep the issue limited.' He glanced at Vonheim. 'Needless to say, the whole thing revolves around the use of the name and the endorsement.'

The maestro spoke quietly. 'What endorsement?'

Erlich glanced from the conductor to Richmond. In the silence that followed, he seemed to pale visibly. 'I thought you understood, maestro. Hasn't Greg discussed this with you?'

'No. None of this has been brought to my attention. What exactly are we talking about?'

Erlich hesitated. 'The scheme I've been outlining. It's supposed to bear your name. We want to call it the Vonheim Collection.'

All attention was focused on the maestro. After a moment, he spoke quietly. 'I'm afraid that would be out of the question.'

Erlich stammered, 'But I thought Greg explained. The whole plan depends on you. Nothing would be offered that doesn't have your personal approval.' He shot Richmond an anguished glance. 'I've been lining up designs for you to look at, and there's a series of perfumes and cosmetics called "Francesca", to accompany Miss Noble's launch on the concert stage . . .'

'Then I'm afraid you've been wasting your time.' The conductor addressed Richmond. 'You weren't seriously proposing to involve me in something like this? Perhaps you're expecting me to model the costumes on television!'

'Of course not, Karl. Don't over-react.' Richmond spoke smoothly.

'As Howard says, the industry's changing, and we ought to move with the times. We're not suggesting some cheap mail-order business, and everything would be presented tastefully and handled with style. The sort of merchandise Howard's suggesting would only be available in a carefully limited number of exclusive stores. It's a very interesting concept.'

'Not to me.' Vonheim spoke mildly, but his expression was set.

'Well, at least take a little time to mull it over. There's no hurry.' He smiled easily. 'To be honest, I anticipated your initial reaction, which is why I didn't forewarn you. When you've had a chance to think it through, and when you see the sort of material we've selected, I think you'll see that there's nothing tasteless or undignified about it. We're talking about a multi-million-dollar luxury industry, involving only the highest standards.'

The maestro shook his head slowly. 'I've thought all I need to. Furthermore, I must expressly forbid you to mention either my name or Francesca's in association with such a scheme.' His voice was cool. 'It may have escaped your attention, but I am a conductor, and that is all. My life is dedicated to the interpretation and performance of great works of art, and I have absolutely no interest in selling clothes, jewellery, after-shave or even toothbrushes that are the Rolls-Royces of dental hygiene! I would have thought that occupation suited some huckster who has achieved prominence as the host of a television game show! Frankly, I'm astonished that you would want me involved.'

Richmond's complexion darkened. 'Very well. We'll leave it there, for the moment. However, now that you've had your say, I'd like you to think about . . .'

'I'm sorry, Gregory. The matter is closed.'

There was a long, uneasy silence. At length, Alex Kostiras shrugged. 'Well, I guess that's it!'

Vonheim stood. 'Thank you for your hospitality, Mr Kostiras.' He ignored Richmond and Erlich. 'We'll leave you to return to your games.'

'Oh, don't go yet. Let's have a drink and relax, to show there's no hard feelings. I understand your view, and I respect it. Greg should have talked to you first. Anyway, we won't discuss it further, and as far as I'm concerned, neither you nor Miss Noble will be mentioned again, I give you my word.'

126

'Thank you.'

'Let me at least offer you a drink. I'm sorry your journey's been a waste of time, but maybe you can enjoy the rest of your visit. I've invited one or two friends over, and they'll be very disappointed if you leave before they get here. Won't you stay a while?'

The maestro hesitated. 'Very well.'

'Great!' He signalled to one of the girls and, almost immediately, a white-coated steward appeared. 'You must let me show you both round my little power-boat.' A casual gesture took in the ocean-going vessel. 'It has a couple of interesting gizmos that might amuse you.' He grinned. 'I guess I should put on some clothes, too. Give me five minutes!'

Over the next hour, Alex, now dressed in a blazer and cream-coloured slacks, was an attentive and suitably respectful host. He kept a firm hold on Francesca's arm, and the conducted tour included a visit to the bridge, which displayed almost as many controls and electronic devices as a jumbo jet, the engine-room, a fully equipped gymnasium and a master bedroom which, with revolving circular bed and electrically operated curtains, might have been designed for the Playboy mansion. A steward, following behind them, refilled their glasses regularly and Vonheim, the earlier incident apparently forgotten, finally relaxed. He seemed fascinated by the gadgetry with which the ship bristled, and Alex was a cheerful and well-informed guide. At one point, he engaged the maestro in a discussion regarding the technical aspects of various Ferraris, nodding in deference to the older man's expertise, and they discussed the comparative merits of compression and gear ratios with the enthusiasm of dedicated collectors. Francesca found that she only understood the occasional phrase, but the wine was cool and refreshing, and she was content to listen.

When they returned to the stateroom, it was crowded with guests. She wondered whether they had been standing on the quay, awaiting a signal to board.

Richmond, his composure restored, approached Vonheim. 'Karl, I wonder whether you could spare me a few minutes before I leave? Howard and I are taking the late flight to Paris, and there are a couple of things I need to discuss before I go.'

The maestro surveyed the room. 'This would hardly seem an appropriate time. Can't they wait?'

Alex was standing between them. 'Use my office if you prefer. There's a telephone and a fax, if you need them.' He led the way.

Francesca was joined by Suzie and Colette who, despite their names, were from London. They worked in the fashion industry as models.

'We're just here for a few days' holiday. We did some swimwear stuff at St. Tropez, and Alex asked us over. He's a scream! Are you really a classical pianist?'

'Yes. Why do you ask?'

'You don't look like one. Mind you, I've never met one before, so I don't know what they look like!' Suzie was flat-chested. 'If I had a figure like yours, I could double my income! Come and meet some people.'

Most of the guests were either English or American, and were in their twenties and early thirties. Few had heard of Karl Vonheim when Colette mentioned his name, and displayed little interest. Sipping steadily from her glass, Francesca wondered, with a hint of disloyalty, whether Howard's unacceptable scheme might have some merit after all. The two girls, who maintained an engagingly wry running commentary, made her laugh frequently and, suddenly surrounded by people of her own age, she felt light-headed and slightly skittish. A momentary vision of Karl in a television commercial, holding a product in one hand and pointing at it with the other while staring earnestly at the camera, made her giggle.

'What's the joke?' Alex was standing next to her. He took her arm and drew her closer.

'Nothing. I had a funny thought. It's too complicated to explain.'

'OK. Are you having fun?'

'Yes, I think I am.' The thought surprised her. Life had been very serious for the past few months. It had been a long time since she had unwound.

'Well don't let it worry you. You shouldn't waste such a beautiful smile.'

'Thank you.'

He lowered his voice slightly. 'Listen, Fran, why don't you stay? We can dump the old man back at his hotel and have a party. Howard and Greg are leaving.' His thumb gently massaged the skin of her arm. 'You're among friends.'

'Well, I . . .' She looked up, and saw that Karl had re-entered the room.

'What d'you say? I'll make sure you get home.' Alex hesitated suggestively. 'Sooner or later.'

Karl smiled at her. 'Shall we go?' He looked very handsome and distinguished. Compared with him, Alex and his friends were tawdry.

Before she could reply, the younger man interjected. 'I was hoping Miss Noble would stay on for a while. My friends would love to talk to her.'

Vonheim looked at her. 'As you wish.'

'I think I should leave.' By way of explanation, she added, 'It's been a long day.'

Alex was visibly disappointed. 'It's still early.'

'I know, but I'm a little tired. Thank you, all the same.'

'I'll take you ashore. There's a car . . .'

'Don't worry. We'll find our way. Thank you again for your hospitality.'

When they reached the quay, Karl said, 'Shall we walk? The hotel's at the top of the hill.'

'Yes, I'd like that.' She was glad that he took her hand and tucked it into the crook of his arm. The evening was warm and sultry, and she felt a little unsteady.

He breathed deeply. 'The fresh air is welcome after that floating gin palace. I still can't imagine what Gregory and his henchman were thinking about.' He walked at a steady pace, and she clung to his arm.

'Were you very angry with them?'

'Perhaps not as much as I suggested. As I warned you earlier, those hyenas are always dreaming up new ways to manipulate you.' He chuckled. 'They call it being creative! The Vonheim collection! It makes me sound like a museum!'

'You should have seen the expression on your face.'

'Suitably frightening?'

'I think thunderstruck would be a better description.'

'Let's hope it will make them think carefully before they come up with their next plan.' They walked in comfortable silence, and the exercise helped to clear her head. As they approached the brow of the hill, his expression clouded. 'We still have one more gauntlet to run.'

'Gauntlet?'

'The spectators' gallery in the Place Casino. There's always a group milling around in the square outside the Hotel de Paris.'

'Why?'

He shrugged. 'Apparently, they have nothing else to do with their time. They watch who goes in or out of the hotel and the Casino; I can't tell you why. They just stand there and gape. The public is fascinated by fame or success. That's something you'll have to get used to.' He shook his head sadly. 'What a dreadful place this is!'

'You seem to take it all in your stride.'

He smiled, apparently flattered by the comment, and placed his hand over hers. 'I've had rather a lot of practice.'

They rounded the corner, and she found that the conductor's prediction was accurate. People congregated outside the Casino, watching the human traffic in the square. The police had erected portable barriers to keep them off the road. Walking quickly, Karl led her into the foyer of the hotel.

The concierge recognised him immediately. 'Maestro! I'm so pleased to see you here again!' He bowed grandly to Francesca. 'May I show you to your suite?' Uniformed attendants scattered as he led the way, and she suppressed a smile. It was like a scene from a Ruritanian musical. In the lift, he asked, 'May I reserve a table for this evening?'

'No, I think not. Perhaps we can have something sent up?'

'With great pleasure!'

When he had departed, Karl held both her hands. 'I hope you don't mind if we eat up here. I hate to feel I'm on display.'

'I'd rather stay here with you.'

'Good. You'll enjoy the food. They used to make a superb soufflé of langouste. May I choose for you?'

They dined by candlelight. 'Are you looking forward to Bern? *Jeunehomme* has always been a favourite.' She nodded. 'You know, of course, that Mademoiselle Jeunehomme was a French harpsichordist. There's some indication that she played the concerto on that instrument. People very often assume that Mozart wrote it only for the piano.'

'I didn't know.' She drank some wine.

'I'll give you some material to read. You should know the background. It explains the ornaments in the second movement.'

'Yes. I hope you'll approve. Will you come to the rehearsal?'

130

'I won't be at the concert.'

'Oh.' For a moment, she felt apprehensive.

'I have to be in New York. Richmond has several plans for our début together, and I have two weeks with the Philharmonic, so we'll discuss the arrangements while I'm there. Zoltán will look after you in Bern, and Simon will shoot a couple of sequences for the documentary about you.' He looked at her. 'Are you worried?'

'No.' She was irritated with herself. It wasn't necessary for Karl to monitor everything, but she had hoped he would be present. She wanted to please him.

'I think it would be better if I stayed in the background. I don't want people to feel they should come and hear you because of me. Your performance alone is sufficient reason. You have several more weeks to prepare.' He refilled her glass. 'And your appearance will not be accompanied by fanfares, mass-marketing, and a special-offer set of matching luggage personally autographed by me!'

She smiled. 'I was looking forward to free samples of an exclusive perfume called "Francesca"!'

'I've asked Zoltán to call me directly after the concert.' He reached across the table so that his hand could caress her cheek. 'It's an important occasion!'

'Don't remind me!' She placed her hand over his, pressing it to her face.

'You have nothing to worry about. Just concentrate on your work, and don't let any outside interference get in the way.' He hesitated momentarily before speaking again. 'Forgive me for mentioning it, but you shouldn't let Mr Meredith distract you, either.'

'Peter? I don't understand.'

Karl's voice was soft. 'Please don't think that I've been spying on you, Francesca, but I couldn't help noticing that he's been writing to you. I read his first postcard by accident. I thought it was for me, but I've also seen that there have been several more. His handwriting is somewhat distinctive.'

She felt her colour rising. 'They don't mean anything. He's taken to dropping me a line from time to time, with the latest gossip from the music world.'

'It's none of my business. I mentioned it because I thought you should be cautious. Meredith wanted to write my biography, you know. He once pushed his way into my dressing-room and tried to talk me into it.'

'Yes, he told me.' She wondered whether she should tell him about the earlier encounter at the recording session, but decided against it.

'I would hate to suggest that his friendship has an ulterior motive, but I know he's still interested in writing that book. It could be a motive for gaining your confidence.'

'I never thought of that.'

'Perhaps I'm being ultra-sensitive. For some reason, the press are determined to document my life to the last detail. I would hate to think he was using you.' He smiled bitterly. 'I can recognise ruthless ambition. As a young man, I was cursed with the same affliction.' Vonheim watched her face. 'I'm sorry to mention any of this. I have no right to pry into your personal life.'

'Peter's just a casual friend. I only met him the one time in Vienna.' She wondered why her explanation felt dishonest.

Later, they sat by the window, their shoulders touching, watching the lights of small boats far across the water. Soft candlelight illuminated the room. A combination of fatigue and more wine than usual made her drowsy.

'Will Dorothea go to New York with you?'

'No.'

'Then I hope she'll come to hear me in Bern. It would be good to have her moral support.'

'I wouldn't count on it.'

'Why not?'

'My wife lives her own life. I can't tell you where she'll be.'

'Well, if she's free . . .' The conductor had leaned forward, breaking any physical contact between them. 'Have I said something wrong?'

He spoke in a low voice. 'No. I had assumed you were aware of her problem.'

'I don't follow you.'

He hesitated before continuing. 'Dorothea is an alcoholic.' For a moment he was silent. 'It's a disease, like any other. The problem is that the public doesn't recognise it as such. They still look on it as a sort of uncontrolled vice.'

'I didn't realise . . .'

132

He shrugged. 'It's not an unusual complaint. I believe the statistics are quite surprising.' He glanced at her. 'I thought you would have guessed. It may also explain why I'm so protective about my private life.'

'I'm so sorry.' Her hand rested on his arm. 'I guess I just didn't think about it.'

'Dorothea manages to keep the situation under control. You may have noticed that she goes away quite frequently.' Francesca did not reply. 'There's a clinic in Solothurn. When things become . . . difficult for her, she spends a few days there. The Swiss are very discreet.' He relapsed into silence.

'I don't know what to say.' She took his hand. Perhaps it was the wine, but she felt a sudden wave of tenderness towards him.

'You don't have to say anything.' He sighed. 'I don't know why it started. When I first met Dorothea in Buenos Aires she was a beautiful, vivacious and witty woman. Maybe she shouldn't have married me. We came from very different worlds. I was an extremely ambitious young man in those days, and I was attracted by her wealth and the influential contacts her family offered.' His voice was bitter. 'I didn't have time for her problems. I was too busy developing my international career! Now, we live in friendly separation, unable to help each other.'

'It wasn't your responsibility.'

'If I had chosen a different profession, I might have been more understanding.' His mood changed abruptly. 'It's late. We have to return to Lausanne early tomorrow.' He faced Francesca and, taking her in his arms, kissed her gently on either cheek. It was like a lover's embrace, and she clung to him. He moved back. 'Please forgive me for burdening you with my problems.'

In her bedroom, Francesca undressed slowly. She was angry with herself, frustrated that she had been unable to offer the right words of comfort. Karl was a brilliant, attractive man, forced to withdraw from any personal relationship and guarding the secret of his wife's illness, and she had been childishly tongue-tied, aware of his self-imposed isolation, conscious of his loneliness, and yet unable to offer sympathy or understanding. He had given her so much, asking for nothing in return. She lay on the bed, staring at the ceiling, searching for something to say to him.

An hour passed, and she remained awake, scarcely moving. There

133

must be some way to let Karl know and understand her feelings. He was so locked away, forced to disguise his real emotions. She wanted to tell him that he was not totally alone; show him how much she cared. Quite suddenly, the answer seemed simple.

Francesca walked quickly through the darkened sitting-room of the suite, instinctively finding her way past the heavy furniture. Her breathing felt shallow when she reached the door to his bedroom. The curtains were still open, and the night sky provided enough light to show the outline of his bed.

He must have been sleeping lightly. 'Who's there?'

'It's me – Francesca.' Her voice trembled.

He turned towards her. 'What is it? Is something the matter?'

'No.' She faltered. 'I wanted . . . I wanted to . . .'

For a moment, he was silent. When he spoke, his voice was cold. 'I don't expect you to behave like this, Francesca. It was not a part of our arrangement. I thought I made that clear to you in Geneva.'

Francesca stood very still, shocked by the sharpness of his voice. She searched for words, but her mouth was dry, and she did not trust herself to speak.

When he continued, Karl's voice was milder. 'I think you'd better go back to your room and sleep off the effects of too much wine.' He turned away, and lay motionless.

Francesca fell into a restless, fitful sleep when grey light was already visible in the sky. The tears had long since dried on her face. Brilliant sunshine awoke her several hours later. Her head ached, and she opened her eyes cautiously. There was an envelope on the pillow next to her, and she recognised Karl's handwriting. Inside was a single page:

'My dear Francesca,
Forgive me. To have responded to your generosity in such an unfeeling way was thoughtless, and I am ashamed. I hope you will understand. Neither my self-pity nor my inability to accept your affection must stand in the way of our life together. You mean very much to me. More important, you have a great and unique musical gift, and I want more than anything to bring that to full bloom. Always remember that.
By the time you wake, I will have gone. I must return to Lausanne early, before going on to New York. Anyway, it would be better for us not to have

to face each other this morning. I am not very good at handling such personal situations! The concierge has your return ticket to Switzerland, and will look after your transport to the heliport. Erich will meet your flight in Geneva.

Work hard, and practise! You should know by now that nothing comes easily. I will be thinking of you, and living through every bar of Mlle Jeunehomme's concerto. I hope you like the conductor I have chosen for you. Don't let him argue with you over the tempo of the finale!

Forgive me again. Until our next meeting,

I send you my love.

K'

13

Max found Gisela in the kitchen, seated at the table. The room was chilly, and she cradled a coffee-mug in her hands to warm them.

'What are you doing up so early?' He was wearing a dressing-gown over his trousers.

'Couldn't sleep.'

'Are you feeling bad?'

'What do you think?' She glared at him, her hands massaging her distended belly. 'It's no fun having to wander round like this. I'm uncomfortable if I lie down; I'm uncomfortable if I stand up, and when I do find a slightly easier position, the little bastard kicks the shit out of my stomach-lining!'

'It won't be for much longer. Did you take your pills?'

'Yes!' Her anger passed. 'Don't mind me. I'm just feeling sorry for myself. Men don't know how lucky they are. All you do is stick it in at the right moment, and wait around for nine months looking pleased with yourselves!'

'I'm sorry.' He sat at the table with her. 'Little Gerda's giving you a hard time!'

'You're so bloody sentimental! Little Gerda! Whatever I've got in there feels like a baby elephant trying to stampede its way out! No wonder doctors give them a good slap on the bottom when they appear. The way I feel at the moment, I'd take the little bastard and give it a thrashing to remember! D'you want some coffee?'

'I'll help myself.'

'Wipe the counter if you slop on it. You leave the place looking like a pig-sty!'

He smiled. Gisela kept the entire house sparkling clean. He had never suspected that she would acquire such domesticity.

'I don't think I'll go into town today.'

'Why not?'

'Because you're due. The doctor said it could be as early as today.'

'That's no reason. I've got the number of the taxi service, the hospital's round the corner, and I don't want you hanging about the place. Christ, if I'm not careful, you'll start boiling water, just in case!'

'All the same . . .'

'No.' She waited until he was seated again. 'Aren't you supposed to meet that Korean today?'

'Mr Kim? He can wait. We only have a provisional appointment. I'll make another.'

'No, Max. See him now. It's important. He could make a hell of a difference to the business.' He would have replied, but she continued, 'Home computers are going to take over in the next few years, and you're a fool if you don't take up his offer. You'll never get anywhere if you stick with the plastic junk you've been buying.'

He frowned. 'I don't know anything about computers.'

'You don't have to. Anyway, you can learn. He'll tell you what machines people want, and you'll get them from him and supply them at half the price the big boys are asking. If you don't, somebody else will.'

'Maybe. It still sounds like a risky business to me. I'd rather keep to the things I understand.'

'Bullshit!' She heaved herself out of her chair, and paced back and forward, to ease her discomfort. 'Everyone has to take a chance, and there's very little risk involved. Listen, Max, we're going to need the extra income from now on. The only thing that worries me is how you're going to manage over the next few months, with me out of the office.'

'We'll manage. I'll get a temporary . . .'

'They're more expensive than a full-time girl. You should look for a kid just out of commercial college, without too many fancy ideas.'

'I know, I know!' He raised his hands in a placatory gesture. It was a subject they had discussed frequently in the past month. 'I'll find someone.'

'Right. Then before you see this Mr Kim, call up an agency and tell them what you're looking for. You should have done it weeks ago.'

'I'll do it tomorrow. I think I should stay home.'

'No.' She stood by his chair. 'I don't need you here, and I don't want you getting under my feet. I can tell better than you if anything's about to happen. The most useful thing you can do is see that Korean and talk him into a deal.'

He placed his arms around Gisela's waist and drew her closer. 'You're quite a businesswoman! I never expected that.'

'It's not business, Max. It's good sense. Half the people you deal with are switching to computers. If you supplied them alone, we could double our turnover and make some real money.'

'We make enough.'

'Not if we're going to find a decent home. I don't want to spend the rest of my life stuck in this lousy suburb. We've got to start thinking about better schools and a nicer neighbourhood for a kid to grow up in.' She returned to her seat.

Max capitulated. 'All right, I'll see Kim. Will you call me if anything starts to happen? You can leave a message. I'm supposed to meet him at the Vier Jahreszeiten at eleven.' He was silent for a moment, watching her. 'You're a very independent woman, Gisela. I would have thought you'd prefer to have me here.'

'Don't start sulking on me. I'll manage perfectly well. It's simply a matter of priorities.' She looked at him earnestly. 'I want you to make that deal, Max. It's really important. I can look after myself.'

He spoke quietly. 'Not always.'

She paused. 'Yes, I know.' She glanced at her left arm, slightly bent, which she usually held against her body. She had never fully regained use of it. 'You think I forget?'

'That bastard! Do you still not remember exactly what he looked like? The police said you could call them any time if . . .'

'It's too long ago.' She sighed. 'The doctor seems to think I've developed some sort of a mental block about him. I just can't picture his face any more. God, you'd think I'd never forget it! I remember that he was handsome and spoke nicely, but that's about it. Besides, you know how dark Willi always keeps the club. The whole idea is that visitors can be there without drawing attention to themselves. I never got a really good look at him at the Acapulco, and I drank too much. By the time we left, I wasn't thinking or seeing clearly.'

'How about Willi? He must have seen the man.'

'He never looks at their faces. He's too busy watching the money! The police weren't that helpful, for all their kind offers. They sent a detective round to see me but he more or less told me it was my own stupid fault. He as good as asked what else I expected if I picked up strangers in a place like that. Bloody hypocrite! He probably goes to the same bars himself!'

'What about the reporter from the newspaper?' They had discussed it all many times before, but Max knew that talking helped to distract her.

She was contemptuous. 'As far as that shit was concerned, it was just another nice juicy story for his readers! When he came to the apartment, he worked his way through all my old pictures, and chose the sexiest shot he could find! It was taken six years earlier.' She lit a cigarette and, seeing the disapproval on Max's face, stubbed it out again. 'Don't talk to me about the bloody press. He dropped more than a few hints that I was just another Reeperbahn whore who picked up the wrong customer!'

Max held her hand. 'It's all ancient history. Willi's place was another life. I'm sorry. I shouldn't have reminded you, Gisela. We've got so much to live for.'

'Careful, Max. You're getting all sentimental again!'

'I mean it! Don't laugh at me. We've got a whole new life ahead of us. I'm not ashamed of being a contented, expectant father. I'm very happy, and I'm proud of you. You're a wonderful wife, and you're going to be a fine mother.'

She laughed. 'Poor Maxie! Whatever made you get yourself tied up with a woman like me? You could have done better than that!'

'I'm not complaining.'

'That would be too much trouble! The problem with you is that you're getting old and fat and lazy!' She leaned forward, and poked a finger in his spreading stomach. 'You should get out and take a bit of exercise. God, you've got yourself such a big paunch that anyone would think you're the one that's having this damned baby! You're bursting out of those trousers!'

He shrugged. 'So I'll buy a bigger size.'

She shook her head. 'As soon as I get back to normal, you're going on a diet. We'll get rid of the stretch marks together! I don't want you looking like the kid's grandfather.'

'Rubbish! I'll look very distinguished.'

She eyed him critically. 'If you lost a bit of weight, you'd be all right. You're not such a bad-looking fellow, you know. Bald men are supposed to be sexy.' Some of her old spirit returned. 'Are you feeling sexy, Maxie? You haven't been getting any lately; well, not from me, at any rate. I could give you a hand-job under the table, if you'd like. It used to be a speciality of the house!'

Max looked embarrassed. 'You shouldn't talk like that.'

'Why not?' The hand on his stomach began to search lower. 'You're dealing with a professional. I'll do it nice and slowly, and you'll be all calm and relaxed for Mr Kim!' She saw the expression on his face. 'What's the matter?'

He held her hand to prevent it from touching him. 'I don't like it when you talk like that, Gisela. It worries me.'

'Why? I was only joking, for God's sake!'

He spoke hesitantly. 'Well, I sometimes wonder whether you miss your old life. I know it's not very exciting here, and I'm not the most dazzling companion. You used to laugh at me when I came to the club to see you, and you'd tell me about some dashing Prince Charming who was going to ride into the place and carry you away.' He smiled ruefully. 'I don't really fill that role very well, do I? I worry whether you won't get bored with living here, stuck out in the suburbs with a house to clean and a fat little husband and a squally kid to feed. It's very different from what you used to want.' He would have said more, but gestured helplessly, unable to find the appropriate words.

For a moment, Gisela did not speak. She rose again from her chair, and went to her husband, pressing his face against her swollen breasts. When she spoke, her voice had lost its characteristically hard edge. 'You silly old fool! What on earth are you talking about? Don't you realise that you're everything I could ever ask for or need, paunch and all? How could you even wonder? Before you started coming to the club, I was a nothing, Max: a cheap bar-girl, on sale to anybody for the price of a stinking drink! I didn't have a life. It was an existence, and a lousy, ugly one at that. The policeman who came to see me was right. He said something about a woman like me only getting what I deserved, and he told me I should count myself lucky to have come out of it alive. You should have seen the expression on his face, Max. He looked at me with such contempt! And he was right. I got what I asked for, and I certainly didn't deserve you.' Her voice grew softer. 'You were Prince Charming, Maxie. I didn't know it at the time, but I do now.

Don't mind me when I tease you. It's just that I spent so many years saying stupid, sexy, affectionate things I didn't mean that I find it hard to say them now, when they're the truth.'

Her mood changed, and she let her hand rest between his legs, pressing gently. 'Now, you'd better get the hell out of here before I rape you!'

The baby was born five hours later. Max arrived at the hospital, breathless, to find her sitting up in bed.

'I'm sorry! You should have let me stay!'

She was slightly groggy with sedatives, and smiled vaguely. 'It was easy, Maxie; nothing to it!'

'But I wanted to be with you. How are you feeling?'

'Wonderful! We must do this again! Did they show you?'

'Not yet. I came straight here, and . . .'

'We're going to have to do something about the name, Maxie. It's a boy.'

'Yes, they told me.'

'And he's so beautiful!' Her eyes focused on him for a moment. 'You can't call a boy Gerda!'

'No. We'll think of . . .'

'We're going to call him Günther, Maxie. That's a good name.' She nodded to herself sleepily. 'Günther. I like that. And he's going to have the best of everything, Maxie: all the things you and I didn't have.' The idea pleased her, and she sighed contentedly. 'The best!'

14

'I do hope I haven't dragged you too far across town.' Richard Templeton smiled deferentially. He gave the impression of being a shy, retiring man, but it occurred to Peter that, as the chief editor of a publishing house, he was aware that he held a position of some influence. An invitation to a writer for a bite of lunch at The White Tower on Percy Street was not unlike a summons to an ambitious politician for drinks and a chat at Number Ten. Why apologise for the location of the restaurant, which was in central London?

He played along. 'Not at all.'

'Good.' Templeton surveyed the cosily elegant dining-room from his habitual corner table. 'I always try to eat here. Unless the weather's awful, it's a pleasant walk from Bloomsbury, and it gives me time to digest the meal on the way back. I do a lot of walking.' He peered over the tops of his half-glasses. 'We put out a book of country rambles a few years ago. It was rather well done, telling you where to park and sending you on a circular route, so that you ended up in the same place, so to speak. I tried a few of the walks myself.' He looked apologetic. 'I had to leave the directions to my wife. I usually got lost after the first half-mile!'

'I don't get much exercise. Too much time behind a desk.' Peter sighed inwardly. Why did the English insist on small talk? Americans managed to get down to business between the first martini and the starter.

'Ah.' Templeton considered his statement carefully. A small man in his late forties, with thinning brown hair, his manner seemed to vacillate between ponderous comments and a general vagueness which Peter suspected was contrived. 'You should try walking. I find it allows me to think; something I rarely do at the office. With so much travel, you'd expect to have plenty of time when you're

142

sitting on aeroplanes, but people constantly come and pester you, don't they?'

'I suppose so. Do you travel much?'

He became vague again. 'Publishing houses keep amalgamating or buying each other up. You're never sure who is working for whom. It's all rather incestuous, really. Shall we order?' He studied the menu, with its colourfully exaggerated descriptions of each dish, then set it aside. 'I don't know why I bother to read this. I always have the same thing. It would probably throw the kitchen into disarray if I asked for something different!'

They chatted casually throughout the meal, mostly about the theatre, and Peter began to wonder whether the editor had mistaken him for someone else. The lunch invitation had arrived unexpectedly and, although flattered, he was still curious to know why he had been asked.

During their second cup of coffee, Templeton glanced at Peter. 'I read your piece about Karl Vonheim's press conference in Vienna. Very interesting.'

'He's an interesting man.'

'Is he really as good as you say? I don't know much about conducting.'

'If anything, he's better. There's no-one quite like him.'

'What makes him so different?'

Peter shrugged. 'It's hard to say. I don't think anyone really knows what makes a conductor. It's not technique. Most of the great ones of the past had rather unorthodox styles, and several were quite hard to follow, if you're talking about the way they waved their batons. It's not the expressive side, either. Leonard Bernstein leaps about like a man possessed. I think he once described himself as the only person he knew who was paid to have a fit in public! On the other hand, Fritz Reiner scarcely moved, Herbert von Karajan stands with his head bowed and his eyes closed, and Hans Knappertsbusch looked almost indifferent to what was going on. Each one gets results in a different way.' Peter hesitated, searching for an explanation. 'It's an extraordinary power to communicate, either by gesture or expression, combined with the ability to command respect and the obedience of the players.'

'You make it sound almost metaphysical.'

'I sometimes think it is. Training doesn't come into it either. I've seen conductors who are excellent academicians. Their knowledge

143

and understanding of music is absolute, yet when you put them in front of an orchestra, nothing happens. They simply don't come across. But there are conductors whose techniques are all over the place, whose knowledge is questionable and whose gestures border on the ridiculous, yet their instincts are so right that orchestras will do anything for them. The same seems to apply to certain actors. They have a kind of animal magnetism that attracts the audience. They really don't have to do anything more than stand there.'

Templeton nodded. 'I've seen that.'

Of course, most of the real work is done at rehearsals, but not every conductor relies on that. Toscanini went through every detail, but Beecham treated them in the most perfunctory way.' He smiled. 'You can't hope to achieve very much in London, where most conductors get one rehearsal and a general run-through on the morning of the concert.'

'Why is that?'

'It costs too much. I'm always amazed that London players can do anything except find their way through the notes, but they seem to manage. But a great conductor can come up with spontaneous ideas and get them across at the concert itself.'

'And is this what makes Karl Vonheim so special?'

'No. He's got the lot: technique, knowledge, gut-reaction, spontaneity, and a magnetic personality. That's what puts him in a class of his own.'

The editor was thoughtful. 'It sounds as though there's a book in that.'

'There is, but he won't allow it to be written.'

'Why not?'

'Who knows? A lot of us have approached the maestro, asking permission to write his biography, but he's not interested. In Vienna he told us he'd write his own story when he retired, but I doubt whether he will. For years, he's refused all interviews. He says his music-making speaks for itself and he doesn't like journalists!'

'Do you believe him?'

'Only the part about not liking journalists!' Peter leaned forward, caught up in his favourite subject. 'I want to know how he gets those results. I'm not allowed to attend his rehearsals, although I doubt whether they provide most of the answers. I want to know the man himself! I've talked to orchestra musicians and soloists who have played for him, and none of them seems to be able to put it into words. All they say is that some sort of magic happens when he steps onto the podium. I've approached him myself but he wouldn't give me the time of day. He's a very private man.'

'You sound as though you've made an intensive study of him.'

'I have, for twenty years, but I'm no closer. I've seen Karl Vonheim whenever it's been possible and I've collected material about him wherever it's appeared. I've built quite a file on him.' Peter grinned. 'I'm not sure whether he's a hero or an obsession!'

Templeton was silent and it struck Peter that his vagueness had gone. 'Your comments about his manager – Gregory Richmond? – aroused my curiosity. You suggested some dirty work at the crossroads.'

'I hope I didn't make it that obvious.'

'I was reading between the lines. What's it all about?'

'Richmond runs Telmusik, a company devoted to filming Vonheim's concerts. Although he denies it, it's been suggested that foreign appearances by Vonheim and his orchestra are only guaranteed if the countries he visits agree to buy the Telmusik films for television. It's a sort of blackmail, accompanied by very high fees.'

'Can you prove it?'

'Not really. I don't have all the facts, and I've never had the chance to talk to the television people, most of whom are in the Far East. Telmusik's latest scheme is looking for government funding of new projects. The organisation's very successful, worth millions, so there's something rather fishy about it.'

'That sounds like another good story.' Templeton stared at Peter for a moment. 'Tell me about Francesca Noble.'

Peter hesitated. He was suddenly aware that he was being gently cross-examined. 'There's not a lot to tell yet. They handed out a press release with the bare bones of her background. Francesca's a young American pianist. Vonheim heard her in Switzerland and decided to sponsor her career. I haven't heard her play. Nobody has, except for a few obscure concerts and recitals in America.'

'How would you describe her?'

He laughed. 'For starters, she's very beautiful. If she plays the piano anything like the way she looks, she'll be a knockout! What fascinates me is that a great conductor like Vonheim should be interested enough to take her under his wing.'

145

'Maybe her beauty had the desired effect.'

'I can't believe that. You have to understand his dedication to his work.'

Templeton sipped coffee. 'It's been known to happen to the most dedicated of men. Are you in touch with Miss Noble?'

'Me? No, not exactly.' Peter found himself colouring, and wondered whether it showed. 'We talked for a while in Vienna. I think we got along rather well. I've sent her the odd postcard since. I'm very interested to hear her.'

'When will that be?'

'She's due to play a concerto in Bern later this month.'

'Will you be going?'

He smiled. 'I'd like to, but I'm not sure whether my budget runs to it. I'm hoping to persuade the editor of my magazine that it's a worthwhile story.'

Templeton looked pensive. 'I think that can be arranged.'

'I don't understand.'

The editor spoke briskly. 'It's clear to me that there should be a book about Karl Vonheim, and that you're the man to write it, Mr Meredith. From what you say, you've already collected a lot of the background material. You need an entrée into the Vonheim household and Miss Noble appears to be the answer. By developing your association with her you may find what you're looking for.'

Peter was thoughtful. 'Possibly. I don't know her very well.'

'I'm sure she'll remember you. It shouldn't be too difficult to extend that friendship. That's up to you, but a visit to Bern would be useful.'

He frowned. 'I liked her when we met, but I'm not very happy about using Francesca to get to Karl Vonheim.'

'I'm not suggesting that you should, but it seems that Miss Noble has become an element in maestro Vonheim's life, and therefore part of his own story.'

'True, but I don't like the idea of manipulating her.'

Templeton laughed. 'I'm not proposing that you should, but you may well find that, through her, you'll meet and talk to Karl Vonheim. He obviously thinks a great deal of her and might welcome your assistance in promoting her career. After all, if you can get to know him as a friend rather than as a journalist, you might persuade him to relax his ban on interviews.'

146

'Perhaps.' Peter was unconvinced.

'The public is fascinated by legends, Mr Meredith, and the more elusive they are, the more attractive they become. That's why Karl Vonheim's aloofness intrigues us all. In this age of instant television interviews and chat shows, of endless articles in magazines and newspapers, a genuine mystery man is a rarity.'

'You don't believe we should respect his request for privacy?'

'No more than you do, or you wouldn't have approached him in the past. We should certainly respect his private world. I'm not suggesting that you should write an exposé, but I think readers are entitled to a carefully considered biography – authorised òr not – of a well-known public figure who earns his living by appearing before audiences all over the world. If there are certain aspects of his private life that you don't consider appropriate to reveal, you have the power to exclude them.' He smiled. 'In your article, you wrote that maestro Vonheim doesn't consider himself to be a very interesting person. Maybe it's true.'

'That would be hard to believe.'

You never know. Specialists in any field aren't necessarily so fascinating when you remove them from their chosen work. You'd be surprised by the number of autobiographies by famous men that I've rejected over the years! I think Karl Vonheim will make a very readable book.'

'So do I.'

Templeton's eyes narrowed. 'It could be that a little investigative work into the operations of Telmusik will come up with some interesting disclosures. It's been my experience that great men are often surrounded by somewhat parasitic characters, without ever realising it. By looking into that, you might be doing maestro Vonheim a favour.' He paused. 'Should you unearth something, the Sunday supplements might show an interest.' He spoke quickly. 'I'm not suggesting there is anything, of course, but you never can tell. Who is your agent, by the way?'

'Mark Shepperd.'

'I know him. Please ask him to get in touch.' He became businesslike. 'Once the contract is signed, you must let me know whether you would like a further advance. We'll put in a separate clause to cover travel and research expenses.'

147

'Yes.' Templeton's change of personality was slightly bewildering but Peter's initial reaction was one of pleasure at the thought of seeing Francesca again.

The editor smiled. 'Becoming better acquainted with Francesca Noble will be a pleasant aspect of your job. She's very lovely.'

He was surprised. His article had no picture of her. 'You've seen her?'

Templeton became vague again, searching the room for a waiter to bring the bill. 'Yes. I was in Vienna for the conference, you know. Didn't I mention that?'

'No.'

'Perhaps I should have. I was tucked away at the back of the room.'

'Why didn't you speak to me there?'

'I wanted to see what you wrote.' He lowered his voice confidentially. 'Besides, I couldn't help noticing that you seemed rather preoccupied with the young woman.'

15

Francesca slammed her hands down on the keyboard, letting the angry discord reflect her frustration, and leaned forward so that her forehead rested against the hard edge of the piano. She would never get it right!

It wasn't the goddam notes. She had learned K 271 weeks ago, memorising every page, and her fingers controlled every phrase until she could play the entire Mozart concerto with her eyes closed. That was the easy part. It was that goddam, stupid slow interlude in the middle of the Rondo of the third movement! Why did he have to put it there, for Christ's sake? It was elegant and beautiful and witty and wonderful — and it just wouldn't come out the way it should! She couldn't find the right tempo, the right mood, that made it fit against the rest of the movement. First it was too slow; then, too affected. Then it became offhand and trite. No matter how she played it, it didn't work!

For once, Karl had been no help. In a moment of self-pity, it seemed to her that he had taken pleasure in watching her struggle. She had played the concerto for him before they had left for Monaco. After the first two movements, he had been constructive and encouraging, adding useful suggestions, but at the end of the third, he had shaken his head.

'I don't like the slow interlude.'

'What's wrong with it?'

'It's too self-conscious. You're over-phrasing it.'

'But I see it as a kind of funny aside, as though Mozart's enjoying some sort of private joke.'

'I think he is, but you're making it too . . . cute. The humour lacks grace.'

'Then should I play it more straight, and let the music speak for itself?'

'Yes, I think so, but there's no harm in bringing out the playful quality as well. Haydn used the same trick dozens of times. The movement's a Rondo. It's supposed to make you smile.'

'It's about to make me vomit! What should I do?'

'You must work that out for yourself. Just don't overplay it. The audience will understand the joke if you don't over-stress it. Like all humour, it's a matter of timing. Don't worry. I trust your judgement. Let your musical intelligence guide you.'

Intelligence! She left the piano and wandered restlessly across the studio. Outside, late afternoon sunlight slanted across tranquil green hills speckled with cattle. A distant tractor inched its way across the horizon. The room was pleasantly cool, and the gentle swish of air-conditioning maintained an even temperature. It was the only sound she could hear. The pale wood panelling and the parquet flooring gleamed warmly, and rows of neatly bound scores on the bookshelves added a flash of colour. It was a beautiful, airy studio, overlooking an idyllic Swiss pastoral scene, but she felt angry, trapped and isolated.

Maybe she should listen to one or two records. There was a Murray Perahia recording of the concerto in the library. He was one of her favourites, with a lyrical, singing tone unlike any other pianist she knew, and there were probably several others if she wanted to make comparisons. No. Karl hadn't exactly forbidden listening to them, but he had advised her never to audition other performers' interpretations until she had already formulated her own.

'Make your own decisions and solve your own problems. When you play this concerto, I want to hear your reading; not some re-hash of other people's ideas.'

Except that Karl wasn't going to hear her play the goddam concerto. He was in New York, and she was left alone, in solitary confinement, to wrestle with Mozart's stupid goddam joke!

For a moment, her thoughts turned to the last time she had been with Karl, and she stared at the pattern of polished wooden rectangles on the floor. Why had she done it? It had been so humiliating. Her behaviour had been recklessly immature. Had she really believed a great artist like Karl Vonheim would want her? She should never have drunk so much wine, and the heady atmosphere of Monte Carlo had made her behave like a fool. She remembered the awful silence of his room, her sense of shame, and the rigidness of Karl's body as he had turned away from her. Later, she had fallen asleep wondering whether she had enough money to buy a return ticket to the States. Her only thought had been to run away.

150

But Karl had understood, apologising for his own self-pity and thanking her for her generosity. She should have known he would find the right words and, by blaming himself, forgive her. On the return flight to Geneva, she had resolved that, if she wanted to express love and gratitude, she would do everything in her power to live up to his musical expectations. That was what he wanted from her.

Francesca spoke aloud. 'So why the hell are you slumping around like this, feeling sorry for yourself and blaming everyone else? Get back to the piano, you jerk!'

Half an hour later, she was so absorbed in the music that she did not notice the door to the studio open. The Rondo was taking shape, and the interlude beginning to work. It needed just the slightest exaggeration; a pause that could scarcely be measured. She felt a sudden elation.

'Do you mind if I listen to you for a while? You play so well. It's very lonely when Karl's away.'

Dorothea Vonheim was leaning against the doorpost, smiling. She was a small, almost petite, woman whose age was hard to guess. Francesca assumed that she was somewhere in her middle sixties. Her hair was dyed jet black and held tightly against her head in a bun at the back. She had obviously been beautiful as a young woman, with high cheekbones over a heart-shaped face, but her skin was now puffy and her eyes seemed sunken and deeply shadowed. Her body, disproportionate to her head, was thick and shapeless.

Francesca stopped playing. 'I hope my practising hasn't disturbed you.'

The older woman held a tall glass filled with colourless liquid and took a sip from it. Then she gestured with her hand, spilling some of the drink. 'I can't hear you from my side of the house. The whole place is so well insulated, it's like living in a tomb.' She giggled stupidly. 'Either a tomb or a prison.' She paused to consider her words. 'A prison, I think. We're both prisoners, aren't we?'

'I'm sorry.' Francesca stared at the keyboard, uncertain whether a reply was expected.

'Oh, don't apologise. There's nothing that either of us can do about it. Would you like a drink? You must be very warm. Your forehead's all wet.' Dorothea crossed the room unsteadily. It was apparent that she had been drinking for some time. She continued to smile hazily.

151

'No, thank you.' Francesca wiped her face and hands with a towel. 'I guess I work up a sweat when I'm playing. It takes a lot of physical control, especially the slow parts.'

'I suppose it does.' The woman leaned on the end of the piano to support herself, then spoke confidentially. 'To tell you the truth, I don't know very much about music. Of course, I pretended I did when I first met Karl in Buenos Aires, otherwise I don't think he would have bothered with me. He was always so wrapped up in it! But I do know that it seems to make people all wet and sticky!' She giggled again. 'I used to think it made Karl very sexy. He'd come to the dressing-room, all hot and shiny from conducting, and I'd be waiting there for him. You'd think from his appearance that we'd been . . .' She interrupted herself, feigning embarrassment, then laughed. 'Well, you're old enough to know what I'm talking about. How old are you, Francesca?'

'Twenty-five.'

Dorothea drank again, emptying the glass. She tried to place it on the narrow edge of the piano, but it fell to the floor, shattering on the wooden surface. She did not seem to notice. 'Twenty-five! That's how old I was when I first met Karl. It's a lovely age to be in love, isn't it? First me, and then you.'

'I don't understand what you mean.' Francesca felt herself blushing.

'Oh, it's all right. I don't mind.' Dorothea gestured vaguely. 'We're all in love with Karl. Everyone loves him! We're all in love, and we're all prisoners of love, for all the good it does us. And we're all happy; happy, loving prisoners!'

'Why do you say prisoners?'

Dorothea gestured broadly, swinging round to take in the room. The motion made her stumble, and she fell into an armchair. 'Look at us both: you locked away with your piano, and me locked away with . . .' She glanced at the broken glass on the floor. 'Just locked away.' For a moment, she was silent, apparently staring at a Pissaro landscape hanging on the wall facing her. Then she sighed. 'It wasn't always like this. When we lived in Buenos Aires our house was full of people all the time: visiting guests, friends, musicians, servants. I used to complain to Karl that it was more like a railway station than a house, but we did have fun!' Her expression saddened. 'We should never have left.'

152

'I guess his work brought him back to Europe.'

'Oh yes.' Her voice hardened. 'We must never forget Karl's work! It's the centre of our universe; the axle of the wheel round which we all spin. Nothing must be allowed to stand in the way of that!' With alcoholic illogicality her mood suddenly softened again. 'How we travelled! First London, and then Lausanne, and then town after town. Everyone wanted to hear Karl conduct. You know, at one time, we lived in so many different hotels that I had to look at the stationery to remember where we were! I told Karl we were the most elegant gipsies in Europe!' Her head began to loll and, as if taking control of herself, Dorothea struggled out of the chair. 'Excuse me. I must find something to drink. I'm very thirsty today. I think the air-conditioning dries the atmosphere. Are you sure I can't bring you something?'

'Quite sure, thank you.' For a moment Francesca was tempted to say more and to persuade the woman to stay, but decided against it. Apparently, Dorothea blamed Karl for her isolation, but didn't most alcoholics need something or someone to blame for their affliction? She watched Dorothea make her way slowly from the room, then returned to the music, hoping to recapture the elusive mood of the Rondo. It was as though it had been at her fingertips before the other woman had entered.

Dorothea returned quite quickly, carrying another glass. This time she stood next to Francesca, leaning against the upper half of the keyboard. 'I want to warn you about Erich. That's why I'm here.'

Francesca watched her face. 'Erich?'

'Yes.' She was standing very close, and lowered her voice. 'Be very careful with him.'

'What do you mean?'

'He spies on us; both of us. Did you know that?'

'No, I . . .'

'He watches me all the time. Nasty, ugly little creature, creeping around the house on those rubber-soled shoes of his! He's always sneaking from one room to another, following me. He doesn't think I know what he's doing, but I know.' She nodded solemnly. 'I know!'

'But why would he do that?'

'Because he's a spy; a mean-hearted cheap little spy! I told you that already. He's always hanging around, waiting and watching me. You too! I've seen him sneaking round your room, poking his ugly

153

little nose into your things.' Dorothea looked round, as though to make sure they were not overheard. 'He's gone into Lausanne today, to do some shopping. That's why I thought it would be safe to come and warn you.' Her words were slurred, and she pronounced them with difficulty. 'He reports everything you do.'

'But I'm not doing anything! Who does he tell?'

'Karl, of course! Who did you think? He's Karl's spy! That's why he works here.'

'Perhaps you're imagining it. Erich's just an employee.' She smiled. 'I guess he is a bit creepy at times, but that's just the way he is.'

'Don't be so naïve!' For a moment, Dorothea was angry. 'Karl uses him to spy on us. He reports back on everything we say and do, I'm telling you! The pair of them are like thieves together.' She swayed slightly. 'They're like characters in one of those Verdi operas, lurking behind screens and whispering to one another!'

The image of Karl Vonheim and Erich as characters in a Verdi sub-plot was so ludicrous that Francesca laughed. 'Oh, come on! Erich just works for Karl. He's – I don't know – what you call a manservant. You're imagining things.'

'No, I'm not! Karl uses him to find out what's going on. He spies on me all the time, and reports what I do to Karl.' She sniffed. 'You call him a man?'

It occurred to Francesca that there might be a grain of truth in Dorothea's paranoia. Perhaps, because of his frequent absences, Karl had asked Erich to keep an eye on his wife, especially if she was drinking heavily. Francesca did not like Erich. There was something sinister about his behaviour and she sometimes had the impression that he was watching her, too. At the same time, on the few occasions when they had spoken, she detected a note of patronising arrogance in his expression, as though he regarded her as a poor relation. She had attributed his attitude to European snobbery.

'Have you ever talked to Karl about it? If Erich's getting on your nerves, you should ask him to find somebody else . . .'

Dorothea laughed. 'Somebody else? He'd never get rid of that cunning little faggot! Erich's been with him for years. He's always there, fetching and carrying, driving the car, chasing after little boys! He disgusts me!' She glowered at Francesca. 'Karl would get rid of me before he'd lose faithful Erich!'

'I think you're exaggerating.' To divert her drunken anger, she asked, 'How long has Erich been with you?'

'He's not with me. I won't have anything to do with him. He's Karl's.'

'That's what I meant. When did he start?'

'I don't know. Years ago.' Dorothea drank again, emptying her glass. 'He must have started the year Karl set up Telmusik. There'd been some sort of trouble in Hamburg and Erich came to work for him.'

'What sort of trouble?'

'I don't remember. You'd have to ask Karl. Erich just showed up at our hotel and Karl arranged for him to have the room next to ours. I told him it was ostentatious to keep a servant like that, but we were only there for a few days.' Dorothea's concentration seemed to be fading rapidly. 'The little sneak's been with us ever since. He's always at Karl's side, whispering in his ear and standing there with that self-satisfied expression on his face! I hate South Africans!'

'Why do you say that?'

'Erich. He's from Johannesburg. Didn't you know?'

'No. I thought he was German.'

'Couldn't you tell from his accent?'

'No. It sounded a bit strange, but I didn't realise . . .'

'He's South African Dutch, which made German easy for him to learn.'

'What was he doing in Hamburg?'

'I don't know. I think he worked as a steward on a ship.' She peered through the window. 'I'd better go. He'll be back soon.'

Francesca watched her. 'Well, if he gets out of hand, you should confront him; tell him to stay out of your way.'

She shook her head vaguely. 'He's too sly to let me catch him. You don't know what he's like.' She paused at the door. 'Be careful!'

Francesca was relieved that the woman was going. 'Sure. I guess I'll see you later.'

'No. I think I'll lie down. This weather disagrees with me. Tell Madame Chauvet to send something to your room if you're hungry.'

Francesca dined alone in the small apartment that had been furnished for her use. A concert on Radio Suisse Romande kept her company. It was a warm evening, and she considered taking a swim in the heated pool in the garden, but she was tired from practising. Sometimes, she went for a late stroll across the meadow that

155

stretched beyond her window. There was a village at the bottom of the hill, and she liked to walk to it, stopping at the small café that was the meeting-place for the local community. Her presence there seemed to embarrass the habitués and, although they greeted her politely, they discreetly avoided her and their conversation became subdued. It was clear that they regarded her as the local 'gentry', and resented her intrusion.

The concert on the radio ended, and she switched on the television, but there was nothing of interest: cycle racing on the French channels, a discussion on the German, and an old Italian movie. When she turned it off, the room seemed very silent.

On her desk there was a card from Peter Meredith. It had arrived that morning. It may have been her imagination, but she thought she had left it face up, displaying a photograph of Buckingham Palace and the slogan 'Greetings from London'. It had been turned over. Had someone been reading it? She hesitated, remembering Dorothea's warning, then shook her head with an irritated frown. The woman was obviously overwrought. Anyway, if the wicked Erich had been reading her mail, he must have been very disappointed with its contents. She read the card again:

'Looking forward to seeing (and hearing) you – at last! – in Bern. Peter.'

Peter had not written to her for several weeks. His previous cards had always contained fragments of musical gossip, designed to amuse her. They had usually begun: 'Just thought you'd like to know . . .' followed by some minor item of news from London. It seemed to her that this message was on a slightly more personal level, which pleased her, but she felt a twinge of guilt. Karl disapproved of 'distractions'. But Peter's cards had been innocent enough; almost impersonal. Why, then, should she feel guilty?

Anyway, she was glad that he would be there for the concert. At least, she could count on finding one friend in the audience. She wished he had given her his address or telephone number in London. She would have liked to reply with her own news, or even call him. For all its comforts, Chateau Beethoven was cut off from the rest of the world. Perhaps Dorothea was right.

Then again, she knew nothing about the Englishman, except that he had been pleasant and amusing for the few minutes they had spent together in Vienna. It was odd that he had taken the time to

156

write to her. Karl had suggested an ulterior motive, or was he just being over-protective too?

She wished there was someone to talk to. Mike had finished his tour with the orchestra in Geneva, and had returned to New York, and she had spoken to her family in Connecticut two nights earlier. For a moment, she thought of calling Karl. The sound of his voice and the absolute logic of his thinking would be certain to reassure her. But there was nothing to tell him. He had already promised her that the Rondo would work if she stuck with it.

Besides, to disturb him for no reason would be childish. She had already made a fool of herself once. She didn't need reassuring, for Christ's sake! And she was glad that Peter, whatever his motive, was coming to Bern.

16

'I hate having to do the backstage bit.' Rachel pulled a face.

'You used to enjoy it.' Simon placed a proprietary hand in the small of her back, urging her past the orderly line that had formed in the corridor outside the conductor's dressing-room. They had already fought their way through the departing audience at the Royal Festival Hall to reach the door leading to the musicians' area.

'It's all so phoney.'

'Nonsense!' He ignored the glares of the people waiting ahead of them, and went to the front of the queue. 'It only takes a couple of minutes, and musicians love being told how good they were.'

'Even if they weren't?'

He grinned. 'Then you have to come up with a suitably worded phrase. My favourite is: "You should have been in the audience!" '

'Yes. You told me.' Inwardly, she added, 'Several times!'

'Anyway, he was good. Anyone who can make Hindemith sound interesting can't be all bad. God, it's a long bloody piece!'

'I didn't really notice.'

'That's because you slept through most of it.'

'I was late last night.'

'Anyone I know?' He saw the expression on her face. 'I'm sorry. That wasn't very kind.'

'No, it wasn't.' She knew Simon wanted her to elaborate on the reason for her late hours but she remained silent. He had already asked her whether she had been busy and she had replied with a monosyllable. Most of the evening had been spent doing washing and ironing, but John from the tennis club had called, and they had talked for over an hour. She had agreed to meet him on Sunday evening for a drink.

Simon spoke softly. 'I promise to make it quick.' It was a peace offering. He had used that particular phrase when they had first been lovers in Venice. They had been late for a morning appointment with maestro Vonheim, but Simon had wanted to make love before they left the hotel. At the time, she had replied: 'So what else is new?'

'You always do.' She returned his smile, forgiving him. It seemed to Rachel that they had been bickering all evening over unimportant matters. Why did Simon always have to play Mr Big? 'Is he a good conductor?'

'Not bad. Vonheim asked him to conduct Francesca's concert in Bern next week. If Uncle Karl's prepared to entrust the girl to him, he must be all right. As a matter of fact, I was on the jury of some competition he entered a couple of years ago.'

'Did he win?'

Simon laughed. 'No! Just goes to show you how much I know, doesn't it?'

Rachel softened. When Simon laughed at himself he was very endearing.

The door to the conductor's room opened and Simon stepped forward, brushing past the young man who was there to prevent a rush. Rachel followed a few paces behind. Simon greeted the conductor effusively. 'Louis, *mon cher*! Bravo!' He clasped the Frenchman in the traditional embrace that musicians reserve for one another, brushing cheeks and clapping the young man on the back. Rachel noted with slight satisfaction that the conductor seemed a little surprised by his enthusiasm. The young man at the door, who was his lover, watched suspiciously. 'That was an outstanding performance. He's a greatly under-rated composer.'

'Thank you.' The conductor brightened. 'It has not been performed here since 1946.'

'Really? That's ridiculous!' Simon looked to Rachel for support. 'It's no wonder half the programmes they do here put the audience to sleep! You know, I should put you in touch with a friend of mine at the BBC. It's high time they made a documentary about Hindemith. Hasn't he got some sort of anniversary coming up?'

The young man standing next to Rachel said, 'He was born in 1895.'

'Well now's the right time to start planning something. We'll have to talk about it. You've met my assistant, Rachel, haven't you?' He paused to let the conductor bow in her direction. 'Listen, we won't keep you now. There are dozens of people waiting outside to congratulate you. We'll see you next week in Bern.'

'Ah yes.' It seemed to Rachel that the young man had finally placed Simon. 'Will you be filming the whole concert?'

'Probably not all of it. We're putting together sequences for a piece about Francesca Noble. Apart from a backstage scene, I'd like to get one of the rehearsals and maybe the whole of the Mozart concerto.'

'Oh. You see, I will be conducting the *Symphonic Metamorphoses* in the second half. If anyone is interested in making a documentary, it would be very useful to have . . .'

Simon was already shaking his hand in farewell. 'Why don't we talk about it in Bern next week? We'll be there by Tuesday. See you then.' Before the conductor could reply, he had already breezed out of the dressing-room.

'Was that quick enough for you?'

'Yes.' She was about to comment that the Frenchman had clearly not known who Simon was until he had mentioned Bern, but decided to let it pass. 'I noticed that you said *we* would be in Bern.'

'Of course. You didn't think I was going to leave you out, did you?'

'I suppose not. You hadn't mentioned that you wanted me to go.'

He placed an arm around her shoulder. 'There was never any question. I can't be expected to work without my faithful assistant!' Rachel was silent. He continued, 'It gives us a chance to spend a few days together – and nights. I don't know about you, but I feel as though we've been bottled up in London for ages.'

'It's not so long since Vienna.'

'It is as far as I'm concerned. I've booked us into a nice little hotel almost opposite the Casino, where the concert will be.'

'I wish you'd told me sooner.'

'I didn't think I needed to. You'll love Bern. It's one of the most charming and civilized cities in Switzerland. Some of the greatest antique shops I've ever seen. It's a shame it has to be wasted on a lot of boring Swiss.'

'When are we supposed to go there?'

'I'm flying to Hamburg on Sunday. I want to talk to Hans Wolpert about budgets. D'you want to come with me?'

'No.' She replied so quickly that he turned to look at her. 'I'll meet you in Bern.'

His tone was reproachful. 'It would give us an extra day together.'

'There's too much to be cleared in the office before I leave. I wish you'd warned me sooner. You don't need me for Wolpert. Besides, I thought you hated Hamburg.'

'I don't like it very much, but it would be fun if you were there. It's not such an awful place.'

'Then why don't you like it?'

'Bad memories. You're not going to show up late in Bern, are you?'

'No. I don't make a habit of missing planes. Please let's not drag that up again.'

When they reached the door of her flat in Putney, Simon parked the car. 'Are you going to invite me in for a coffee?'

'Not tonight, if you don't mind. I'm tired.'

'It isn't very late.'

'It's already after ten. What time do you have to report in?' She regretted the words as soon as they were spoken.

'That's not your problem. I thought we'd agreed on that some time ago.'

She faced him, half-turning in her seat. 'It is my problem, Simon. Don't you understand? If I ask you in, and we relax and stop niggling at each other, I'll want you to stay.'

'So I'll stay.'

'But for how long?'

'I don't know. As long as you like.' His laugh was forced. 'You make it sound as though we're bargaining.'

'I didn't mean to.' She placed her hand over his. 'I'm sorry, but there are times when the situation gets me down. It's not much fun having to be a lady-in-waiting.'

'I know. I'm sorry, too.'

She spoke softly. 'We're neither of us much good at facing up to reality, are we?'

'Meaning what?'

For a moment, she was irritated. 'Oh, come on! You know what I mean. You also know that I . . . care about you, so don't pretend. Look, we like the same things. We enjoy working together. We even laugh at the same jokes, as long as you don't repeat them too often! In fact, we spend most of our waking hours with one another. But at the end of the day, you go home to Richmond, and I'm left to my own devices in beautiful downtown Putney!'

'You said that was the way you wanted it.'

'Not exactly. I said I didn't want you to change your life because of me. That's slightly different. If you're not happy with your

161

domestic situation, you should do something about it, Simon. It's not fair to use me as the excuse.'

'That's a cop-out. You're perfectly well aware that it's because of you that I'm not happy with my "domestic situation", as you so discreetly describe it. I assume you don't mean I'm unhappy with the au pair girl.' Simon waited for her to reply, but she remained silent. At length, he spoke again. 'Listen, if I weren't married, would you live with me?'

Rachel hesitated. 'I don't know. I'm not sure.'

'Oh.' Simon watched her face. 'Are you gently trying to say good-bye?'

'No, I'm not. Don't be dramatic, darling. It comes out sounding like a soap opera. It's just that you make me feel that I'm at your beck and call, whenever you've got the time for me. And when we're not together, it's as though I'm under a microscope, being watched by you. I'm not allowed a life of my own.'

'I don't know what you're talking about.'

'I think you do. For a start, there's the daily catechism every morning: What did you do last night? Who did you see? Where did you go? I don't enjoy being interrogated.'

'I don't mean to. It's just that I'm interested. Isn't that what caring for somebody is about?'

'Not if it ends up with a question and answer period every morning. I gave up Show and Tell in kindergarten! I don't mind telling you what I did, but I don't like being cross-examined. It makes me want to rebel and say nothing out of bloody-mindedness.'

'All right. From now on, I won't display interest in anything you do.'

'Don't sulk, darling. I'm just trying to tell you how I feel.'

'You already know how I feel.'

'Yes.' She stared out of the window. 'I do.'

'Then what do you want?'

'Space. You're crowding me. I'm not asking you to get a divorce, Simon. That's your responsibility and, if you decide it's what you want, it's got to be your decision alone. Don't use me as the reason. On the other hand, if you want things to stay the way they are, you should say so. I'll understand. I don't want to tell you how to live your life, but you mustn't tell me how to live mine.'

'I don't.'

162

'You do, in a way. I feel that you've got me in some sort of emotional stranglehold. I want to be free to meet other people and have a life of my own.'

'By other people, I assume you mean other men?'

'Not necessarily, but, yes, if the situation arises.'

'And has that situation arisen? Did it delay your arrival in Vienna?'

'Oh, for Christ's sake, stop it!' She moved away from him, leaning against the door of the car. 'Look, if I start seeing someone else, you'll be the first to know! OK? I'm not planning to get involved with anyone at the moment. I just don't want to feel that everything I say or do depends on you. I'd like to be my own mistress – for a change!'

Simon stared out of the window. A car passed, and his face was lit in profile. It seemed to Rachel that he looked very sad and very vulnerable. When he eventually spoke, his voice was low. 'I'm sorry. It's a lousy situation, and it is my fault. I didn't mean to pressure you.' He turned towards her. 'It's just that I do care – desperately! – and I don't know what to do about it. I know that if I don't sort my life out soon, you'll get sick of hanging around. I'm not that stupid! You know that I love you.'

She spoke softly, 'Yes, I do, but that doesn't solve anything, does it?'

'No. Will you at least give me some time to work it out?'

'Now you're being dramatic again! We're not facing any deadlines, and I'm not giving you any ultimatums.' She smiled. 'Should I have said ultimata? It sounds funny. I'm just asking you not to get so heavy with me.'

'I won't. Don't you realise that I ask you all those questions because I'm afraid of losing you?'

'I guessed it was something like that.'

'When you didn't arrive in Vienna, I was convinced you'd met someone . . .'

'That's ridiculous! What sort of person do you think I am? Anyway, if I had, I wouldn't have come to Vienna at all.'

'I suppose not.'

'I'm just not the handmaiden type, and I'm not prepared to follow behind you, at a suitable distance, awaiting your pleasure. There are girls like that. They make marvellous secretaries! If you want one, you should advertise.'

'You know I don't.'

'I'm also doing my best not to put any pressure on you, although I think it's about time you made up your mind as to what you really want. You'd be much happier if you did, and we'd both be spared another of these discussions.'

'Yes. You're right – as usual! Listen, when we finish in Bern, let's go away for a few days. It's ages since we've had any real time together, away from work.'

Rachel laughed. 'Darling, we've never had any time together. It's always been while we were working.'

'Then let's do something about it. The concert's on Thursday. Why don't we stay on for the weekend? Switzerland's lovely at this time of the year, and the Bernese Oberland is glorious.'

'What will you tell you-know-who?' She never used Ann's name.

He shrugged. 'That I'll be working until Sunday evening. Will you stay?'

Rachel hesitated. A few stolen days, playing at being married, would only draw her closer to Simon. It resolved nothing, and made the situation more complicated than before. Betty would be furious with her for giving in! But then, without the pressures of time and work, perhaps they could recapture some of the excitement that had originally drawn them together. She doubted it.

'Well?'

'Why not? I've never seen Switzerland in the summer.'

'You'll love it. I promise.' For a moment, he held her in his arms. 'Don't worry. It will all work out.'

The telephone was ringing in her flat and Rachel hurried to un-lock the front door. It stopped before she entered the room, and she switched on the answering-machine to see if there was a message, but the caller had not bothered to leave one. She wondered whether it might have been John.

164

17

When Zoltán Teleki put his head round the door to inquire, for the third time in ten minutes, whether she had everything she needed, Francesca smiled with some effort.

'Everything's fine, thank you. The Haydn sounds great.' The concert was being relayed on a small monitor near her dressing-table, and the programme opened with an early symphony.

'Louis is an excellent young conductor.' Teleki paused for a moment to listen to the music. 'I have big plans for him next season.' He straightened his old-fashioned dinner jacket, shiny with age. 'Would you like a glass of water, perhaps?' She shook her head. 'Waiting to go on must be the worst part of the evening.' He looked solicitous. 'You're not nervous, are you? There's nothing to fear. If it goes as well as this morning's rehearsal, it will be a triumph! You mustn't worry.'

'I won't.' His presence was making her increasingly apprehensive.

He paced across the large ante-room that served as a dressing-room for visiting artists. It seemed odd to Francesca that the Casino did not offer properly designed accommodation. 'You'd be surprised how upset performers can be before they go on stage. I knew one young violinist who threw up every time he had to play, but when he walked out, he was as calm and collected as a seasoned veteran!'

'I'll certainly try not to do that.' She wished he would go away. 'Are you sure there isn't anything you would like?'

'Positive.' Her hands felt damp, and she dried them on a towel.

'Then I'll leave you alone. I promised Karl I would make sure you weren't disturbed. I want to talk to Ravenscroft. He's set up his camera in the corridor outside, to catch you as you leave the dressing-room. Did he warn you?'

'No, I don't think he did. I can't remember.'

Teleki clicked his tongue with disapproval. 'He should have told you! I'll tell him he's not to shine those lights on your face. You don't want to be blinded as you walk out.'

'Thank you.' When he had gone, Francesca closed her eyes and breathed deeply, trying to concentrate her thoughts. 'Ignore the audience. Just go out and play the way you did at the rehearsal. Remember to watch for Louis and, for Christ's sake, relax!' Looking down, she found she was still clasping the towel tightly, and threw it aside, angry with herself. She wished Karl were there. A nod of approval or a quick smile of encouragement would have dispelled any anxiety. After all, this was no different from any concert she had played in the past. Except that she was now Karl Vonheim's protégée, and the audience knew it. She had wished all day that he would telephone from New York.

There was a tentative knock on the door. 'Yes?' She hoped her voice sounded controlled.

Rachel entered, looking apologetic. 'It's only me. I'm sorry to barge in, but Zoltán's giving Simon a hard time about the lighting. They're trying to shout and whisper to one another at the same time! We wanted to get a quick shot of you coming out of the dressing-room on your way to the stage. Is that OK?'

'Sure.' She smiled nervously. 'I think he's afraid I'm going to stumble blindly into the double-basses!'

'Something like that.' She gave a quick intake of breath. 'You look gorgeous! Where did you find that dress?'

'It was chosen for me. Karl . . . maestro Vonheim . . . saw it in Milan and had it delivered. Do you like it?'

'It's fantastic!'

Francesca stood before the mirror. The dress was of pale ivory silk, cut simply so that it clung to her body, with slightly padded shoulders and a plunging neckline. 'I feel a little naked. She rummaged in her bag. 'Maybe I should wear some pearls. There's an awful lot of bare flesh showing.'

'No, leave it like that. It's sensational!' She giggled. 'Every woman out there is going to hate you!'

'You don't think it's too much?'

'I think it's beautiful. You look marvellous!'

'Thank you.' She looked again at the mirror. 'It doesn't feel like me.'

Rachel pretended to pout. 'It's really not fair: looking like that *and* playing like an angel. I'm developing a mega-inferiority complex. You're sure you don't mind about the cameras? If they put you off, we can shoot it later.'

'No. It's all right.' Rachel turned to leave. 'Don't go.'

'I thought you'd prefer to be alone and contemplate your navel, or whatever musicians do.'

'I tried that. My navel's tied in knots! I'd rather talk to someone.' She smiled. 'Have you been with Telmusik a long time?'

'About three years. I'd met Simon when I was working at the Beeb, and when he advertised for an assistant, I got the job.'

'It must be interesting.'

'It's fun, and it's much better than working! Simon's the best.'

'So I heard. He seems to know everybody. Weren't you with him in Vienna?'

'Yes, but I missed the press conference.'

'I thought I saw you the next day, but nobody introduced us.'

'My fault. I should have come over and said hello. If Simon's around, I'm usually hovering somewhere in the background.'

'I guess you two are pretty close.' It was pleasant to gossip with someone of her own generation. Besides, Rachel was a fellow professional, and was probably accustomed to musicians with pre-concert nerves.

Rachel seemed to hesitate. 'Does our association look that obvious?'

'Not really. I guess I noticed that you were close. He's a very attractive man.'

'Mrs Ravenscroft seems to think so.'

'Oh shit! I'm sorry. I think I said the wrong thing. I didn't mean to . . .'

'Don't apologise. I told you. Anyway, it's not exactly a state secret. I hoped it wasn't too obvious.'

'It isn't. I simply noticed that you seem to make a good team together.'

'We do. That's what makes it difficult, sometimes.'

Francesca nodded. 'I guess it must.'

'We manage.' Rachel listened to the music coming from the monitor. 'I'd better get out of your way. They're into the last movement

167

of the Haydn. Zoltán will come and fetch you. He's run through the order of service four times!' At the door, she smiled. 'Good luck, or am I supposed to say "Break a leg"? I'll see you later.'

'Yes, and thank you.'

'What for?'

'Being a friend in need at the right moment. I forgot to get nervous.'

Within moments, Zoltán appeared. 'Everything's under control outside. I have Ravencroft's personal assurance that they won't disturb you. Are you ready?'

'Yes.'

'In that case, we have just enough time for me to give you this.' From behind his back, he produced a small package.

'What is it?'

'A present from Karl. He gave me strict instructions to hand it to you five minutes before you begin. You'd better open it quickly.'

It was a small velvet-covered box. The diamonds in the necklace it contained glittered like shooting-stars. A card in the maestro's handwriting bore a short message:

'I think this should complete your ensemble. Tonight, I hope you will play Jeunehomme just for me. Love, K.'

'Oh my God!' She stared at it. 'It's beautiful!'

Teleki peered at the stones. 'Magnificent!' For a moment, he looked as though he might produce a jeweller's loupe and value them. 'May I put it on for you?' He stood behind her, fastened the clip at the back of her neck, then looked over her shoulder at her reflection in the mirror. 'You look like a princess!'

Francesca gazed at herself, feeling almost detached from the elegant young woman in the looking-glass. In the distance she could hear the audience applauding the end of the symphony. She felt unexpectedly relaxed. It was as though Karl Vonheim's presence surrounded her with a protective shell.

'Are you ready?'

She nodded, and followed Teleki into the brightly-lit corridor where the conductor and the film crew awaited her.

For the first few moments she was totally absorbed in the technical demands of the concerto. There were two phrases to be played after which she could settle back and let the orchestra take over. If

168

the musicians had seemed slightly lacklustre at the rehearsal, they now played with an extra edge of concentration, and she listened with growing pleasure as the young conductor led them through the opening themes. It was a brisk, muscular performance, still retaining a lyrical quality that inspired new ideas, and the trills which heralded her return matched their mood perfectly. She felt totally in command, letting the music breathe and, to her delight, discovered that she was enjoying herself. Adrenalin flowed, and her pre-concert nerves were replaced by an exhilarating sense of new-found strength. Everything seemed to fall into place. Karl had lent her a book by Alfred Einstein, in which the musicologist had written about the intimate relationship between the soloist and the orchestra, and she was caught up in the interplay between piano and players: a duet with the oboe; another with the horn. At one moment the piano was alone, singing to them. Then the orchestra replied and the music surged onward. It was almost with surprise that she found herself embarking on Mozart's virtuoso cadenza, and her fingers flew through the brilliant runs and displays. The orchestra returned, there were trills and some delicately moulded arpeggios to manipulate, and the movement came to an end.

She was aware of a slight shuffling in the auditorium, but did not turn towards the audience. She looked up to see the conductor, his face shiny with sweat, nodding encouragement, and there were smiles on the faces of the violinists beyond him. It was going well! Then she closed her eyes, awaiting the introduction of the slow movement in which the piano, like the heroine of a tragic opera, carries a serenely extended aria with dark undertones. The melody flowed at an unhurried, measured pace and she resisted the temptation to move it forward too quickly, letting the full dramatic weight of the music make itself felt. When she was a student, Mozart's piano concertos had seemed to her to be delightful, airy concoctions, designed to charm the listener, but she was now conscious of the deeply-felt emotions that lay beneath the surface. The movement ended with two solemn chords and, after only the briefest of pauses, she swept into the Rondo.

Suddenly, it all seemed easily simple and she felt herself smiling. Her fingers sped over the keyboard and she looked up to see the conductor grinning broadly. It was no longer a matter of notes and pauses, and worrying and counting measures. It was uninhibited joy. The slow interlude became a gracefully balanced Minuet requiring only the most delicate emphasis. There was no need to underline the humour, and pizzicato strings added a delightful accompaniment. Karl had been right: it was a matter of understatement, and she had found the answer. She felt a surge of excitement as she led the orchestra back into the Presto finale and, almost before she knew it, the concerto was over.

For a moment, the hall was silent. She heard the final chords die away and stared at the keyboard, the sound still ringing in her ears. Then a great roar of approval engulfed her. The conductor stepped from his podium to take both her hands and bowed low over them. She could not hear what he said. Then he straightened and turned with her to face the audience. The sound was thunderous. Cheers mingled with applause as people rose to their feet. Behind her, the orchestra had set aside their instruments to clap their hands and, feeling slightly dazed, she remembered to thank the leader. The conductor took her hand again and, gesturing broadly, pointed her in the direction of the exit. She walked offstage as though carried by the wave of sound.

The conductor escorted her to the door of her dressing-room. They had returned to the stage for four or five calls, each time to be greeted with renewed vigour. When, at last, she had laughed and said, 'No more!', he had shrugged good-naturedly.

'I was afraid you were going to do a Vonheim and disappear immediately. Would you like to play an encore? They adore you.'

'No. Right now, all I want to do is collapse.' She was breathless with elation.

'You were wonderful.'

'So were you. Thank you for everything.' She kissed him on the cheek, hugging him.

'We inspired each other. My God, when you attacked that Rondo, I thought I was never going to catch you!'

'Was it too much?'

'No, it was perfect! You took such incredible risks.'

'I guess I thought it was now or never. I just forgot everything and let go. Jesus, it was exciting!'

'Unbelievable!' He paused. 'Will you be speaking to maestro Vonheim?'

'I hope so. I want to tell him about it: every detail.'

'Will you be sure to send him my best wishes?'

'Of course.'

'And tell him how well we collaborated? I would like him to know what a fine partnership it was.'

'I'll tell him you were great!'

'Thank you.' For a moment, his expression was earnest. 'It is very important to me that he should know.' Teleki was approaching, his face wreathed in smiles and his arms outstretched like a revivalist minister. The young Frenchman stepped back. 'I'd better go and change. I still have the second half to conduct!'

'I'll try to sneak in at the back of the hall and listen.'

'I doubt whether you'll have the opportunity. I have the feeling that half the audience will be coming to see you. In fact, I may find myself conducting to an empty house!' He took off his jacket, and she saw that his sodden shirt clung to his body. 'We'd better go and dry ourselves.'

'Yes.' Her neck and shoulders were wet with perspiration. She hadn't noticed until that moment. What was it Dorothea had said? As though she had been making love. It was almost the same sensation! Almost.

Teleki stood between them, taking each of them by the hand. 'Bravissimi! I've never heard such playing! Karl will be proud of both of you.'

'Will you speak to him?'

'I'll be calling him shortly. He's waiting to hear from me. What a performance!' He turned to the conductor. 'Louis, you should go and change. The interval's half over.' Then he led Francesca to her room. 'Let me know when the first guests may come in. I'll stand guard until you're ready.'

'What will you say to Karl?'

'That you were extraordinary – far better than any of us imagined. I should have believed him when he said you were special!'

'Will you send him my love?'

'Of course. I expect he'll call you later.' He glanced down the corridor. 'Now hurry! You shouldn't keep your public waiting.'

171

The conductor's prediction had been correct. When Teleki opened the door, a flood of visitors filled the room. They surrounded Francesca. Members of the orchestra looked in to congratulate her; total strangers embraced her, greeting her in a variety of languages; programmes were thrust in her hands with requests for her autograph, and she found herself drawn from one enthusiastic visitor to the next with disconcerting haste.

Rachel embraced her. 'God, you were incredible! I never realised Mozart could sound like that!' She looked at the necklace. 'Where did that come from?'

'It was a last-minute surprise from Karl. Zoltán gave it to me as were leaving.'

She looked closer at the diamonds. 'They're real! I noticed you'd put something on, but I thought it was just costume stuff. They must be worth a fortune.'

'I guess so. Aren't they beautiful?'

She laughed. 'To die for! When I get home, I'm going to take piano lessons!'

The room slowly emptied, and she sank into a chair. Teleki hovered nearby.

'Are you tired?'

'Not really. Part of me is physically exhausted, but I'm on such a high that I won't sleep for a week!'

'Erich is waiting to take you home, when you're ready.'

'So soon?' She was not prepared to return to the austerity of Chateau Beethoven.

'Karl's instructions. He thought it would be better for you to unwind back at the house. Otherwise, I would have suggested that you join us for dinner. I've booked a table here at the Casino for Louis and his ... colleague. The food's very good.' He looked slightly embarrassed. The only thing is that they've asked a couple of their friends to join us. You might feel a little uncomfortable . . .'

'Because they're gay? It doesn't bother me.'

'Well, in that case . . .' He hesitated.

At that moment, Simon entered, accompanied by Peter Meredith. The director beamed. 'That was tremendous, Francesca. You brought the house down! Now I'm sorry we filmed the rehearsal,

172

but I wanted the backstage sequence in costume. You should have warned me you were going to take off like that!'

'I didn't know I would until it happened.'

He saw the direction of her gaze. 'This character claims he's an old friend of yours but I never believe a word he says. He's a journalist.'

'Yes, I know.' Francesca stood to meet Peter. 'Hi!' She wondered why she felt slightly self-conscious.

He held her outstretched hand, then drew her close and kissed her cheek. 'That was a marvellous performance. I've been trying to think of something original to say about it but I can't.' His face was still pressed against hers. 'It was magical, from beginning to end.'

'Thank you.' She hugged him briefly. 'It's good to see you again! I'm glad you came.'

'Wild horses wouldn't have stopped me!' As she stepped back, he turned to Ravenscroft. 'What was that crap of yours about the public being suspicious of beautiful musicians? I think it just went down the drain.'

Francesca laughed. 'He told me. Sexist!' She crossed her arms so that they covered her exposed flesh. 'I must admit I felt naked enough when I walked out there tonight. From now on, I'm going to wear a sack.'

'Please don't.' When Peter looked at her again, she noticed that his eyes were hazel-coloured.

'Now you're embarrassing me.'

Simon shrugged. 'If you insist on parading round like a fashion-model, what do you expect?'

'I'll have you know that the rest of my wardrobe consists of T-shirts and jeans.'

Peter smiled. 'And a Pucci dress.'

'Yes. I forgot that.'

Simon asked, 'Have you seen Rachel anywhere?'

'She was with the camera crew, outside in the corridor, a few minutes ago.'

'Good. I need her.' He went in search of her.

Peter's voice was intimate. 'Lucky girl!'

'We're not supposed to notice. I said the wrong thing earlier.'

'Never mind. It's a little hard to miss!'

173

'I guess so.' She was surprised how easy it was to talk to him. It was as though they were old friends. Her hand rested on his arm. 'I didn't thank you for your cards.'

'I hope they amused you.'

'They were great, and very welcome. They kept me in touch with the outside world.'

He seemed puzzled. 'Outside world? Doesn't maestro Vonheim let you out from time to time?'

'Yes, but Lausanne's pretty quiet. Nothing much happens there.' His comment had touched a nerve. 'We did go to Monaco for the day.'

'Was it fun?'

'Not bad. It was just a flying visit. If you'd given me your address, I would have written you.' She smiled. 'I could have sent you a card.'

'I'll make sure you have it from now on. As a matter of fact, I tried to call you a couple of times. I had a hell of a job getting hold of your number. It's very definitely unlisted!'

'How did you find it?'

'A friend of mine manages the British Symphony Orchestra. He owed me a favour!'

She was pensive. 'I didn't know you'd called.'

'A couple of times. I think I got that sour-faced chauffeur.'

'Erich?'

He nodded. 'He said you were out – both times.'

'He didn't tell me.'

'Well, I said not to worry and that I'd call back.'

'But he should have told me, just the same.'

'It doesn't matter. I'm here now, so there's no problem. I wouldn't have missed that performance for anything. I'm surprised the maestro didn't come.'

'He's in New York at the moment.'

'What's he doing there?'

'Concerts with the Philharmonic.'

'Oh. When does he get back?'

'I'm not sure; sometime next week. Why?'

'I was just interested.' He grinned. 'I'm a fan, if you remember.'

'And a journalist?'

174

He shrugged. 'I have to earn a living. Anyway, tonight I'm just here as a fan.'

'And I thought you were going to give me a rave review!'

He leaned towards her. 'I'll do that, too.'

Teleki approached. 'Erich is waiting for you, Francesca.'

Peter groaned. 'Not again!'

'I'm sorry. Karl thought it would be better for me to go straight back to the house.'

'Won't he allow you to take a couple of hours to celebrate? What does he expect you to do: go home and practise?' She was silent. 'I came all the way from London to hear you. The least you can do is let me take you to dinner.'

'Well . . .'

'I've hired a car. I'm going to be here for a couple of days.' He smiled encouragingly. 'Listen, Miss Cinderella, if I promise to deliver you home by midnight, will you have dinner with me?'

Simon had reappeared, accompanied by Rachel. 'Did someone mention food?'

'Yes. Why don't you and Rachel join us?' He turned to Francesca. 'Don't say no. This is your big evening, and you have to acknowledge it in some way. I'll see you home, I promise. Do you know somewhere good, Simon?'

'Lots of places.' He eyed Francesca critically. 'You're a bit overdressed for the one I have in mind, but it doesn't matter. The natives will enjoy watching you spill *Fondue Bourgignonne* down your cleavage.'

She laughed. 'I can always change.'

Teleki looked uneasy. 'What about Erich?'

Peter guided him to the door. 'Tell him to go away. I'll bring Miss Noble back, safe and sound, after she's eaten.'

The Hungarian shot a nervous glance in Francesca's direction, and departed. Peter smiled. 'That wasn't so difficult, was it? I hope your place is good, Simon. I'm starving. Do you want to change, Francesca?'

She nodded. 'I'll be more comfortable in jeans.'

'OK, but don't take too long.' He paused. 'You can leave that necklace on, if you like. It'll add a bit of class to the present company.'

Rachel bridled. 'Speak for yourself!'

Simon selected a traditional Swiss tavern with chequered red tablecloths and large antique cow-bells decorating the panelled walls. 'I thought you'd enjoy a touch of local colour.' He indicated the bells. 'They'll come in handy if you feel like a quick run-through of the Mahler Seventh. Anyone for fondue? It's the best way to get to know your neighbours.'

'Why.'

'Their skewer technique. It reveals their character. I have a theory that you can tell where a person comes from by the way he wields a fondue stick. The British are inclined to be terribly polite about it, putting themselves carefully into a vacant space without touching anyone else. The Germans bash their way in like conquerors, and the Italians are all over the place!'

Francesca asked, 'How about Americans?'

'Oh, they're just plain folksy and snuggle up close!'

'Gee, I never realised Swiss food was so sexy!'

'That's because you live in never-never land. I bet Uncle Karl insists on separate pots.'

She laughed, feeling slightly disloyal.

The evening passed quickly. The food and wine were excellent and, as Simon had promised, sharing fondue was both intimate and amusing. He and Peter entertained them with endless anecdotes from the music world. It was a popular pastime among musicians. They led nomadic lives and their paths seldom crossed, so they made up for close relationships by exchanging jokes. The director had a vast fund of stories, which he told extravagantly. It appeared that every well-known artist was a personal friend, and his impersonations were sometimes cruelly accurate, but they made Francesca smile. She felt suddenly liberated from the responsibilities that had weighed upon her for the past few months. It was like being a student again. The evening's concert seemed far removed. Peter's humour was kinder and more reserved. He did not compete with Simon, who dominated the conversation, but she was acutely aware of his presence at her side.

During a pause in the stories, he asked, 'How did you actually meet Karl Vonheim?'

'You asked me about that in Vienna. I was fooling around on the piano in Victoria Hall. I didn't know he was listening to me.'

'But what were you playing?'

176

'The Schumann concerto. He started asking me questions about it and, before I knew what I was doing, I was auditioning for him. I was terrified!'

Simon interrupted. 'I suppose you know the story about Zubin Mehta and Daniel Barenboim playing that concerto?'

Rachel raised her eyes to the ceiling. 'Not again!' She had been subdued throughout the meal.

'I don't think I do.' Francesca noticed his irritation.

'It happened at a concert in Israel. Daniel was still adjusting his stool, and Zubin forgot to look at him, to see whether he was ready. He brought his hands down for the opening of the Schumann, and poor Daniel had to move like greased lightning to reach the key-board for his opening chords!'

'Jesus!'

'That's not the end of it. When the movement finished, Zubin looked round. Daniel, with his hand that wasn't visible to the audi-ence, beckoned to him. So Zubin leaned over to ask what he wanted and, as he did, Daniel looked up at him very innocently and played the opening solo of the second movement!' He mimed the four-note phrase. 'Caught totally off-guard, Zubin had to jack-knife round to bring the orchestra in!'

They laughed. Rachel said, 'I don't believe that really happened.'

'Daniel swore it did. He told me so himself.'

'It makes a good story anyway.' Peter looked at his watch. 'If I'm going to deliver you home as promised, we ought to leave soon.'

'I guess so.' The prospect of returning to the isolation of Chateau Beethoven was depressing.

Rachel was watching her. 'It's not very late. Be a devil and stay!'

'No. I think I'd better go.'

'Why?'

She was embarrassed. 'Well, for starters, I know it sounds silly, but I don't have a key. I forgot to bring one with me. They'll be waiting up for me.'

Simon signalled a waiter. 'In that case, we'd better leave. Other-wise, that zombie Erich will put you on bread and water for three days.'

'It's not like that.'

'I know, but I think it would do you good to spend time with your friends. I hadn't seen you laugh before. It suits you.' He brushed aside

Peter's offer to share the cost of the meal. 'This one's on Telmusik. Next time, you can take us to Fredy Girardet's in Lausanne.'

'Thanks a lot! Anyway, you have to book three months ahead.'

'If tonight's concert is anything to go by, we'll be back.'

The two women waited by the door of the restaurant while the men fetched their cars.

'Will you go back to London tomorrow?'

'No. Simon and I are staying on for a few days. Why don't we meet again? You'd be doing me a favour.'

'How?'

'Simon's in one of his heavy moods. If you were there, he'd be easier to handle.'

'Are things not going so well? You seem a little down.'

She shrugged. 'Occupational hazard. I don't feel like playing Juliet at the moment, but he's determined to be Romeo if it kills him. It can get to be a strain.'

'I'm sorry.'

Rachel smiled. 'It's not the end of the world, and we should have sorted ourselves out a long time ago. It may pass. If it doesn't . . .' She left the sentence unfinished. 'I like Peter. He's just about the only straight music critic in London. It's a gay old world! Have you known him long?'

'No. We met in Vienna and sort of stayed in touch. He's nice.'

'And single. Give thanks for small mercies.'

'How come?'

'He had a live-in for a long time. I heard that she died.'

'Oh.'

'Look, I'd be grateful if you wouldn't say anything about me and Simon. We'll work it out, one way or another.'

'Of course.'

She smiled. 'It's just that he's so pitifully eager to prove his love, and I'd rather have a good night's sleep!'

They talked quietly during the drive between Bern and Lausanne, and Francesca found herself falling asleep. In the warm intimacy of the car, she fought to remain awake, but her eyes kept closing.

'I'm sorry. It all seems to be catching up on me.'

'You don't have to apologise. One way and another, it must have been a hell of a day.'

'It's been wonderful. I can't believe it's all happened.'

'I was about to say the same thing! Will you call Vonheim?'

'Yes. Tomorrow. Some time.' She yawned and stretched luxuriantly. 'I'm too tired to think about it. I have to sleep.'

'Go ahead. I'll wake you before we reach Lausanne and you can give me directions.'

'That's not fair.'

He smiled and reached for her hand. 'I'm happy.'

'Me too.'

Peter parked the car by the entrance gate at the end of the drive. Lights were still burning in the ground-floor windows of the mansion. 'It's not quite midnight, as promised. Is this where you turn back into a princess?'

'I hope not.'

'Will I see you tomorrow?'

'If you would like to.'

'I'd like to.'

'I'm glad. I should really practise for a while, but I guess I can play hookey for one day. Maybe I'll get up early.'

'No. Indulge yourself for twenty-four hours. You earned it.'

Her hand rested on his. 'Don't go yet. I don't want today to finish.'

'I'll be back before you know it. What would you like to do? Have you seen anything of Switzerland?'

'Not much. I stayed in Geneva for a while, but I never went anywhere else.'

'In that case, we can explore it together: just point the car down the road and see what happens.'

'I'd like that.'

He kissed her and, for a moment, she held him. 'Maybe I should go after all.'

His smile was illuminated by the lights from the dashboard. 'I'm in no hurry.'

'It's a long drive back.' She was slightly breathless. 'Thank you, Peter. I'm glad you're here.'

'So am I.' He kissed her again. Then she gently released herself. 'Don't forget your fancy dress. The maestro would never forgive you if I drove off into the sunset with it!'

As Francesca approached the front door it opened. A shadowy figure was silhouetted against the light.

179

'Hi, Erich. I'm sorry if I kept you up.' He did not reply. 'Have there been any calls?'

'Maestro Vonheim – twice. He expected you back much earlier.'

'Oh. I decided to stay in town and have dinner with some friends.'

Erich ignored her explanation. 'He asked you to call him as soon as you returned.'

'Right now?'

'New York is six hours behind us. He's waiting in his hotel room to hear from you. The number's written down next to the telephone.' He eyed her coldly. 'Do you want me to get him for you?'

'No, thank you. I can do that for myself.'

'Very well.' After a pause, he said, 'The maestro's waiting.'

She dialled the hotel and asked for him. After a moment, she was connected to his suite. 'Karl? It's Francesca.'

'You're finally home.' His voice sounded remote.

'Yes. I decided to stay in Bern for dinner. Zoltán had booked a table at the Casino.' She bit her lip. It was only a small white lie.

'Erich explained.'

There was a long silence. 'Hello? Are you still there?'

'Yes.'

'I hope I haven't kept you waiting at the hotel. They asked me to stay in town – sort of a celebration.'

'You should have told Erich to wait. He's there for you.'

'I didn't know how long I'd be. Some friends who were coming this way dropped me off. Did you speak to Zoltán?'

'Yes.' His voice lightened. 'He said it was a triumph. What did you think?'

'Oh, Karl, it was wonderful! Everything went the way it should have – even the Minuet in the last movement. It was so exciting!'

'I'm looking forward to hearing it tomorrow.'

'Tomorrow?'

'Yes. The performance was taped. I have arranged for it to be sent to me by courier. Didn't Zoltán tell you?'

'No.'

'When I have had a chance to hear it, I'll call you, and we can talk about it more coherently.'

'Yes. Of course.' She suddenly felt that all the emotion and excitement of the performance was about to be dissected and exam-

180

ined in a cold-blooded post-mortem. 'You'll find I took the last movement a little faster than before. It seemed . . . right.'

'Why not? That's what a try-out is for. How was the conductor?'

'Fine. Great. Terrific. I really enjoyed working with him. He asked to be remembered to you.'

'Tell him not to worry. I'll remember him.'

She sought to recapture some of the evening. 'I had a wonderful time, Karl. I hope you're pleased.'

'I'm sure I will be, Francesca, but try to remember that this is just the beginning. The hard work starts now.'

'Yes.' She could not escape the feeling that she was being gently chastised.

'I'm glad you enjoyed your celebratory dinner, too. When you become more accustomed to the life, I think you'll find that it's better to leave quickly and return to the peace and quiet of your own surroundings.'

'I guess so. I just wanted to unwind a little.'

'I understand.' His voice grew softer. 'I know how hard you've worked towards this moment and I'm very happy that it was such a success. I'm sorry I wasn't there.'

'So am I. I think you would have been pleased. Oh! In my excitement, I almost forgot! Thank you for your present. It's beautiful! I don't know what to say.'

'I hope it went well with the dress.'

'It was perfect.' She smiled. 'Zoltán thought I looked like a princess. I certainly felt like one.'

'Then I'm pleased. Forgive me, but I must go. Rest well, Francesca. Tomorrow marks a new phase of your life. I want you to be prepared for it. There's so much to be done.'

'I know. It's been an unbelievable day, Karl.'

'There are many more to come.' He chuckled. 'Are you tired?'

'Exhausted!'

'Then go to bed. I'm looking forward to that tape. You sound very happy.'

'I am.'

'Then so am I. Goodnight, Francesca.'

'Goodnight, Karl, and thank you. Thank you for everything.'

When she replaced the receiver, she looked up to find Erich still standing in the room. He was watching her with a contemptuous expression.

'What are you doing? Why are you still here?'

'I didn't know whether you needed anything else before retiring.' He spoke politely but the contempt remained in his eyes.

'No, I don't need anything. I'd also prefer that you didn't eavesdrop on my private conversations.'

'I'm very sorry. If you had asked me, I would have left the room.' She faltered. 'Well, next time, please don't listen in.' He inclined his head without speaking. 'Incidentally, I understand a friend of mine called from London a couple of times. Mr Meredith; Peter Meredith.' Erich nodded. 'Why didn't you tell me he rang?'

'He told me not to bother you and that he'd call back at another time.'

'You could have told me.'

His servility was openly insolent. 'I was following his instructions.'

'Well, if he calls again, I want to know, whatever he says. OK?'

'As you wish.' At the door, he paused. 'Madame Vonheim will be away for a few days. She's having a short . . . holiday. If you will let Madame Chauvet know what you would like to eat . . .'

'I'll be out tomorrow.'

'Oh?'

'I'm spending the day with a friend. I'll eat out.'

'The maestro said you were not to be disturbed. He . . .'

'I said I would be going out. When Mr Meredith calls for me, please let me know.'

'Yes.' A supercilious smile spread on his face. 'I'm glad the concert was a success tonight, Miss Noble. I managed to hear your performance. May I add my congratulations?'

'Oh. Thank you. I didn't know you were there.'

'I usually try to attend when the maestro plays, too. I'm sure he'll be very impressed with your reading.'

'Thank you.'

His voice softened. 'I hope you enjoyed your dinner with . . . Mr Teleki. Maestro Vonheim thought you would want to rest tomorrow. I was only trying to pass on his message. He thought you would be tired.'

'I'll be fine in the morning. Please let me know when Mr Meredith gets here.'

'Very well.' Erich left the room, closing the door very quietly behind him.

18

The maestro greeted Richmond at the door of his suite. He was in high spirits.

'Come in, Gregory, come in.' He looked at his watch. 'When it comes to punctuality, I can rely on two things: Swiss trains and the President of U.S. Artists! I've ordered coffee for you.'

'Thank you, Karl. You're very chipper this morning.'

'Why not? It's a beautiful day.'

'Don't let the view from the Carlyle Hotel fool you. It's like a steam-bath out there. New York in July is not a happy place! You should be grateful for Salzburg in a couple of weeks.' He placed an elegant briefcase next to his armchair. 'That was a superb concert last night. I haven't heard the Philharmonic play like that for years.'

'Thank you. It's a good orchestra.'

'Sometimes. The players can also be the most independent in the world. I've seen strong men rehearse them with tears in their eyes. They can be hell! Do you remember that ringleader in the horn section who used to strike terror in the heart of any unfortunate guest who earned his disapproval?'

'No, I don't think so.'

'He was murder! Years ago, there was an idiot who had the audacity to rehearse them without a score. He thought he'd impress them with his knowledge, and prided himself on a photographic memory. Anyway, halfway through the first session, this horn player – what was his name? – put up his hand and said, "Excuse me, Sir. The third bar of letter K, fourth note; what do I play?", and the conductor made a great show of closing his eyes to picture the measure in question. Eventually, he called back, "F-Sharp," and the horn player looked triumphantly at his colleagues and said, "Wrong!". He never took a rehearsal without a score again!'

Vonheim smiled. 'My sympathies are with the horn section. Professionals hate to work with amateurs.'

'They sure as hell knew who was in charge last night!'

'I hope so. However, Avery Fisher Hall's acoustical problems remain. It sounds a little better but there is a hard edge to it that worries me. I still prefer Carnegie Hall.'

Richmond nodded. 'Some wag's been suggesting that Isaac Stern should play a series of concerts to save Lincoln Center, but I doubt whether even he can do that!' He sipped some coffee and smiled approvingly. 'Maybe I should quickly brief you on what I propose for Magnum Records before their people get here.'

'Magnum?' The maestro looked pained. 'Not that awful little man with the artificial smile and the loud shirts? He doesn't know anything about music.'

'Perhaps, but he'll be willing to meet our terms and his corporation's got the best distribution. As far as repertoire is concerned, you simply tell him what you're going to do.'

'It's easier to deal with a European company. Their engineers are more sympathetic, and I can talk to the producers. The last young man from Magnum spoke nothing but English, and that not very fluently! We did *Gioconda*, and he couldn't even pronounce the names of all the characters!'

'I think I have the solution to problems like that.' He paused momentarily. 'It may also have certain tax advantages. I'm having one of my colleagues look into certain aspects of it. From now on, I'm proposing that we produce the records ourselves and lease the material to Magnum. This means that you can select whichever producer and engineers you prefer.'

'Doesn't that mean a financial risk for us?'

Richmond grinned. 'Not if they pay the kind of advance against royalties that I'm going to ask for. Furthermore, as owner of the master-tapes, our royalty will be higher than before, *and* the tapes will revert to us at the end of a specified period.'

'You think they'll agree?'

The American shrugged. 'If they don't, we'll consider the other offers I've had. Three companies have written in the past month. Magnum begged me for a first refusal, which is why I said you would see them. You shouldn't overlook their sales force.'

185

'Very well. I'll leave it in your hands. As a matter of fact, it is their sales and promotion which interest me most.'

'They're more than eager to please. I've already had five calls from the Art Director, begging for photographic sessions. I said I'd let him know.'

Vonheim shook his head. 'You don't understand, Gregory. I'm not thinking about myself. My concern is for Francesca. If we're going to launch her career, we must have the best possible compaign on her behalf.'

'Ah.' Richmond paused. 'We haven't talked about a contract for her thus far. I thought it would be wiser to have your own deal signed and sealed before we do that.'

The maestro frowned. 'I made it clear that she must be included in any contract involving me. Haven't you explained this to them? They have to offer Francesca a contract; otherwise, I'm not interested.'

'That may be a little difficult to arrange. I'm already demanding a lot for you.' He saw the maestro's expression and continued smoothly, 'I can't help feeling that we're being a little premature in her case, Karl. In all fairness, nobody's heard her yet.'

'I have. I would have thought that was enough.'

'Well, your opinion is very important and will weigh strongly in her favour, but I can't offer a guarantee.'

'I can. Are you questioning my judgement?'

'Of course not, but I am trying to be realistic. Francesca's unknown. At this moment, nobody in Magnum's heard of her.'

Vonheim grunted. 'Nobody in Magnum's heard of Palestrina or . . . or Bellini, from the way they talk! It was your job to tell them.' His voice hardened. 'Why haven't you done so?'

'First, because I've had nothing to work with; and secondly, because I didn't consider it opportune. We're in the process of a delicate negotiation, Karl.'

'If Francesca's not included, the contract's worthless, as far as I'm concerned.' He stared at the American. 'You'll have to do better than that.'

Richmond's suntan appeared to darken. 'For heaven's sake, you're not on the podium, Karl, and I'm not one of your players!' With an effort, he checked himself. 'How did Bern go last night? Have you heard from anyone?'

186

'It was an unqualified success. I spoke to Zoltán. I've arranged for a tape of it to be flown over by courier. As soon as I've heard it, I'll pass it to you. Have copies made, and send them to every major orchestra, with a request for an early engagement.' He walked to the window and stared down at the street. 'My next concert here will be in February, and Francesca will make her official debut as my soloist, after which I expect her to play at least thirty or forty American concerts in the 1990–1991 season. Don't worry about the repertoire. I'll give you a list of the concertos she'll have ready by then.'

Richmond laughed uneasily. 'You're joking!'

'What makes you say that?'

'I can't set up a deal like that with some total unknown! It's hard enough to arrange tours for some of our top names.'

'But you supposedly have the most powerful management in the world?'

'Be reasonable! U.S. Artists carries a lot of clout, but we're not omnipotent. We don't run America! You can't expect me to call people like Henry Fogel in Chicago or Tom Morris in Cleveland, and tell them they've got to take Francesca Noble.'

'Why not?'

'Because!' He smiled thinly to cover his irritation. 'These guys have their own plans and commitments. Many of them are already made for '91–'92, and they have their own music directors to accommodate. I don't control them, and I sure as hell can't order them to take a young, untried girl simply because you want it.'

'I would have hoped my endorsement stood for something. If it will help, I'll dictate a personal letter. You have a machine in your office which reproduces my signature. A copy of the letter can be included with each cassette.' He paused. 'Tell them that if they want me to appear with their orchestras again, they must find a space for Francesca.'

'It wouldn't help, Karl. We have to build her up first.'

'I was coming to that. I made it very clear to you that no press statements about Francesca were to be issued without my prior approval, but nobody has sent me anything. Does this mean that nothing has been done?'

'We haven't released anything yet. There's nothing to say.'

'On the contrary, there's a great deal, unless you feel my name no longer stands for anything in your organisation.'

Richmond showed exaggerated patience. 'We have enormous respect for you and your name, Karl, but you can't expect me to put the entire resources of U.S. Artists behind one very beautiful and, no doubt, talented female on the strength of your say-so!' He stood. 'I have a multi-million-dollar corporation to run, with half a dozen divisions and hundreds of artists to look after. I can't neglect their careers to satisfy some personal whim of yours.'

'Personal whim?' The maestro stared at him. 'Is that what you think this is about?'

The manager shrugged. 'What else can I think? You've kept her under wraps until now. Nobody's been allowed near her and, after one obscure concert in Switzerland, you expect me to launch her on the American music scene with a coast-to-coast tour! It won't work, Karl. I'll look after Francesca and see that she gets a proper hearing, but in matters like this, you should rely on my professional judgement. I know what works.'

'Like that vulgar merchandising scheme you proposed in Monaco?'

Richmond paled. 'There was nothing wrong with that idea. You rejected it out of hand because of some sort of misplaced European snobbery . . . '

'It was appalling! Neither Francesca nor I will be sold like bargain basement items at Macy's!'

'Nobody suggested any bargains. A great deal of time, money and effort were wasted on that project, Karl, and I didn't expect to see them dismissed in such a perfunctory manner.'

'I'm not prepared to see my name used for some cheap sales campaign!'

'There was nothing cheap about it, and while we're on the subject of selling, I haven't heard any complaints about the income you enjoy. It's easy to sneer at your management because it has to dirty its hands with the commercial side of the music world while you live in splendid isolation in Switzerland. You enjoy the benefits!'

Vonheim spoke coldly. 'I enjoy those benefits because of my

talent: my name, my reputation, my interpretations. The public comes to hear me because of who I am and what I do. Do I make myself clear? It has little to do with U.S. Artists, its divisions, its mainly incompetent staff, or its President! I don't need any of you and, judging by the offhand treatment my requests have received, neither does Francesca Noble.' He paused, as though making a decision. 'Very well. From now on her management and my own will be administered by my secretariat in Hamburg, until alternative arrangements have been made. You can communicate with me through Hans Wolpert or Zoltán Teleki.'

There was a long silence. At length, Richmond spoke. 'You're not seriously proposing to sever connections with my organisation, are you, Karl?'

'I should have thought that was patently obvious.'

'I think you'll find there are a number of obstacles.'

'Such as?'

'For a start, you have a contract.' He smiled crookedly. 'If you'd care to read it, you'll find that the clauses covering your services are specifically binding. I employ a very expensive team of lawyers to prepare those documents.'

'Contracts can be contested.'

'There are other factors.' He spoke softly. 'We go back a long way together, Karl. It would be foolish to let a minor disagreement destroy a mutually profitable collaboration. I've fulfilled every commercial obligation and my corporation has supported your career at every level.' Vonheim was silent. 'Apart from looking after your professional needs, I've gone to enormous lengths to protect your personal privacy. You seem to have forgotten that I bought off that writer who prepared an unauthorised biography a few years back. It was an expensive item.'

The conductor looked up sharply. 'What do you mean?'

'Don't concern yourself. The material was destroyed, and he was well paid for his trouble.' His smile was forced. 'Some of it made interesting reading. I guess we all have a few skeletons in the closet.'

'Are you trying to suggest . . .?'

The manager raised his hand. 'I'm not suggesting anything except that we both calm down, take a deep breath, and start again. Every-

189

thing's under control.' He seated himself, adjusting the razor-edge crease of his trousers. 'I'm sorry about Francesca. I guess I didn't fully appreciate her importance to you, but we can make up for any lost time. It's only a couple of months since the Vienna conference. So, I'll get my people on it right away. They'll fax material to you in the next few days, and if you don't like their press releases, I'll bring in a specialist.'

The maestro was considerably subdued. 'And her recording contract?'

'It shouldn't be a problem. I've left space for a few concessions on your part. If necessary, we'll make them, provided she becomes part of the overall package. Magnum's not going to give me a hard time if they think they've signed you.'

Vonheim was thoughtful. 'Possibly. I think you should insist.'

'I will, once they've signed you.'

'What about her public appearances?'

'I'll see what I can do, but I'm not offering iron-clad guarantees I can't fulfill. As far as concert dates are concerned, I think we should move carefully. The press and public are suspicious of overnight wonders. The fact that you're sponsoring her is enough to establish her presence. The rest will be up to her.'

'You still have to provide the opportunities.'

'We will. Zoltán's doing the groundwork in Europe. You know about the Paris recital?' The maestro nodded. It's the next step in the progression. I've been in touch with a couple of Scandinavian orchestras and I'll make sure that any concerts are covered by reputable critics. If necessary, I'll fly them in. Once the word spreads, she'll get all the offers she can handle. Let me do it my way.'

'Very well.' He stared at the American. 'Just make sure you do.'

The telephone rang and Richmond, his composure restored, asked, 'Shall I take it?' The maestro was lost in thought. He was about to repeat the question but Vonheim indicated with a wave that he should. He cupped his hand over the mouthpiece. 'It's the delegation from Magnum Records. Can they come up?'

'Yes. Do I have to stay?'

'Just to shake their hands. It makes them feel important!' He spoke briefly into the phone before hanging up. 'Once you've said hello, you don't need to be present. However, in view of Francesca's contract, it might be a good idea.'

Mel Strich, Vice-President of Artists and Repertoire, was a small, compact man in his forties. Almost entirely bald, and with deeply set eyes, his teeth were unusually large, giving his face a skeletal character when he smiled. He was wearing a beige tropical suit, and the stripes on his custom-made shirt clashed violently with a florid tie. He advanced purposefully into the room.

'Hi, Karl! It's great to see you again!' He did not see Richmond wince at the use of the maestro's first name. 'That was a terrific concert last night. I tried to find you backstage, but they wouldn't let me through. Listen, do me a favour, will you? If we're going to be working together from now on, I'd be grateful if you'd tell the guy on the door I'm kosher.' Vonheim glanced towards Richmond, but said nothing. 'Let me introduce Larry Stein. He's my Vice-President of Business Affairs.' Mel winked. 'Larry dreams up all those boilerplate clauses that drive Greg here crazy!' He laughed confidently, and the young man behind him fingered his rimless glasses nervously. Mel rubbed his hands together. 'Do I see coffee?'

'Please help yourself.'

'Thanks.' The Vice-President of A & R seated himself. 'I like this place. It has real class.'

Vonheim remained standing. 'Thank you. If you have everything . . . '

'Don't go. I've been looking forward to the chance to talk to you.'

'I thought you would prefer to discuss the contract with Mr Richmond . . . '

Strich waved problems aside. 'Don't worry, we'll work something out. I know you're expensive, Karl, but we can afford you.' He grinned mischievously. 'Like the old joke goes, we've established who you are, and all we're trying to do is fix the price!'

'I don't think I know the joke.'

Under his breath, Richmond muttered, 'That's probably just as well!'

'I'm only kidding. Listen, I was talking to Larry on the way over, and we both agreed that we need to get things off the ground with

191

something big: some sort of major project that would make the public aware of you.'

For the first time, there was a slight smile on the maestro's face. 'If you will forgive a small conceit, I thought the public was already aware of me.'

'Sure they are.' He gulped some coffee. 'But not on Magnum. It's been years since you did anything for us.'

'We recorded *La Gioconda* about five years ago.'

'That's what I mean. Believe me, Karl, in our business, five years is a lifetime. Anyway, a one-off of some unknown opera doesn't amount to much. Marketing was disappointed with the results.' He lowered his voice confidentially. 'To be honest, we took a bath on it, but I figured it was an investment in goodwill. It got great reviews. Did you see them?'

'No.'

'I'll have my secretary send them over. You came out smelling like a rose, and it was a prestige item.' He smiled. 'You know the definition of prestige? It's a show that closed in New Haven!' He leaned forward. 'I'm talking about a major project, like a multiple set we can launch at a special price: something with mileage.'

With a straight face, Richmond asked, 'Like a compact car?'

Mel's bonhomie faded, and he stared at the other man. 'Good, Greg, but your timing's off.' He smiled. 'I'm talking compact discs! What d'you say?'

Vonheim considered the problem. 'Perhaps we should consider Mozart. 1991 is an anniversary year, and there is a young pianist I . . .'

'Mozart's out, Karl, for a number of reasons.' Strich counted them on his fingers. 'One, we're too late. We'd never get anything finished on time. Two, I already agreed to a deal with somebody else. Three, I wouldn't do it in this country.'

'Why not?'

'Too expensive. Don't you know the union rules? You have to pay the whole orchestra for the first two hours of any recording session, no matter whether you use the players or not. I don't want to end up paying a hundred and ten men when I'm only using thirty-five or forty. It's not worth it. Anyway, 1991 is going to be one great big overkill. Everyone is going to issue every goddam piece Mozart ever wrote. We'll have his music coming out of every orifice! Believe me, Karl, if you want a hit, you'll steer clear!'

'I see.' Vonheim looked at Richmond. It seemed to the manager that the maestro was showing extraordinary restraint. 'Should we work in Europe?'

'Later, maybe. I want something big, and I want to do it here, Karl, where the action is! Anyway, I get the feeling I'm being ripped off every time I go to Europe. The dollar isn't what it used to be, and bands like the Berlin Philharmonic charge an arm and a leg. I don't want to get hit with a bill like that on top of your fees. Let's forget about Mozart, and talk about the big stuff.'

'What exactly do you have in mind, Mr Strich?'

'You can call me Mel.' He paused dramatically. 'Tchaikovsky! Now hold on. Don't tell me he's old hat and everyone's done him already. The public loves that music, and it's years since you recorded any.' He winked. 'I've been doing my homework on you, Karl. The last time you recorded Tchaikovsky was 1982.'

The maestro's voice had cooled. 'Which works did you have in mind?'

'I'd like to start with a three-record set – maybe two sets – containing all the big pieces. It would be a kind of survey of Tchaikovsky's greatest hits.' Richmond watched the maestro's face uneasily. 'Later, we can break out the individual records and re-couple the best pieces. I've got a marketing man who's an expert at re-packaging the same repertoire twenty different ways. That's what I call mileage!'

Richmond interrupted smoothly. 'I assume you would pay an advance on each record, including reissues?'

'Maybe not the full amount, Greg. You already got paid the first time around.' He turned to his Vice-President of Business Affairs, who whispered inaudibly. 'We can haggle over that one later. What d'you think, Karl?'

For a moment, the maestro was silent. 'I'm not against it. You know, George Szell was once criticised by a rather pushy young man for performing Tchaikovsky on tour, on the grounds that it was too familiar. His reply was: "Just because a great work is popular, it doesn't cease to be a masterpiece." Of course, it will depend what you want me to record.'

Strich was enthusiastic. 'I knew you'd understand, Karl. Listen, don't worry about the programme. I've got computer read-outs of all the best-sellers. We can make up a list in ten seconds flat.'

'Possibly, but I would have to insist on including certain works.'

'OK. What I really need is a catchy title for the series. We call it a hook.'

'Ah.' The maestro glanced at Richmond. Strich probably did not notice a slight dryness to his voice. 'Something like the Vonheim Collection?'

The record executive's face lit up. 'Now you're talking! I love it! Maybe we could use your autograph across the front cover of each set, like a kind of logo.'

'Maybe. I would have to see the designs. I will consider your programme. I assume you'll want the last three symphonies?'

'Sure, but I've got to have *1812*, *Romeo and Juliet* and *The Nutcracker Suite*. They're basic.'

'We should include the famous concertos.'

'Great! You're firing on all cylinders, Karl! I knew we spoke the same language! We could back the piano concerto with the violin concerto, and . . . '

'No. I would want to record all three piano concertos.'

'Three?' Strich frowned. 'I didn't know he wrote more than one. The violin concerto makes a better coupling. I'll see if I can get . . . '

'As far as soloists are concerned, you should leave that to me. I would only record with artists I consider suitable, Mr Strich.'

'Mel! Use my first name. We'll talk about soloists later. I guess you know everybody. Maybe you could help. I mean, if you could get Perlman . . . '

'It's worth considering. The violin concerto and *Meditation* could be recorded with the *Rococo Variations*, so that you would have the piano concertos on one record, and the string concertos on another.'

'That sounds a bit esoteric.' He brightened. 'I guess we could always re-couple the blockbusters later. You know, Karl, the more we talk about this, the better I feel. I've got half a dozen other composers ready for the Vonheim treatment!'

194

'I'm sure you have.' The telephone rang and he signalled to Richmond.

After a brief pause, Gregory said, 'It's Erich, in Switzerland. He's sorry to disturb you, but it's important. Will you speak to him?'

'Yes. Excuse me, gentlemen.' Taking the receiver, Vonheim spoke in German. 'What is it?' He listened for a moment, then frowned. 'What do you mean? I gave strict istructions that she was not to be disturbed today.' He listened again, his expression grave. 'I see. Did you talk to her? Did you try to dissuade her?' There was a long silence. 'Where are you now? Good. Don't lose them. I am relying on you to make sure she returns. Yes, if necessary. It is essential that this nonsense is ended before it goes any further . . . Very good. I will have to make some alternative arrangements. I'll call you later.' He replaced the receiver.

Mel Strich had been watching him. 'Not bad news, I hope? If there's anything my people can do . . . '

The maestro ignored him, addressing Richmond. 'I will be returning to Switzerland tonight.'

'What?' His manager rose to his feet.

'A domestic crisis. My presence is needed there.' He glanced at his watch. 'I'm too late for any of the morning flights.'

'But you have a concert here tomorrow night. I have the contract!'

'Please extend my apologies. Unfortunately, I have to leave.'

'What am I supposed to tell the Philharmonic?'

He spoke testily. 'Tell them anything you like. I won't be here!'

Strich said, 'Jesus!' Vonheim glared at him.

As the maestro crossed the room, Richmond caught up with him, placing a restraining hand on his arm. 'Karl, I really think we should discuss this. It's very serious. You can't just walk out! What's going on?'

The conductor eyed him coldly. 'I am taking the evening flight to Zurich. Is that clear enough for you?' He looked down at the man's hand, waiting for him to remove it. 'I suggest you contact the Philharmonic immediately, so that they can find a replacement. As my manager, I'm sure you'll come up with a suitable explanation for my absence.'

'For God's sake, Karl! You can't expect . . . '

'In the meantime, I have a number of appointments to cancel. I would be grateful if you will call me this afternoon, before I leave for the airport.'

When he had left the room, Strich looked at Richmond and grinned. 'Holy shit, Greg! There are times when you really have to earn every lousy dollar you make!'

Francesca waited in the large drawing-room which overlooked the sloping lawns leading to the front gate. She did not trust Erich to admit any visitors. When Peter appeared in the drive, she ran to the front door.

'Hi!'

He kissed her. 'Did you sleep well?'

'Dead to the world. I woke at seven, had a swim, and ate a huge breakfast!'

'Seven?' He grimaced. 'I bet you then practised for a couple of hours.'

'No. I declared today a national holiday.'

'Good for you.' He glanced past her. 'So this is where the legendary Karl Henrik Vonheim lives. Aren't you going to invite me into the holy of holies?'

She took his arm. 'Let's get out of here before the alarm goes off!'

'Now you do make it sound like a prison.'

'I was kidding. Where are we going?'

'Anywhere you like. Simon and Rachel left a message at my hotel. They're going to be in Thun, and wondered whether we'd meet them there.'

'I'd like that.'

He looked disappointed. 'You'll have to listen to all those stories again.'

'They make me laugh. Anyway, I promised Rachel we'd try to meet up before they leave. How long will it take to get there?'

'About an hour on the motorway.'

'We can see them this afternoon. Is there a slower road?'

He nodded. 'Along the lakeshore, through Vevey and Montreux. You must have been there.'

'No. I don't go out much. I didn't even get to see Bern properly. We arrived in time to change for the concert.'

'You make that place sound even more like a prison. Doesn't the maestro give you time off for good behaviour?'

'It's not like that. There's always something else to do.'

'Like what?'

'Practising, mostly. I really have to work at it. When I was in music school, there were kids who could play anything you put in front of them. Jesus! I used to envy them. I guess I'll always have to do it the hard way, and for every five minutes of music, there's ten hours of sweating it out.'

'You make me think of poor old Grieg, proudly showing his Piano Concerto to Liszt, who sat down and sight-read his way through the whole thing. It must have been shattering. But you must do something other than practise all day.'

'There's a lot of reading. Karl says that if you want to play a work properly, you have to understand where it comes from.' She sighed. 'There's so much to learn! And I'm trying to brush up on my German and study French, and . . . '

'You're making me tired just by talking about it!' They drove in silence, and she leaned back, closing her eyes against the sunlight. She felt very contented.

'Do you see much of the maestro?' His voice disturbed her reverie.

'I guess not, over all. He's usually around the house when he's in Switzerland. He doesn't go out much. He has an office and a study at the back, but I rarely see them. I have a kind of apartment of my own in the other wing, and he gave me the use of his studio and piano. We eat dinner together. Otherwise, he mostly looks in to see how I'm doing. He listens to me play, and we talk.'

'What about?'

'What I'm playing. He likes to ask a lot of questions, like why am I doing this, or why don't I do that. I guess he's helping me to come up with the answers for myself. He'll never say I must do any one thing. The farthest he'll go is to suggest something, but he always says the final decision is mine, and that he doesn't want to tell me how to play. Sometimes, he talks about other pianists, and how they solved the same problem.'

'It must be fascinating.'

'It's incredible. Karl says he's not a teacher, but I've learned more in the past few months than I thought possible. There are times when he freaks me out. He knows so much, it's scary!'

198

'Do you talk about other things?'

'Sure. He tells me about places to visit, and food he thinks I'd like, and people I should meet.' She smiled. 'Then there are all the books I ought to read, and the museums I should visit, and works I must study. The day doesn't have enough hours.' She paused, taking a deep breath. 'Am I babbling?'

'No. It sounds as though you're getting a fantastic crash course in the arts from a great master. Does he ever talk about himself?'

'Not often. He told me about his early years, when he studied with some old German conductor I'd never heard of . . . Otto somebody.'

Peter smiled. 'Klemperer?'

'I'm not that dumb! This was some conductor in Munich who introduced Karl to a record producer in London. I guess he died a couple of years after Karl moved to England. And he and Dorothea sometimes talk about life in Buenos Aires when they lived there.'

'I find Madame Vonheim interesting. Nobody ever sees her, except maybe sitting at a concert. Even then, she's up in one of the boxes and he spirits her away as soon as the music's finished. What's she like?'

For a moment, Francesca hesitated. She was tempted to confide in Peter, but remembered that he was a journalist and, despite their new-found friendship, almost a stranger. 'She's very kind and hospitable. She's made me feel welcome in the house. I don't see her very often.'

'Living under the same roof?'

'It's a big roof.' She looked out of the window. 'Where are we?'

'Heading towards the lake. We go past miles of vineyards, planted on very steep slopes. I'm told some of the best Swiss wines are made here, but they only bottle enough for local consumption. There's a village called Saint Saphorin, just off the road, where we could stop for a few minutes. I seem to remember it has a shop with all sorts of antique wine-making gadgets on display.'

'I'd like to see that.'

'OK.' He reached into a pocket and handed her a small card. 'Before I forget, I wrote down my phone number and address, in case you ever want to get in touch with me. I didn't have too much luck reaching you.'

'Yes. I talked to Erich about it, and told him that if you ever called again, he was to tell me.' She shivered slightly. 'He's a creep!'

'I wasn't very impressed. Do you think he will?'

'I don't honestly know. I guess so. If he doesn't, I'll talk to Karl about it.'

'How about other friends? Does he tell you when they call?'

She hesitated again. 'I don't really have any other friends.'

'I see. Doesn't that make life a little lonely?'

'I guess I'm too busy to think about it. Besides, it's such a fantastic opportunity . . . '

'Of course.' Peter spoke gently. 'Anyway, you've got a friend now.'

A narrow road, climbing steeply into the carefully terraced hillside, ran parallel with the highway, and he parked next to several other vehicles.

'We have to walk from here. The village streets are too narrow for traffic.' As they left the car, Peter took her hand, pretending to pull her up the sharp incline. He did not release it when they were amid the picturesque cluster of houses.

'This is beautiful.' She gazed at the tumbledown buildings. At first glance, they seemed inappropriately ramshackle for Switzerland, but on closer inspection she found that they had been carefully restored, their brickwork arches reinforced with steel beams. The street was deserted, except for an elderly dog sunning itself.

'It's mostly been taken over by wealthy businessmen from Lausanne, but a few of the farmers still live here.'

'Where's the place you were talking about?'

'Round the next corner.' He led her to a small shop whose window was filled with antiques: wooden farm implements and ancient vintner's equipment. All the items were worn with age and dust-covered. They looked as though they had been there, scattered at random, for many years.

Francesca stared at an unidentifiable contraption of stained wood and rusty metal. 'I wonder what that's for.'

'I think it's an old-fashioned machine for putting corks into bottles.' He peered at the instrument, explaining its function, and she leaned against him, enjoying the sensation of his closeness.

'You've been here before.'

He nodded. 'I covered the Montreux Jazz Festival a few years ago, and we did some exploring during the day.'

'We?'

200

He spoke quietly. 'The woman who used to live with me. We made a holiday out of the trip.'

'I'm sorry. I didn't mean to . . . '

Peter smiled at her, but his eyes were sad. 'That's all right. There's no reason you shouldn't know. As a matter of fact, I was going to tell you about her.'

'You don't have to. It's none of my business.'

'I wanted you to know. Besides, it occurred to me that you might wonder why I wasn't married. Single men of thirty-four arouse suspicion these days!'

It would have been too difficult to explain her conversation with Rachel. 'I didn't think about your age.'

He drew her close for a moment, and their cheeks brushed. 'I do, sometimes. Anyway, her name was Elizabeth – Liz, most of the time – and we lived together for about five or six years. We always talked about getting married one day, but we never got round to it.'

'What happened?'

'Traffic accident. A drunk driver. She was crossing the road, and he didn't stop; claimed he didn't see her in the rain.' His voice became matter-of-fact. They found her address in her bag, and came and told me. It was a bit complicated because I wasn't her next of kin, but everyone was very sympathetic.'

'I'm sorry.' Her head rested on his shoulder.

'It was quite a long time ago; several years. It's the sort of thing that happens all the time to people. You read about it in the paper, and never think about it when it's somebody else. She was just a statistic.'

'Maybe we shouldn't have come here today.'

'No. I think it was a good idea. It happened in the past. To be honest, I don't know whether I brought you here because we once . . . or because I thought you'd like to see it.'

'Do you think about her often?'

'Not so much any more. Sometimes I remember something, or a word can trigger an image in my memory, but it's over. I don't want to spend the rest of my life living out memories.' He faced Francesca. 'But I wanted you to know.' They walked on, their bodies touching. 'I wanted to fill in the spaces for you, and I want to know everything about you.' His voice lightened. 'Were you a spoiled brat

201

when you were young, or were you always so calm and beautiful and serene?'

'Is that how you think I am?'

'I can't make up my mind. Not when you play the piano, and . . . '

She stopped suddenly and, as he turned towards her, a puzzled expression on his face, placed her arms around his waist, drawing their bodies together, and kissed him. Peter responded immediately, and her lips parted, her tongue probing and tasting his. He held her tightly and, as she pressed herself against him, she could feel him hardening against her stomach. After a moment, she pulled herself free.

She laughed breathlessly. 'Relax. I'm not going to ravish you in broad daylight!'

'Too bad. It would have given the dozy old Swiss something to think about.' He reached for her again, but she stepped back. 'What brought that about?'

'As if you didn't know!' She became serious. 'I'm not a delicate piece of Dresden china, Peter, and you're not the first man I've kissed.'

'A woman with a past?'

'No. Just average, I guess, with normal, healthy feelings. Don't patronise me.'

'Was I?'

'Sort of. I'm glad you like the way I look, but it shouldn't be the basis of any friendship between us. OK?' He nodded, and she took his hand. 'Let's go look at Vevey. I could use a cup of coffee.'

They found an old-fashioned hotel on the lakeshore, and sat in a high-ceilinged dining-room overlooking the water. It was still quite early and the tree-shaded promenade was almost deserted.

'What was the name of the conductor who gave Vonheim his start?'

'Otto somebody is all I can think of. It was like another first name. He was pretty old.'

'When was that?'

She shrugged. 'Soon after the war ended. Karl said he hitchhiked across Europe to find him.' She thought for a moment. 'Thomas! That was his name: Otto Thomas.'

'Good Lord! I haven't heard him mentioned for years.'

'Was he famous?'

'At one time. He made a lot of records in the 1930s but they were never reissued.'

'Why not?'

'Because of his wartime associations. He was supposed to have been one of Hitler's favourite conductors. I wonder why Vonheim went to a man like him.'

'Karl said he was one of the great conductors. He taught him everything he knew.'

'I find that hard to believe but it certainly makes sense. Did Thomas introduce him to Lancelot Gordon?'

'I guess so. He arranged a concert in Munich and Gordon came to hear him.'

Peter was thoughtful. 'I wonder whether the old man had any family.'

'Karl didn't say. Anyway, he died years ago. Why did you want to know?'

'Just curious. He might have left behind some fascinating corre-spondence. He was a very important musician in his time. The maestro didn't mention his name at the conference in Vienna.'

'Should he have?'

'Not necessarily, but he was a major musical figure. Any of the older journalists would have picked it up immediately.'

'You seem very interested.'

He smiled. 'It's an intriguing revelation. I'd love to ask the maestro about it. You seem to forget that I'm a Vonheim specialist.'

Francesca watched his face. 'Is that why you asked me out today?'

'No, of course not.' He looked away, signalling to a waiter. 'Where shall we go next?'

'What about Bern? I'd like to see more of it than the dressing-room of the Casino and that restaurant. It was fun, wasn't it?'

'Yes, but there's plenty more. I'll show you a wonderful street, filled with antique shops; and there's a bear pit.'

'With real bears?'

He nodded. 'You can feed them, if you want.'

'I wish I'd brought my camera.'

'I've got one in the car. You can use that.' He smiled. 'I want some pictures of you, even if I'm not supposed to mention the fact that you're beautiful.'

'The bears are more interesting.'

'I'm not into bears.'

'Really?' She looked at him innocently, leaving the rest of the question unspoken.

'They're lousy pianists!'

They explored the Kramgasse and Gerechtigeitsgasse, busy with tourists, and she was pleased to find that their tastes in furniture and decorations were similar. The prices were shocking. In one shop Peter found an old print and asked the owner how much it cost. When he told them, they left the store giggling like school-children.

'You'll have to find a cheaper souvenir of our visit.'

'I don't need one.' She squeezed his hand. 'But I appreciate the thought. Where are the bears?'

'At the bottom of the hill.'

'Let's look at them, and then we can eat. I'm starving.'

'After your huge breakfast?'

Her lips brushed his. 'I have healthy appetites.'

They ate lunch at an outdoor café in the broad square facing the parliament building. The tables were busy in the warm sunshine. Two young men in jeans and open shirts were playing chess with huge plastic pieces, as big as themselves, on a gigantic board made of black and white paving stones. A small crowd had gathered to watch. In another corner, some musicians in their late teens were playing a woodwind quintet. The sound drifted across the square.

'What does Dorothea Vonheim do all day with her time?'

'I don't know. She goes shopping sometimes, and I guess she reads a lot.'

'Does she have many friends?'

'She may have, but I don't get to meet them. I'm tucked away in my studio at the back, so I don't really know what's happening in the rest of the house.'

'Does she mind having you around?'

'I don't think so. I guess she thinks of me like one of the servants. I mean, I'm just part of the household. Our paths don't cross. She's always pleasant and friendly when we meet.' Francesca's thoughts moved to their last conversation, but she remained silent.

'You don't think she regards you as an intruder?'

'No. Why should she?'

204

Peter shrugged. 'It would be natural if she did. I have the impression that the maestro decided to bring you in without discussing the matter with her. It's not as though he's accustomed to having people around the place. There was an article a few years ago that criticised him for not taking on students. Most conductors have an entourage of scholars and apprentices, but he's always avoided them.'

'I don't know whether he asked her or not. Dorothea's always charming . . .'

'And almost as isolated as he is.' Peter was silent for a moment. 'I wonder why.'

She placed her hand over his. 'Peter, don't let's talk about the Vonheims. OK?'

'What do you mean?'

'You've done nothing but ask about them all morning.' She hesitated. 'I have the feeling that you're trying to pump me for information. Look, Karl's been wonderful to me: kind, thoughtful, generous with his time; eager to help me every way he can. Dorothea's the same, in her own way. She's not a musician, so we don't have a lot to talk about, but she's friendly and hospitable. She couldn't be nicer. I don't want to discuss them. It makes me feel . . . disloyal.'

'I'm sorry. I didn't mean to spy. I told you I wanted to get to know you better. Asking about them gives me a better picture of your day-to-day life. That's all.'

She placed both her hands in his. 'Then why don't you ask me about me? I'll tell you anything you want to know.'

'All right.' He paused. 'Aren't you lonely?'

'Sometimes. It would be nice to have someone my own age to talk to. I miss my old friends.'

'Close friends?'

She smiled. 'If you mean other men, no. Not really. There have been a few, but nobody very special; at least, not any more. I was sort of living with someone in Geneva when Karl met me, but it wasn't important. We'd agreed to avoid getting serious.'

'Do you stay in touch?'

She shook her head. 'He went back to New York. I think he was a little hurt that I just walked out on him, even though we'd . . . ' She was silent for a moment. 'Anyway, Karl is a wonderful companion. He knows so much, and he shares it with me whenever he can.'

'It's not quite the same thing.'

'I know.' She had a fleeting memory of the night in Monaco and stared at her hands which were entwined in Peter's.

'Wouldn't you like to get away for a while, and live your own life?'

'I do live my own life. I know we joke about it, but I'm not a prisoner.'

'Would you come to London?'

She paused before replying. 'I guess so. Not right now.'

'Why not?'

'I have too much to do. Besides, I don't think Karl would want me to.'

He spoke softly. 'Always Karl! What do *you* want?'

Her eyes met his. 'I want to become a concert pianist, Peter. Karl's offering me the opportunity of a lifetime.'

'Don't you believe you could do that anyway, with or without him?'

'Yes, I guess so, but I have a lot of studying and practising to do. At this particular point in my career, Karl doesn't approve of ... distractions.'

'Meaning someone like me?'

'Something like that.' She did not mention that Karl knew he had been writing to her. 'Don't give me a hard time, Peter. It's not for very long.'

'I understand.' His mood seemed to change. 'Shall we move on to Thun? It will take about half an hour to get there.'

'Do you know where to find them?'

'Rachel left the name of the hotel. It's a very small town. We'll probably run into them.'

'Jesus, this is beautiful!' They had parked the car and were walking towards Thun's main shopping street, set on two levels.

'It's the real picture-postcard stuff that brings tourists from all over the world.' As they crossed a square that might have served as a Hollywood set for a historical romance, he pointed to a charmingly proportioned building whose many window-boxes were filled with bright clusters of geraniums. 'That, believe it or not, is the local police station.'

'It's almost worth getting arrested. That castle looks like something out of a fairytale. Remind me to buy some cards. I want my family to see this.'

'Do you stay in touch with them?'

'Yes. We talk on the phone every week.'

'How do they feel about your living here?'

'They're very pleased for me. You know, Karl wrote my dad when he first invited me to Chateau Beethoven. He was very sweet and concerned and old-fashioned, in case they might get the wrong idea.'

'Does he ever talk about his own family?'

She shook her head. 'I once asked him but he said Norway was another life that he preferred to forget. God! It must have been a horrifying experience to see his family cut down by machine-guns. He must have been incredibly strong.' She smiled, taking Peter's arm. 'Now I'm the one who's talking about him.'

'It's understandable. He's a major influence on your life.'

'I know. It's strange, but most of the time, I don't think of him as a great conductor or a world-famous musician. He's more like a family friend; someone who knows just about everything there is to know. I guess it's because he treats me like an equal.'

'Despite those discourses on what to do, where to go, whom to meet?'

'It doesn't come out that way.' She glanced at him. 'You sound a little jealous.'

'You can't blame me. I'd like the opportunity to monopolise your time, too.'

On one of the many bridges over the river Aare, she stared down at the crystalline water. Swans glided smoothly over its swiftly flowing surface. 'It's all so clean and tidy!'

'And horribly dull.' Simon Ravenscroft was standing beside them. 'That's Switzerland's secret weapon. Nothing ever happens here. You can set your watch by the trains, you can eat off the pavement, you can live in peace and prosperity for the rest of your life, and you can go stark raving bonkers with boredom!' The director seemed nervous and depressed.

'Hello! Where did you spring from?'

'We spotted you from the dining-room.' He gestured towards a modern hotel across the water whose plate-glass windows commanded a view of the river and the town beyond. 'Did you read the reviews?'

For a moment, Francesca looked blank. 'I forgot all about them.'

'That's a refreshing oversight. Rachel's bringing them. She went up to our room to fetch them.' Despite his edginess, he managed a benign smile. 'You were a big hit. One of the critics described you as a major musical discovery. Another made an oblique reference to Uncle Karl but added that you fulfilled every promise.'

'I guess I'm going to have to learn to live with that kind of thing.'

'For a while. Once the dust settles they'll judge you on your own merit.' He glanced towards the hotel with an irritated frown. 'What the hell's keeping her now?'

When Rachel joined them, they sauntered back along the river in search of a café. Simon and Peter walked together while the two women followed, stopping occasionally to window-shop.

'Have you spoken to the maestro since yesterday?'

Simon shook his head. 'He doesn't expect to hear from me. Zoltán's the one who reports in. I'm just one of the hired hands.'

'Don't you deal with him directly?'

'Not really. I attend the odd planning meeting, but I report to Greg Richmond. He gives me a free hand at Telmusik, as long as it's a Vonheim special, and Wolpert writes the cheques.' He seemed preoccupied.

'Don't you work on other projects?'

'Apart from the Francesca Noble Saga, no.'

'I thought Telmusik was planning to diversify.'

'So did I. That was always the original plan.' His voice was bitter. 'Unfortunately, it hasn't worked out that way. I've submitted dozens of different ideas, but once Greg and Uncle K have sifted through them, we end up with yet another Vonheim film. I've shot the maestro from so many different angles that I could make a three-dimensional picture of him.'

'At least you get the chance to see him work. I'd love to watch him rehearse.'

'So would I.'

'What do you mean?'

'I'm not included, and it's been made patently clear that my presence is neither required nor appreciated. We attend the final rehearsal as a lighting and camera run-through, after which I'm supposed to do it all at the concert.'

'That must be difficult.'

'Not if you've done it for as long as I have. It doesn't allow much leeway or imagination. My job is to record the legend without editorial comment.'

'I see.' Peter walked in silence. 'I'd hoped to ask you about his working methods.'

'I can't really help you. By the time I get to him, it's all prepared.'

'What's he really like?'

'Vonheim?' The director stared moodily into space. 'I don't honestly know. He's always polite: cool, calm and collected; the way he was in Vienna. He's pleasant and witty, although I wouldn't say he has a real sense of humour. I've never seen him lose his temper. Perhaps it's something to do with the Scandinavian personality. He's totally controlled; always in charge. Charming too, when necessary, but ice-cold until he gets his own way, which is inevitable. Nobody wins an argument with Uncle Karl! I've worked with him for about twenty years, but I still don't know anything more about him other than that he's the greatest bloody conductor in the world!'

'What do you think made him choose Francesca?'

He shrugged. 'You've heard her play.'

'But she's so different: vulnerable, passionate, lively . . . '

Ravenscroft looked at him. 'It sounds as though you've been doing some homework.'

'We're getting to know each other a little. She's so open and companionable and . . . ' He searched for a suitable adjective.

Simon's expression was morose. 'Give it time.'

When the men were out of earshot, Francesca asked, 'How's it going?'

'*Comme çi, comme ça.* A bit tense. Poor Simon! He's doing his utmost to be the perfect, thoughtful lover. He's terribly sentimental.' She held out her arm. 'Do you like my watch?'

'It's beautiful. Was it a present?'

'A souvenir of two idyllic nights in Thun. It was horribly expensive and he'll expect me to wear it forever.' She shook her head sadly. 'Everything has to be a symbol.'

Francesca was thoughtful. 'I think I might like that.'

'Oh, he's very sweet, but it can get to be an awful strain after a while.' Rachel lowered her voice. 'He's pissed off with me at the moment, although he's trying desperately not to show it, because I wouldn't make love last night.'

'Why not?'

'I was tired, and I wasn't in the mood. I can't just turn on at the drop of a hat. Besides, he doesn't seem to understand that there are times when I'd be much happier to curl up and fall asleep next to him. He has to keep proving himself! As a matter of fact, you just saved another little contretemps. Because I'd said I was tired last night, he was dropping heavy hints about an afternoon siesta if you didn't show up.'

'You could do worse. It's such a beautiful, romantic place. With the right companion, this could make an ideal weekend.'

Rachel sighed. 'I know, but on Sunday evening we fly back to beautiful, romantic London and my lousy little flat in Putney, and we're back to square one all over again. Nothing's changed. I'm glad you're here.'

'So am I.'

'Oh?' Rachel noted her expression. 'Are things going well with Peter?'

'I guess so. I like him.'

'I had that impression last night. Are you . . .?'

Francesca smiled. 'Not exactly. Like the papers say, we're just good friends.'

A cup of espresso and the afternoon sunlight restored Simon's good humour. 'Why don't I take you on a tour of the district? I know it quite well. I was once here with Antal Dorati and we found a superb little inn a few miles in that direction.' He pointed vaguely towards the mountains that formed a backdrop. 'He told me he'd just received a visit from a record producer who wanted him to make Beethoven's *Wellington's Victory*.' Simon gave a fair imitation of a Hungarian accent. ' "I said: my dear young man, I expect, in the not so distant future, to come face to face with my Maker, and when I do, I hope that I can look Him in the eye and tell Him that I have served music with honesty, probity and dignity. I can hardly do so if you expect me to record a piece of crap like that!" '

They made a circuit of the lake, stopping in Interlaken, before driving into the hills. Their route meandered past small hamlets of wooden houses and carefully cropped fields, climbing steadily. At the village of Blumenstein, he left the main road and took them through grassy alpine meadows until they reached a church nestling beneath a tall mountain. A waterfall cascaded into a shallow brook.

210

'I thought you might like the view from here. The church has excellent acoustics. Several record companies use it.'

'What a heavenly place!' She inhaled luxuriantly. 'The air smells so good!'

Simon nodded. 'We might shoot a little sequence here. If I'd thought about it sooner, I would have told the crew to stay on an extra day.'

Peter walked with Francesca up the steep, fir-covered slope bordering the stream. 'How does it feel to be back in the real world?'

She laughed. 'You call this real? I feel as though I just stepped into a sequence from *The Sound of Music*!'

'Wrong country.'

'Don't quibble. Any minute now, I'm going to look up at the sky and see a great big sign reading "The End", while an offstage orchestra builds to a big finale!'

Beneath the trees and in the shadow of the hillside the light was subdued. He drew her closer. 'I was hoping we'd only reached the opening credits.'

She was about to respond, when Simon called from below. 'Are you ready to move on? Our restaurant's a couple of miles up the road.' His voice barely disguised frustration. 'Rachel says she's being bitten to death by midges.'

Peter smiled. 'That sounds like the real world!'

The restaurant was an old coaching inn with heavy wooden beams supporting the ceilings. Despite summer weather, the temperature had cooled considerably after the sun disappeared behind the high ridge of the mountains, and a log fire burned in the open hearth of the dining-room. Rich food and heavy wine made them sensuously sleepy, and Simon's constant anecdotes dwindled to an occasional story. The atmosphere softened Rachel's mood, and she sat close to Simon, her head resting against his shoulder. It was late by the time they left.

As they re-entered Thun, Simon turned to Peter and Francesca in the back seat. 'Why don't you two stay over? It's a hell of a long drive to Lausanne at this time of night. There's sure to be room at our hotel.'

'We didn't bring any overnight things with us.'

'It wouldn't matter. If I know the Swiss, they can probably rustle up a toothbrush for you. What else do you need?'

Rachel glanced at Francesca. 'Do stay. I can lend you something to wear.' She had drunk a lot of wine during the meal, and giggled. 'If you feel you must!'

Peter looked at her. They were sitting very close, and he spoke softly. 'What do you think?' His smile was barely visible. 'It is a long drive.'

Simon was persuasive. 'You don't want to go all that way, do you? Nobody's going to miss you. Besides, you don't have to ask anyone's permission.' He chuckled. 'I promise not to tell!'

Peter's face was very close, and Francesca leaned towards him so that their cheeks brushed. 'I'd like to stay.'

'That's settled, then.' Simon faced the front, apparently concentrating on the unlit road.

Peter's voice was barely audible. 'Are you sure?'

She understood the implication of his question. In reply, she pressed her face against his.

Simon parked outside the darkened hotel and switched off the headlights. 'I'll go ahead and find the night porter. There won't be anyone else around at this hour. His English is almost non-existent but I can fake my way in German.' He left the car and walked briskly away.

Rachel followed with Peter and Francesca a moment later. As they approached the front door of the hotel, another car suddenly drew up, momentarily blinding them with its powerful lights. The vehicle stopped at the entrance, blocking their path. Its electric window glided open and, in the pale reflection of the light, Francesca recognised the driver. It was Erich.

She did not move. 'What are you doing here?'

His face and voice were expressionless. 'I've come to take you home.' After a fractional pause, he added, 'Madam.'

'I . . .'

'The maestro will be expecting you.'

She whispered to Peter, 'How did he know where to find me?'

'I'm not sure, unless he's been following us since this morning.'

'Oh Christ! He couldn't have been!' The thought seemed to drain the day's pleasure.

Peter approached the car. 'Miss Noble's decided to spend the night here.'

Erich looked at him blankly. 'I don't think so, sir. Maestro Vonheim gave explicit instructions that I was to bring her home.' He nodded towards the interior of the limousine. 'I spoke to him earlier.'

'You phoned him?'

'Yes, sir. He was very concerned that I should take care of Miss Noble.'

'But she'd prefer to stop over.'

'I don't think so, sir.' Erich looked past him, speaking directly to Francesca. 'Maestro's on his way back to Switzerland. He'll be here early in the morning.'

'But I thought he was ... '

Erich interrupted. 'When he heard that you had ... left, he was very upset and cancelled his New York concert. He's on the overnight flight.'

'Oh God!' She felt a sickening panic.

Peter stepped in front of her, blocking Erich from view. 'What do you want to do? Let me tell him you're staying here. He can't make you go.'

She started at Peter. 'You don't understand. Karl cancelled his concert.'

'That's his problem. I'm more concerned with what you want.'

She closed her eyes. 'It's not what I want. You don't realise ... '

'Francesca, please don't go!'

She shook her head and was silent. When she spoke, her voice was toneless. 'I have to. I'm sorry.' She looked at Peter. 'It wouldn't be any good, now, if I stayed.'

'You don't have to do what he tells you. It's your choice.'

'Yes.' Peter's hand was on her arm, but she ignored it.

'Then stay!'

'I can't. I have to go back.'

'Don't let him do this to you! He doesn't own you, for God's sake!'

'I know that.' She was close to tears. 'I'm going because I want to. I'm sorry, Peter. I would have stayed, but not now.'

Watching her, his anger diminished. 'I think I understand. You're wrong, but you've got to work it out for yourself.'

She took his hands. 'Don't ... '

'It's all right. Will you call me?'

213

'Yes.' She walked to the door of the car. Erich did not bother to open it for her.

'When?'

'Tomorrow. Some time. Where will you be?'

'London. I'll fly back in the morning.'

'OK. Tomorrow.'

She entered the limousine and the heavy door clicked shut. Peter turned to speak to Erich, but the tinted window had closed, obscuring his face. He watched the heavy vehicle reverse smoothly into the street, its headlights blazing in his eyes. Then the car turned and disappeared from view. Enveloped in the darkness, the two circles of light left their image burned into his vision.

20

Gisela walked to the foot of the stairs and shouted, 'Where are you, Maxie, for God's sake!'

'I'm on my way.'

'I'm not going to call you again! Your coffee's cold.'

When he finally appeared, dressed in the smart dark blue suit that she had recently chosen for him, she glanced in his direction. 'What's the matter with you, then?'

'I don't know. I feel lousy. I'm still getting over the flight. Maybe I should take the day off.'

'You always want to take the day off! You spent half the weekend in bed. What's wrong?'

He sighed. 'Nothing. I probably ate something that disagreed with me. I hate all that oriental food.'

'You more likely made a pig of yourself on it, if I know you.' She ran a wet cloth across the work space of their newly fitted kitchen. A variety of electrical gadgets, uniformly black and arranged like display models in a shop, adorned the gleaming white counter. As she poured a fresh cup of coffee, she eyed him critically. 'If you took more exercise, instead of filling your face all the time, you'd feel better.'

'There's nothing wrong with me. I'm just tired. Those damned Koreans ran me off my feet from the moment I landed. If they weren't showing me round one of their factories, they were holding endless meetings to talk about production figures. I only understood one word in ten. And, what with the time change, I was up half the night, trying to get to sleep, and fighting to stay awake during the day. I don't know why the hell I went there in the first place.'

'Because goodwill is very important to them, and you're a major purchaser and valued customer. You should be flattered.'

215

'I don't see why I should have to go halfway round the world to hear that. Next time, they can put it in a letter!'

'Oh, you're always grumbling. The trouble with you, Max, is that you're just plain lazy. If you took more care of yourself and drank less beer, you'd have some energy.'

'That's your answer to everything.'

'I mean it. Look at you! Carrying all that extra weight around is bound to make you tired.' She softened a little. 'Maybe you need some vitamins. You're not getting any younger. When was the last time you went for a check-up?'

'I don't need to see a doctor. I'm just suffering from jet-lag. That's all.'

'You don't have to snap at me.' She addressed an imaginary audience. 'My husband, the international traveller!'

'I wish you'd leave me alone. I don't go on at you every time you light a cigarette. You're doing yourself just as much harm.'

'Bullshit! Besides, I don't spend all day moaning about it. Eat your breakfast and try not to spill it all over your tie.' She smiled. 'You're supposed to look like a successful businessman.'

He took a sip of black coffee and pulled a face. Gisela had forbidden sugar. 'Where's young Paganini?'

'Having a bath.' She hesitated. 'I wish you wouldn't call Günther that, Max.'

'Why not?'

'Because he's sensitive about it. Kids of his age are easily hurt.'

'He knows I'm only joking.'

'I hope so. You're always picking on him these days.' She sat opposite him across the glass-topped breakfast table. 'It would be nice to see you take a little more interest in what he's doing. You hardly ever talk to him.'

'Of course I do. You're the one who spoils him. A twelve-year-old should be out with his friends, kicking a football; not sitting around the house with a bloody violin stuck under his chin. Your pampering has got him so concerned with himself that he's turning into a real little prima donna. Look at the fuss you made when I wanted to buy him a bicycle for his birthday.'

'He didn't want a bicycle. Anyway, they're dangerous. Drivers don't make allowances for them on the streets. There's nowhere for him to ride one. It's not the same as it used to be.'

'The other kids seem to manage well enough. Anyone would think he was made of glass. If you ask me, he could do with a good haircut and a few hours out in the fresh air.'

Gisela laughed. 'Look who's talking!' She leaned forward, and gave his shiny forehead a good-natured pat. 'I'll allow you the haircut, Maxie, but I haven't noticed you heading for the wide-open spaces lately. Your idea of exercise is the long hike from the front door to your car!'

'We're not talking about me.' Max was unwilling to be mollified. 'Anyway, I don't want my son to become a musician.'

'His teacher says he has real talent. He's better than any of the other kids in his class.'

'Then I'm glad I don't have to listen to them!'

'You haven't heard Günther play for ages, Max. He's really good.'

'So what have you got planned for him: an international career as a celebrated virtuoso?'

'It's not a bad ambition. I'd sooner see him become an artist than waste away his life in the business world.'

'Don't sneer at the commercial world, Gisela. It's been good to us. We didn't get this house, or the car, or the offices in Frankfurt and Munich, by standing around corners, playing the fiddle!'

'I didn't mean that.'

'It took a hell of a lot of hard work and long hours, and it paid off.' He seemed irrationally angry. 'We're doing all right!'

'I know we are. Don't get yourself all worked up.' She spoke softly. 'You appear to have forgotten that I was the one who pushed you into it.'

'Then what have you got against the business world, for God's sake? Is our son too delicate to get his precious hands dirty?'

'No, Max. You don't understand. I simply meant that having talent is important. I want Günther to be somebody special. His teacher says he has a real gift. It's too early to know whether he's good enough to become a proper musician but I'd be very proud of him if it happened.'

Max finally relented. 'So would I.' He exhaled heavily. 'I don't know what's the matter with me today. I suppose I'm just overtired.'

'We'll have an early night.' She moved round the table and stood behind him, massaging his shoulders. Her thumbs probed the thick flesh. 'My God! You are all tensed up.'

'I told you I was.'

She laughed. 'I'll think of something to relax you!'

He chuckled. 'We could always go back to bed.'

'Not a chance!' She leaned forward and planted a kiss on his bald head. 'You've got work to do. We're going to need every penny we can lay our hands on, Maxie.'

'Money! Are you still thinking about that house in the Hochkamp district? We've only just finished doing this one up.'

Gisela shrugged. 'We'll get a better price for it. I drove over to look at the house again, Max. It's still on offer. The agent said they'd probably accept a lower bid.'

'What's wrong with what we've got?'

'Nothing, but it's not the same class of neighbourhood, and the schools there are better. It would be good for Günther.'

'Won't he miss his friends?'

'He'll soon find new ones. Kids adapt quicker than you think. He gets along well with everyone.' She massaged the back of his neck again. 'Will you at least think about it?'

'I suppose so.' His body sagged forward under the gentle pressure of her fingers. 'The Koreans made me an interesting proposal while I was there. They wanted to know whether I was prepared to take them on as full partners. They backed up the offer with a lot of money; more than I expected.'

'Why didn't you tell me about it?'

'I am telling you. I was too tired to talk about it over the weekend.'

'But you've said nothing until now.'

'I know. I wanted to think about it for a while, and I need to talk to our lawyer. This sort of thing's beyond me. It's going to involve pages and pages of legal language.'

'Why don't we see him together?'

'All right.' He smiled. 'You've got a much better head for business than I have.'

'I learned the hard way! Would you still be in charge of everything?'

'Here in Germany? Yes, as far as I can see. I told them I'd be happy to restrict my activities to a domestic arrangement. I've got enough on my plate already.' He spoke slowly. 'I must admit it's a generous offer.'

'We'll let the lawyer take it apart before we sign anything.' She spoke softly. 'So, all things being equal, we could afford that house?'

He nodded. 'And that damned violin you've been hinting about for the past couple of months!'

'Oh Maxie!' She hugged him.

'So the business world has a few advantages, doesn't it? I haven't said yes yet.'

'But you're going to?'

'If the lawyer approves.' He tugged at her hands to extricate himself. 'You always get your own way in the end, don't you?'

'How much are they talking about?'

Max smiled. 'I'll let that come as a surprise.'

'You sly old bastard! How could you keep something like that from me all weekend? I would have told you as soon as I walked through the door.'

'No, you would have worked out how you were going to spend all the profits first!'

'What's wrong?' Günther was standing in the doorway, watching them. He was a tall, handsome child with sharply defined features: pale brown eyes, fair skin, a broad forehead, high cheekbones and dark curls that reached almost to his shoulders. It was the current style for his generation, and most of his friends wore their hair like pageboys. They reminded Max of old lithographs of nineteenth-century poets.

Gisela busied herself, taking food from the refrigerator. 'Nothing. Your father and I were discussing his trip to Korea.' She glanced at the clock. 'You're going to be late.'

'Do I have to drink milk?' His face registered anguished self-pity.

'Yes, of course you do. And eat. You can't work on an empty stomach.' Max caught her eye and winked.

The boy sat obediently. Max watched him. He felt slightly self-conscious, aware that Gisela expected him to start a conversation. Much as he loved his son, they had become strangers. 'How was the video game from Korea?'

'Good. It took a while to work it out. There weren't any instructions.'

'Oh. They must have forgotten to include them.' Günther did not offer any additional information. 'How's school?'

'Fine.'

'Are you playing football this term?'

'No.' He glanced at his mother. 'I asked to be excused.'

'Why?'

'I don't like it.'

'What do you do instead?'

'Watch. Sometimes we have to run round the edge of the field.'

'Would you rather do that than play? It's more fun to take part.'

'I'm no good at it.' He looked at his father solemnly. 'What's Korea like?'

'Quite interesting; very different from here. I didn't like the food.' He searched for something additional to say, and Günther waited politely. It saddened Max to think they had so little in common. He wanted to tell the boy how much he loved him. 'How are the violin lessons? I thought I heard you playing something new.'

Günther became more interested. 'I have two new pieces and some different exercises. They're much harder.'

'Will you play them for me when I get home this evening?'

He looked pleased. 'I'm not very good at them yet.'

'It doesn't matter. I'd like to hear what you can do.'

'All right.' The boy spoke shyly. 'I missed you. I'm glad you're back.'

'So am I.' He gripped his son's arm for a moment. The boy's hands were pale, the fingers short and stubby. He had always imagined that musicians would have long, slender fingers. 'I missed you, too.'

Gisela finished her housework and was about to leave the house when the telephone rang. She had arranged another meeting with the agent, hoping to learn whether the people in Hochkamp would reduce their asking price. In view of Maxie's news, it was no longer so important. Not bad for a girl from the Reeperbahn! The sound of the telephone cut across the melody of the new piece Günther was practising. It had been running through her head all morning. She couldn't wait for Maxie to hear him play it.

'Frau Weidlich? It's Verena . . . Verena Zorn from the office.' The woman sounded strange.

'Yes, Verena. What is it?'

She spoke with difficulty. 'I'm sorry to trouble you. I . . . '

220

'That's all right.' Maxie's secretary was usually so efficient on the telephone. 'Is my husband there?'

'No. You see, I'm sorry to tell you . . . he was taken ill.'

The words were a physical shock. 'Ill? What do you mean?'

'He was sitting at his desk, and . . . ' The woman sounded as if she was crying. 'He had an attack.'

'What sort of attack?'

'I don't know for sure. It must have been his heart.'

'Oh God!' She spoke quickly. 'Did you call his doctor? The number's in his address book, on the desk.'

'No. I called for an ambulance. I thought it would be quicker.'

'Yes, you're probably right. Where is he? Can I speak to him?'

'They took him in the ambulance . . . '

'Yes, but where did they go? Which hospital?'

'To the General . . . ' Her voice broke. 'They were too late. He was . . . ' She was again silent.

'What are you saying?'

'I'm very sorry, Frau Weidlich. Your husband died before the ambulance arrived.' After a pause, she spoke again. 'I'm so very sorry . . . '

Her words were cut off. Gisela had replaced the receiver.

The young man sitting opposite her did not look old enough to be a qualified lawyer, despite the wisp of moustache he affected. He removed his glasses and smiled nervously. 'It's kind of you to see me, Frau Weidlich. I hope you will forgive my intrusion at a time like this.'

For a moment, she was irritated. It was such a familiar cliché that she felt cheated. On the other hand, what else was he supposed to say? From the look of him, it was probably his first time, too. She nodded graciously. 'It was my suggestion that someone from your office should come here. We have to go through my husband's things sooner or later. I'd like to see them sorted out.'

'Thank you. Herr Mangelsdorff sends his condolences. He would have come himself, but he's away from Hamburg at the moment.' He reached into his briefcase to remove a file. 'I'll leave all the documents with you. I think you'll find the conditions of the will are quite simple.'

'I suppose so. It's strange, but Max never bothered to discuss wills with me. I suppose we didn't want to think about them, so he went ahead without me. We always talked about the office. I used to work there so I know how the company operated. I never thought about what would happen if . . . ' She paused. 'Would you like some coffee?'

'No, thank you.' His eyes avoided hers, and Gisela wondered whether he was afraid she might break down or become hysterical. 'Would you like to read the material? I have familiarised myself with the details, so I can probably answer any immediate questions.'

'No. Why don't you just give me a general outline.'

'Yes.' He kept his eyes on the papers, although it was clear that he was not reading them. 'The estate passes to you, of course. There is a clause covering the eventuality of your predeceasing your . . . Herr Weidlich, but that's inapplicable. Also, he did not include anything directly for your son, except in the event of you both . . . ' He glanced at Gisela who nodded and then looked away. 'If I may make a generalization, your husband was a careful man. He left you very well provided.'

'Really?' Since the death of Max, she had not given much thought to the future. There was enough in the bank to cover immediate needs, and there had been too many other problems to deal with. And there was Günther. Telling him had been the hardest part.

'Yes.' The lawyer's voice cut across her thoughts. 'His life was quite heavily insured. Didn't he tell you?'

'No.' Max had never talked about pensions or insurance. She realised, with the same pang of regret that had tortured her many times in past weeks, that it was yet another subject they had never discussed. They had wasted so much of their time with useless, unimportant matters. If only they hadn't bickered on that last morning! She should have listened to him!

'You'll find the details in the file. There are also some bonds and share certificates that he purchased some time ago. I can't tell you their exact value on today's market, but they appear to have increased substantially over the past ten or twelve years.'

'I see.' Twelve years? He must have bought them when Günther was born.

'I would be happy to wait while you read them, in case you have questions.'

'No. I'll go through it all later.'

'Very well. Perhaps I should say that even after death duties, your husband's estate is worth a considerable amount — perhaps more than you think.' He seemed relieved to have passed on the information, as though ridding himself of a guilty secret. 'There is one other matter, but I'm not sure whether this would be an appropriate time to discuss it.'

His caution was infuriating. 'What is that?'

'When your husband's death was announced a number of organisations expressed interest in taking over the company. They did not, of course, know the exact structure but wrote letters inquiring about future ownership.' He smiled bleakly. 'It is evidently a greatly respected operation.' He looked at Gisela earnestly. 'I hope you don't find it presumptuous that they should ask . . . '

'No. I find it very flattering.' Gisela paused for a moment. Max was gone. Nothing would bring him back. She had spent many hours alone, once Günther was asleep, accepting the finality of it. From now on, it would just be Günther and herself.

The boy had taken the news in silence, offering no comment. He seemed to have withdrawn into himself. Efforts on her part to talk about his father had been fruitless. They had continued, day by day, almost as though Max were away on one of his business trips. A week after the funeral he had returned to school. They had not discussed the matter beforehand. She had found his bedroom empty and a note on the kitchen table to say he would be home late because of a violin lesson.

The lawyer was waiting for her reply, unwilling to press her for an answer. 'Have you included the correspondence?'

'Yes. I hope you don't feel it was precipitate of me.'

More carefully chosen words! Precipitate! She was tempted to say something rude; a vulgar expression, to shock him into talking like a real person. She had the vocabulary! 'I'll let you know. I may need advice on which offer to take.'

He seemed surprised. 'You wish to sell? Forgive me, Frau Weidlich, but you mentioned that you used to work . . . '

'I'm not interested in going back. You see, I expect to be fully occupied over the next few years. I have my son's future to consider.'

'Yes?'

223

'He is a very talented musician. I expect to devote my time to helping him develop his career.'

'Oh. I didn't know. In that case, we will await your instructions. In the meantime, if I can be of any assistance . . . '

She wanted to shake the young man, interrupt his carefully chosen pompous phrases and professionally sympathetic manner; knock some life into him. Didn't he understand about Günther? Now she would be free to concentrate her life on her son and devote herself to his future. Max, dear old faithful Max, with his crumpled suits and his shiny bald head and his paunchy, misshapen body, had set her free! And Günther would become a musician: a great virtuoso violinist. She would ensure it. It was what Max would have wanted.

21

Francesca was aware that the maestro was standing in the doorway of the studio, listening to her. She continued to play, concentrating on the music in an effort to ignore him. The first movement of Beethoven's *Appassionata* was demanding enough to exclude everything.

When she finished, he crossed the room and stood, facing her. 'Are you very angry with me?' He spoke quietly.

She stared at the keyboard, unwilling to look at him. 'I don't really know, to be honest. Yes, I'm angry, but I'm not sure if it should be with you.'

'What do you mean?'

'Erich. He had no right to follow me. Did you tell him to?'

'No. He did it entirely on his own initiative. It never occurred to me that he would. I'm sorry if it upset you. He was under the mistaken impression that he was doing the right thing.'

She stared at him. 'For Christ's sake, Karl! He spent the whole day spying on me: sneaking up on me, monitoring everything I did, reporting back to you. He had no right! I'm not an irresponsible teenager. I'm entitled to my own life!'

'I hope I've never suggested otherwise.'

'Then what was he doing, for God's sake?'

'I've already explained. He thought he was looking after you.'

'It was none of his goddam business, and I can look after myself. Was he instructed to intercept my phone calls, too?'

'Of course not.'

'But people have been calling me and he told them I was unavailable. He didn't even bother to inform me. Am I not allowed to speak to my friends?'

'Friends?' Vonheim watched her face, and she felt herself colouring.

225

'All right, one particular person. Why shouldn't Peter call me? This isn't supposed to be solitary confinement.'

He smiled. 'Now you are talking like a teenager. Erich gave me a different version of the incident.'

'So he discussed it with you?'

'He mentioned it on the way back from the airport this morning. He apologised to me for upsetting you. According to Erich, Mr Meredith only called once and, when he learned that you weren't there, told him not to bother you.'

'I think he called more than once.'

'I don't know. We can talk to him about that, if you like. I must also take some of the blame. I instructed Erich to allow you to work undisturbed. He may have misunderstood me. Anyway, it hasn't happened again since you spoke to him.'

'No. Instead, he took it upon himself to shadow us all day, to report my movements to you, and to come and fetch me from Thun. He shamed me in front of the others, insisting that I came back here.'

'Then why did you go with him? You were under no obligation to do so.'

'I know.' She hesitated, remembering Peter's words. 'Then he told me you'd cancelled your concert. He said you were very concerned.'

'I was.' He was silent for a moment. 'I still am. Was that the only reason you agreed to return?'

'Under the circumstances, what else did you think I'd do?'

The maestro left her and paced across the room. He paused to stare out of the window. Slanting afternoon shadows cross-hatched the meadows.

At length, he spoke. 'I'm very sorry, Francesca. Erich had no right to interfere and I certainly don't want to impose myself on your life. Please forgive me.' His voice softened. 'That's the second time I've had to beg your forgiveness, isn't it? I must confess that I'm not very good at apologising. Conductors are too egocentric to humble themselves!'

Her anger was replaced by guilt and she regretted her outburst. 'Why do you say you're concerned?'

'Because, at the risk of sounding obsessive, everything that happens to you matters to me. Being a pianist isn't your keyboard

226

technique or memorising scores, Francesca. It's a state of mind; a way of thinking. You're at a critical moment in your career. I know Bern was a success but, as I warned you on the phone, it simply marked the beginning of a new phase in your life. This is the time to consolidate everything you've learned so far and move on to the next level. Where you go from here depends on a number of important decisions that only you can make. My role can only be that of an advisor.'

He sat close to her on the piano bench, his hand resting lightly on her shoulder. 'I'll try to explain. You'll always be a fine pianist and an instinctive musician. That's an inherent gift. I recognised it the first time you played for me. But what you do with that gift hangs in the balance. If it's all you want, you can settle for a comfortable, successful life of regular concerts and — with time — recognition and respect. Perhaps that's all you really want. If so, I can arrange concerts with influential conductors, myself included, to guarantee such a life and career.'

He paused before continuing, 'I believe you're destined for much more. If you can clear your mind, set aside distractions, concentrate all your faculties and totally dedicate yourself, you have the potential to become a great artist; perhaps the foremost musician of your generation. That's why I invited you to live here. If I'd believed less, I wouldn't have bothered. But you won't achieve anything if you allow yourself to be confused by all the inner conflicts of an emotional attachment.' He smiled. 'I'm not proposing that you take a lifelong vow of abstinence. If you do that, you won't mature and develop as a complete human being. I'm talking about now. It's a matter of timing.' The pressure of his hand on her shoulder increased. 'This isn't the right moment to take a lover.'

'He isn't my lover!' She was telling the truth, but the words felt false.

'I'm relieved to hear it.' The maestro rose from the bench and resumed pacing. 'You see, I heard some disquieting news about your Mr Meredith when I was in America. It appears that he's preparing a biography of me.'

'What do you mean?'

'I learned about it by accident. The people who commissioned him work for a publishing house owned by an American corporation. When I was in New York I received a call from its president, telling me how delighted he was with the good news. He wanted to know whether I would find time to sit for some portraits. He also asked whether I had any childhood pictures or family photographs they could use.'

Francesca closed her eyes. 'Oh my God!'

'I think I told you that I've encountered Mr Meredith before. It seems that he's a very persistent man.' Vonheim paused. 'It may be churlish of me, but I have resisted all previous attempts to sift through my personal life. I just don't happen to share the view that, because I'm a public figure, I'm public property. Privacy is very important to me, and the last thing I want is to have some muck-raking journalist from the British press routing out my family history. And because I have always refused, I know that most of it will have to be fabricated or suggested by innuendo. In this particular case, they haven't even had the good taste to approach me first, or to propose an established serious writer. They know that I can't prevent them from preparing a book, however much I disapprove.' He lowered his voice. 'When we were in Monaco, we talked about Dorothea's . . . problem. Her illness is of no concern to the outside world. Agreed?'

'Yes.' She mouthed the word inaudibly.

His voice was bitter. 'I'm sure it will make fascinating reading when the gutter press gets hold of it!'

'Are you sure it's true? I just don't believe Peter would do something like this without asking you first.'

'He has already asked me and I refused him.'

'But he told me you were the greatest conductor in the world. He's admired you all his life.'

'How very kind of him! No doubt he asked you all about me, so that he would have first-hand information about his idol.' He watched her reaction. 'Are you sure you're not being rather naïve about his interest in you, Francesca? Didn't it occur to you that by gaining your confidence, he was hoping to extract information about me?' When she did not reply, he continued, 'I've been trying to decide what to do. Of course, I can ignore the whole matter, and let him dig up whatever he can find. After all, I've been on display for about forty years. If he wants to fabricate gossip about me, he'll need a vivid imagination. However, there are other people to consider. I think I'd prefer that he wrote the whole truth. It's preferable

228

to a series of half-truths and suppositions to whet the appetite of a public that likes to assume the worst.'

'Peter wouldn't do that. He thinks the world of you.'

The maestro's expression was pitying. 'Then I fear you're even more gullible than I suspected, Francesca. Do you really believe he's being paid a handsome advance to write a five-hundred-page tribute to my inestimable talents? The press departments of any of my record companies would be only too happy to do that for nothing!' He shook his head. 'I think the best compromise would be for me to swallow my pride and agree to collaborate with him on an official biography. It would guarantee the truth, and protect you and Dorothea.'

'Protect us?'

'Certainly. If we work together, I can ensure that any references to Dorothea are controlled. There is something desperately ugly about feeding off the weaknesses of a person who cannot fight back. That's why I despise the press so much. As far as you're concerned, you'll be free to work and concentrate without being emotionally manipulated by an ambitious opportunist.'

'But he's not like that! I don't believe any of this.'

The maestro pointed to a telephone. 'Why don't you call him? Ask him whether or not it's true. Do you know where to reach him?'

She avoided his eyes. 'Yes.'

'Good.' He walked to the door. 'I'll leave you alone.' He indicated the illuminated plastic buttons on the instrument. 'I'll see you when you have finished.'

Francesca dialled the number slowly. She had already memorised it.

Peter answered immediately. 'Hello?'

'It's Francesca.'

He sounded relieved. 'At last! I've been waiting here for your call. I only got in about an hour ago. My flight was delayed.' She said nothing. 'What's wrong?'

'Karl told me about the book.'

'Oh.' He hesitated before asking, 'What did he say?'

'That you've been hired to write his biography.' She kept her voice neutral. 'He heard about it by accident. The publisher in New York thought he already knew.'

'I see.'

229

'Then it's true?'

'Yes.'

Her voice trembled. 'Why didn't you tell me?'

'I was going to, as soon as the opportunity arose. Yesterday didn't seem the right time.'

'Or the night before, when we had dinner in Bern? Or when we drove back to Lausanne? Weren't there any opportunities then?'

'I suppose so. I just didn't know how to tell you. I was afraid you'd misunderstand.'

'Misunderstand what, Peter? Your questions about Karl: What was he really like? What did he talk about? What did he eat for breakfast, lunch and dinner? And Dorothea: how about her? What did she talk about? What does she do with her time? Why is she always kept hidden away? You should have written out a list of questions, and asked me to dictate them into a tape recorder!' He did not reply. 'What didn't I understand?'

'You've just told me.' He spoke quietly. 'When we were together yesterday and the evening before, I wasn't thinking about Karl Vonheim, or his wife, or any lousy book. Please believe me. I was with you: talking to you, thinking about you, trying to picture your life in that house; getting to know you. You've been in my thoughts ever since Vienna. I really was going to tell you about the damned book.'

'When? Before we went to bed, or after? Or were you going to mention it casually at breakfast, somewhere around the second cup of coffee?'

'I don't know. All I can say is that I was going to explain before I left Switzerland, and I was also going to promise you that anything you said would never find its way into the Vonheim biography. As far as I'm concerned, yesterday was for us, Francesca. That's why I told you about my life with Liz, and what happened to her. You talk as though we spent the whole day discussing Karl. I thought we were talking about us. That's all I cared about.'

She felt herself wavering. 'You asked an awful lot of questions about Karl.'

'Of course I did. He's a terribly powerful influence on your life at the moment. You must know that. I watched your face every time you mentioned his name. It was only natural that he should domi-nate our conversation. I learned how important he was when that

230

little shit Erich showed up at the hotel and took you away. How did you think I felt?'

She spoke softly. 'No worse than I did, Peter. I wanted to stay.'

'And I wanted you, not just to make love, but to hold and to comfort and be close to. You must have known that, too.'

'I thought I did. Then Karl told me, and . . . you should have warned me, Peter.'

'I would have. Listen, Francesca, I'll talk to the publishers and ask them to let me set aside this whole thing for a while. God knows, it's waited long enough already. Let's get our own lives sorted out first. If necessary, I won't do it at all. They can find someone else. The only thing I can say in my defence is that they chose me because they know how much I admire the man. I'm not preparing some sort of exposé. Karl Vonheim's a great conductor.'

'Would you do that?'

'Yes, if it's what you want.'

She hesitated. 'I don't know what to say. I know what that book means to you. Oh shit! Why did it have to be like this?'

'It's my own fault. I should have told you straight away. I'd even hoped that, because of our . . . friendship, Karl would be less hostile towards me.'

'That makes me feel I'm being used.'

'No, I simply meant I hoped he'd accept me because of the way I felt about you.'

She spoke slowly. 'I'm beginning to wonder whether I do know how you feel, Peter.'

'What do I have to do to prove it?'

'I don't know.'

In the pause that followed, neither spoke. Finally, Peter said, 'When will I see you again?'

'I'm not sure. Maybe we should leave things for a while.'

'Is that what you want?'

'I don't know what I want, Peter. That's part of the problem.'

'It doesn't sound very hopeful.'

'I didn't mean it that way. I just want to think things through. I guess I'm confused.'

'Will you call me?'

'Yes.' She made her voice lighter. 'I might even send you a card.'

'I'll send the pictures we took. The film can be developed tomorrow. Francesca . . . '

231

'Yes?'

'Please believe me. I meant everything I've said.'

'I want to believe you, Peter.' She replaced the receiver without saying good-bye.

Karl returned. 'Did Mr Meredith confirm or deny?'

'He explained about the book.'

'He could hardly do otherwise.'

'He also said he would drop all work on it if I asked him to.' She felt defensive. 'He doesn't want it to stand in the way of our friendship.'

'Good. Then it appears that I'm to be spared from wasting a lot of time and energy.' The maestro saw her expression. 'There's no reason why he shouldn't remain your friend. That's for you to decide. Let's hope he'll be a little more open with you in the future.'

'Yes.' She was about to say more on Peter's behalf but decided against it. Karl would not understand.

'In the meantime, you have a lot of work to do.'

'I guess.'

He studied her. 'You're still not happy about it, are you?'

'Not very.'

'Because he betrayed your trust?'

'He didn't. At least, he says he didn't. He was going to tell me.'

'When? On the inside cover of the first copy?'

'No, sooner.' She gestured helplessly. 'I hoped you might hear his side of the story. I guess I'm just not sure what to believe.'

The maestro placed his arm around her shoulder. 'Don't allow it to upset you, Francesca. There's too much else to think about. You have a long musical life ahead of you. Worry about that!'

'I'm sorry about your New York concert, Karl. I feel very guilty.'

'That doesn't matter. Neither New York nor its orchestra give me much pleasure. They both offer too few returns for all the effort required.' He smiled. 'I was grateful to have an excuse to escape early. Richmond looked after everything.' For a moment, his expression was sombre. 'You're tired. I think you should take a few days' rest. You've been working very hard and, coupled with a concert, a situation like this can be wearying. I blame myself. I should have been here when you needed me. And I sometimes forget what it's like to be young.'

'I wish I had your self-discipline.'

232

He laughed. 'You will, if you trust me and listen to my advice. I'm not sure whether it's self-discipline or simply a lifetime of set routines. They bring about a reassuring hardening of one's emotional arteries. I sometimes feel like a battle-scarred old veteran of a thousand wars!'

'Even when you conduct?'

'No. That's when I'm released. It makes all the hours of study and preparation worthwhile. Didn't you feel that when you played?'

'Yes, I did. It was like riding a roller-coaster. I was flying!'

'You're learning quickly.' His mood seemed to change quite suddenly. 'Tell me, have you ever seen Venice?'

'No.'

'You'll adore it. It's one of the most beautiful and romantic cities in the world, unlike anywhere else. We could drive there in a couple of days. I think I would enjoy that. I haven't had the chance to air my beloved Ferrari for months. Shall we go? There's plenty of time before I have to be in Salzburg.'

'When?'

'Tomorrow. The day after. Does it matter?' His enthusiasm was infectious. 'I promised the manager of La Fenice that I'd consider a new production for him. It's one of the most charming opera houses in the world. You feel as though you're in the interior of a superbly designed doll's house. What do you say? Shall we pay him a visit?' He was like a small boy, and Peter Meredith was already forgotten.

Her mood lightened. 'I'd love to.'

'Wonderful. I'll make all the arrangements. We'll stay at the Principe, and I'll treat you to a personally conducted tour!'

He bowed so ostentatiously that she laughed aloud. 'Why Venice, all of a sudden?'

'That's an excellent question and the answer is that I haven't the slightest idea, except that I think you need cheering up, and it gives me a chance to drive a magnificently designed and extremely powerful piece of machinery. The gentlemen of the press love to gossip about my fast cars, so we'll oblige them with something to write about.'

'I thought Venice was all water. There are no cars.'

'True, but we have to get there. We'll drive to Milan on the first day, to alert the *paparazzi*. It will be fun watching them try to catch us on the autostrada.'

'I'm beginning to think you secretly enjoy the notoriety.'

He smiled. 'No, but I love foiling their efforts! Now, if you'll forgive me, I'll leave you to work. The Beethoven sounds good.' He grinned. 'Perhaps you shouldn't attack it quite so violently. Ravenscroft's waiting for me.'

'Simon? Give him my love. Shall I come with you to say hello?'

'No.' He steered her towards the piano. 'If we're both going to play truant for the next few days, your conscience will feel clear if you give your piano a few minutes of your time. I won't be very long with him, after which I'd like to hear the whole sonata.'

'Slave-driver!' She returned to the piano and, after a moment, began to play.

Simon Ravenscroft was waiting in the living-room, idly leafing through a magazine. When Vonheim entered, he half rose from his chair. 'Good evening, maestro. I got your message just in time. We were leaving for the airport.' He smiled, but noted that the conductor did not return his greeting. 'We shot some excellent stuff backstage with Francesca. It will dovetail nicely with ... '

The maestro's voice was cold. 'I gave you and Teleki explicit instructions to look after Miss Noble and make sure she wasn't disturbed.'

'Yes.' He stopped smiling. 'We took a trip through the Bernese ... '

'Despite which, you ignored my request, sent the driver home, and blatantly contributed to a shabby liaison with a cheap, scandal-mongering journalist!'

Ravenscroft stood. 'Hold on! Peter Meredith's a friend of hers. He's a perfectly respectable ... '

'Furthermore, having masterminded this sleazy relationship, you deliberately placed her in a compromising situation which, had it not been for Erich, might have had serious consequences.'

'You're overstating the case. What consequences? I didn't compromise Francesca. She's perfectly able to make up her own mind. I didn't encourage anything. It was late by the time we finished dinner and I simply suggested she spend the night in Thun. Good Lord! She's not a child. Are you criticising me because she decided to stay?'

'I'm blaming you because I expected you to act responsibly, instead of which you behaved like a prurient whorehouse pimp! How dare you influence her in this way?'

Ravenscroft turned pale. 'I did nothing of the sort! Just because

234

she felt like relaxing among friends of her own age, for a change, you're assuming . . . '

'Her own age?' The maestro's voice was cutting. 'You're old enough to be her father: something you've managed to overlook in the shoddy little affair you've been carrying on with your personal assistant. You've always followed the same unscrupulous, self-serving pattern. I should have recognised that when you first started in Hamburg. Perhaps, if you cleaned up your own salacious activities, you'd be less eager to corrupt other people's!'

'My private life is none of your business!'

'It becomes my business when you attempt to induce the same gutter-level morals.'

The director raised his voice. 'Gutter . . . Jesus Christ, Karl! You can't talk to me like this!'

'I'll talk to you any way I choose.'

'In that case, I'm leaving.' He walked towards the door.

The maestro spoke calmly. 'Correct, and you will not be coming back.'

Simon paused. 'Are you telling me I'm fired?'

'With immediate effect. Please make sure that all filmed material is returned to the Telmusik office.'

'My contract has another year to run.'

'Hans Wolpert will make the necessary arrangements. I seem to remember a cancellation clause. Now go.'

Ravenscroft hesitated. 'Look, Karl, perhaps we should discuss this at another time. I think we're both somewhat overwrought at the moment.'

'There is nothing further to discuss. Kindly leave.'

'I'm sorry if . . . ' He would have spoken further, but the maestro had turned his back.

After closing the front door, Simon walked slowly away from the house. Rachel, watching him from the car, was puzzled by the expression on his face.

235

22

Arthur Sinclair tilted his chair so that it rested against the wall of his cramped little office in Bedford Square. It was a habitual pose, and Peter noted that there was a discoloured patch where he had worn away the paint. Framed posters advertising concerts in various languages occupied every other available space behind him. They were the traditional trophies of past tours.

'So what brings you to the palatial home of the British Symphony?' He had a youthful, unlined face, but unruly grey hair gave a better indication of his age.

Peter smiled. 'I needed the exercise!' He had just climbed three steep flights of stairs in the antiquated Victorian building that housed the organisation.

'Can't afford anything better, old boy. Office space costs a bloody fortune these days. Have you any idea what it takes to keep a London orchestra alive? Still, it has its advantages. The thought of coming here puts off a lot of unwanted visitors. Only the young or the very ambitious last the course. Which are you?'

'It's September, so I'm doing my usual piece about the new season.'

'Didn't you get an invitation to our press conference? You could have ridden up in the lift and enjoyed the view.' Like several of London's orchestras, the British Symphony held its press receptions in the Martini Terrace, on the top floor of New Zealand House in the Haymarket, which gave a breathtaking panoramic view of London.

'Too late for my deadline.'

'No wonder nobody asks intelligent questions by the time we get there! Mind you, I can always count on one eager beaver who wants to know what we're doing for contemporary music. One of these days, I'll tell them: playing to empty houses! You remember that series we did on new music from Eastern Europe? Great reviews, and we lost our bloody shirts on it! Half the sponsors wouldn't take my phone calls for the next three months. I swear they thought I'd conned them into it out of spite!'

'Are things that bad?'

'Not really. I'm feeling sour because we had a board meeting last week. They complained about poor attendances last season and, in the next breath, proposed that we should do a Schoenberg retrospective. I ask you! I've never been able to fathom why London orchestras have to be run by committees of elected players. They're lovely people, but they have this happy illusion that concert audiences are made up of other musicians. How I envy those big American bands, with their millions of dollars and boards of governors. Not a player in sight! You're not going to quote me, I hope.'

'No. I leave the shock-horror pieces to my distinguished colleagues.'

'Thank God for that! There are a couple of your fellows who seem to think there's an evil conspiracy every time we put on a concert. One of the record companies did a special promotion for a new artist last year, and it was like a red rag to a bull. They attacked the poor lad unmercifully; said he was little better than an amateur. They implied the whole thing was a put-up job. What's the matter with them?'

Peter shrugged. 'It gave them something different to write about. Besides, I suppose they want to be the sole arbiters of taste. It ruffles their feathers if somebody else discovers talent first. They're always suspicious of young musicians, especially if they make a successful record. You've got to be eighty years old and slightly gaga before they have any real respect.'

'Maybe I should be quoting you!'

'I see you've got Karl Vonheim in November. That's quite a coup.'

Sinclair sighed. 'And a headache. He's our lifetime conductor emeritus, dating back to Lancelot Gordon's time, but he seldom comes here. This year, he's doing a local European round-up: Paris, Amsterdam, Hamburg and London. He's usually too busy for us, thank God!'

'What's the problem?'

'Cash flow. Old Karl may be our distinguished alumnus, but it doesn't change his fee by one penny. I've been fighting his office for weeks. As a matter of fact, Hans Wolpert's on his way here now.

237

On top of that, the maestro wants three extra rehearsals, which puts paid to any profits we might have made.'

'You'll get a full house. That should please your committee.'

'Maybe, but I can't go above a certain level on the ticket prices, so I'm still losing. The operation was successful, but the patient died!'

'What's the answer?'

'Go after the sponsors, as usual. You don't win in this business.'

'What's Vonheim's programme?'

'Strauss and Mahler, thank God. Nothing to frighten the horses.'

Peter kept his voice casual. 'I wondered whether he might include a piano concerto. It's time he let us hear Francesca Noble.'

'Oh, so you already know about her?'

'I was at her press conference in Vienna, and I heard her in Bern this summer. She's marvellous.'

'So I understand.' Sinclair rummaged through a pile of papers on his desk. 'I've been deluged with stuff about her. American managements send out more junk mail than Diner's Club and American Express put together. There's a PR lady in New York who sends me a three-page story every time her damned violinist sneezes. When I see her name on the envelope, the letter goes straight into my circular file!' He indicated the wastepaper bin at his feet. After a search, he found the documents he wanted, and stared at the photograph. 'She's good-looking. Maybe the old man's human after all!'

'Don't let appearances fool you, Arthur. She's an excellent pianist.'

'We've booked her for next year, provided they're realistic about her fee. Richmond and his boys are demanding a bloody fortune, considering she's unknown.'

'I think you'll find she's worth it.'

'She may be the greatest thing since sliced bread but, as far as I'm concerned, she's not going to put backsides on seats!' He frowned. 'That's the least of my problems. Suddenly, out of the blue, Vonheim's asked me to change some of the orchestra personnel. According to him, their playing was unsatisfactory last time. Very odd! I explained that you just can't do that in London, but he brushed it aside.' He smiled. 'In Ireland, I think they call that chutzpah!'

'Did you talk to him?'

Sinclair sighed. 'Karl Vonheim talks to you. It's a one-way flow. I explained that London players, despite their official free-lance status, are permanent members of each orchestra, but he said he was sure I would find some way of working it out. End of conversation!'

'I see. Is he very difficult to deal with?'

'No, he's always courteous and extremely correct. He's like the French: very cooperative, as long as you do it their way!'

'I'd love to attend one of those rehearsals. I suppose you have.'

The manager smiled. 'From a well-concealed place.'

'What happens?'

'Nothing you'd notice immediately. He doesn't start and stop all the time like some conductors, and he seldom speaks. It's nearly all done by gesture and what the Americans call eye-contact. You forget that I used to play in the orchestra, in the viola section.' He raised a hand. 'Spare me the latest joke!'

'Why are there so many viola jokes?'

'Who knows? Every group needs a scapegoat.'

'What makes his rehearsals so different?'

Sinclair considered his answer. 'A feeling of intense involvement. It was always as though every faculty I possessed was sharply focused on what he was doing, to the exclusion of everything else. It was a bit like being hypnotised.'

'And the reason for no visitors?'

'To avoid breaking the chain, I suppose. There were times when I felt he was controlling me by thought transference, and the sensation carried over to the concert. At the performance, I hardly noticed there was an audience.'

'Really?'

Sinclair leaned back again. 'I remember one rehearsal when a cleaning-lady walked through the stalls at the Festival Hall. Nothing very terrible, and with any other conductor it wouldn't have mattered. But, working with Vonheim, her presence was almost shocking! You know how it is in the normal way with a rehearsal. There are the odd spectators; student conductors following scores; librarians checking parts; players discussing a point or marking changes in bowing; people from the management wandering in and out. There's sort of undercurrent of movement. But when Vonheim rehearses every outside distraction is removed and your attention is drawn down a kind of laser beam of concentration. By the end of a three-hour rehearsal I used to feel mentally exhausted. Maybe that's the answer. He certainly gets the results.' He noticed that Peter was writing in his notebook. 'Is this the real reason why you came to see me?'

'No, but I'm fascinated. I've been watching Karl Vonheim for years.'

'Are you going to write a book?'

'I'd like to, one day. I started to work on one, but decided to set it aside for the moment. It doesn't stop me from doing the research.'

'I can understand. It's strange. I've either played for or worked for Karl Vonheim for twenty years, but I still can't tell you anything about him.' The telephone rang, and he listened for a moment before cupping his hand over the mouthpiece. 'Wolpert's outside. D'you mind if he comes in?'

'No. Would you prefer me to leave?'

'Let's see what he says.' He looked at Peter. 'Off the record?'

'Of course.'

'I've known you long enough to trust you.' He grinned. 'I was rather hoping you'd do a nice little puff piece about the orchestra in your magazine.'

'Give me the details and I will.'

He winked. 'In that case you're on!'

Wolpert entered hurriedly, looking flustered. 'I am sorry to disturb you.'

'That's all right, Hans. Would you like a coffee?'

'No, thank you. I will make my visit brief. I am already late for another meeting.' He looked at his watch fretfully. 'As you know, Eva Lindtman is supposed to sing the Mahler Fourth here in November.'

'Yes. I'm waiting to hear from her agent.'

The German looked irritated. 'I'm not surprised he hasn't contacted you. I learned this morning that Miss Lindtman has already signed a contract to appear in Munich on the same evening.'

'Oh Lord! Has the maestro chosen someone else?'

Wolpert looked surprised. 'Someone else? That is out of the question.'

'But if she's already signed herself away, she can't sing here.'

'It should not be a problem. She must obtain a release.' He hesitated. 'The difficulty is that the conductor doesn't wish to let her go.'

'I don't blame him. Who's she supposed to be appearing with?'

'Andras Hortávanyi.'

'Oh, shit!' He glanced at Peter. 'The original Hungarian goulash. He's a real pain in the you-know-what. The last time he was here he wanted us to fetch him in a Rolls-Royce. I took him to dinner after the concert and he invited three Hungarian friends who ate their way through the menu!'

Wolpert looked uneasy. 'Maestro Vonheim has a solution to the problem. He proposes a little quid pro quo.'

Sinclair eyed him suspiciously. 'How little?'

He spoke rapidly. 'In return for releasing Miss Lindtman, he wants you to offer Mr Hortávanyi an engagement with your orchestra.' Sinclair tried to speak, but he continued, 'It is absolutely essential that Miss Lindtman performs the Mahler. The maestro says there is no suitable alternative.'

'There must be someone. I don't think my board would be prepared to have Hortávanyi back. His last appearance was not a success.'

'I don't think you have much choice. The maestro says that if Miss Lindtman does not sing, he will regretfully have to cancel the concert.'

There was an uneasy silence. Sinclair said, 'That gives us little choice.'

'Maestro Vonheim felt sure you would understand.'

'I understand all right, Hans. It's the usual give and take of the concert world, but I don't see why I should always have to do the giving!'

'If you wish to make alternative arrangements . . . '

'What about a change of programme? There's still time.'

'I don't think that's possible.'

Sinclair restrained his temper. 'I'll put it to the board. Will Hortávanyi insist on London? We have a couple of engagements outside that aren't yet fixed.'

'That's up to you. When the maestro spoke to him, he didn't specify London.'

Sinclair's complexion darkened several shades. 'They've already talked?'

241

'He thought it wise, in case it is necessary to make alternative plans.'

'I don't suppose he'd consider substituting Francesca Noble, would he?' Peter asked the question innocently.

Wolpert looked up sharply. 'Miss Noble? No.'

'It would introduce her to London audiences. Everyone's eager to hear her.'

'I don't think the maestro believes she will be ready by November. He wants her to make her debut with him in New York. After all, she is an American.'

'It was just a thought. How is she doing?'

'Very well. She has a number of recitals this autumn, and we hope to present her with the maestro early next year.' He removed a file from his briefcase. 'Would you like a copy of her current itinerary?'

'Very much.'

'You will see that she has an important recital in Paris next month. Preparing for it would hardly leave enough time for a concerto in November.'

'Not even the Mozart? It went so well in Switzerland.' The list showed only a few engagements, each separated from the next by several weeks.

'I couldn't say. All decisions like that are made by the maestro.'

'And, presumably, Miss Noble?'

'Naturally.' He watched Peter cautiously. 'She is working in Switzerland at the moment. They were all away during August.'

Peter nodded. 'I must give her a call.'

Wolpert turned to leave, but Sinclair said, 'I hope you can spare me a couple of minutes more, Hans.'

'As you wish.'

'First, there's the matter of the maestro's fee. My board feels . . .'

Wolpert raised a hand to silence him. 'I regret that you are speaking to the wrong person. The secretariat does not make those decisions. Fees should be discussed either with Mr Teleki in Vienna or Mr Richmond in New York.'

'If you say so. The other matter is this request to replace a number of players in the orchestra.'

'Ah yes.' He seemed uneasy. 'The maestro gave me a list for you.'

'I should explain that a request like this is, frankly, very embarrassing. We can't remove players like that, Hans. It's unheard of.'

'Well, maestro Vonheim did not actually request their removal. He simply made the suggestion. The last time he was here he felt that the musicians he has mentioned were unsatisfactory, reducing the overall standard of the orchestra.'

'Nobody else has complained. Maurice Levinson is getting on a bit, but he's still an excellent cellist. They're all good, reliable players.'

Wolpert avoided Sinclair's gaze. 'I could not offer an opinion. I am sure you understand that I was passing on a message. I believe it was a constructive suggestion.'

'That's all very well, but it places me in a difficult position. I haven't discussed it yet with the orchestra but I think they'll be very offended. The maestro has a lifetime position with us, of course, but he's an honorary guest.'

'Should I tell him this?'

'Of course not! It would be better if we just finessed the whole subject. If necessary, I'll speak to him when he gets here. It's possible that certain alternate players will be available at the time, but I wouldn't want a story like this to circulate.' He looked at Peter, who nodded. 'It would be particularly unwelcome in view of the fact that all the players in question happen to be Jewish.'

Wolpert was astonished. 'Are you implying the maestro is anti-semitic?'

Sinclair laughed. 'I hope not. My family's name was Sinzheimer when they came here in 1937!'

Wolpert fiddled with the clip of his briefcase. 'I will leave the matter to your discretion. As far as I'm concerned, I have passed on the message. Maestro Vonheim takes a direct and personal interest in every player who performs for him. He has an uncanny knowledge when it comes to strengths and weaknesses in an orchestra, and his memory of players is . . . ' he searched for the word ' . . . photographic. Any requests or suggestions he makes are always in the best interests of the orchestra.'

'I'm sure they are, Hans, but in this particular case I'm not prepared to do anything.' Sinclair spoke quietly. 'If the occasion arises, I'll pass on his thoughts to the board, but I think they'll be surprised and upset by them.'

'I understand.' Wolpert was eager to change the subject. 'May I assume there will be no problems with the extra rehearsals?'

243

'I'll do my best. The maestro's stretching our finances to the limit. Even with specially priced seats, the concert will create a deficit. The people at the South Bank have already called to say that I'm charging more than I should.'

'For an appearance by Karl Vonheim? You surprise me.'

'It's an age-old London problem: too many concerts and too few rehearsals.'

'With respect, Mr Sinclair, that is not the maestro's problem. He is accustomed to working in a certain way. That is why he achieves such extraordinary results.' He stood. 'You must forgive me, but I am late.'

Sinclair took his hand. 'Goodbye, Hans. Tell the maestro we're looking forward to seeing him. I'm sure it will prove worthwhile in the end.'

'Thank you.' He nodded to Peter.

'I'll give Francesca a call. You did say she was in Lausanne?'

'As far as I know. She is preparing for her Paris recital.'

When Wolpert had gone, Sinclair smiled wryly. 'Aren't you glad you earn your living pushing a pen?' For a moment, he was serious. 'I'm trusting you to keep everything you heard to yourself.'

'Absolutely.'

'Thanks. Does it give you a better picture of the glamorous concert world?'

'Yes.' Peter was thoughtful. 'He's a pretty demanding man.'

'And he always gets what he wants, but when it comes to the crunch, he delivers, and that's what it's all about. Now, what about my article?'

Peter smiled. 'You'll get it. Have you got a list of programmes?'

The manager handed him a printed leaflet. 'Every last detail. Don't you want to do a quick interview?'

'I'll make it up as I go along.'

'Then make sure you tell your readers how conscientious, hard-working and dedicated I am, and for Christ's sake spell my name right!'

'All right.' He pretended to write. 'That's S – i – n – z . . .'

'Don't you bloody dare!' He was laughing. 'Do you want tickets to any of the concerts?'

'All of them, probably.'

'In that case, I expect rave reviews!'

As soon as he reached his flat, Peter dialled Lausanne. He thought he recognised Erich's voice. 'This is Peter Meredith. Miss Noble, please.' He spoke firmly, indicating that he would not accept a refusal.

There was a pause before the man replied, 'I'll see if she can be disturbed!'

'Thank you.'

'Peter!' She sounded delighted. 'I wondered whether I'd ever hear from you again.'

'I would have called sooner but I didn't know where you were. When I rang Lausanne there was a recorded message, in three languages, to say that everyone was away until September and to call Wolpert in case of an emergency.'

'We were away all summer. Did you get my cards from Venice and Salzburg?'

'Yes. They were very welcome.'

'I feel as though I've been on the road forever! I wanted to call you, but it was . . . difficult.'

'I thought that might be the case.' He hesitated. 'I've missed you.'

She spoke softly. 'Me too. I'm sorry things were such a mess the last time we talked. I wanted to say a lot more, but I guess I was very confused.'

'I understand.' He lightened his voice. 'How's everything going?'

'Great! I've been working like a slave, but Karl's been wonderful to me. I've never seen so many places or met so many people. I don't know where to begin.'

'You can tell me all about it when we see each other.'

'When? Soon?'

'How about Paris? I'll be at your recital.'

'Will you? That would be so good!'

'It's a date. Incidentally, I saw Simon at a concert last week. His behaviour was very odd. He scarcely spoke to me and couldn't wait to get away.'

'Didn't you hear what happened? Karl fired him. He thought Simon was responsible for . . . ' she laughed nervously, ' . . . leading me astray.'

'That's ridiculous!'

'I know. I told him, and I've asked him to take Simon back. He

245

didn't have anything to do with us. I felt awful about it! Karl said he'd consider it.'

'How magnanimous of him! You know, I'm beginning to have second thoughts about the great Karl Vonheim. He's not quite such a hero any more.'

'Don't say that, Peter. You just don't understand how he thinks. He's been so good to me. I wish you knew him better.'

'At this moment, that seems highly unlikely!'

'I guess so. It's just that . . . ' She paused. 'Let's not talk about Karl. It's good to hear your voice again!'

'And yours. I want to see you, Francesca.'

'I'm glad. I feel the same way. I was afraid you were still mad at me.' After a moment, she asked tentatively, 'What happened to your book?'

'I've set it aside for a while. I'm still fascinated by the man. I suppose I always will be. Maybe one day I'll do something more about it. I just hope that by the time I get to it I won't feel my idol has feet of clay.'

'Why do you say that?'

'Nothing specific. He's a great musician. That's never changed, but there are little details that keep emerging. They bother me. For a start, he's more of a dictator than I'd ever assumed. Perhaps there's a touch of megalomania inside every conductor; otherwise, they couldn't be who they are. Anyway, I'm not writing anything.' When she said nothing, he asked, 'Are you still there?'

'Yes.' She spoke quietly. 'You've been very generous, Peter.'

'I gave you my word, and the past few weeks have given me time to decide what my priorities are. I meant what I said when we last spoke.'

'Yes. I know that now. I should have known then.'

'We'll talk about it when I see you in Paris. Save some time for me.'

'Oh yes! I can't wait for that!' Her manner suddenly changed. 'It's very kind of you to call. The summer has been busy. I really ought to go now.'

He spoke quickly. 'Has someone come into the room?'

Her voice remained impersonal. 'That's right.'

'The great man himself?'

'Yes.'

'And he's listening?'

'Right.'

'Shit! Can you call me back?'

'No, I don't think so; not for the moment, anyway.'

'All right. I'll see you in Paris. I'll find you backstage, or somewhere. Don't worry; I'll be there.'

'That's good. Thank you for calling.' Her voice showed no emotion. He might have expected her to add, 'Have a nice day!'

23

Seated at his desk in the living-room, Simon stared at the blank sheet of paper in his typewriter, searching for an appropriate opening sentence. What the hell was he going to say? Karl Vonheim didn't offer second chances.

Maybe he should try phoning again. On the previous occasion, the maestro had refused to accept his call. He could not be disturbed. At least, that was what his smarmy little bastard of a manservant had claimed. But that was nearly two months earlier. Now that the dust had settled and he'd had a chance to think things over . . . No! That was wishful thinking. It was up to him to make peace. Anyway, it was easier to put it in writing: apologise for his lack of discretion, point out that he had never encouraged anything between Francesca and the journalist. For God's sake, he'd been close at hand to make sure they behaved themselves! Why take it out on him because they'd fancied one another?

The words wouldn't come. It was ridiculous! He'd spent years knocking out scripts, ad-libbing in front of a camera, taking part in round-table discussions, adjudicating competitions, making informal speeches; and now, when he needed a well-turned phrase, when his whole bloody future depended on it, his mind was a blank!

It had been a long, uneasy two months. On his return to London, Simon had been convinced that a break with Telmusik was a blessing in disguise. He had spent too many years going through the same routine, concert after televised concert, to the point where he no longer thought about it. Going back to the real world of television, the daily examination and rejection of a hundred exciting new projects, would start the old creative juices flowing again. He still had the London office. Wolpert had advised him that he was contractually obliged to continue for a further three months, during which he would be expected to edit and complete all the existing material, with the exception of the Francesca Noble documentary. He was not to see her again. Karl's orders!

But that was two months ago and, over the following weeks, he had discovered that the 'real' television world was not very concerned with his availability. He had mistakenly assumed that a few discreet calls would be met with all sorts of interesting offers. After all, he was a well-known television personality.

The BBC wasn't interested. That had been the first shock. It had not occurred to him that in the intervening years a new generation of producers and directors had emerged. There were younger, equally articulate presenters who now featured regularly on the box, but Simon had been too busy to notice them. Two weeks earlier, he had visited Music and Arts in their offices at Richmond Way. The young man who met him had been a trainee when he'd left to become a freelance.

'You've directed all those Karl Vonheim concerts, haven't you?'

'Nearly fifteen years of them.'

'They're a bit on the old-fashioned side, aren't they? I mean, they're marvellous performances, of course, but . . .'

He hadn't bothered to explain the circumstances surrounding the filming and, anyway, he had seen no reason to make excuses. It hadn't been any better at the independent television offices. The girl on the switchboard had asked him to repeat his name twice, and most of the current staff were strangers. With an increasing sense of uncertainty, he had become aware that over the years he had lost touch with the industry. For nearly two decades, he had viewed it from the safety of a highly-placed position at Telmusik.

He had also called several European organisations. Following the recent death of Herbert von Karajan, Telemondial had been non-commital, with no definite future plans. Unitel in Munich had finally agreed to see him after weeks of repeated calls. He had returned from their offices two days earlier with nothing: a few vague possibilities in 1990. Please stay in touch. He had contacted several others, but they had been closed for summer holidays.

In about four weeks, by mid-October, he would be unemployed. It had never happened to him before. He would still have an income for a while, but no office, no telephone, no expenses, and no assistant.

He stared out of the open window, which overlooked the garden. Sarah, leggy in tight shorts and a T-shirt, was sprawled on the grass reading the supplements. Richard had taken his bicycle apart to clean it. In a far corner, Ann was cutting back the buddleia, hacking away the younger branches. Overhead, there was the constant drone of aircraft; on Sunday afternoons there was always an endless flow of air traffic heading to or from Heathrow. A few years earlier, he had spent a fortune having the house double-glazed. For a moment, he was tempted to telephone Rachel, then remembered that she was supposed to be spending the afternoon with her mother and would not be home before five. If that was really where she was going to be. He was no longer sure.

Rachel's reaction to his dismissal had been curiously impersonal.

'Does that mean I'm busted too?' No words of condolence. No sympathy. Not even anger on his behalf!

'I don't know. I doubt whether he thought about you. Would you want to stay on?'

'I can't afford to walk out, if that's what you're suggesting. I still have to pay the rent.'

'I wouldn't worry about it too much. I'll include you in any new job. After all, I'll need an assistant.' She had been silent. 'You would come with me, wouldn't you?'

'I suppose so. It would depend on the salary.' He had felt betrayed. Later, on the drive to the airport, she had softened. 'I'm sure you'll soon find something else. With your background and experience, it shouldn't take long.'

'Let's hope.'

'I do love my new watch.'

'Good.' For a moment, he had regretted the expense.

Simon stared at the typewriter, not even sure how to open the letter. Was 'Dear Karl' too pushy? Surely, after twenty years, the maestro would accept him as a colleague. They had never disagreed before. If only he hadn't answered back that day . . . but the man had been outrageously insulting. Jesus Christ! You don't call someone a whorehouse pimp just because . . . When he had told Rachel, much later, she had laughed.

'You could always consider taking it up, darling, if all else fails. It probably pays rather well, and you'd get away with murder on your income tax returns!' Her disloyalty had stung, but he'd not mentioned Vonheim's contempt for their own 'shoddy little affair'. Perhaps he had feared her response.

So what should he do? Crawl back like a mangy dog and throw himself on the maestro's mercy? It was so bloody unfair! Maybe he should try the Americans. He'd met dozens of them over the years and, even though they did relatively little in the classical field, there was enough to keep him fully occupied. Besides, a new life, with Rachel by his side, in New York ... In the past it had been a pleasant daydream. What was the name of that man from PBS who had hinted at something? He remembered a letter, a few years ago, inviting him to 'drop in for a chat the next time you're on this side of the pond'. At the time, he hadn't given it a second thought.

What about Rachel? Ever since Switzerland, he had been convinced that she was avoiding him. Between phone calls and editing, he had hardly seen her during the day, and she had asked for two weeks' holiday in August.

'Where are you going?'

'I told you. I'm staying with my mother, and we're going to take day-trips all over the place. She doesn't drive, so I'll run her down to Brighton. We might try a quick look at Devon and Cornwall for a few days; take pot luck with bed and breakfast places.'

'Why do you need to stay with her?'

'It saves dragging back and forth between Putney and Highgate. I haven't spent any time with her for ages.'

'You haven't spent any time with me, either.'

'Don't be silly, darling. We only just got back from Switzerland.'

'That was nearly a month ago. I've got tickets for half a dozen Proms.'

'Then you should go. I hate the Albert Hall in the summer. It gets unbearably hot.'

'We wouldn't necessarily have to go. You could tell your mother you were there.'

'I'm sorry. I want to spend at least a week with her.'

'How about the rest of the time?'

'I'll be in and out of the flat. As a matter of fact, I've got a couple of interviews lined up.'

'You didn't tell me.'

'I didn't want to bother you. I thought you had enough to worry about already.'

'What sort of interviews?'

251

'Nothing very interesting. I'm just sort of shopping around. Don't look at me like that, darling. I'm not deserting you!'

'Really?'

'No. I'm not actually planning to take anything. I thought it would be a good idea to see what was going.'

'Look, as soon as I find something, you'll be included. You know that.'

'Yes.'

'Then what's the problem?'

'Well, to be honest, I'm a bit worried for both of us. Nothing much seems to be coming in your direction.'

'It's the summer. Everyone's away.'

'I suppose so. I'll call you regularly while I'm gone, to keep in touch. I thought it might make life easier for you, without having me hanging over you.'

'I'm more concerned with you than anyone else.'

'Then don't look so mournful, darling! I'll be back.'

She had telephoned, twice, but there had been nothing to tell her. He realised, with a sense of guilt, that he would have been happier if she hadn't called.

'Why don't you go into the garden for a while? It's a lovely afternoon. You never talk to the children.' Ann had entered the room. She was carrying a large cut-glass vase filled with freshly picked chrysanthemums. Dressed in a flowered shirt and an old pair of jeans, she was still as slim as a boy.

'I'm trying to write a letter.'

'You don't have to snap at me. I thought the fresh air would do you good. You've been cooped up in here for hours.'

'The only thing that would do me good would be a little peace and quiet!' He stared at the blank page.

'Nobody's disturbing you. We've all had to tip-toe round you for weeks. Who are you writing to?'

'For God's sake!' He vented his anger on the paper, tearing it from the machine and throwing it on the floor. 'If you must know, I'm trying to compose a letter to that bastard Vonheim.'

'Will it do any good?'

'I haven't the vaguest idea, but it doesn't help if you breathe down my neck while I'm doing it.'

'Don't take it out on me, Simon. I'm trying to help.'

'You're not doing a very good job. I need to be left alone.' After a moment, he relented. 'I'm sorry. I'm just worried.'

'That's apparent to everybody in the neighbourhood.' She watched him. 'What exactly happened between you and Vonheim?'

He exaggerated an impatient sigh. 'I told you. We had a disagreement.' He had never discussed all the details with his wife. Too much of the information needed editing.

'What about?'

'It's not important. We had an argument and he fired me.'

'There has to be more to it than that. For the past month you've been prowling around the house making veiled comments about the future, hinting that we're going to have to watch the budget, and generally upsetting everyone. Richard and Sarah are worried. They're scared to come anywhere near you, and you bite my head off every time I speak to you. What's going on?'

He turned on her angrily. 'In four weeks' time, I'm out of work. That's what's going on! I've spent the last two months calling every contact I know and I'm no better off than I was at the beginning. So, despite the fact that the son of a bitch behaved like a shit and accused me of all sorts of crimes and misdemeanours for which I was not responsible, I'm trying to compose an arse-licking letter of apology in the hope that he'll take me back. Does that satisfy you?'

Ann sat on the arm of the sofa. 'What did he accuse you of doing?'

'Various things, none of which was true. You wouldn't understand.'

'I might. What sorts of things?'

'For a start, encouraging a friendship between Francesca Noble and a writer called Peter Meredith.'

'Is she this young pianist Vonheim's interested in?'

'Of course she is! If you took any interest in what I do for a living, you'd know that.'

'Please don't start that again, Simon. Half the time you don't tell me where you are or what you're doing, but you still expect me to know the names and details of people I've never heard of. Did you encourage this friendship?'

'No, I did not. My God, you're already taking Vonheim's side!'

'I'm not taking sides. I simply asked. How old is the girl?'

'I don't remember. Twenty-four or twenty-five; something like that. She lives with the Vonheims in Lausanne and he keeps her practically under lock and key. He expects her to be as isolated and remote as he is. It's a very unhealthy set-up.'

She nodded. 'How did you come into it?'

Simon became more subdued. 'I had dinner with them after her concert in Bern. It was a harmless evening. Vonheim was angry because she decided to stay and eat instead of going straight back to Lausanne with his driver. I thought she'd prefer to unwind because it had been a big night for her, and that Peter should drive her back. They already knew each other. It wasn't as though she was committing some sort of horrendous crime and it seemed to me that she was old enough to make her own decisions. Vonheim blamed me.'

'Is that all that happened?'

Simon avoided her eyes. 'Not entirely. Peter arranged to spend the following day with her. He offered to take her on a sight-seeing tour of the district. She's never been anywhere. It sounds weird, but Vonheim expects her to live and work in Chateau Beethoven all day, every day, without even a glimpse of the outside world.'

'That's up to her, surely. She doesn't have to live there.'

'I know, but you have to understand what the music world's like. Having the legendary Karl Vonheim as your sponsor is a hell of an opportunity if you're an aspiring musician. He has enormous influence, and he can open every door to a concert career. I was filming a documentary about her until we had this stupid bust-up.'

'Did you see the two of them again?'

'Yes. I ran into them in Thun. We did a little tour of the area, and had dinner at a local inn. It was late by the time we finished, so she thought it would be easier to stay over at the hotel and go home in the morning.' He paused uncertainly.

'I see.' Ann's mouth was set in a firm line.

'No, you don't see. Jesus Christ, you're as bad as Vonheim! Francesca's not a child. She's old enough to make up her own mind.'

'Then you didn't encourage her to stay?'

'Me? No. It was none of my business. Why do you always have to assume the worst?'

'But Vonheim thought you did? Is that it?'

'That's exactly it. He sent for me, raved and ranted like a maniac, and accused me of master-minding the whole thing. He behaved appallingly! Then, when I started to argue with him, he threw me out. The whole incident was unreal. If it hadn't had such serious consequences for me, it would have been laughable, especially as she went home anyway.' When Ann did not comment, he explained, 'The old man's chauffeur had been following them all day, without their realising it. He showed up at the hotel to take her home, so her virtue went untarnished!'

After a moment's silence, Ann asked, 'What were you doing in Thun?'

'What do you mean?'

'The concert was in Bern. That's twenty miles away.'

'Twelve, actually. I was having a look at it with the crew. There were a couple of locations that interested me for the documentary and I wanted to check them out with the cameraman.' His eyes met hers for a moment. 'Why do you ask?'

She spoke quietly. 'The crew came back to London the morning after the concert. I know, because Mike Bailey called me that evening. He had some questions for you and assumed you'd come back on a different flight.' Simon was silent. 'So you weren't in Thun with the cameraman. Who were you with?'

'Are you sure you've got the dates right?'

'Positive. Mike told me all about the concert.' She watched him. 'So what were you doing in Thun, and who were you doing it with?'

'Don't be silly!'

'I'm not a fool, Simon. The concert was on a Thursday evening, the crew flew back on Friday, and you didn't arrive home until Sunday. I know you well enough. You hate to go anywhere alone, and you sure as hell wouldn't have spent two days by yourself in Thun. Anyway, you had no reason to be there. In addition to that, I can't see you making up a jolly threesome every time this pianist and her boyfriend had a meal. You obviously had someone with you.' Simon did not reply, and she sighed. 'It's happened before, so you may as well tell me. Who is she this time?'

'I don't know what you're talking about. I needed to stay in Switzerland. I had to see Karl on the Saturday evening.'

255

'No, you didn't. He sent for you. Those were your own words, and he wouldn't have needed to do that if you'd come home on Friday with the others. If Mike hadn't called me, I might have believed the story about choosing locations.' She stood. 'I'll tell you what I think happened. You went off for a dirty weekend in Thun with someone, got caught up with this Francesca girl and her boy-friend and, to ease your own guilty conscience, persuaded them to do the same thing. That's why Vonheim kicked you out.'

'You don't know what you're talking about.'

'I've got a pretty good idea. You've had a long succession of accommodating little bimbos on the side for years. Don't insult my intelligence by denying it, Simon. I can always tell when you've got yourself involved. Who is it this time: the pouting one with the big boobs?'

'Who do you mean?'

'Your assistant. Rachel what's-it. She's the young, pneumatic type you usually run after.' Her voice was contemptuous. 'You're such a vain little peacock! You always need some mindless, adoring twenty-year-old to massage your overworked ego. Why can't you grow up?'

'Oh, for God's sake! I've got enough on my mind without you making hysterical accusations. Every time I work with someone of the opposite sex, you automatically assume that I'm jumping into bed with her.'

'That's because you usually are, and if you're not actually doing it, you're certainly trying to. It's so bloody . . . undignified!'

'Is that what you're worried about: what the neighbours will say? God knows, I get little enough care or attention around here!'

'You get a great deal more than you deserve. This entire house-hold is organised around your self-serving comings and goings, whether it's a hot meal for the few occasions when you condescend to grace the dining-room, or a freshly-ironed shirt for your next technicolour public appearance. My God, you're nothing more than an ageing Peter Pan with a constant erection!'

'How would you know? The last time you saw one, you locked yourself in the bathroom and prayed for an earthquake!'

'You bastard!' Ann had turned very pale. 'I've had enough. If you want to shack up with Miss Big Tits, you can go ahead, but don't expect to find me here. I'll go.'

256

'What does that mean?'

She faced him with her arms folded. 'I assume you're madly in love with this . . . sex-kitten?'

'What are you talking about?'

She ignored his question. 'Tell her she can move in here. It will save all those trips back and forward to her place. I'm sure you'll find a suitable explanation for Sarah and Richard. You were always a great communicator. It says so on that ridiculous biography you had printed up!'

'For God's sake . . . !'

Ann spoke briskly. 'I'll leave a list of minor chores for her to look after. Richard will need a clean shirt for school every day, and fresh underwear. Sarah usually manages her own clothes, but she's inclined to leave them lying around. I'm sure your competent little helpmate will soon get the hang of the washing-machine, and the ironing doesn't take long. The children like to have dinner around seven, and she'll need to supervise their homework; otherwise, it won't get done. During the day, of course, there are the beds to make, house-cleaning and laundry, but if she gets an early start, she'll have plenty of time for shopping in the afternoon. As for meals, she'll soon get to know their individual requirements. Now that Sarah's toying with becoming a vegetarian, the choice is more limited, and Richard doesn't eat French beans or broccoli. But I'm sure she'll cope. I assume she's terribly efficient around the house as well as being sensational in bed?'

Simon was subdued. 'Where are you going to be?'

'Me? Oh, I'll be living somewhere else, close enough for the children to visit me. You'll have to pay for it, of course, but that's your problem. Maybe I should take over Miss Big Boobs' flat. I suppose she has one. Is it all right? I mean, I know she must have a nice, comfortable bed, but does it offer all the normal mod cons? You may not need to worry about an allowance, although I'm probably entitled to something after twenty years as an unpaid housekeeper. I'll get a job. I had a call from the BBC last week, asking if I'd like to go back on a part-time basis, so at least one of us will be working for the old firm.'

'For God's sake, shut up!'

'Why?' She exaggerated her innocence. 'I'm offering you the chance of a lifetime. Isn't this what you want?'

'You know bloody well it isn't!'

Ann's voice hardened. 'In that case, you're going to have to make a choice, because I'm damned if you're going to have it both ways.' She was close to tears. 'How dare you treat me like this, Simon? I'm not your goods and chattel. If you want to run off with some twenty-year-old nymphette, that's your decision. It's your life to mess up, but it's also mine and the children's.'

'She's not twenty.'

'What a pity. It would have given her more in common with your daughter!'

'Don't be such a bitch!'

She stood before him. 'Make up your mind, Simon. I know you always want to please everybody, but for once in your life don't be so bloody weak! I'm offering you the opportunity to make a clean break, but I'd like an answer before the end of the day, so that I can make a few plans of my own.'

'You know I don't want anything like this.'

'I don't know what you want any more. God knows what you've been telling the silly cow up to now, but you're going to have to decide one way or the other. The only thing that's certain is that you can't have us both. Well?'

'You're being totally irrational!'

'No, I'm being realistic. You're the one who's living in cloud cuckoo land.' She paused, breathing hard. 'You'd better go and see her.'

'Look, you've dreamed up an imaginary situation. I don't know why you're raving like this.'

'For God's sake, stop pretending! The least you can do is be honest about it!' She controlled her voice with an effort. 'Go and see her.'

'What for?'

'I've just explained, in detail! Tell her she can move in tomorrow.'

'You know I don't want . . . '

'In that case, tell her good-bye. It's one or the other.' Ann blinked back tears. 'And if you think you can go on playing around with her behind my back, you're wrong. If I have the slightest suspicion that your tawdry little affair hasn't finished, I'll walk out. I mean that. You'd better go.'

'There's nowhere for me to go. I keep telling you . . . '

'Then take a drive. Go for a walk. I don't care. I just don't want you in the house.' He did not move. 'Please, Simon! Just get out of here for a while.'

'Very well.' He walked to the door. 'What time are you serving dinner?'

'Oh, for Christ's sake!' She turned angrily away from him and sat on the sofa. By the movement of her shoulders, he could see that she was crying.

Simon drove slowly in the direction of Putney, trying to clarify his thoughts. This time the shit had really hit the fan! What the hell was he going to say to Rachel? She would be terrified by the thought that Ann had found out. When they had discussed the possibility in the past, she had warned him that they would have to separate immediately. She wanted no part of a divorce.

Except that Ann was the one who was proposing to leave. Surely, that made quite a difference. Secretly, he did not really believe that she would do it when put to the test. She cared too much about the house and the children. When the time came, she would never desert them, whatever she threatened.

Besides, the house was their house. They had painted and decorated it together, finishing it slowly, room by room. Could she really walk away from twenty years of living there? When they were first married, they had gone without many small luxuries to buy the furniture they wanted. He remembered the weekend in Sussex when they had found the little antique table that now stood in the hall. They had slept in the car and used the overnight hotel money to buy it. Rachel was an outsider to their world. She would never have understood a gesture like that. She had a curious disregard for memories and souvenirs, and often teased him for being sentimental and possessive. When she had no further use for something, she threw it away.

He thought about the children. What on earth would he tell them? That Ann was leaving, to be replaced by Rachel? It would never work. He tried to imagine Richard's horrified reaction. Even if he could find appropriate words of explanation, the boy would never accept the idea. It was the sort of situation that belonged in a second-rate American soap-opera! Sarah was at a critical point in her education, with university entrance exams only a year away. He wanted her to try for Oxford, which meant concentrated, undisturbed studies. What was he going to say to her?

It would be so much easier for him to leave and move in with Rachel. The children would hardly think about his absence: it would be as though he were away on one of his business trips. He had thought it all out before. Of course, Rachel had never actually suggested it in so many words, which had been disappointing. On the other hand, she always complained that he left her just when she most wanted him to stay. Now he could do it. If Rachel really cared, and she had assured him frequently that she did, this would be her chance to prove it. After all, they didn't have to talk about divorce for the moment. It was a different issue. A trial separation didn't count.

The Sunday afternoon traffic was light and, almost before he knew it, he had reached the house in Putney. Rachel's flat occupied the first floor of a converted Edwardian villa, just off the high street. There was a narrow parking space outside and, as he edged the car into it, he paused again mentally. Even if Rachel did agree, was this what he really wanted? The situation between them had not been happy for some time. Was it simply because he was not free to be with her, or had the original infatuation passed? He still wanted her physically, but there had been too many little frictions and irritations between them; too many times when they had seemed less ideally suited to one another than he used to believe. More important still, did Rachel still want him?

He switched off the engine and stared through the windscreen at the rusty old banger parked in front. There was one easy way to find out!

It was not yet five o'clock and it occurred to him as he pressed the intercom button that she might not be back. She might still be in Highgate with her mother.

'Who is it?' Rachel's voice sounded slightly metallic on the speaker built into the wall.

'It's me. Simon.'

There was a longer pause than he expected. 'What are you doing here?' She seemed annoyed.

'I want to talk to you.'

'It's not very convenient right now.'

'Why not?'

'You didn't tell me you were coming. You should have called.'

'I didn't think about it. Does it matter? I'm here.' Why was she being so evasive?

'I didn't expect you.'

'Next time, I'll send a telegram first! D'you mind pushing the button for the front door? I feel stupid, standing here talking to the wall!'

After another pause, she said, 'I'll come down.'

'Why?' There was no reply. She had replaced the phone upstairs.

Rachel partially opened the door, blocking the entrance. Her hair was tousled. She had thrown on her old dressing-gown and he could see, where it hung loosely, that she was wearing nothing beneath it. It made her look very sensuous and desirable. Conscious of the direction of his glance, she pulled the gown together.

'Why are you here?' She was angry.

'I needed to talk to you.'

'It's Sunday. You're supposed to be at home.'

'I know, but I have things I want to discuss with you.'

'Can't they wait until tomorrow?'

'No. What's the matter?'

'You should have warned me.' She was silent and Simon noticed that her lips did pout slightly. He had never thought about it before Ann had mentioned it.

'I'm sorry. Did I wake you?'

'What?' She seemed distracted, then noticed that he was looking at her dressing-gown. 'No.'

He laughed uncertainly. 'Aren't you going to invite me in?' He moved to pass her but she held the door firmly.

'Not now.'

'I don't understand.'

'I'm sorry.'

Simon became impatient. 'What the hell's the matter with you?' Rachel did not reply. Instead, she shook her head, apparently at a loss for words. 'Why can't I come in?'

She stared at the ground. 'Somebody's there.'

'Somebody?' Then he realised. 'Oh Christ!'

Still avoiding his eyes, she spoke in a small voice. 'I'm sorry.'

He was silent for a moment, watching her face, but she would not look at him. 'D'you mind if I come inside?' She started to protest but he added, 'Just as far as the hall. This isn't the sort of thing you talk about on the doorstep!' Rachel turned and entered the narrow entrance-hall, then sat at the bottom of the staircase. 'How long have you been seeing this . . . somebody?'

'Not long. I was going to tell you.'

He felt unexpectedly calm. 'Anyone I know?' She shook her head. 'But it's been going on for a while?'

'No. We met some time ago, but we didn't . . . ' Inconsequentially, she added, 'His name's John.'

'Oh.'

She seemed to regain her composure. 'I'm sorry, darling. We always said the time might come when . . . After all, you are married, and . . . and with the trouble at the office, it's probably better this way.' She relapsed into silence.

'I expect you're right.'

'I really was going to tell you.' She attempted a smile. 'It's not the easiest situation to explain. I didn't want to hurt your feelings. I mean, I know things have been a bit tense between us. I thought you probably guessed . . . '

'I should have.'

'Are you cross?'

What a stupid question! She was like a child who had been caught misbehaving. 'No. Disappointed, obviously.'

'I'm sorry.'

'It's all right.' There seemed nothing further to say and he turned to leave.

'Will I see you tomorrow?'

'Tomorrow?' He had forgotten about the office. 'Yes, I suppose so.' He nodded in the direction of her flat. 'Is this why you've been looking for a job?'

'Yes. I was going to tell you about that, too. I've been offered something at London Weekend. It's not very exciting but, under the circumstances . . . '

'When do you want to start there?'

'The beginning of October. D'you think it would be all right? It means leaving a couple of weeks early.'

'Don't worry. I'll tell Hans. He won't care.'

'Thanks.' She hesitated. 'I'm awfully sorry, darling.'

'You don't have to keep saying so.' He looked at her for a moment. 'And I'd rather you called me Simon from now on.' As he closed the front door he decided that it had been an appropriately dignified exit line.

In the car, to his surprise, his immediate reaction was one of relief. He felt no anger towards Rachel. 'The poor kid! She's probably been psyching herself up for days to face me with it. She should have realised I would understand.' Another thought occurred. 'Thank God I didn't tell her my news first!' His only regret was that he had not realised sooner and more calmly. She must have seen the initial shock on his face.

He settled back in the driving seat, opening a window to allow cool air into the cabin. Now he could tell Ann absolutely truthfully that the affair was over. Furthermore, Rachel was leaving the office. For a moment, he felt a stab of jealousy. Had she immediately returned upstairs to the arms of her lover? What had she said to him? Had they laughed together, like conspirators, the way he used to when they were first lovers? He set the thought aside. It no longer mattered.

Richard was in the living-room, watching television.

'Where's your mother?'

He did not take his eyes off the screen. 'Went for a walk. She said she'd be back in half an hour.' For a moment, he looked up uncertainly. 'Is it all right if I watch the end of this? There's only ten minutes left.'

Simon laughed. 'Help yourself. I have to make a phone call. I'll use the one in the bedroom.'

He dialled the number in Switzerland, wondering whether he would be granted a moment to speak. Erich answered.

'Hello. This is Simon Ravenscroft. Is maestro Vonheim free?' He felt unexpectedly light-headed.

'I'll ask him.'

He waited impatiently, mentally composing his opening words. Should he tell the maestro that he had just sorted out his private life, as requested? Not immediately.

'Yes?' The conductor's voice betrayed no emotion, so there was no indication of his mood.

'Maestro? It's Simon. I'm sorry to disturb you. I was hoping you would permit me to come and see you. I'd like to explain a number of things, and . . . '

'When do you wish to come?'

Did he detect a trace of warmth in the voice, or was it false expectation? 'Whenever you like.'

There was a pause. 'I am here all week. Why don't you make it Wednesday?'

'Yes. Thank you. Thank you very much.' His sincerity was genuine.

'Give Erich details of your flight. He'll meet you at Geneva.'

Simon was about to say more, but the line was already disconnected.

24

'Hey, Peter!' Miss di Bonaventura's strident voice rang out above the general hubbub of the crowded foyer of the Théâtre des Champs-Elysées. She elbowed bodies aside to reach him and planted a kiss on his cheek. 'I thought I'd find you here.' She used her thumb to erase a trace of lipstick from his face. 'Just about all the European music press has made it, except for that sourpuss from Vienna. Trust him to ignore her! This place is like a madhouse!'

'It's a big occasion. I didn't see you in Bern.'

'I know. It's the only concert I didn't get to. Jesus! I never realised there were so many summer festivals to cover. How was she?'

'Terrific. She's a wonderful pianist.'

The reporter from the *Herald-Tribune* nodded. 'I'm sorry I missed her. As you can see, the word's out on Francesca Noble. The house sold out as soon as the box-office opened. This has to be the smartest event of the new season. I'll be doing a side piece about the clothes. It's the hottest ticket in town.'

'Don't tell me! I had to beg, borrow and blackmail my way in.'

She had to raise her voice above the general din of conversation. 'I'm not surprised. Everyone who's anyone is here. The bush telegraph's been working overtime. I had a sense of déjà-vu, looking at the gang from the press corps. It was Vienna all over again.' She grinned. 'I just saw your favourite boy, complete with hangers-on.' When Peter looked blank, she explained, 'Karl Vonheim, dummy! As I was coming in, he was walking down the alley to the artists' entrance, along with Mrs V, Greg Richmond, Simon Ravenscroft, that funny little guy Wolpert, and a couple of characters I know from Magnum Records. I don't know how they got in on the act so quickly, but I can guess.'

'Was Simon with them? I thought he was supposed to be out.'

'He was there, large as life.' The crowd was moving towards the auditorium. 'Where are you sitting?'

'Somewhere at the back. It was the best I could manage.'

'You should have called me.' She frowned. 'It's not a very daring programme.'

'I didn't expect it to be. Vonheim probably chose it for her, not that it matters.'

'You don't approve?' She scrutinised him with her myopic stare.

'Yes, of course I do.' Glancing past her, he nodded to Arthur Sinclair and the manager of another London orchestra. 'I thought he'd put her through her paces with standard repertoire. This is her official solo debut.'

'I guess so. There's one piece I didn't recognise in the second half. She'd better be good after all this build-up.'

'Don't worry, she will be.'

'Did you talk to her in Bern?'

'Yes, we had a chat.' He spoke casually.

Miss di Bonaventura would have asked more, but found herself being pushed through the door to the hall. 'I'll look for you in the intermission.' She turned to an elderly Frenchman in a dinner jacket and snarled, 'Quit shoving, Mister! I'm doing the best I can!'

Peter watched her departure and allowed himself to be urged forward. He was still searching for a way to make contact with Francesca. He had telephoned her twice at the Plaza-Athénée, but all calls to the Vonheim suite were being monitored by the hotel switchboard, and he had been advised that she was unavailable.

The recital started late. Despite their enthusiasm, the elegantly costumed patrons were slow to find their seats, many of them pausing frequently to greet equally fashionable friends en route. There was a high-pitched babble as fur-clad and bejewelled women vied with one another for attention, while their escorts, most of them in black tie, patiently steered them with the skill of harbour tugs nudging an ocean liner into a narrow berth. The level of conversation was slightly reduced as the house lights were dimmed, and slowly dwindled as the auditorium became dark.

Sitting at the back of the stalls, next to the stairs leading down to an exit, Peter could feel the undercurrent of excitement. Apart from the professionals from the music world, this was not a very discerning audience. They had been warned to expect a new young virtuoso, personally selected by the great Karl Vonheim, and it was a gala occasion, offering an excuse to dress up and be seen in chic society. For most of them, it was less boring than the opera, and it

266

had a distinct advantage over the old Domaines Musicales, for those who remembered the Sixties, when smart Parisians arrived to have their ears assaulted by the most outrageous pieces of contemporary music. The French put up with a lot in order to be in the swim.

Finally, near-silence descended and, after a further pause, Francesca entered. There was a gasp of admiration as she walked quite quickly to the front of the stage and stood next to the piano. Her full-length dress was black, fashioned from a soft, clinging material that emphasised her slim, athletic body. It was severely cut, following the natural lines of her shoulders, with a gentle curve across the generous swell of her breasts. A diamond necklace, set in gold, glittered at the base of her throat. The simplicity of the outfit underscored her beauty, and as the applause rose to greet her, Peter was conscious that some of the women in front of him were leaning towards one another, exchanging comments. They recognised style when they saw it. Francesca smiled nervously, inclining her head, and turned quickly to seat herself before the applause died. It seemed to Peter that she looked pale and uneasy. After a further murmur of conversation, the hall was silent.

The three Scarlatti sonatas with which she opened the programme were sparkling and subtly moulded, with beautifully balanced and even finger-work that drew nods of appreciation from the more knowledgeable listeners. The second, with darker overtones, was charmingly lyrical, and the third, a brilliant toccata of repeated notes and spectacular runs, brought an immediate response. The audience applauded enthusiastically as Francesca stood, and she rewarded them with a smile before leaving the stage. The 'warm-up' had achieved exactly the right reaction.

When she returned almost immediately, Francesca scarcely appeared to notice the renewed burst of applause, and seated herself again, her head bowed and her hands on her lap. There was absolute silence. It was as though the instant was suspended in time. Peter leaned forward in anticipation, and she played the dramatic opening measures of Chopin's G Minor Ballade. Their intensity was almost shocking and the audience became very still. Following this, the work unfolded gently, the ornamentation like gossamer, steadily building to the first powerful climax. The great central melody – first, simply stated, then passionately developed – took command,

267

and the music soared. For a moment, it was thoughtfully introspective; then a tempestuous wave of sound broke over the calm. Her performance was hypnotic, and Peter found himself holding his breath, awaiting each new sequence. Almost unexpectedly, she was coming to the end. Her right hand produced fiercely difficult virtuoso figurations, while the left added accompanying chords. There were two dazzling upward scales; then both hands, from either end of the keyboard, seemed to hurl themselves towards the centre, and the Ballade ended with a triumphant flourish.

Even before the sound had died, people were on their feet, cheering, and the auditorium seemed to come alive like a living organism. The uproar was deafening, and when Francesca looked up, her expression was startled. She had been totally absorbed in the music and, confronted by the thunderous reaction, seemed unable to comprehend what had happened. She stood by the piano, slightly bemused, to accept the ovation, then turned and walked swiftly offstage. The cheering continued, increasing in volume, but she did not return.

Several minutes passed before she reappeared and, once again, the audience rose to greet her. She remained standing, smiling shyly, while the applause continued. As the noise slowly receded she returned to the keyboard and waited for the spectators to settle themselves. Peter was fascinated by the ease with which she commanded their attention. It was as though she now held them in the palm of her hand.

The final work in the first half was Schumann's *Etudes Symphoniques*. Once again, it was a magnificent interpretation, combining drama and poetry. From the solemn opening theme to the heroic, ringing tones of the finale, the audience was held spellbound and, for a while, Peter was so caught up in the music that he was no longer conscious that it was Francesca playing it, or that he desperately wanted to be with her. Secretly, he had doubted whether she would recapture the uninhibited joy of the Mozart concerto, but he was now aware of a richer maturity and a greater depth of feeling than he had anticipated. Whether it was in the isolation of her own studies, or because of Karl Vonheim's influence and advice, she had been transformed into a great artist, and he listened with wonder as she moulded and shaped Schumann's variations in a performance that he would remember for the rest of his life.

When it ended, the house again came wildly alive, and it was as though every person present physically wanted to express joyous acknowledgement of both music and performer. The sound was overwhelming, and the cheering was sustained as Francesca left the stage and returned many times. When finally, she did not reappear, the lights were turned up, and an excited, animated throng surged towards the exit doors.

'Jesus H Christ, that girl's unbelievable!' Miss di Bonaventura buttonholed him as he entered the foyer. She looked reproachful. 'You didn't warn me she was that fantastic!'

'I knew you'd have to hear her for yourself.' He felt illogically proprietary.

'I peeked up at Vonheim during the Schumann. He was grinning like the Cheshire Cat. He must be pretty pleased with himself. Your conductor sure as hell knows how to pick himself a winner.'

'He's not mine, but you're right. She's come a long way since I last heard her.'

She laughed. 'How do you think he does it: blood transfusions?'

'No. Her talent was always there. You can't teach anyone to play like that. He simply found a way of bringing it out.'

'Well, however he did it, it's too bad he can't find a way to patent it. He'd be a millionaire!'

'He's a millionaire already.'

'True. I saw the whole party heading backstage through a side door. The guys from Magnum Records looked slightly punch-drunk.'

'I'm not surprised.' Peter smiled. 'In a couple of weeks, they'll be telling the world they discovered her.'

'You'd better believe it! If they haven't signed her yet, they'll be sorry. There was a gleam in Greg Richmond's eye that looked like a dollar sign.'

They were joined by Arthur Sinclair and the man from *Le Monde* who, for once, was remarkably friendly. Moments later, the journalist from *Der Spiegel*, the reporter from the *Züricher Nachrichten* and one of the Japanese interviewers from Vienna came over.

Peter laughed. 'You don't often see the press take over the foyer of a concert hall. They usually eye each other from a discreet distance. We should do this more often!'

Le Monde gave a Gallic shrug. 'There is no need for caution tonight. Our opinions are unanimous. Mademoiselle Noble is a miracle! Her Chopin combined the fire of Horowitz with the poetry of Rubinstein!' At his side, the Japanese hissed slightly and nodded his head vigorously.

Miss di Bonaventura faced them. 'Peter has an unfair edge on us. He went to the concert in Bern.'

The Swiss said, 'I was there, too. It was not as good as this.'

'I could still kick myself for passing it up.' She turned to Peter. 'Are you going backstage after?'

He hesitated before replying. Karl Vonheim had almost certainly issued strict instructions forbidding journalists, himself especially. Then an idea crossed his mind. 'I might. On the other hand, it would be an excellent opportunity to speak to maestro Vonheim again. After this, he won't be able to resist saying a few words about his protégée.'

Der Spiegel looked pleased. 'That's right! We could catch him on the way out. My God! Imagine persuading the great man to grant an interview twice in six months. It's unheard of!'

The man from *Le Monde* nodded weightily. 'Speaking for myself, I would like to hear what he has to say. This is an important occasion. Perhaps, if we station ourselves next to the door that leads backstage, we will be able to approach him. Shall we agree to wait there?' There was general assent, but the Japanese looked crestfallen. 'What is wrong?'

'I did not bring my tape-recorder!'

At the end of the interval, Miss di Bonaventura walked with Peter back into the hall. She glanced at him, lowering her voice. 'You're up to something; I can tell. What gives?'

'Nothing.'

'Who are you kidding?'

'Well, if you must know, I want to see Francesca before Vonheim gets to her. I'm not exactly welcome in his circle.'

'So why the . . . ?' Then she understood. 'I get it. A little diversionary tactic!'

'I still don't know if I'll be able to reach her. Zoltán Teleki's probably standing guard. Say you'll help.'

She looked suspicious. 'Just how well did you get to know this broad?'

'Not what you're thinking, unfortunately. If she says anything interesting, I promise to share it with you.'

'From the look on your face, it won't be repeatable! I didn't think you Englishmen were like that.' She was amused.

'I just want to talk to her. She's got more bodyguards than Madonna! Will you help?'

Miss di Bonaventura shrugged. 'Who am I to stand in the way of true love! Listen, if she stands you up, I'm still available. I'm not proud.'

The second half of the concert was an even greater triumph. Three exquisitely coloured Debussy Preludes were followed by the only rarity on the programme: John Corigliano's *Fantasia on an Ostinato*, a fascinating experiment in minimalism, by a fellow American, based on the second movement of Beethoven's Seventh symphony. Peter listened with interest but his mind wandered. He was too concerned with finding a way to reach Francesca backstage. Once again the audience, even if it was slightly puzzled by the new music, responded ecstatically. The final work, Prokofiev's rugged Sixth sonata, demanded his attention, and again he became totally involved in Francesca's playing, marvelling at its combination of strength and lyricism. There were moments when the music seemed to call upon every physical resource, but she played with sustained power and passionate energy. As the last blazing chords announced the end, the auditorium erupted again, and the audience rose for a standing ovation, cheering louder than ever. He slipped quickly from his seat, the sound ringing in his ears, and ran to the exit.

A small side street, adjacent to the theatre, led to the musicians' entrance and he hurried down it. The man on the door looked up as he passed, but made no comment. The audience was still applauding inside and he assumed that Peter, who nodded briskly in his direction, was part of the backstage management. There was a sudden hush and, in the distance, he heard Francesca play again. As an encore, she had chosen a Chopin waltz, and he tiptoed towards a darkened recess by the rear wall, making sure he was well clear of Zoltán Teleki, who was waiting by the door leading to the stage. The piece ended to loud cheers and Peter remained immobile in the shadows hoping that his presence had not been noted by the stage-hands. Eventually, he watched Teleki walk Francesca to her dressing-room and, having seen her into it, post himself outside the door. In the auditorium the cheering continued, accompanied by

271

rhythmic stamping of feet, but it was clear to Peter that she would not reappear on stage.

He waited a few seconds more, then walked towards the Hungarian. 'Good evening. Marvellous, wasn't it?' He smiled amiably.

For a moment, Teleki did not recognise him. 'Yes. Magnificent!' He saw that Peter was walking directly towards him, and straightened uneasily. 'Oh, it's you. I'm afraid you can't go in . . . '

'Nonsense!' His hand was already on the handle. 'Francesca's expecting me.' Still smiling, he stepped inside.

Francesca was standing in the centre of the room, her eyes closed. In her hands was a small towel with which she had been wiping her face, and she was grasping it so tightly that he could see tensed muscles in her forearm. Away from the lights, her face was pale and drawn, and there were dark shadows beneath her eyes. She was shaking uncontrollably. The sound of the door disturbed her, and she looked round, seeing him.

'Peter!' She ran to him, flinging her arms about his neck, and buried her face against his shoulder.

For a while, he said nothing, but held her gently until the trembling eased. He spoke softly. 'Are you all right?'

She nodded. 'You weren't supposed to see me like this. I'm expected to be cool, calm and collected at all times!' She clung to him. 'Oh Peter, I've missed you so much! I was afraid you didn't want to see me again.'

'I wanted to more than ever, but I couldn't reach you.' He smiled. 'I even considered pitching a tent in the road outside Chateau Beethoven!' She said nothing, but he could feel her relaxing. 'The concert was wonderful.'

'It felt like a nightmare. I thought I was going to collapse out there.'

'But why? You had the audience spellbound. It was incredible!'

'I guess I was overwrought. I've been working non-stop all summer.' She spoke quickly. 'I thought if I could go out there and play like a machine . . . sort of programmed . . . I wouldn't have to worry . . . I guess it doesn't work like that . . . Karl told me to forget about everything . . . to ignore everyone and just play . . . I couldn't. It's not like a concerto . . . the conductor, and the orchestra . . . The keys in front of me started to blur, and . . . ' Once again, she buried her face against him.

'You've worked too hard. There's a limit to how much you can do.'

'It doesn't matter, now that you're here. Oh Peter!' The pressure of her mouth against his was fierce, as if driven by desperation.

After a moment, he drew back, holding her face in his hands. 'I'm worried about you.'

She had grown calmer, and attempted a smile. 'I'm all right again. I guess the pressure built up in me. Don't worry, I'm not going to attack you!'

'I'm not complaining. Will you have a rest now; get away for a few days?'

'I can't. Karl says this is just another beginning.' She spoke without emotion. 'Everything is a stepping-stone, moving to the next stage.'

'Not without a break. You can't keep it up all the time.'

'I'll be fine by the morning.' She was slightly self-conscious. 'I guess I let it all get to me. Karl says . . . '

'To hell with Karl! I'm thinking about you.'

She released herself from his arms. 'I'm OK. Everything's back to normal. It was just reaction.' Her hands gripped his tightly. 'I'm glad you're here!'

'So am I.'

There was a tap at the door and Zoltán Teleki appeared. He looked anxious. 'I really think it's time for you to go. The maestro will be here any moment. He gave strict instructions . . . '

'One more minute, please?' Her voice was pleading. 'Peter's just going.'

The Hungarian looked uncertain. 'Very well. He's going to be angry if he finds . . . ' He closed the door again.

Peter spoke quickly. 'When will I see you? Is there a reception this evening?'

'No. We'll be returning to the hotel. It's just down the road.'

'I know. I tried to call. Are you leaving immediately?'

'No. Karl says I can receive visitors for half an hour maximum. He's arranged a supper upstairs when we get back, and I have to be in my room by twelve.' She repeated the instructions like a child. 'It's a routine he always follows.'

'But you're not Karl, Francesca. Doesn't he let you decide things like that for yourself?'

273

'He says it's better that way. I trust his experience. I have to.'

'When do you leave Paris?'

'Tomorrow. Erich's picking us up around noon.'

'But we have to see each other again!'

She hesitated. 'Yes. We have to.'

'How?'

'I'll meet you later. Karl and Dorothea will go to their rooms at twelve.'

'Rooms?'

She nodded. 'They sleep separately. Once they've gone to bed, I can get away. Where are you staying?'

'At a hotel called the Queen Elizabeth. It's not far from here, on the corner of the George Cinq and the Avenue Pierre Premier de Serbie. It's just around the corner from the George V. Do you know where I mean?'

'I guess so.' She looked uncertain. 'I've seen the hotel.'

'There's a little bistro opposite called Calavados. It's on Pierre Premier. Shall I find you there?'

She nodded, repeating the name. 'I'll be there some time after twelve. Will you wait for me?'

'Of course.' He kissed her again. For a moment, she held on to him, pressing her body tightly against his. 'I'd better get out of here.'

'I'll come to you as soon as I can.'

At the door he turned to her again. 'You played like an angel!'

'Thank you.' She smiled. 'It doesn't matter any more.'

As he closed the door, Peter paused. A party of people was walking across the backstage area in his direction, led by Karl Vonheim. Seeing the journalist, the maestro halted, indicating to the others that they should continue without him. Only Gregory Richmond remained. Peter stood aside to let the well-wishers past.

Vonheim approached him. 'I wonder if we might have a word, Mr Meredith.' He walked a few paces away from the dressing-room, out of earshot, and Peter followed, accompanied by Richmond. Then he turned. 'It appears that you're very persistent.'

Peter looked at him calmly. 'Not really. Miss Noble is a friend. I wanted to offer my congratulations.'

The maestro's voice was icy. 'No doubt hoping to question her about my latest movements?'

'No. We didn't talk about you. I came to see her.'

'You don't really expect me to believe that?' Vonheim's voice was contemptuous. 'I'm not a fool, Mr Meredith, and I'm well aware of the sort of shoddy tricks journalists employ.'

Peter felt his temper rising. 'I'm not very concerned with what you think, maestro. I simply wanted to talk to her.'

Richmond interrupted smoothly. 'This is hardly an appropriate time to get into an argument, Karl. Mr Meredith is leaving now. I think we . . . '

The maestro ignored him, concentrating his attention on Peter. 'What are you doing here?'

'I would have thought that was self-evident. I wanted to congratulate . . . '

'So much so that you didn't bother to wait for her encore? I watched you sneaking out of the hall after the Prokofiev.'

Peter stared him down. 'I'm flattered. I thought you would have been more interested in the music.'

The maestro's face darkened, and he started to speak, but Richmond intervened. 'Look, there's no point in . . . '

'Be quiet!' Vonheim turned on him angrily. 'If I want you to interrupt me, I'll tell you!'

'For heaven's sake, Karl! This is totally unnecessary. In my opinion . . . '

'I'm not interested in your opinion, or your interference. I think I made that perfectly clear in New York.' He turned again to Peter. 'You are not going to pry into my private life. Do you understand?'

'I've already explained to Francesca that I . . . '

'Explained!' He spoke in a low, harsh voice. 'Explained what? That you're using her? That you've been sniffing around her like a dog on heat to mislead her? That you've been asking sly questions, carefully concealed, prying into my life; gathering dirty little bits and pieces of information, so that you can twist them into some sleazy, muck-raking little . . . '

'Karl, please!' Richmond had raised his voice. Several bystanders, waiting at the door to the dressing-room, looked up curiously. 'This is getting ridiculous! You're making all sorts of assumptions and suppositions that are totally unfounded. I think we should leave this to another time.'

The maestro suddenly focused his anger on Richmond. 'You won't tell me anything! I will protect my name, my life and my privacy as I see fit, and I don't need the incompetent manipulations of a grubby little New York upstart to guide me!'

The American had turned pale. 'Be careful what you say, Karl. You could regret it.'

'I regret nothing. Go and join the others. I don't want you here, and I don't need you. I can defend myself against trash!'

'Very well. Have it your own way.' As Richmond turned to leave, he spoke softly. 'Don't worry, maestro. Your secrets are safe with me!' His gaze did not falter. He straightened the sleeves of his well-cut dinner jacket and walked swiftly to the dressing-room.

Peter listened to the exchange in silence. He was puzzled by the maestro's sudden fury with his manager, and wondered what had taken place between them in New York.

When Vonheim faced him again he seemed to have regained his composure. 'Mr Meredith, setting aside your unhealthy interest in me and the money you have been paid to write about me, I must make it clear that you are meddling with the life of a brilliant young musician who is on the brink of an important career.'

Peter spoke quietly. 'I have no wish to hurt Francesca's life, and I share your belief in her.'

'What would you know about it! If you care about her, stay away from her!'

'Why? Because you want to dominate her life? Are you afraid she might listen to someone else? Is that what worries you?'

The maestro's voice was cold. 'I'm not prepared to discuss any aspect of her life or her career with you, Mr Meredith. You wouldn't understand, anyway. You have no part to play in it, and I'm warning you to stay away from her.'

'Warning me?'

Vonheim ignored the question. He spoke coolly. 'I will not tolerate any interference. You are playing dangerous games with an extremely vulnerable and impressionable young woman. Don't provoke me, Mr Meredith. I will not tell you again.' He stared at Peter for a moment, then turned and walked to the dressing-room. A number of guests, still waiting to be admitted, stood back respectfully to let him pass. As he disappeared from view, Peter heard a short burst of applause to acknowledge the maestro's presence.

Francesca arrived at the bistro well after midnight. She was wearing an old raincoat, beneath which were an oversized man's shirt and

276

jeans. Her mouth brushed against Peter's. 'I'm sorry. I had to wait longer than I expected. Karl felt like celebrating. He was in a wonderful mood, like a kid with a new toy.'

'Not when I saw him!'

'Why? What happened?'

'I ran into him outside your dressing-room.'

'Oh no! What did he say?'

'Quite a lot. For starters, he accused me of latching on to you so that I could unearth all the murky secrets of the Vonheim household. I tried to explain, but he wouldn't listen to me. I've never seen him lose his temper before.' She turned pale. 'Then he rounded on Gregory Richmond, and went for him because he tried to introduce some semblance of calm. What's going on between those two? I thought they were supposed to be friends.'

'I don't know. Greg hasn't been around for weeks. He flew in specially for the concert.' She remembered Monaco. 'I don't think Karl likes him very much.'

'It was strange. Vonheim started to slag him, but instead of backing off, Richmond sounded as though he was doing the threatening, telling Karl that he might regret what he was saying. He looked like a cornered rattlesnake.'

'What then?'

'Vonheim told me to stay away from you. In fact, he warned me.'

'Warned you? Why?'

He shrugged. 'I don't know. I think he was just trying to get the message across, but he made it sound very sinister.'

'God!' Her fingers were interlaced in his. 'I tried to explain to Karl. I told him you'd decided not to write that book. I thought he believed me. I hoped he'd feel better about you.'

'He's not going to feel better about anyone who comes near you. Don't you understand? You're letting the man control your life.'

'It's not like that. Karl's kind and generous. He does everything for me. I still can't believe that someone like him can give up so much of his time and attention to help me. I owe him everything, Peter. I sometimes feel I'm his creation.'

He spoke quietly. 'No. He didn't create the pianist I heard this evening. Nobody can do that. He gave you the freedom to study and work, and he offered you new thoughts and ideas about what you played, but the rest came from you. Don't turn him into some sort of a god, Francesca. He didn't create you, and he doesn't own you.'

She shook her head. 'You don't understand. He isn't like that. I wish you could see us together. Don't be jealous.'

'I'm not; believe me. Won't you leave Chateau Beethoven for a while? Come and live in the real world.'

'I can't.'

'Why not? You can't spend the rest of your life shut away with Karl Vonheim.'

'I don't intend to.' She chuckled. 'You make me feel like a character in a fairy story. I'd better grow my hair longer so you can climb the tower!'

'I'm not joking. I wish I were. When will you leave?'

'When it's right. We're going to appear together soon. After that, he won't expect me to stay. Don't you see? I owe it to Karl to fulfil his belief in me. It's my way of repaying him.' She leaned forward so that her cheek touched his. 'Let's not talk about it any more, Peter. We have so little time to be together.'

He sighed. 'You're right, and I'm sorry. He seems to overshadow everything we say to each other. Would you like a drink?'

'No. We had champagne back at the hotel.' She smiled 'You-know-who insisted on vintage Dom Perignon. I drank a lot.' She leaned closer. 'Did you say your hotel was opposite?'

'Yes.'

'Let's go there now. We have some unfinished business from Thun.' Her voice became a whisper. 'I want you!'

In the hotel room they faced one another. Her raincoat slipped to the floor. 'I suddenly feel a little shy.'

He kissed her. 'Shall I turn off the lights?'

'No.' Her fingers fumbled with the buttons of his shirt, and her hands stroked his chest and shoulders. 'I want to see everything!'

She was wearing nothing beneath her shirt, and Peter stooped to kiss the space between her breasts. She held his head closer, moaning softly as his mouth explored her flesh, and trembled when his lips moved to arouse her nipples. For a moment, he wrestled with the buckle of her belt, and she giggled. 'Need any help?'

'I seem to be managing. I'm out of practice!' His hands caressed her and, as his face moved lower, his tongue searched and tasted.

278

She gave a sudden intake of breath as her senses responded to his embrace. He savoured the earthy perfume of her body, and she writhed sensuously, her breathing growing rapid. Then he lifted her in his arms.

'You'll hurt yourself!' She laughed as they fell together on the bed, and her arms enfolded him. 'Oh Peter, I've wanted you so much! Ever since that first day, when . . . ' The words were cut off as his mouth found hers, and his fingers touched and teased until her body strained against him with mounting excitement. 'Oh, now! Don't wait! Now!' As he entered her, she pressed herself closer, arching her back to draw him deeper. She felt herself starting to climax and called out, her hands clutching his shoulders, unable to repress the involuntary paroxysm that swept through her. His movements complemented her own, and he responded, thrusting deeper until, with a sudden cry that combined anguish with pleasure, he seemed to explode inside her. He lay very still, deep within her, his face against her shoulder, as the compulsive spasms that racked her body slowly ebbed.

When her breathing had returned to normal, Peter kissed her tenderly. 'You're so beautiful . . . and exciting . . . ' He kissed her again. ' . . . and delicious!'

He moved to lie next to her, but she held him. 'Stay where you are.' Her legs clasped him gently.

'I'm heavy.'

'That's what I like.' She sighed contentedly, her fingernails lightly scraping against his back and shoulders. 'It didn't feel like the first time for us. I guess I thought about you so often and wanted you so much that I'd imagined it all before.' She smiled. 'I got it wrong. It was much better than any of my erotic little fantasies!'

'I wish you'd stayed in Thun. Then we wouldn't have lost all this time.'

'Maybe. Now I'm glad I didn't. Waiting for you made tonight all the better.'

After a while, he lay at her side, watching her. She pretended to pout. 'Are you leaving me already?'

'No. I want to look at you: memorise every part of you.' His hands caressed her body slowly.

'You have.' Her fingertips traced the lines of his eyes and mouth. 'When you touch me, I feel as though you know where to find every secret place and nerve-end in my body.'

279

'I'm only just beginning to discover them.' Her breath quickened again as the tip of his tongue explored the aureoles of her breasts, and his hand cupped the gentle curve of her stomach.

Her voice trembled as he searched lower. 'You know what's going to happen if you do that?'

She could feel his face move against her skin as he smiled. 'I have a rough idea.'

She reached down to touch him. 'So I see!'

This time they made love slowly, moving together languourously to prolong the pleasure, but quickening passion inflamed their senses and desire was beyond control. Their cries blended, and they lay breathless in each other's arms, laughing like children.

Later, Peter turned off the lights and they talked in whispers, exchanging memories and recalling moments they had spent together. The darkness was like a warm blanket.

He cradled her in his arms. 'You must sleep. It's been a long day.'

She snuggled against him. 'The most beautiful of my life! What time is it?'

'About three.'

'Then sleep with me.'

'No. I'd rather hold you. I don't want to lose a minute of this night.'

She smiled happily, her eyes already closed. 'You're very romantic. I like that. Maybe we should set an alarm. I'll have to leave about five-thirty.'

'Do you have to go?'

'Yes. I have to be back in my room before anyone wakes.'

'You could call them tomorrow morning and say you'll be there by noon.'

'I can't, Peter. You know that.'

'I suppose I do. One day, it's going to be different. You'll just fall asleep in my arms, and we won't need to think about tomorrow. Let's not wait too long for that.'

She did not reply and, by the evenness of her breathing, he knew that she was sleeping.

He woke her gently a little after five. Grey light filtered through the curtains.

Francesca opened her eyes and smiled. 'Now you know what I look like in the morning. I have no secrets left!'

'Nor I.' He held her. 'In case you're interested, you look more beautiful than ever. I'll take you back to your hotel.'

'No. I'd rather go alone. Stay and sleep.'

'When will I see you again?'

Her face was sad. 'I don't know. Karl has a tour coming up. He's doing a whole lot of guest appearances. I don't know whether he expects me to go with him. I doubt it. He was talking last night about choosing our concerto for New York. I'll have to start working on it.'

'Come to London with me. You can work there.' She shook her head. 'He's not even going to be around, so you won't be missing anything. You could . . . '

She placed her fingertips on his mouth to silence him. 'I can't, Peter. I have to go. Please be patient with me.'

'It could be weeks before we're together again.'

'I know.' There were tears forming in the corners of her eyes. 'I've been trying not to think about it.'

'Then why stay with him?'

'I must. Please help me.' For a moment, she held him tightly. 'I want to be with you more than ever, Peter, but I can't. Please say you'll wait.'

'You know I will.'

'I'll call you, and write. I'll be thinking about you all the time. It may sound stupid, but I don't think it really matters if we're not together for a while, as long as I know you'll be there when it's over. Does that make sense? After that, I'll be with you for as long as you want me.'

'Do you mean that?'

'Yes. Just go on wanting me. Please!'

'How long?'

'We're heading towards the end of October now. I'll be playing in Bergen at the beginning of January.'

'Christ! That's two months!'

'I know, but they'll pass quickly enough, if we want them to. I can't get away before then.' Her voice was pleading. 'Say you'll wait for me!'

He held her in his arms. 'I'll wait.'

At the door, she clung to him for a moment. 'I'm sorry, Peter. Don't be angry with me.'

281

'I'm not angry.' He drew her close. 'I love you, Francesca.'

'Oh.' She closed her eyes. 'I was afraid you weren't going to say it.'

He smiled. 'Why? I thought it was obvious.'

'Because I love you too. I have for a long time. That's why it hurts so much!' Before he could speak, she pulled herself free, and ran from the room.

Heavy curtains made the living-room of the hotel suite dark. Francesca felt along the wall for a light switch. As she was doing so, the door to Vonheim's room opened, and she saw a shadowy figure momentarily silhouetted against pale light. The door closed again, and she found the switch. Erich, in a dressing-gown and pyjamas, was standing there. He blinked slightly in the sudden glare and stared at her in surprise.

Francesca spoke first. 'What are you doing here?'

The man paused before replying. 'The maestro needed some refreshment. He couldn't sleep.'

'Oh. Are you staying here?'

'I have the room next door.'

'I see. I didn't know.'

He spoke softly. 'I always stay nearby.'

'Oh.' She was aware that he was watching her with a curious expression. 'I couldn't sleep either. I went for a walk.' He did not reply. 'I'll try to doze for a while.'

'Would you like me to leave instructions not to call you too early?'

'No.' She replied quickly. 'I'll manage. I slept earlier on.'

'Very well.' He padded past her in slippers and let himself out of the room. Much later, when she was in her own room, Francesca wondered why the maestro had not taken a drink from the bottle of Evian water next to his bed.

25

Richard Templeton's office, overlooking Russell Square, was furnished like the reading-room of a small but exclusive gentlemen's club. Bookcases filled two walls, and there were heavy armchairs and a sofa upholstered in dark leather. An upright reading desk, which might have belonged to Charles Dickens, occupied a corner of the room, and an ornate but dusty chandelier hung from the ceiling. Beneath the window, a shelf was littered with files, books, magazines, typescripts tied together with coloured ribbons, and assorted trays of correspondence. He worked, however, behind a circular Sheraton desk whose surface was completely bare. From the rich patina of the wood, it looked like a genuine antique, which might have explained its pristine state, and to avoid damaging the deep polish, a telephone stood on a small cabinet next to his chair.

'It's terribly kind of you to come over at short notice. Can I offer you some coffee?' As before, he gave the impression that his summons was an imposition.

'No, thank you. You sounded worried on the phone.'

'Did I?' He peered over the tops of his half-glasses. 'Perhaps intrigued would be a better word. I sometimes think I should have devoted myself to crime fiction. I love a good mystery.'

'What's happened?'

The editor carefully rested his elbows on the surface of the table, his fingertips touching. 'I'm afraid our little secret didn't last very long. You may remember that I mentioned our affiliation with an American publisher?' Peter nodded. 'Myron Kirschbaum, the President of Farsight Publications in New York, seems to have let the cat out of the bag.'

'I heard that Karl Vonheim had learned about the book. As a matter of fact, he confronted me on the subject last week in Paris. He was very angry about it, to put it mildly.'

'Oh dear. Perhaps I should have said that our Mr Kirschbaum set the cat among the pigeons. It's resulted in what might be described as discreet harrassment for the past couple of months.' Templeton's brow furrowed. 'I can't think what prompted Myron to telephone Mr Vonheim in the first place, except that he does love to mingle with the rich and famous. He obviously misunderstood my conversation with him. I thought I was being diplomatic at the time. I should have spelled out the situation in words of one syllable.' He shook his head sadly.

Peter restrained his impatience. 'What sort of harrassment?'

'It started off with a phone call from Gregory Richmond. I expect you remember him from Vienna.'

'Very well.' Peter smiled. 'He invited me to come and see him next time I'm in New York. He hinted that he might have a job for me.'

'As a writer?'

'No. He used some general phrase about finding a place for me in his organisation. I think he was trying to buy me off because of those embarrassing questions about his handling of Vonheim's business affairs.'

'Yes. I do recall the exchange. Anyway, Richmond called Myron and, without actually threatening him, made it very clear that he was getting into deep water if he had anything to do with a book about his client. He didn't say anything specific, but the words libel and lawsuit kept turning up in the conversation. It was all very polite, but with somewhat sinister undertones.'

'That sounds like Richmond. He's a powerful man in his own field. No matter what they say, most musicians do their best to stay on friendly terms with him.'

'Possibly, but I wonder whether his influence extends to the world of publishing. American laws covering libel give the author a great deal more freedom than our own. It made me wonder what you could write about Mr Vonheim that could give rise to such an accusation.'

'I can't think of anything. What happened next?'

'Nothing, for a while. Myron forgot all about it. Then he received a phone call from some lawyer, who told him that Richmond had asked him to get in touch. He wanted to know whether we still intended to pursue the publication of the book.' He looked up for a reaction, but Peter remained impassive. 'Myron called me in something of a panic, saying that he didn't want to find Farsight Publications in the middle of an expensive legal dispute. He was in favour of dropping the whole project.'

'On the strength of two phone calls?'

He shrugged. 'Legal disputes in America can go on forever, and cost a fortune. According to Myron, sales predictions for the book did not warrant the time or the expense. I'm afraid music is not one of his interests. However, I reminded him that, despite our association, we enjoy a certain autonomy in this country and, as far as I am concerned, that you and I have a signed agreement that I propose to honour. I also assured him that we are perfectly capable of editing sensitive material, should there be any, so that it cannot be regarded as offensive.' He sighed. 'I think our American colleagues are inclined to forget that we have been issuing books for a great deal longer than they have.' Peter was about to speak, but he continued, 'Then, after another silence of several weeks, something rather unexpected occurred. Mr Richmond called again. This time, he was most cordial; couldn't have been more friendly.'

'I understand that's when he's at his most dangerous.'

'Ah.' Templeton took a moment to digest the information. 'You could be right. He called to say that Mr Vonheim had decided, after some deliberation, to write an autobiography and would begin working on it almost immediately. He was therefore passing on this fascinating information to Myron so that we would avoid the emabarrassment of producing a book which, by the time it appeared in print, would be completely overshadowed by the conductor's own testimony.'

'Bullshit! When did he call?'

The editor seemed shocked by Peter's outburst. 'About two weeks ago. Is it important?'

'Very. I saw Vonheim in Paris last week, and he made it clear to me that he had absolutely no intention of revealing anything of his personal or public life to anyone. He was in the process of calling me a sleazy little muck-raking journalist from the tabloid press, when Richmond intervened to stop him from making a scene in front of strangers. After that, he bit off Richmond's head for daring to interrupt him, and the two of them had a fight.'

'What fun!' Templeton suddenly smiled. 'Curiouser and curiouser! Tell me, have you started to write anything?'

'Not yet. I've been meaning to talk to you about that.'

285

'Oh?'

'I'm in a rather ticklish situation at the moment.' Peter could feel himself colouring. 'You see, I've given my word to Francesca Noble, the young pianist who . . . '

'I know who she is.' The smile had faded.

'I told her I wouldn't work on the book for the moment.'

'You've set it aside?' His voice hardened.

'Not exactly. Vonheim told Francesca my . . . friendship with her was motivated by the hope of digging up information about him. He was very persuasive. It wasn't true, of course, although I admit I did ask her a lot of questions about him. I know you talked about gaining his confidence through her, but I now believe that any interest I show in her will infuriate him further. He's warned me to stay away.' Templeton watched him in silence. 'Vonheim's a dangerously possessive man and has a very unhealthy hold over her. We've become . . . close, and I had to persuade her that I wasn't using her. It was important.' He paused. 'I told her I wouldn't write the book, if that was what she wanted.'

'Oh.' The editor blinked. 'Then you're not going to write it?'

'Not immediately.'

'I don't understand what you're trying to say.'

'I know it sounds as though I'm hedging my bets, but I want to delay work on the book for two or three months. You see, she's living with the Vonheims at the moment. In February of next year, she'll make her international debut with him, after which she'll feel free to leave the house and lead an independent life. Once she's no longer directly under his control, I can convince her to let me go ahead.'

Templeton was silent for a moment. 'I'm not happy about this development. What if she still doesn't want you to write it?'

'It won't be a problem.'

'I hope you're right. There's something rather odd about this whole situation. I don't enjoy being threatened, however gently, and I don't like the pressure they've been putting on Myron in New York. I was hoping you would step up your efforts. In fact, I want to make a public announcement about the biography in the trade press. Since Vonheim knows already, there doesn't appear to be any further reason to pussyfoot around. I'm interested to see how he'll react.'

'I'd rather you didn't.'

'Why not?'

'First of all, he'll close up like a limpet, and forbid anyone to talk to me.'

'From what you've said, he'll do that anyway.'

'Perhaps, but I don't see any reason to bait him. He's always resisted any intrusion into his privacy.' He paused. 'My main reason is that I don't want to go back on my word to Francesca.'

'On the other hand, you have signed a contract with us. Forgive me, but I don't fully understand what you have promised. Has she actually asked you not to write this book?'

'Not in so many words. I offered to stop.'

'But only provisionally? In two or three months, you hope to start again?'

'Yes.'

'And in the meantime?'

'I'll continue to work on him. We're talking about a short delay.'

'What will you do if Miss Noble still asks you not to write? You say that Vonheim exerts a great deal of power over her.'

Peter hesitated. 'I'd prefer to cross that bridge when I get to it.'

Templeton sighed. 'Very well. We'll do it your way. I'm disappointed. I prepared a delightfully provocative press statement, but I suppose it can wait. When do you hope to see Miss Noble again?'

'Not until the beginning of January. She has a concert in Bergen, which will be useful. It should give me an opportunity to do some research into Vonheim's childhood. He grew up in the mountains not so far from there. His family was wiped out during the war, but there could be some relatives.'

'Very well. It will be November next week. What will you do in the next two months?'

'Keep going. I want to contact some people I know in Munich. That's where he began conducting. He worked with a very distinguished old conductor who found himself in bad odour after the war. I'd like to look into that. Despite his reticence, I've built up quite a history on Vonheim. I have several thick files at home: one filled with reviews of his concerts over the years; another with articles about him, and a third with ideas and impressions of my own. The picture's beginning to fill out nicely.'

'Good. Have you got a title for the book?'

'Not really. I like "Karl Vonheim – The Ultimate Maestro", but I thought I should leave it to you. I do have one other suggestion. I wondered whether you might like to write to him. It occurred to me that you could point out that this is a respectable publishing house, interested in producing an accurate and suitably serious biography, with no wish to peddle sensational or distasteful material. A word from you might make him feel better. I'd be prepared to submit the manuscript to him for approval, if he wants.'

'Perhaps. It's not a bad idea. If you'll leave his current address with my secretary, I'll think about it. I can't help wondering whether he isn't trying to hide something. Otherwise, why is he so secretive?'

'I'm not sure that secretive is the right description. He's just a very private person. Even when he's rehearsing a full orchestra, he objects to the kind of public examination to which most public figures are subjected. It's become almost a fetish. You saw him at the conference in Vienna. It seemed to me that he was prepared to answer questions when they were put to him.'

The editor looked doubtful. 'He didn't appreciate inquiries about his wife. As Myron would say, he clammed up rather abruptly.'

'She's part of the private world he wants to protect. You can't blame him.'

'You sound sympathetic.'

'I think I am.'

'Despite the way he's treated you?'

'I've tried to look at it from his point of view. After all, apart from a couple of uneasy meetings, he doesn't know me from a bar of soap. All he does know is that I've been chatting up his protégée. British journalists don't have the best reputation in the world. Which reminds me that I ought to look through the music magazines dating back to his early years in London. Maybe he wasn't quite such a recluse in those days. I can't imagine that Lancelot Gordon would have wanted to keep him tucked away. It's a shame he died a few years ago. He could probably have told me everything I wanted to know.'

Templeton rose to indicate that their meeting was over. 'It sounds to me as though you've got plenty to keep you busy in the next two months. Please keep me advised.'

'I will.' They shook hands. 'I'm sorry about the delay.'

'It's not very serious.' He permitted himself a bleak smile. 'In matters of personal affection, one can make all sorts of rash promises!'

Peter hurried towards his flat in a quiet road bordering Camden Town's high street. It was after five, and Francesca sometimes chose that time to telephone him. The sky was already dark, and a thin drizzle of rain made him turn up the collar of his raincoat and lean into the wind. He disliked the city in autumn. The damp and the mist made him discard any thoughts of mellow fruitfulness.

The bulb in the hall had gone out, and he cursed under his breath, feeling his way up the staircase. It was a sturdy old Victorian building, converted into flats, and the caretaker was not very efficient. Fortunately, a light on the top floor provided enough illumination to guide him, and he fiddled with the key to his front door. There had been several burglaries in the neighbourhood, and the other residents had agreed to replace their old-fashioned mortice locks with newer models. He entered the flat, removing his raincoat, and reached to turn on the wall switch.

For a brief instant, his eyes took in the scene. The living-room had been ransacked. Drawers had been pulled from the desk, their contents strewn on the floor, a chair was overturned, the pictures hung at eccentric angles, and cushions from the sofa had been scattered. As he stepped forward, an angry exclamation on his lips, he failed to hear the swish of sound as someone hit him at the base of his skull. He was conscious of a movement behind him, the sudden blow which made him stagger forward, and a flash of white-hot pain. His assailant struck him a second time, his senses reeled, and his legs refused to support him. He fell heavily against an armchair, unconscious.

There was an insistent throbbing in his head, which sent punishing shocks through him. For a moment, Peter lay absolutely still, sprawled across the arm of the chair, waiting for the internal thudding to stop. As his senses returned, he was aware that, somewhere in the distance, a telephone was ringing. It seemed to be the cause of the hammering pulse inside his brain, repeated with each ring of the bell. He revived slowly and with care, afraid that any sudden movement would amplify the pain. As his thoughts came into focus, the sound of the phone grew louder, and he realised that it was his own instrument, standing on the top of the desk a few feet away. He opened his eyes cautiously, wincing as bright light burned them, and willed his limbs to respond. At first, they would not, and he rolled from the chair to the floor, using his hands to break his fall, and lay face-down on the carpet. The phone stopped ringing, and he remained immobile, trying to regain control of his body.

After a few minutes, he raised himself on one elbow and, using the chair to support himself, stood. The room swayed drunkenly round him for a moment, and his neck and shoulders ached, but the sharp twinges had dulled, and he was able to totter to the kitchen and put his head under the cold water tap. Exploring the nape of his neck gingerly, he was relieved to find no blood on his fingers.

When he felt steadier, he walked to the kitchen door and surveyed the room. Nothing appeared to be broken and, at first glance, nothing was missing. The television set stood in the corner and green digits on the videotape recorder indicated that it was 5:20. He calculated that he must have been unconscious for less than ten minutes. His glance took in the contents of his desk drawers, scattered like debris across the floor. His camera was there, as well as an expensive gold cigarette lighter that dated back to the days when he had smoked. On the reading-table by the bookcase, an antique brass carriage clock ticked quietly. The thief had apparently taken nothing, and he wondered whether he might have surprised the intruder and frightened him off. The flap of the desk was open and, next to his typewriter, he could see that papers and envelopes, unanswered correspondence and bills, had been thrown aside as if by a wilful child. His eyes continued to search through the mess, making a mental inventory and looking for the absence of some familiar possession. Then, quite suddenly, he realised what was missing. The three Karl Vonheim files were no longer there.

He moved unsteadily across the room, peering amid the discarded items, but he knew, long before he reached the desk, that they had been taken. Years of collected material: old concert programmes, photographs, magazine articles and record reviews that he had carefully preserved, together with his more recent notes and lists of subjects that might be of interest; they were all gone.

He sat for a moment, staring at the keys of his typewriter. Someone had removed all trace of Karl Vonheim. He – or she – must have been leaving the flat when he had walked in. Hearing his key in the lock, the thief only had to stand behind the door and, as he entered . . .

He wondered vaguely whether the telephone call that had revived his senses had been Francesca. If only she had rung a few minutes earlier! Peter hesitated. What was he going to tell her? He had promised to set the book aside. Would she understand when he explained that he had continued to gather material?

It no longer mattered. For a moment, he felt despair, and then a wave of anger swept through him. Who did that arrogant bastard think he was? What right did he have to . . . ?

After checking in his address book for the number, he dialled Templeton's office. The editor's secretary connected him.

'This is Peter Meredith. I've been thinking about your press release. Go ahead and issue it!'

'Ah. Well, perhaps we should wait a little longer. I like the idea of sending the great man a letter. I should have thought of that myself. If he thinks . . . '

'Write if you want to. I don't give a shit what he thinks!'

'Really?' Templeton seemed shocked by his vehemence. 'I thought . . . '

'I've changed my mind. Listen, I'm going to write this damned book anyway, no matter what anyone says or does!'

'I see. And Miss Noble?'

'She'll understand. She'll have to!'

There was a pause before Templeton spoke again. 'I'm surprised. However, I'm also delighted to hear the news. If I'm not being too inquisitive, what made you change your mind so dramatically?'

'I'll have to explain at another time. I just thought I'd let you know.' Peter replaced the receiver without waiting for the editor to speak again.

26

When Gregory Richmond saw his secretary hovering by the door, he motioned to her to come forward. He was in the midst of a telephone conversation, apparently listening. She placed a leather correspondence folder, filled with newly-typed letters awaiting his signature, on the desk. Still holding the receiver against his ear, he read each one quickly, added a scribbled signature, and returned the documents to her. Then he cupped his hand over the mouthpiece.

'Goodnight, Shirley. I won't be in before lunchtime tomorrow. I'm seeing the Russians in the morning.'

'OK, Mr Richmond. Enjoy your concert.' She smiled when he shrugged nonchalantly, and left the room.

On the other end of the line, Mel Strich's voice had increased in volume by several decibels. 'Shit, Gregory, you're crucifying me! Here I am, paying this friggin' broad a goddam fortune, and now you're telling me I don't have the home video rights!' When Richmond said nothing, the record executive continued, 'You can't sell her out from under me like that. We have a contract.'

'Which doesn't include video rights. I removed the clause. Check it with your boy in Business Affairs.'

'I did. When you and I talked about it last time, you said there wouldn't be a problem. Now you're telling me I can't have her. Why not, for God's sake?'

'Because Miss Noble signed a deal with Telmusik. They have distribution of all her video material.'

'And if I record her for discs, they can still make movies of the same repertoire?'

'That's right.'

'So give me the home video distribution on the movies. You control the goddam company!'

'I've already offered them to you.'

'Yes, but for what? I can't afford to pay that kind of money! Jesus Christ, you've already got me over a barrel on the audio deal!'

Richmond spoke smoothly. 'You didn't have to sign her, Mel. When you heard her in Paris, you said you wanted her. I turned down offers from other companies.'

'Maybe, but you didn't warn me you were going to film her playing the same stuff. I want exclusive rights, goddamn it!'

'You have them.'

'Not if you sell those goddam videos to someone else.'

Richmond purred. It was the sort of situation he enjoyed. 'I've already offered them to you . . . '

'At an asking price that's five times as high as the record deal. It means I'm paying six times over to protect my own investment. That's blackmail!'

'No it isn't.' He spoke calmly. 'Filming's expensive. It involves all sorts of technical costs that you don't have to think about. You're not obliged to buy.'

'But you'll offer them elsewhere.'

'Naturally, if you won't take them. Telmusik has to recoup its investment. There are plenty of interested parties. I've already been approached.'

'And they're prepared to pay that kind of money?'

'We haven't reached a final figure. I thought you'd want to put in your bid first. After all, you've got more to protect.'

'Now wait a minute! Are you trying to tell me you're offering that stuff elsewhere for less?' His anger seemed to have reached bursting point.

'Not necessarily. It depends what else goes into the agreement.' He smiled contentedly. 'Maybe you'd like to reconsider my original proposal.'

Strich took a deep breath. 'Look, I already told you. We can't afford the Vonheim movies. The deal on him is crazy! By the time we finish paying, it would take twenty years to make our money back. My people would never buy it. Nobody would!'

'Oh, I don't know. The Japanese are very interested, and they're determined to corner the world market. Of course, they see the institutional advantages, not to mention the kudos. As a matter of fact, I had a call from Tokyo this morning. They said . . . '

'I don't give a shit what a bunch of goddam Japs had to say! You can't do this to me!'

Richmond's voice hardened. 'I'm afraid you're wrong, Mel.

When it comes to video, I can make any deal I choose. If you're not interested, say so, and I'll make alternative arrangements.'

There was a slight pause. 'I didn't say I wasn't interested.'

'I've told you the terms. Now, we can either make a deal for Francesca Noble alone, or we can talk about a Telmusik package. If that's what you'd like, the royalty would be a little steeper, but you'll have access to some of the Vonheim movies . . . '

'Some? I thought you were offering all of them.'

Richmond chuckled. 'I don't think Magnum could afford that, but I'd be prepared to consider an offer.' He paused to add weight to the next sentence. 'Of course, when Francesca makes her debut with the maestro next February, that's a different ball game. Whoever has the rights to Karl gets her as a bonus.'

From the spluttering sounds at the other end of the line, Mel Strich appeared to be having an apoplectic fit. 'You're going to film them?'

Richmond kept his voice light. 'I certainly hope so. It's going to be a major musical event. I've been talking with WNET about it. They're hoping that with some support from WGBH in Boston they can . . . '

'But I've already booked a recording for the following day. You can't do this to me!'

'I don't see why not. On the other hand, maybe we can work something out.' Having dropped his bomb, he spoke quickly. 'I must run. I have a concert tonight, and I want to go home first. Why don't you think it over and give me a call some time tomorrow afternoon? You'll want to talk to your people about it.'

Strich ignored the comment. 'You didn't tell me about this.'

'Didn't I? There's nothing definite yet, of course, but I fully expect it to go ahead. The Japanese were very interested. They were talking about some sort of satellite link-up.' Strich was about to reply, but he continued, 'We'll have to talk about it tomorrow, when you've had a chance to explore all the possibilities. Goodbye.' He replaced the receiver.

By the time he had reached the street, Richmond had forgotten Mel Strich and Magnum Records. As far as he was concerned, they were small potatoes, and Karl kept the lion's share of any of the income. It had been a pleasant diversion to string Mel along, seeing how far he could tantalise him. He had already accepted the Japanese offer.

294

He was more concerned with Germany. Earlier in the day, Hans Wolpert had called from Hamburg. There were serious changes on the way, and it might soon be necessary to re-think the situation concerning Eastern Europe. Berlin was a powder-keg, and Hans had been receiving daily reports that the wall was about to come down. If that happened, God knew what it would do to all his carefully laid plans for 1990. During the summer, he had made several trips to East Berlin and Dresden, bargaining with the local bureaucrats for tours by two orchestras and an opera company. Each would net a very handsome profit for U.S. Artists, and it worried him that any change in the political climate could affect his plans. With the exception of Karl Vonheim, Richmond seldom bothered any more with individual musicians, except for courtesy appearances at an occasional dinner or reception. The corporation had enough managers and divisions to look after their needs, leaving him free to organise major international tours by groups and companies which generated profits far in excess of anything enjoyed by solo performers. A recent visit to Japan by a European ballet company had brought a net income of more than a quarter of a million dollars. If someone was going to upset the Eastern European applecart, it could result in serious losses and involve months of negotiations with a new cast of characters. Richmond was not interested in politics, unless they conflicted with his plans. With any luck, the East Berlin police would quickly put down any demonstrations that got out of hand.

He was distracted by these thoughts when he drove his car from the parking lot, and scarcely acknowledged the salute from the young Puerto Rican who controlled the exit barrier. His parking space was rented on a monthly basis, but he often tipped the kid on the way out. He directed the Cadillac towards Central Park in heavy traffic, leaving sufficient space for yellow taxis, their horns bleating, to duck in and out like boxers weaving and feinting for a superior position. He admired their arrogant impertinence. At a red traffic light, he leaned forward to turn on the radio in case there was any change in the news. So far, it had all been rumours. There were flecks of snow in the rain, and he turned on the wipers. For early November, the weather was bad.

He took the 72nd Street exit to the East Side, waiting patiently as the rush-hour flow of traffic edged its way towards the lights. He was only a few blocks from his apartment on Park Avenue, with

plenty of time to wash and change for the concert. He was a fastid-
ious man and disliked going from the office to the concert hall
without changing suits. It would be a dull evening, which would
give him breathing-space to think through a number of current
problems. A newscaster droned monotonously, and he was relieved
to hear that there had been no change.

The Dutch conductor he would hear that evening was a boring,
taciturn man, but he was developing a good reputation, and Richmond had arranged to take him and his dumpy wife to dinner
afterwards. One of his minions would be there to supervise the
entertainment and talk to them, giving him a chance to assess the
man's social acceptability and decide which orchestra he should
direct. Depending on various factors, there were at least three
middle-ranking American orchestras that would be needing new
music directors, and since he represented all three of the departing
conductors, it would be a simple matter to substitute the Dutchman.
Richmond knew that the boards of each orchestra relied on him both
for patronage and for a supply of the better soloists represented by
U.S. Artists. Despite their supposed power to vote for the new man,
they would accept whomsoever he chose as replacement. It was an
influence he enjoyed, and he settled himself comfortably in the
driving seat, mentally sorting out the possibilities.

As he turned left into Park Avenue, a voice behind him whispered,
'Keep going. Drive on past your building.'

Richmond was shocked and would have looked back to identify
the intruder, but cold metal, placed firmly against his cheek,
prevented him from turning his head. The car was moving quite
slowly and as he jerked at the steering-wheel a taxi swerved to miss
him, blasting its horn derisively. 'Who are you? What do you want?'
He looked into the rear-view mirror, but found that it had been
twisted out of position.

'Just drive.' The pressure on his cheek increased slightly. 'This is
a gun, if you didn't know it, and it's silenced, so keep your eyes on
the road. I'll tell you where to turn.' The voice was muffled but
sounded vaguely familiar. For the moment he could not place it.
'I'll be moving back, out of sight, but don't try anything clever. I
can just as easily shoot you through the back of the seat.'

Richmond tried to remain calm. There had been endless police
warnings about muggers. Don't fight them. Give them what they

296

want. Don't risk your life for a few bucks. 'Look, if you want my money, you can have it. There's a billfold in my pocket.' He started to reach inside his jacket.

'Leave the money where it is.' The voice was little more than a husky whisper. 'Make a right on 96th Street and go up the Drive.'

Traffic was lighter than usual on the East River Drive and he accelerated to stay in the flow. As they passed one of the exits to Harlem, he asked, 'Where do you want to go?'

'Up the Deegan.'

'Why?' He was about to look round but decided against it. 'Look, I've got an appointment this evening. Can't you just take the damn money and go? There's a couple of hundred dollars, and my credit cards ...'

'Just keep driving.' The voice was slightly scornful. 'You'll have to be late for your appointment. And don't talk. We have a long drive ahead.'

'Where are we going?'

'Katonah.'

'Katonah? Good God, that's miles! Why the hell are we going there?'

'I'll tell you when we get there. Now shut up and drive!'

'Won't you at least tell me what this is about?'

'You'll know when we get there. Just drive. You can leave the radio on.'

They travelled the length of the Major Deegan Highway, one of the main arteries heading north out of the city. The rain had become heavier, but the queue of cars and trucks moved steadily. Towards Yonkers, the traffic thinned a little as commuters took various exits. As they approached the toll booths on the New York Thruway, the man spoke again.

'Just remember what's pointing at you back here. A bullet would go straight through the seat and break your spine, so don't get any smart ideas. I'm not afraid to do it. Understand?'

The menace in his voice was chilling, and Richmond found that he was gripping the steering-wheel so tightly that his arms were trembling. His nerves were tightly stretched. 'Won't you explain? We could work something out.' His voice was pleading. 'I won't make any trouble for you.'

'Keep going, and there won't be any trouble. Do you have change?'

He felt in his pocket. 'Yes.'

'Good. Pay the man and keep going. Take the Cross County, and go north on 684.'

'Please! Can't you be reasonable?'

'Just shut up and do it!'

The Cross County Parkway was busy with commuters, and he stayed in the right-hand lane, driving at a slower pace. He considered various possibilities. Should he throw the car into the grass verge, and jump for safety? There was a chance that it would take the man by surprise. He rejected the plan. The car was big and, despite its powerful engine, cumbersome. If the man was pointing a gun at him, he would not have time to open the heavy door and leap out. His body was held in place by a seat-belt. There was no way of releasing it without drawing attention to the fact. Richmond stared out of the window, almost hypnotised by the rhythm of the windscreen wipers. His body was damp with sweat, and he wiped his face with the back of his hand.

Route 684 was comparatively empty, with wide spaces between the vehicles. 'You don't have to crawl. Use the accelerator!'

'I'm sorry. I'm not good in bad weather. The rain . . . '

'The sooner you get to Katonah, the quicker we can be finished.'

He accelerated, moving to the outside lane, and the big car picked up speed. What was it about the man's voice that sounded familiar? Maybe it was his accent. He spoke like an American and yet it did not ring true. Was it to disguise his identity or was he a foreigner; a European who had settled in America some years earlier? The car was travelling at seventy miles an hour, over the limit. A new idea occurred, and he gently pressed on the accelerator, edging the speed up to eighty. At this time of the evening, with the heavy flow of cars, the police were frequently on the look-out for dangerous drivers.

'Slow down.' The voice was almost bored. 'If you're hoping to bring in the cops, I'll finish you now.'

Richmond eased his foot back, and a new thought struck fear in him. What did he mean by 'now'? Had he used the word in place of 'later'? His voice was shaking. 'We're almost at Katonah. Won't you tell me why we're going there? What do you want?'

'I'll explain in a while.' He sounded more reasonable. 'When we get there, make a right and head for Pound Ridge. You know where it is?'

'Yes.' The Pound Ridge National Park was a favourite tourist spot, not far from the centre of Katonah.

'OK. Listen, you're doing fine so far. It won't take much longer.'

Richmond relaxed for a moment. For the first time since the journey had begun, the man sounded quite pleasant. 'Do I know you?'

The gruffness returned. 'Just drive!'

When he left Route 684, he found himself on a smaller country highway, and there were few cars travelling in either direction. The rain had stopped and the heavier clouds had lifted. Glancing past trees to his right, he could see occasional reflections in the water of a reservoir that bordered their route. His headlights picked up the last of the brown and yellow leaves still on the branches of trees, and the tarmac was covered with a thick carpet of late autumn foliage. It was a beautiful, tranquil area, populated by wealthy landowners. Large houses, set well back from the road, commanded views across substantial tracts of land, most of which had been left to grow wild.

'Slow down. We're almost there.'

He reduced his speed to a gentle pace, following the curving, narrow strip of road that wound round the reservoir. At one moment he pressed on the brake pedal suddenly when the headlights of an approaching car blinded him. They came towards a clump of trees growing by the water. A grassy border, ten feet wide, stretched towards them.

'Park here. That'll do fine.' The man spoke quite gently.

Richmond brought the car almost to a halt, then edged into the grass. A wire fence indicated where the water began. He could see another car, already parked, about twenty yards away. Its lights were turned off and he wondered whether he had been brought to the place for a secret meeting. But why at gun-point? He sat, with the engine running, awaiting the next instruction.

'Good.'

'Should I turn the engine off?'

'No. We won't be long. Maybe you should kill the lights.'

'What happens now?'

'We walk the rest of the way.'

'Where to?'

'I'll show you. Get out slowly, and head towards those trees.' He paused. 'Don't try to be a hero.'

As he released the seat-belt and turned towards the door, Richmond looked round. For a moment, he was shocked. The man was wearing a black woollen ski-mask, with slits for his eyes and mouth. It made his head grotesque. The rest of his body was hidden beneath a dark raincoat, and he was wearing gloves. He motioned with the gun. 'Keep going.' It was a small, old-fashioned revolver, with a circular chamber to hold six bullets. The long tube of the silencer looked out of proportion with the rest of the weapon.

He stepped out of the car and shivered as cold air met him. Under foot, the grass was soaked. His shoes seemed to sink into it. He wondered whether he should break away and start running. If another car appeared from either direction he could aim towards it, waving for help. The road remained silent and empty.

'This way.' The man was waiting by the front of the car. Although it was dark, there was still enough light reflected from the water and the night sky to see his outline clearly. 'You go first.'

They walked through the trees towards the water, stopping at the edge. He found himself standing on a small spit of ground on which gravel had been tipped. The road was no more than a few yards away but they were hidden behind the trees. The man stood nearby, gazing across the reservoir, and pulled his ski-mask off. He seemed to be speaking to himself. 'Nice place.' Richmond stared at him, but there was not enough light to distinguish his features. He was shaking with cold.

'Are you going to tell me why we're here?'

The man spoke mildly. 'In a moment. I was just enjoying the clean air.'

A distant car was moving down the road towards them, its headlights occasionally visible between the trees. Seeing it, the man moved closer, raising the revolver so that the end of the silencer touched Richmond's right temple. He flinched, but the man stayed next to him. 'Stand very still.'

'But why . . .?'

'Quiet!' He hissed the word sharply.

The car passed them slowly, its lights throwing strange shadows through the trees. Richmond looked at his captor. The lights momentarily illuminated the place where they were standing.

He recognised the man. 'My God! You!'

A moment later, they were plunged into darkness again. The end of the silencer touched his temple.

The man seemed to chuckle. 'Good-bye, Mr Richmond!' He squeezed the trigger.

The silenced gun made very little noise in the open air, and the bullet passed through Richmond's brain, taking part of his skull with it as it exited. He made no sound and fell, face-down, on the gravel. For a moment, his body twitched, then was still.

The man leaned down and carefully fitted the gun into Richmond's lifeless hand. Pointing it towards the water, he pressed the dead man's finger so that it fired a second time. Then he produced a small torch and, using a pencil, removed one of the spent cartridge cases from the chamber and put it in his pocket. He replaced it with a fresh round of ammunition, then placed the revolver on the ground, next to Richmond's hand. He adjusted its position, so that it appeared to have fallen from the dead man's grasp. He let the beam of the torch explore the area round his feet and, having satisfied himself that there were no footprints, switched it off and made his way back to the road by a different path.

The motor of Richmond's Cadillac was still running, and he opened the door and reached in to turn it off. He left the key in the ignition and pushed the door shut. Then he walked quickly down the road to where the other car was parked. The engine came to life immediately and, having checked that no other vehicles were nearby, he turned on the lights and drove away.

27

Gisela looked into the living-room to make sure, yet again, that everything was tidy. She had already checked the room twice that afternoon and, on each occasion, had found some small detail that needed attention. The flowers in the Chinese vase by the window were arranged perfectly, the magazines on the coffee-table positioned to give the impression of being casually scattered, and the silk cushions on the settee were free of wrinkles. She nodded to herself. As good as anything you'd find in a magazine! She walked over to the baby grand piano and, taking a duster from the pocket in her apron, wiped its varnished surface to remove specks of dust that had settled. Black was an impossible colour!

On the mantelpiece, there was a silver-framed photograph of Günther, and she paused to admire it. It had been taken the previous month to celebrate his fifteenth birthday. He was so handsome! He had posed for a photographer who specialised in portraits of professional musicians, and he smiled out of the picture, slightly self-conscious, cradling his precious violin in his arms. The instrument had cost a small fortune, but it was worth it. She polished the glass protecting the photo, which looked just like the cover of one of his record albums, except that she thought Günther looked more sensitive and 'artistic' than most of the musicians in his collection. His delicate features and long hair were 'poetic', and she indulged in a familiar daydream: Günther walking onto the stage of a famous concert hall to be greeted by thunderous applause. This evening would be the first step towards that moment.

She made a mental check-list of her preparations. The cakes and biscuits were set out on plates in the kitchen; she had ground fresh coffee ready for the machine and she had washed all the best china and glasses. Her guests were due to arrive at eight o'clock and, if everything ran with the precision she hoped for, Günther and Erwin would begin their recital by nine. There would only be a dozen people, including Günther's violin teacher and Erwin's parents, which made it easy to handle. However, they had persuaded Herr Weissman, a junior music critic on the *Hamburger Morgenpost* to come and, notwithstanding his teacher's enthusiastic reports, Günther would now be playing for a professional journalist whose opinions carried weight with the public. It was almost as good as a real concert and, if the programme was a success, Herr Weissman might even be persuaded to write a letter of recommendation. How proud Max would have been!

She checked the entrance hall again. There were enough coat-hangers to accommodate all the visitors. That was the sort of small detail that gave people a thoughtful first impression. The house was not large, but substantial enough to create an appearance of refined taste and unostentatious wealth. After Max died, she had set aside plans to buy the mansion in Hochkamp, but had chosen a good neighbourhood, better than the old one, and had been readily accepted by the other families in the street. It had been easier than she suspected to shed all the trappings of the Reeperbahn. Now that she had learned to drive, there was a new Audi 100 in the drive outside. She saw no reason to buy a more expensive car, and it would not help Günther's career if she appeared too pushy. A grandfather clock struck four and, satisfied that everything was in place, she returned to the kitchen to watch the television.

It was extraordinary. All those happy faces, slightly bewildered, as thousands of East Germans poured across the border, free to travel unhampered. Strangers embraced them and thrust bottles of champagne into their hands, families were reunited, and the young people sang and danced. Gisela felt a lump in her throat, and tears formed in her eyes. She had turned down the voice of the television commentator, and was content simply to watch the now-familiar images, endlessly repeated in regular bulletins. She had never thought much about politics. Germany had always been divided and, because she had no relatives living on the other side, she had seldom considered the situation. As far as she was concerned, East Germany was another country, on the wrong side, and although Max had talked about it, she had never listened very carefully to what he was saying. With a house to run and a son to look after, what did she need to know about things like that? When the news had broken, and those amazing pictures of people dancing on the Berlin wall had flashed across the screen, she had watched with Günther, drawing pleasure from his excitement. He had told her that both Leipzig and Dresden possessed wonderful orchestras, and her first thought had been that, by the time he was ready, he would be able to include them in his concert tours. At the supermarket, one of her neighbours had hinted darkly that the changes could mean higher taxes and unemployment in the future, but she had not been concerned. Everyone was so happy! Old Mangelsdorff had assured her that she and Günther would be financially secure for many years. Her money was safely invested and, provided she did nothing foolish, she would never have to worry. Trust that poor old buzzard to assume that she might suddenly go off the rails! Besides, in a few years Günther would begin playing professionally, and their income would grow by leaps and bounds. Concert artists made a fortune once they were established. Maybe, when Günther had become a household name, they would move to Hochkamp, and she would realise her only other ambition. The bulletin ended, and she switched off the television. If only Max had lived to see it all happen! She lit a cigarette, and settled back to daydream a little longer. Günther was not due home until five.

At five-thirty, she became a little uneasy. Günther had not arrived, which meant that her schedule was beginning to run late. She had prepared a sandwich for him, after which he was to wash and change. His fellow student Erwin had arranged to come round at six-thirty for a final run-through, allowing her to change into the new dress she had bought for the soirée, and still giving her time for a last-minute clean-up in the living-room. The boys were quite tidy, but they were young enough to be careless, and everything had to be perfect for her guests. She lit a cigarette and, leaving it in the kitchen so that the smoke would not permeate the hall, she walked through the house and opened the front door, looking down the street for any sign of her son. He had gone into the city and she wondered whether there had been any problems with the S-Bahn. Back in the kitchen, she turned on the radio. One of the local stations broadcast traffic and travel news. A few more minutes passed, and she felt growing concern. Günther was unusually punctual for a boy of his age. It was not like him to be late, especially on such an important day.

She heard the front door open and close, and ran out of the kitchen. Günther was in the hall. 'There you are! I was begin-

304

ning to worry.' She saw the expression on his face. 'What's wrong?'

The boy was pale and his hair was dishevelled. He seemed distracted. As she approached, he turned away and started up the stairs. 'Nothing.'

'What is it? What's the matter?' Gisela felt a tremor of concern.

'Nothing. Leave me alone!' His feet pounded on the staircase.

'There's a sandwich for you. Don't you want it?'

'No.' He entered his room and slammed the door. A moment later, she heard the key turn in the lock.

She hesitated. Perhaps the boy was nervous. In the past, before school recitals and end-of-term concerts, he had always been unexpectedly calm – like a professional! – but maybe this was different. They had discussed Herr Weissman's visit several times, and he had seemed unconcerned, but it was possible that the importance of the journalist's presence had affected him. Feeling guilty, she blamed herself for making so much of it. After a moment of indecision, she climbed the stairs and knocked on his bedroom door.

'Go away!' His voice was muffled.

'That's no way to talk to your mother. Are you all right? Is something the matter?' There was no reply. 'Open the door.'

'No!'

'What is it?' Silence. 'What's wrong?'

'Leave me alone!'

'Please tell me.' She waited, but he did not reply. 'It's getting late. I've made you a sandwich, and . . . '

'I'm not hungry!'

She paused. If the boy was nervous, he wouldn't want to eat. He had once told her that some of the other students, waiting to perform, had been so worried that they had thrown up. 'If you'd rather not eat, it doesn't matter. You can have something later.' She rattled the handle. 'Please unlock the door.'

'No. Go away! Leave me alone!'

'But what's wrong?'

'I don't want to talk to you!'

'Why? What have I done?' She remembered her hours of preparation. 'You don't have to act like this, Günther. Open the door and let me in.'

'No!' The word was shouted.

Anxiety made her temper quicken. 'Stop this nonsense! It's getting late. Erwin will be here in less than an hour, and you have to wash and change.' There was no reply. 'What's going on?'

'Just go away and leave me in peace!'

'Why? What's the matter with you? Listen, people are coming to the house. If you're not ready by the time they get here, you'll be sorry. Are you going to open this door or not?'

'No!'

She decided to bargain. 'Will you at least wash and change? I want you ready in half an hour.' She waited. 'Well?'

'I'll do it in a while. Now go away!'

'All right. I'm going downstairs. I'll be back in ten minutes, after which I want to see you dressed and ready. I don't know what's got into you! And please unlock this door. Understood?'

After a long pause, he said, 'Yes.'

'We haven't got time for this sort of behaviour; not tonight. I'll be back.'

In the kitchen, she lit another cigarette. What the hell was going on? It was so unlike Günther. She paced back and forth, dragging smoke into her lungs. Why, of all times, did he have to choose now to play the temperamental artist! After a minute, she felt calmer. It was probably just nervousness. Later, they would joke about it, and she would tease him. She removed cling-film from the sandwich and poured a glass of milk. As an afterthought, she put some of his favourite chocolate biscuits on a plate, and transferred everything to a tray. She shook her head slowly. Kids! Even so, he didn't look well.

When she returned to Günther's room, she found, to her relief, that he had unlocked the door. Dressed in a sports shirt and an old pair of jeans, he was lying on the bed. His violin was on a chair, beside him. Günther glowered at her, but said nothing.

His face was very pale, and there were damp streaks beneath his eyes. He looked as though he had been crying. He was trembling slightly but trying not to show it. Gisela avoided his gaze. She pretended not to notice anything unusual. 'Haven't you changed yet? You'd better get a move on!' She made her manner cheerful. 'I've brought you something to eat in case you change your mind.'

'I don't want anything.' His manner was more subdued than before.

'Suit yourself. You'll be hungry later. If you're not careful, your tummy will rumble all the way through the Mozart!' She glanced at him and he looked away. 'What's wrong?'

'Nothing.'

He was lying on his back, staring at the ceiling. For all his poise, he was still a child. In many ways he was young for his age. The room was filled with possessions from earlier years: stuffed toy animals, plastic model aeroplanes, boxes of board games. He had insisted on bringing everything with him from the old house. He had even installed the hooks in the ceiling that were designed to hold his old swing, although he had never used it.

'There must be something the matter. It's not like you to behave like this. What is it?'

He hesitated. 'I can't talk about it. You wouldn't understand.'

'Of course I would. I'm your mother.' She moved towards him, and he drew away, pressing himself against the wall. Gisela stood back, shocked by his reaction. Her voice softened. 'What is it, love? You can tell me.'

He was close to tears. 'I can't.'

'Why not?'

'Because . . . because it's so horrible!' He began to cry, but when she again moved to comfort him, he flinched, putting up his hand to indicate that she should keep her distance.

'Horrible? What do you mean? Has something happened to you?' He did not reply, by she could tell by his expression that her question had struck home. 'Tell me.' He shook his head. 'Where were you this afternoon?'

'I went to . . . ' He shook his head and was silent again.

'Yes . . . ?'

He took a deep breath, as though reaching a decision. 'I went to the concert hall.'

She kept her voice matter-of-fact. 'What was going on there?'

'A rehearsal.' He spoke with difficulty.

'I see. Are you allowed to watch?' It occurred to her that he might have been in trouble with some minor official. They were always throwing their weight around! He was a sensitive boy, and hated to be reprimanded. Once, when he was several years younger, she had lost patience and shouted at him. It had upset him painfully, and she had regretted her outburst for days. Her own childhood had been

307

orchestrated with violent quarrels and abuse. Günther's frightened reaction to her anger had shamed her.

He spoke again. 'Students are supposed to go to rehearsals. We're allowed to sit at the back, so we don't disturb them.' He stopped again and she was conscious that she needed to persuade him to speak.

'How did it go?' He shrugged. 'Did you enjoy it? Was anyone with you?'

He looked at her suspiciously. 'What do you mean?'

'I don't know. One of the other boys. Don't you usually go with your friends?'

'Yes.' Günther seemed lost in thought. 'I was alone today.'

She waited, aware that the time was passing. Erwin would arrive in about half an hour. 'Then what?'

He was having difficulty in bringing himself to speak. 'Someone came and . . . came and . . . sat next to me.'

'Who?' He shook his head, refusing to say. 'Another student?'

'No.'

'Then who? A man? Someone from the orchestra?'

'A man.'

'Did he talk to you?' Günther nodded. 'What did he say?'

'He asked if I was . . . if I was a musician. I said I . . . I played the violin.'

'All right.' She waited.

'We . . . we talked for a while. He said he . . . he knew lots of musicians. He said maybe he . . . he could help me. We had to . . . to whisper, because of the rehearsal. He . . . he asked me lots of questions.'

'What kinds of questions?'

The boy shrugged. 'What I played. What sort of . . . of music I liked.' For a moment, his eyes met hers; then he quickly looked away. 'He was . . . nice to me. I thought he was being . . . being friendly.'

A gnawing suspicion was growing in her mind. Oh God! Don't let it be something like that! Gisela tried to keep her voice calm. 'What then?'

Günther had stopped crying, but his body was occasionally racked by convulsive spasms. 'He . . . he said we couldn't talk properly, because of . . . because of the rehearsal, so why didn't we

308

go . . . go outside. He said there were . . . there were plenty of rooms where we could . . . could have a proper chat.' He made an effort to control his emotions, and she could see the muscles in his jaw working.

'Go on.'

'We walked round to the . . . to the back of the hall, where the . . . the dressing-rooms are.'

'What did he say?'

'He talked about . . . about Berlin. He said . . . said it was a wonderful time in our history!' There was anger in his voice.

'I see.'

'We went into . . . into one of the dressing-rooms.'

'Oh?'

'He said we must . . . we must celebrate. He had a . . . a bottle of something to drink, and . . . and some glasses. He said we must . . . we must drink to the new . . . the new Germany.'

Gisela closed her eyes. 'What sort of drink?'

'I don't know. I think he said it was . . . it was whisky. It was very strong. It made me cough.'

'What happened then?'

'He poured some more. I didn't want . . . want it, but he said I must because of . . . because of what had happened in Berlin.' He paused for a moment. 'It made me feel dizzy and a bit sick.'

Once again, Gisela moved towards him, but he shied away like a frightened animal. His rejection was painful, but she kept her voice calm, and spoke gently. 'Try and tell me about it.'

There were tears on the boy's cheeks, and he spoke with difficulty. He was in severe shock. 'We . . . we drank some more, and he . . . he put his arms round me and . . . and hugged me. He said we must . . . must celebrate . . . celebrate the . . . ' The memory of the experience grew stronger. 'He . . . he kissed me and . . . and touched me!' Revulsion brought a convulsive shudder, and he was silent again.

She waited, but he would not speak. 'Tell me.'

'I tried to . . . tried to leave, but he'd locked the door. I said I . . . He wouldn't let go of me! He . . . '

Her voice was quietly insistent. 'Tell me. You must tell me. Get it out of your system. Tell me!'

Günther was crying freely. He was . . . he was . . . very strong. I . . . I tried to get away, but he . . . he wouldn't let me go. He held

309

me, and . . . he . . . he hurt me! I couldn't . . . He hurt me!' His voice
had risen. 'He hurt me!'

There were tears on Gisela's cheeks. 'Oh my God! The bastard!'

She reached for her son, but he backed away, shouting, 'No!
Don't touch me! I don't want you to touch me! I don't want anyone
to touch me!'

'I want to help you. Don't be frightened. I won't hurt you, I
promise!'

'No! Stay away!'

'Who was he? Do you know his name?' Günther said nothing, but
stared at her, a wild expression in his eyes. 'Tell me! Who is he?'

'I can't!'

'Why not? Tell me who did it!'

'It's no good. Nobody saw us. I told him . . . I told him I would
tell . . . would tell . . . ' For a moment, he could not speak. 'He said
they . . . they wouldn't believe me. He said . . . he said nobody
would believe me. I couldn't . . . couldn't do anything.' For a moment, he sobbed. 'He hurt me!'

Gisela tried again. 'Let me see. Let me . . . '

'No!' He shrank from her. 'Don't touch me! Stay away!'

She watched him, afraid to move. 'What happened to you?'

'He left me there. He said one day . . . one day . . . I'd understand.' His eyes were filled with pain. 'But he hurt me!'

'Günther, tell me who did it. You must tell me! Do you know him?
Do you know who he is?'

The boy was weeping. 'They won't believe me!'

'It doesn't matter. I believe you. Tell me his name!' The boy
shook his head.

Looking at the wall by his head, Gisela noticed that a picture was
missing. In recent years, Günther had taken to pinning souvenirs on
the wall: pictures taken from magazines, publicity photographs of
his favourite artists, concert leaflets and other memorabilia from the
music world. One had been torn loose, leaving only drawing-pins
to mark the space it had occupied. Her eye travelled across the
carpet, and she saw the missing picture – a page from a music
magazine – rolled into a tight ball. It had not been there when she
had cleaned the room that morning. She had hoovered the carpet
when she made his bed. Günther must have removed the picture
since returning home. Moving on her hands and knees, she re-

trieved it from the floor, unrolling and flattening it. Günther watched her.

'Why did you tear this . . . ?' A thought struck her. 'This picture; is he in it? Answer me! Is the man who . . . Is he in the picture?' From his expression, she knew. She glanced down, and saw that it was a photograph of a group of people, apparently taken outside a concert hall.

'Throw it away!' There was fear in the boy's eyes. 'Stop asking questions! Leave me alone!'

'You can tell me . . . '

'No! I don't want to tell you! Leave me alone! Go away!'

Ignoring him, she spread the picture flat and examined it. Her eyes focused on one of the faces and, as recognition dawned, she felt the room around her begin to sway. A pulse beat in her temple. She was still kneeling, and had to reach out with her good arm to support herself.

She recognised him. It was the man from the Reeperbahn who had beaten her. He was older than she remembered, but she knew him immediately. Gisela closed her eyes, and the pounding in her head increased. She looked at the face again. There was no doubt.

Günther was watching her. She held the picture in front of him, a few inches from his eyes. 'Was it . . . ?' She could barely speak. 'Was it . . . ?'

Günther looked at the picture. If Gisela had watched the direction of his gaze, she would have seen that he was not looking at the man she had recognised, standing with the group in the foreground. His attention was held by a shadowed figure at the back of the group, apart from the others. It was a middle-aged man, slightly balding, dressed in a black jacket and grey trousers. He was holding the door of a limousine, apparently waiting for his passengers to enter.

'Tell me!'

'Leave me alone! Go away! Leave me alone, and get out of here!' He was crying hysterically. The full force of the shock had hit him, and he shouted, 'Get away! It's all your fault!'

'My fault?' She stared at him, puzzled. 'What are you saying?' For an insane moment she thought he was talking about the Reeperbahn. 'What do you mean?'

'It's your fault! Everything's your fault! I never wanted to be a musician! You forced me! You made me stay home and practise and

... I never wanted to ... !' Tears mingled with spittle from his mouth. 'They laughed at me, made fun of me! It was your fault!'

'No! It wasn't ... '

'They hated me; called me names! They said I was a sissy and a ... baby ... and a ... a ... ' He could not bring himself to say the word. His thin frame was shaking with sobs and he suddenly looked at her with hate. 'You made me! You told me I had to ... I never wanted it!'

'No! I thought you ... '

'It's your fault; your fault! If you hadn't forced me, I wouldn't have been there! He would never have ... never have ... ' He broke the stream of words to cry out in anguish.

'No!' She was on her hands and knees. 'You don't understand! You mustn't talk like that! Listen to me. Please listen to me!'

'It's your fault!' Günther reached out blindly. His hand siezed the neck of his violin and, using all his strength, he swung the instrument in a wide arc and struck the wall with it. The violent impact caused it to crack and he swung his arm again. Gisela watched, horrified, as the violin shattered into fragments. Screaming unintelligibly, Günther smashed it again and again, until nothing was left.

28

When Peter awoke, light was filtering through a crack in the curtains. The sun, reflected by the snow, was very bright, illuminating the hotel room. It was still early but he could hear a low rumble of traffic outside. The Norwegians took full advantage of their limited daylight hours.

Francesca had turned away from him during the night and lay on her side with the lower half of her body pressed against his. She had thrown off the heavy duvet, and her naked back and shoulders moved in slow accompaniment to her even breathing. They had talked and made love into the small hours, falling asleep in contented exhaustion; he did not remember when.

Awakening to find her there filled him with a wave of tenderness and he stroked the smooth, firm skin. She sighed in her sleep, edging closer, and his arm encircled her, his hand on her breast, to draw her to him. He inhaled the perfume of her body as his fingertips caressed her, tracing the tiny folds surrounding her nipple. Closing his eyes against the light, he let his head fall forward until his lips touched the nape of her neck. It tasted slightly salty.

For a while, he dozed peacefully, but he was physically aroused by her presence, and his hand cradled the warm flesh, his fingers feeling the nipple slowly harden. A flickering of desire stirred him, and his hand moved lower, shaping itself to the sensuous swell below her navel. The depth of her passion was thrilling, and she had given herself totally, using hands and mouth and body to excite him more completely than any other woman he had known. He searched deeper, massaging slowly, and his fingers curved around damp softness, rekindling sensation. For a moment, he thought she was still asleep, and lay still, but she reached back to touch him and, as she re-positioned herself, to guide him into her body.

Later, when her breathing calmed and his own heart-beat had returned to normal, Francesca stretched luxuriantly, twisting her

313

head so that her lips could touch his. 'What a lovely way to wake up!' She kissed him, her mouth lingering. 'Good morning!'

He smiled. 'It sure as hell beats an alarm clock. Do you want to sleep for a while?'

'No. What time is it?'

'Not yet eight.'

'I'm hungry!'

'Shall I call room service, or are we permitted to be seen together in the dining-room?'

'We can eat downstairs. It's not immoral to break bread together.'

'That depends whether the waiter notices how I'm looking at you. The Norwegians are very proper about such things. They're not like the Danes.'

She lay on her back. 'I had a little talk with Zoltán yesterday morning. I explained about us and asked him not to interfere.'

'What did he say?'

'He wasn't very happy at first. He was afraid of what Karl would say, but I told him Karl knows about you and has come to accept the idea that I was going to go on seeing you.'

'He has?'

She giggled. 'Not really, but Zoltán doesn't need to know that. I just told him we'd be very discreet and asked him to act likewise. He argued a bit, but then he came round. After all, what more could a Hungarian from Vienna ask for than a little secret intrigue?'

'I wondered why he was so friendly after the concert last night.' He kissed her. 'On the other hand, how could he refuse you when you gave him that dewy-eyed look?'

'He didn't go along with it a hundred per cent. He's caught between having to play bodyguard and fight you off, or face Karl's displeasure. So he decided to compromise and turn a blind eye.' She hesitated. 'I think he was following us yesterday, after the rehearsal.'

'When?'

'While we were sight-seeing, down by the harbour and the fish market. You know how you get the feeling that you're being watched? It was the same when we were window-shopping on Strand Gaten.'

'You should have told me. I didn't see him.'

'Neither did I, but I had this feeling that someone was following us.'

'Maybe it was guilty conscience. Your friend Karl's got you brain-washed.'

'Let's not talk about it.' She left the bed and stood, naked, by the window, peeping through the curtains. It was only minutes since they had made love, but the sight of her stirred Peter again. 'It's such a beautiful place. I thought Switzerland was great, but this is unbelievable! I adore those wooden houses down by the water. All those reds and browns and yellows, they're like the fall colours back home. Don't you love that snow?'

He sank beneath the warm duvet. 'I prefer to look at it from in here!'

'It reminds me of our house in Roxbury. Will you come and see it one day? I want to show you where I grew up.'

'Of course. I want to know everything about you.'

'You do already.' She took the little Victorian pendant that he had given her as a belated Christmas present, and fastened it round her neck. 'You knew I would love this. Are you sure you want to give it to me? It belongs to your family.'

'As far as I'm concerned, that includes you from now on.'

'Oh.' For a moment, she was silent. 'I'll always wear it.' Then she smiled and struck a pose, letting the pendant hang between her breasts. 'How do I look? Am I suitably attired for breakfast?'

'Perfect. Anything more, and you'll be overdressed! Are you sure you want to eat downstairs? It's more fun in bed.'

She shook her head. 'I'm starving. I hate room service, when everything arrives half cold.'

'You're always hungry!'

'We didn't eat last night.' She returned to him. 'You seem to have forgotten that we dashed out of the Grieghalle as soon as the concert was over and came straight here.'

'I thought that was what Karl expected you to do.'

She joined him under the duvet. 'He does, but not for what we had in mind!'

At breakfast he asked, 'Where is the maestro at the moment?'

'New York, for a couple of days. He wants to supervise all the final plans for our concert.'

'Does he have to do that himself?'

She shrugged. 'Everything's upside-down at U.S. Artists. Ever since Greg Richmond committed suicide, the place has been a mad-house. He doesn't trust the new man.'

'Who's taken over?'

'Howard Erlich. He used to be Greg's chief gofer. I met him in Monaco once. He had some glitzy merchandising scheme, using Karl's name, but it was shot down. According to Karl, there was a real battle in the boardroom, with half a dozen contenders trying to take over. He called it a thieves' carnival. Nobody expected Erlich to come out on top. I guess he knew more about Greg's plans than any of the others. I still don't understand what drove Greg to it. It must have been terrible for his family.'

'Who knows?' They had talked about it several times on the phone. 'It made no sense, but he may have had all sorts of personal problems we know nothing about. It would be hypocritical of me to express any real sorrow. I didn't like him, but I wouldn't wish that on the people he left behind.'

'It's made life very difficult for Karl. He depended on Greg more than he realised. Now he's talking about pulling out of U.S. Artists altogether and putting Zoltán in charge of everything, but he's worried for my sake. Greg was looking after my American concerts, and Karl's afraid Erlich will cancel them if he quits the manage-ment.' Her hand covered Peter's for a moment and he knew that she was offering a further defence of her sponsor. 'He's so thoughtful and unselfish where I'm concerned.'

'Are you sure?'

'Yes. He told me that nothing must stand in the way of my career. He'll work out a deal with Erlich.'

Peter nodded in acceptance. After a pause he asked tentatively, 'Will you stay on for a few days?' He had put the same question several times before.

She was silent for a moment. 'I can't, Peter.'

'Why not?'

'I promised Karl I'd go straight back to Lausanne and work on the Schumann. You know I'd rather stay. I can't.'

'You have nothing to work on. You played it superbly last night.'

She shook her head. 'That was just to make sure I got the notes right. As soon as he gets back we have to start studying in earnest. He's talking about cancelling everything for the next three weeks

316

so that he can be with me every day. Do you realise what that means? Ever since the events across Europe in the last two months, he's been asked to conduct every kind of gala and charity concert. He was supposed to be in Berlin next week and Budapest the week after, with two concerts in London to help raise funds for the Romanians. According to Zoltán, Wolpert's been deluged with requests and invitations. Everyone wants Karl!'

'That's hardly surprising. They'd want him even if nothing had happened.'

'I know, but it means a lot to him, too. He's been very moved by all the changes. I've never seen him quite so emotional. He told me he never believed any of it would happen during his lifetime. He talks about a united Europe beyond his wildest dreams.' For a moment, her face was sad. 'If it weren't for me, he'd be out there every day.'

'But the concerto doesn't need changing. You're not going to play the Schumann differently, are you? It couldn't have been better.'

'I don't know. Karl and I have talked about it a lot since we decided to do it. In some ways, it's the hardest piece I know. Karl says I have to make up my mind whether it's a lyrical, romantic work, like an extension of Chopin; or a noble, heroic concerto, looking forward to Brahms. Both views are totally different, and yet they're both right. I still can't decide.' She looked at him. 'I guess, knowing you were in the audience, it got to be the romantic version!'

'I'm glad.'

She smiled ruefully. 'One thing's for sure. Those goddam arpeggios in the last movement are killers! I'll never get them smooth enough!'

'I think you should play it the way you did last night. It's got to be your interpretation; not Karl Vonheim's.'

'It will be. He's already said he'll accept whatever view I have, but he wants me to consider all the possibilities.'

'Doesn't that make it more confusing than before?'

'No. It's the way we work together. We make a fantastic team; at least, he's a fantastic conductor, and he makes me play better than I knew how.' She smiled. 'Without him, who am I? I think he chose it because that was how we first met. You know, he's really very sentimental when you get under that cool exterior.'

'In that case, you see something that escapes the rest of us.'

317

'Don't be angry, Peter.' Her voice was pleading. 'I know how much you admire him.'

He sighed. 'It's true. I liked him better when it was from a respectful distance. Perhaps he's right to remove himself from the world. Closer acquaintance doesn't make him more loveable!'

'Don't say that. He means so much to me.' She saw his expression. 'It has nothing to do with us. These last twenty-four hours have been so . . . so perfect. I don't want to spoil it by arguing with you about Karl.' She smiled. 'I was going to tell him Simon's story about Barenboim and Mehta, but I thought I'd better leave it to another time. I don't think he's forgiven Simon yet.'

'Then why did he allow him to come back?'

'Because I asked him. I told you, he's very generous.' She watched his face. 'Please be patient, Peter. It's not going to be for much longer. After New York, it will all change.'

He spoke softly. 'Are you sure of that?'

'Yes. If it's what you want, I'll come to London.'

'You know I want.'

'Then we're talking about a few weeks. I wish it were now! Will you be able to get to New York?'

'I think so.' Templeton had already approved the expense. He sighed. 'I hoped you'd stay a little longer. I've hired a car.'

She chuckled. 'If I stayed, we wouldn't need one. We have that wonderful, comfortable bed . . . '

'Don't remind me!'

' . . . and the people would let me use the piano in the hall to practise, if you ever let me go for more than ten minutes! Oh well, I can dream too! Where would you want to drive?'

'I thought we could visit Troldhaugen and look at Grieg's house. It's a museum, furnished the way it was when he lived there. If you've only got one national composer that anyone's heard of, you have to make the most of him!'

'Could we do that this morning? My plane isn't until the afternoon.'

'I suppose so. It's more or less on the way to the airport.'

'I'd like that. I guess there's lots more to see, like the Edvard Munch collection and that funny little funicular railway, but we'll come back. The conductor's talked to Zoltán about it. Yesterday afternoon was such fun, just being together and walking round the town.'

'Despite your shadow?'

'I don't know if there was one, and I don't care. I didn't want to waste time looking at anything except you.'

He smiled. 'You wouldn't by chance be soft-soaping me, would you?'

'No.' Her lips formed the words 'I love you', but she did not say them aloud. It was something they had said to one another during the night, in the dark, but she seemed reluctant to say it in the daylight. 'When will you leave?'

'Not for a day or so. I'm staying on a little longer.'

'Why?'

He spoke casually. 'I want to drive out to Fjordby. It's the village where Karl grew up; the one that was destroyed by the Germans.'

She had become still. 'Why do you want to go there?'

'I'd like to see it. I thought I'd take the opportunity to do a little research.'

'Research? I don't understand.'

Peter held her hands. 'Francesca, I want to write that book.'

'But you said . . . ' From the hurt in her eyes, she looked betrayed.

'I know. I've been trying to find a way to tell you. Listen, you remember that I told you my flat was broken into?'

'Yes.'

'I didn't tell you exactly what happened. The burglar was there when I walked in. He came up behind me and knocked me unconscious. I was out cold!'

'No! Were you hurt?' In her anxiety, other thoughts were set aside.

'Not badly: my pride more than anything else. I was on my way back from the publisher. I'd just finished telling him I was going to set the book aside.'

'Then what are you trying to tell me? You said the thief didn't take anything valuable.'

'He didn't, if you're talking about money, or television sets or things like that.' He looked at her steadily. 'The only things missing where my Vonheim files. They contained all the material I've gathered over the past twenty years or more: everything from pictures to programmes; articles and reviews. That was all he took.'

Francesca was silent, her eyes held by Peter's. After a moment, she looked away. 'What are you implying?'

'I would have thought it was obvious. The burglar wasn't some junkie, looking for a few bits and pieces that would make a quick sale. That's what most of them are. Whoever got into my flat knew what he was looking for. He didn't even try to disguise it by taking anything else.' He waited, but she did not respond. 'Somebody hired him to steal the Vonheim material. It's of no value to anyone except me.'

She spoke quietly. 'You think Karl would do that?'

'It's hard to come up with a better suspect.'

'He wouldn't, Peter. I know he wouldn't!' She spoke passionately. 'I know he's over-protective, and I know he hates the idea of anyone prying into his life, but he wouldn't do a thing like that! You don't understand what sort of man he is. He's an honourable, dedicated . . . ' She searched helplessly for appropriate words.

His voice hardened. 'Now you're being childish! Don't let yourself be blinded by misguided loyalty. Who else would have engineered it?'

'There are others – people around him – who might assume it's what he'd want. Karl would never sanction it, but they might do it without asking him. My God, after what happened in Thun, he told me he'd be prepared to collaborate with you on the book, if only to make sure it contained the truth.'

Peter was surprised. 'He told you that? You never mentioned it.'

'No. When you told me you'd stop work, I passed the message on to Karl, and he said something about not having to waste the time. He didn't want to do it, and he only offered because he was afraid I couldn't persuade you. Then, when you said . . . ' Once again, she gestured helplessly. 'I was all confused about you and about him when it happened.'

'Then who do you think arranged the theft?'

'I don't know. I suppose Hans might have done it, except that he'd be too scared to get involved. Erich, maybe, not that he'd know about it. Karl wouldn't discuss a thing like that with him.' She hesitated, remembering the hotel suite in Paris. What did Karl discuss with Erich? He had never properly explained why he had permitted him to follow her in Switzerland. Another thought occurred. 'How about Greg Richmond? Did this happen before he died?'

Peter thought for a moment. 'Yes.'

'It's crazy enough to have been him. God knows what he was thinking about before he killed himself!'

He hesitated. 'Perhaps. I had the impression that he and Karl were on bad terms when I last saw him. They had an argument backstage in Paris.'

'I know. I think he was afraid Karl was about to dump him.' She spoke quietly. 'Karl told me he didn't need U.S. Artists any more, except for me.'

Peter was thoughtful. 'He made some cryptic remarks about Karl's secrets being safe with him.'

'Then it was Greg. Maybe he thought that by stealing your notes, he was doing Karl a favour that he'd have to repay. That's the way his mind worked! I know Karl wouldn't have had anything to do with it.'

'Maybe. I admit it's possible. You can understand why I thought Vonheim was behind it.'

'Yes, I guess so, except that if you only knew Karl . . . ' Her voice trailed into silence. After a moment, she asked, 'Are you going ahead with the book?'

'I don't know. When my flat was ransacked like that, I was angry. I told the editor I would. I wanted to get back at him.'

'I understand.'

He looked at her. 'Are you sure?'

'Yes.'

'Then you won't mind if I work on it?' She did not reply. 'I know I said I wouldn't. On the other hand, I'm still not convinced. We don't know for certain whether Richmond was the one.' When she remained silent, her eyes fixed on the table-cloth, he gripped her hands tightly. 'Say something!'

There were tears forming. 'I don't know what to say, except that I love you and I want to be with you. I'm sure a man like Karl would never have been involved. I understand why you changed your mind, but I believed you when . . . .'

'I love you, Francesca. That's what I want you to believe. It matters more than anything else.'

They did not say very much when he drove her to the airport. For an instant, Peter was tempted to tell her that he would leave Bergen too. The hell with Karl Vonheim, Fjordby and the book! They mattered much less than his feelings. But he remained silent.

321

She held him very close at the departure gate. 'Will you call me when you get back to London?'

'I'll call you late tonight. I'll want to hear your voice the moment you've gone!'

'I'm sorry. I'd rather stay here with you. You know that.'

He shrugged. 'Karl's orders.'

'No. I'm going back to Switzerland because I must. It's my own decision, Peter. I made it of my own free will. You mustn't try to dominate me any more than you think Karl does.'

'I don't want to dominate you, Francesca. I love you.'

'And I love you.' For a moment, she held him. 'Oh God! Till it hurts! But you've got to trust me, and accept me as I am. I don't want to change my life just to please you. I have to see this through. I owe it to Karl and myself.'

Peter smiled. 'I've started, so I'll finish.'

She looked puzzled. 'What does that mean?'

'I was being flip. It's something that a quiz-master says on a popular TV show.' He kissed her gently. 'We'll see each other in New York.'

'Yes.' She looked at him anxiously. 'But you'll call?'

'Tonight.'

When she walked through the Customs and Immigration barrier, she did not look back.

29

Gisela closed the door to the living-room carefully, and motioned to her guest to seat himself. 'It's very kind of you to come to the house, Doctor. I greatly appreciate your taking the time.'

Dr Senn nodded curtly. 'It's no great problem. I think I explained that it's on my way home. I live nearby.' He made a mental note to charge a little extra for the consultation.

'May I offer you some coffee, or would you prefer a drink?'

'Perhaps a small whisky. It's been a long day.' He was a large, heavy man, with close-cropped grey hair. Gisela noted that the jacket of his tweed suit was neatly pressed, but the trousers were wrinkled and creased. Presumably this was because he wore a white linen coat in the surgery and the jacket hung all day in a closet.

'Water and ice?'

'Just ice, thank you.'

She left the room, and Dr Senn settled back in an armchair, glancing round. The place was comfortable and well furnished, but it had a curiously uninhabited feeling, as though she kept it only to entertain visitors. The silk upholstery and the carpets were expensive. He wondered which member of the family played the piano. The pictures on the wall were nondescript but perfectly appropriate. So what was wrong with the overall effect? Books. That was it. There were no books. Even the magazines on the coffee-table looked as though they had not been opened.

She returned with a cut-glass tumbler, generously filled, but with nothing for herself. It made him feel slightly guilty, but they had agreed when she had telephoned that it was simply for 'a chat'. It was almost a social occasion.

'Thank you.' He sipped appreciatively. It was good Scotch. 'Now, how can I help?'

Gisela seated herself on the edge of her chair, and paused momentarily. She was tense. 'I'll try not to take too much of your time,

Doctor. As I explained on the phone, my son is going through a very difficult . . . experience.'

'Yes.' He glanced at the colour photograph on the mantelpiece. 'The young man in the picture?' At first glance, he had thought it was a girl, but he had caught the direction of her gaze. 'I don't think I've met him, have I?'

'No. He has his own doctor, but he refuses to see him.' She leaned forward earnestly. 'He refuses any kind of medical attention.'

'You shouldn't allow that. How old is the boy?'

'Fifteen last October. Until recently, it was never a problem. He went for regular check-ups and all the usual things. We've had the same family doctor for years.'

'In that case, shouldn't you consult him? If he knows the boy's history, it would be . . . '

'No. Günther refuses to see him. He won't see anyone!' She hesitated for a moment, slightly embarrassed to have interrupted him. 'It's very difficult. Since my husband died four years ago, I've had to manage by myself. Günther's no longer a child, you understand. At the same time he's not an adult, but he's big enough and strong enough to resist me. I can't force him . . . ' She left the sentence unfinished.

Dr Senn watched her carefully. She had only become a patient recently. Apparently, she had lived in another district, farther away, and had decided to come to him because it was more convenient. He had seen her once, briefly, and was still waiting for her previous doctor to forward her files. She was a good-looking woman, somewhere in her late forties, who obviously did little to make herself attractive. There was something odd about her left arm. It looked slightly bent, as though there had been a fracture which somebody had not corrected properly. She seemed unduly nervous.

He took another sip. 'It's not an unknown situation. I think you'll find that boys of his age quite frequently go through a difficult, self-conscious period.' He smiled. 'It's one of the external symptoms of puberty, not unlike all those facial rashes, but slightly deeper rooted. Of course, in the absence of a father, I can fully understand the difficulty. It's so much easier to handle a sensitive change in his life when there's a man for him to talk to.'

'No. You don't understand.' She took a deep breath. 'Last November, my son was assaulted.'

324

'Assaulted? You mean attacked?'

She nodded. 'By a stranger: a man. He was sexually assaulted.'

The doctor set his drink to one side. 'You should have explained on the phone. Please tell me what happened.'

Haltingly, Gisela recounted the events as Günther had described them. He had never repeated them, but his words were etched in her mind. It was strange. In the old days, in her previous life, as she thought of it, it would have been easy enough to describe everything. The gutter language of the Acapulco Club had sufficient words to cover every circumstance. It would not have been particularly shocking. When you worked on the Reeperbahn, every form of human depravity was common currency. But this was her son she was talking about. This was Günther, Maxie's boy, whom she had loved and cherished since the day of his birth, and whom she was determined to protect from all the filth and the ugliness that she had seen. She struggled, searching for language that would not reflect her own past.

The doctor listened intently. When she had finished, he shook his head gravely. 'It is essential that your son receives medical attention immediately. His attacker could have done permanent physical damage.' He saw her recoil. 'When did you say this happened?'

'Mid-November. I don't remember the date, but I can look it up. It was the . . . '

'Good God! That's almost two months! Have you looked at the boy? Have you examined him?'

'No.' She was close to tears. 'He won't let me come near him. He blames me.'

'You? Why do you believe that?'

'It's because of his musical studies. You see, he was studying to become a violinist.' She spoke almost to herself. 'I thought it was what he wanted.'

'Yes?' He glanced at the photograph. The boy was holding a violin.

'The man who . . . This happened at a concert hall, in one of the dressing-rooms. He blames me for it. He said that if I . . . if I hadn't made him study, he wouldn't have been there, and . . . and it wouldn't have . . . '

The woman was distraught and Dr Senn interrupted. He spoke more gently. 'I understand. In a traumatic situation like this, it's not unusual for the victim to transfer blame to someone who is close to him – a friend, or a member of his family – but that's something for a psychiatrist to deal with later. I'm more concerned with the immediate physical repercussions.'

'I don't think he's physically . . . damaged. I believe I would have known by now.'

'Perhaps. Has he displayed any signs of discomfort or pain since that time?'

'No. None.'

'You're quite sure?'

'As sure as I can be.' There was anger in her voice. 'He won't let me near him!'

He kept his voice impersonally calm. 'A normal, healthy child can survive such an attack without permanent damage. You might be shocked to learn how frequently it happens. Nevertheless, it is essential that he has a full medical examination at the earliest possible date.' He opened a diary. 'We should make an appointment immediately.'

Gisela flared up. 'Don't you think I've tried? He refuses! I've begged him to see a doctor – his own doctor, any doctor! – but he won't listen to me! I made appointments, but he wouldn't go! He stayed out half the night before coming home. I was going half out of my mind! I don't know what to do!'

The doctor put out a hand to calm her. 'I understand.' He spoke quietly. 'We have to find a way.' After hesitating, he added, 'There are certain very serious health hazards to consider. I'm sorry to bring this to your attention, but sexually transmitted diseases are not always immediately recognisable. We have to consider such a possibility.'

Gisela fought back tears. 'Don't you think I have considered it? My God! I spend half the night awake, terrified of the thought!'

He waited until she had regained control of herself. 'Where is the boy now?'

'Upstairs, in his room. He just sits there, doing nothing, refusing to talk to me. I've tried everything, but he won't say a word. Sometimes he looks at me as though he hates the sight of me!' She paused again, the tears running down her cheeks. 'If I talk to him, ask him a question, he'll reply, but the rest of the time he treats me as though I don't exist.' She gestured brokenly. 'He's like a . . .

a zombie! He doesn't speak, or shout, or laugh, or cry. He just . . . is!'

'How about his school? Have you spoken to his teachers?'

'No. I called them to ask how he was doing, and they said he was the same as usual. His grades haven't changed. He's always been rather quiet in school, but he works well enough, and they haven't noticed any difference. They were surprised when I asked.'

'Did you tell them what had happened?'

'No. I couldn't.'

'Why not?'

'Because I know schools.' Her voice hardened, and Senn wondered whether there might be some memory from her own childhood. 'Teachers gossip. Someone lets something slip, without meaning to, and before you know it the word spreads like wildfire. I couldn't risk it.'

'How about his friends?'

'He doesn't see them any more. At first, they came round, asking for him, but he wouldn't go out with them. He said he was too busy, or that he had homework. I begged him to see them, but he wouldn't. So, after a while, they stopped calling. I don't know what happens during the day at school. I suppose he just keeps to himself.' Her face broke. 'He's so alone!'

The doctor listened sympathetically. He was painfully sorry for the boy. God knew what was going through his mind. It could take months, perhaps years, to correct the damage, but that was beyond his power. As soon as possible, he would get the child to a specialist. He was equally sorry for the mother. She was living through some sort of private hell, torn between feelings of terror for her son, and unexplained guilt of her own. There was something about her that wasn't right. Even her accent seemed to slip from time to time. Had she suffered a similar experience as a child? Who could tell what was buried deep inside the psyche?

At length, he asked, 'Would you like me to try to talk to him?'

'Oh yes! Please!' She seemed pitifully grateful.

'Very well. I'll see him in a minute. Maybe, if we're alone for a while, he'll find it easier to talk to me.'

'Yes. Anything you say.'

At that moment, there was a distant, muffled sound, which seemed to take Gisela by surprise. With a look of astonishment, she

327

started from her chair and rose to her feet, listening. 'D'you hear that?'

Somewhere outside the room an unaccompanied violin was playing. She ran to the door and opened it, and the music became more distinct. She stood, seemingly transfixed by the sound, and her surprise gave way to delight. 'It's Günther! He's playing! He's playing his violin!'

Dr Senn nodded. He could hear it clearly. Someone was playing the Chaconne from the Bach D Minor Partita. It was not very skilfully done, but good enough. 'Is this a new development?'

'Yes! Since that day, he's never touched the instrument again. This is the first time!' She listened again. 'He broke his good violin; smashed it against the wall. He must be playing the old one: the one he first learned on.'

'Ah.' He made another mental note to ask about the breaking of the other instrument. Gisela seemed hypnotised by the sound. 'Maybe we should let him play for a while. It could be a good sign.' She did not seem to hear him. 'I said . . . '

'Yes. Yes.' She re-entered the room, leaving the door slightly ajar. When she spoke, her voice was lowered, as if she feared that it might be heard upstairs. 'It's so good to hear him play again! D'you think it's a sign that he might be getting better?'

'It's too soon to say. I haven't met your son yet. It could be an indication of recovery. I'm afraid I can't offer you very much advice. You should leave that to a specialist. I would be happy to recommend a number of . . . '

'Listen!' Her head was turned towards the door. 'He plays so well!'

Dr Senn paused. The majestic strains of Bach's great masterpiece were distinctly audible. 'He sounds very talented.' When she turned towards him, she seemed transformed by the music. He spoke gravely. 'Tell me, do you have any idea who might have done this to your son? It's a very serious offence, with severe legal consequences. Did he know who the man was? Would he be able to identify him?'

She concentrated her attention, trying to ignore the music, and her face became sombre again. 'Yes, I think so. I believe I know who it was.'

'Have you contacted the police?'

'Not yet. I've been too concerned with Günther. I know I should have called them long ago.' She shrugged. 'He told me it would be useless to accuse anyone. There were no witnesses. He said nobody would believe him.'

'It should still be reported as soon as possible. If there were no witnesses, it's his word against the man's, but it's essential to tell them and let them make their inquiries. For all you know, the man has a criminal record. If nothing else, you might prevent him from doing the same thing to someone else.' He watched her carefully. 'You say you think you know who it is?'

'Yes.' For a moment, she looked frightened. Dr Senn was puzzled by her reaction. Was it a friend or an acquaintance? Such things had been known to happen before. Perhaps that was the reason for her own hypertense state and the hostility her son apparently felt towards her. God! There were times when he hated to find himself involved in domestic crises . . .

The music suddenly stopped in mid-phrase. Gisela raised her hand, as if calling for silence, and they waited to see whether it would continue. After a while, she turned to him. 'I don't think he's going to play any more.'

'Possibly. It's a start. This is the first time since . . . '

'Yes. It could be a good sign, don't you think?' She was patently eager for his confirmation.

'Perhaps. I would not want to give you a false sense of optimism. As I said earlier, you will need to consult a specialist.'

She closed her eyes, leaning back in her chair. 'This is the first time! It's the first tiny sign that he's returning to normal!'

'Let's hope so.' He smiled at her. 'Both the mind and the body have extraordinary recuperative powers, you know. This could be a beginning.'

'Will you talk to him?'

'Yes. I think I must. I can't promise you very much. He may still reject an outsider like me. Would you like me to go up?'

'No. I'll see if I can get him to come downstairs.' She seemed almost light-hearted. 'Don't worry. If he agrees to see you, I'll stay out of the way.' At the door she paused. 'You don't know how important it was to hear him play again!'

The doctor nodded. Perhaps she was right. When she left the room, he walked to the fireplace and stared at the photograph. It

329

was a pale, sensitive face: handsome but rather too pretty. Highly-strung. All that hair was highly unsuitable for a teenager, in his opinion. He wondered whether she had persuaded the boy to grow it so long.

Gisela climbed the staircase slowly, preparing a suitable opening sentence. Should she introduce Senn immediately as a doctor? The word might frighten Günther back into his shell. Perhaps she should say only that he was a friend that she would like Günther to meet. He was a big, fatherly man, and very sympathetic. Once they started to talk, it might work. Doctors were trained to deal with patients. She should have thought of asking him sooner. For a moment, she stopped. He had played again! In her head, she could still hear the music. It was so beautiful!

She opened the door slowly. 'Günther, I'd like you to . . .'

The thing was suspended from above. A piece of pyjama cord, tightly wound around its neck, was attached to one of the hooks in the ceiling. It was stretched to breaking-point as it held the full weight of the body a few feet above the carpet. It hung very still; lifeless. Nearby, his miniature armchair – the little wooden one that Max had bought for him when he was three – had been kicked to one side. She stared at it. A draught of air, caused by the open door, disturbed the atmosphere. It caused the thing hanging there to gyrate slightly, as though gently disturbed. Gisela looked up and, as it slowly turned, she saw Günther's face.

30

Hostile skies and an icy wind greeted Peter as he left the Norge Hotel and walked across Ole Bulls Plass, past the statue of the violinist after whom it was named. The weather reflected his mood. Without Francesca, the hotel room had been empty and impersonal, and Bergen appeared dull and lacklustre in its wintry setting. The sudden warm spell of the previous two days had melted much of the snow, leaving behind discoloured and dirt-flecked slush. He picked his way through grey mounds of ice that had been shovelled from the street.

He found a bookshop on Sverres Gatt with a display of maps in the window. The one provided by Hertz did not include Fjordby, and the pretty blonde assistant looked uncertain.

'Fjordby? I don't know it.' Her English was perfect. 'Where did you say it is?' She looked about fifteen, but he noted that she was wearing a wedding ring.

'Not far from Finse, in the Hardanga Vidda. It's the village that was destroyed in the war.'

'Oh yes?' She looked blank.

'The Germans razed it to the ground. All the villagers were executed.'

'That's terrible!' She looked apologetic. 'I didn't know.' On a road map of Norway she traced the route from Bergen to Finse with her finger. 'It's not on this one.'

'Really? I thought it was a war memorial. There's a church there.'

'I'll get a map of the area.' She returned a moment later with a large-scale ordnance survey, and spread it on the counter. 'Here it is!' Her index finger identified the symbol for a church. 'There's nothing else there.'

'That's right. Everything else was destroyed. I'm surprised you don't know about it.'

She smiled. 'It was a little before my time!'

*

331

The drive into the mountains should have been beautiful, but the overcast persisted, and Peter kept his eyes on the road, occasionally checking landmarks on the map which lay open on the seat beside him. As his route wound its way up, the snow grew deeper, its whiteness untarnished, but the tarred surface remained clear. It was the main road connecting Bergen with Oslo, on the other side of the country, but there were times when it was little wider than a country highway. The morning traffic was sparse.

It took some time to find the small track leading to Fjordby. There was no signpost, and Peter passed it before he realised that he had driven too far and was approaching Finse. He parked for a moment to check his bearings, then doubled back. What appeared to be a farm lane, cut through a forest of pines, made a gap between the trees. A wooden board, barely visible from the highway, was marked 'Fjordby – 4 KM'. The surface had been cleared some days earlier, but fresh snow left a carpet several inches deep, and he drove slowly, following the tyre tracks of a vehicle that had recently travelled the same way. Tall fir trees stood on either side, their branches partially protecting the road from snow and creating a narrow green avenue which reduced the overhead light. Glancing to the side, he could see no sign of life beneath the forest. Pine needles, generations deep, blanketed the ground, and nothing grew amid the thick grey trunks. It occurred to him that there would be an eerie silence beneath the trees.

There was a brighter area ahead. It looked like the end of a tunnel, and he accelerated slightly, feeling the wheels of his Fiat skid on the icy surface. Quite suddenly the trees came to an end and he found himself in a broad clearing, about fifty yards wide, that ran along the slope of a hillside. Ahead, he could see a small wooden church, which stood alone at the edge of the open space. Beyond it, the upper branches of trees indicated that the forest began again where the hill fell sharply away.

He stopped the car. There was something strangely unreal about the place. From the encircling trees to the church, an area about the size of a football pitch, there was nothing. The land curved gently and tufts of grass were visible through the snow, but the entire space seemed to have been cleared by some giant earth-moving machine. The church, its narrow wooden spire silhouetted against a panorama of mountains and sky, stood by itself. His eyes travelled a few feet from the edge of the road, and he was aware of a series of large, smooth rectangles in the land, which did not follow the natural contours. The snow on them was clean and even; undisturbed. He stared at them, puzzled, then realised that they were all that remained of the houses: a set of flat, concrete tombstones that marked the places where families had once lived; where they had loved, borne children, laughed, celebrated, suffered, died. This was all that remained of Fjordby. The snow provided a gentle covering to hide the scars of wounds out of which the life-blood of the village had flowed. He wound down the window, and cold air filled the cabin of the car. For a moment, it rustled the page of his map, but he could hear nothing else. It was a place of death.

He restarted the engine, and drove to the church. A small car, its bodywork rusty and dented, was parked near the door, and he assumed it was the vehicle whose tracks he had been following. Stopping next to it, he got out and stood for a moment in the brittle air. He turned to face what had once been the village, his eyes scanning the emptiness in search of a movement, but nothing stirred. The wind disturbed the trees on the steep slope on which the building was perched, and he was grateful to hear them rustle.

When he pushed open the wooden door, there was a new noise. At the far end of the church, an elderly man dressed in a heavy overcoat was slowly sweeping the floor. He heard the door close and looked up, nodding in Peter's direction.

He walked forward. 'Good morning. Do you speak English?'

'Yes. A little.' His accent was marked. 'What do you want?'

'I'm from England. I wanted to see Fjordby.'

'You see it; all there is.' The man must have been in his late sixties or seventies; it was hard to tell. 'England, did you say?'

'Yes. Do you work here?'

'I come once a month to clean the church and sweep the floor. I am the . . . ' He paused, frowning. 'What is the word?'

'Verger?'

'Yes. That would be it.' He was silent.

'Do many people come here?'

The question seemed to touch a nerve and the old man scowled. 'No. Nobody comes here any more. I am the only one. In a while, when I am gone, that will be all. It will be the end.'

'But aren't there visitors at other times; in the summer, perhaps?'

333

The man shook his head. 'There is nothing to see. The church is not so . . . unusual.' He spoke slowly, searching for words. His English was limited. 'The people don't like to come here. It is too sad. Why are you here?'

'I'm doing research for a book.'

'A book? There is nothing here for a book.' He seemed bitter. 'People have forgotten.'

'Not everyone. In England, we know about Fjordby, and how the Germans destroyed it.'

'A long time ago. Forty-five years.' He paused, remembering. 'After the war, they cleared the land, and there was a ceremony. It was a ceremony for the dead people. All the people of Finse came to it.' As if in explanation, he added, 'I am from Finse.'

'Yes?'

'Then the people forgot. Nobody came any more. It is a sad place. Not good for tourists. Now, only I come, to clean the church one day each month.' He looked round the empty interior. There were no decorations; not even an altar. High on the wall behind him, there was a simple crucifix, carved in dark wood. 'We do not lock the door. There is nothing to take, and nobody comes here.' He stared at Peter. 'What do you want? There used to be a booklet, but we do not have it any more. When the last one was taken . . . ' He shrugged.

'Are there church records? I want to make a list of people who died.'

'Why? It was a long time ago. The people have gone.'

'There was a family who lived here. Vonheim.'

'Yes. Vonheim. They lived here. They are all gone.'

'Did you know them?'

The man looked surprised. 'I? No. I did not come here in those days. I am from Finse.' He spoke as if that were sufficient reason.

Peter smiled. 'But one of them, Karl Vonheim, is a famous man. You must have heard of him.'

'Vonheim? No.' He thought for a moment. 'It is a very typical name. Norway is full of Vonheims.'

'I didn't know. This one – Karl – became a famous conductor.'

The man shrugged again. 'I don't know about conductors. I don't listen to music.' He thought for a moment. 'It was not Karl Vonheim from Fjordby. He died with the others.'

334

'No. He escaped and went on to become a famous conductor. I've seen him many times.'

'He died.' The old man spoke with conviction. 'I will show you the register.'

'What register is that?'

'From the ceremony. It was a service of remembrance. In 1945. I told you about it.' Peter nodded. 'They wrote the names of the people who died in the register. It was the last time they wrote in the book.'

'May I see it?'

'Yes. Come this way.' The man led him through a door to a small, empty vestry near the back of the church. A wooden cupboard was attached to a wall. He opened it, and lifted out a heavy, leather-bound register which he placed on the deep sill of a window facing across the forest. He wiped the dusty surface with his sleeve before opening it and leafed through the pages until the final entry. From inside his coat he produced a pair of glasses and peered at the sheet. 'That's strange!'

'What is it?' Peter looked over his shoulder.

'A page is missing. It is not here. Someone has taken it!' He was angry.

'Let me see.' Peter opened the thick ledger, stretching the pages wide, then ran his fingernail close to the centre. A tell-tale edge of paper, barely visible, indicated that a sheet had been removed. 'You're right. A page has been taken out. Who would want to do that?'

'Vandals! Souvenir hunters! Young people! They have no respect for property!' He stared at the damaged book. 'This is my respon-sibility. I will have to tell the authorities.' The ghost of an old argument seemed to come alive. 'I warned them. I told them we should keep the church locked. People have no respect!' He glared at Peter. 'You cannot see it. Someone has stolen it!' His expression suggested that Peter was to blame. 'You have wasted your journey. Anyway, Karl Vonheim died here in 1945. I remember his name.'

Peter spoke patiently. 'I think you'll find he escaped.'

'No-one escaped!' His face was grim. 'The Germans were very thorough! You're thinking of another Karl Vonheim. There must be hundreds of them in Norway.'

335

Peter turned away. There was no point in arguing with the old man. 'I suppose so. I'll have to find other records.' He walked back into the church while the man returned the heavy book to its resting-place.

At the door, he shook the verger's hand rather formally. 'Thank you very much for your help. I seem to have wasted my time. I wanted to make a list of all the names of the people who died.'

'Then look at the grave.'

'I don't understand.'

The old man treated him like a child. 'The grave! There is a grave in the churchyard, under the trees. I will show you.' He made his way cautiously down the steep, snow-covered bank of the hillside bordering the church. Then he crossed to the nearest patch of fir trees and waited for Peter to join him.

'When the Germans left, it was decided to bury all the people of Fjordby here, in a communal grave, where they fell. This is their grave.' He pointed to a small wooden obelisk, planted at the foot of the trees. Its surface was roughened with age, and part of it was barely visible beneath coarse grass that had sprung up around its base. It blended so well with the scenery that Peter hardly saw it.

The verger spoke in a low voice. 'This is the memorial. It was made from a fir tree that once stood in the village. They decided it would be right for the men and women who died here.' He grunted. 'I think they chose it because wood is not so expensive. They did not want to spend money on strangers!' He stood aside. 'You can read the names of the people who died.'

Peter leaned forward. There was a short phrase, written in Norwegian, followed by a date: February 11th, 1945. Below, in a single column, were the names of the villagers, accompanied by the years of their lives. It was difficult to read. The wood had suffered badly. Constantly attacked by the elements, its varnish had cracked, and the list, shallowly carved into the surface, was gnarled and disfigured. He worked his way down. A.J. Andersen (1896–1945); R.L. Gjierset (1889–1945). Others followed, usually in pairs: L. Halvorsen, P. Halvorsen; A. Haugland, P. Haugland; Larsen, Lindgren, Nansen. His eyes reached the bottom of the column, and he pushed the grass aside to read the remaining inscriptions. E.J. Vonheim

336

(1887–1945), I.K. Vonheim (1895–1945), and finally K.H. Vonheim (1922–1945). He read them again. There was no doubt.

'So. Do you believe me now?' The verger was watching him.

'Yes.' Peter stood back, frowning. 'I was certain the Vonheim I wanted came from here. I thought he got away.'

The old man's face cleared. 'Now I know who you mean! Karl Vonheim did survive the others.'

'Then why . . . ?'

'He was the one who crawled from the place where they were all shot. I remember now! He dragged himself from the other bodies and managed to reach the church.'

'Yes?' Peter felt a sudden excitement.

The man shrugged. 'He died a few hours later. There was no reason to put him in a separate grave. He had lost a lot of blood, you see, and he left the door of the church open. It was a very cold night.' The memory seemed suddenly to affect him and he shook his head slowly. 'He froze to death.'

Peter drove through the dark tunnel of trees leading back to the main road. He had taken a few minutes to copy down the list of names from the memorial and, after a second farewell, had left the verger standing by the door of the church. The man was still upset.

'Vandals! People have no respect. That was church property!'

He was relieved to come away from Fjordby. Despite flat space, open to the sky, it felt menacing and claustrophobic, as though the ghosts of all those villagers and their German executioners still hovered over the silent ground.

Something was wrong. Karl Vonheim must have escaped. The story of his miraculous survival on the night of the massacre was part of the folklore of the music world. He could not remember when he had first heard it, but he had known it for as long as he had been aware of the conductor himself. It was one of the few things that everyone had always known about Vonheim's life. The gaps came later and, unless he had a change of heart, would remain undisclosed until he decided to reveal them.

Peter frowned. He had just seen a memorial plaque that included Karl Vonheim's name. The dates were right, too. The verger had confirmed that he had escaped as far as the church, but only to die a few hours later. Who, then, had survived? Was there a second son, a brother perhaps? If so, which man died in the church? And who had removed the page from the register? Why? It was unlikely that vandals would choose only that one sheet. Besides, he had not bothered to point it out to the old man, but the page had been carefully removed, using a sharp blade, so that its absence was barely noticeable. Why?

He rejoined the main road. The sky was growing darker and sleet was starting to fall. He reduced speed, turning on the windscreen wipers to remove spray thrown up by faster-moving vehicles. His headlights picked up flecks of snow in their beams.

There couldn't have been a second son. It was a wild theory. And, if there had been, why should he bother to assume Karl's identity? It made no sense! He stared at the highway, thinking aloud. 'Start at the beginning. Karl Vonheim escapes from the massacre at Fjordby, hides in the mountains and, when his wounds have healed, finds his way across Europe to study in Munich under Otto Thomas. Thomas introduces him to Lancelot Gordon, who takes him to London, and the rest is history.' He frowned angrily. 'But it isn't history! I've just seen his grave and spoken to a man who remembers how he died! He says that Vonheim is a very common Norwegian name. Therefore, it must be some other Vonheim who went to Munich and emerged as a conductor. Why did he want the world to believe he was a survivor from Fjordby? Personal glory? A glamorous background? Bullshit! Vonheim spends his life avoiding publicity!'

The car was entering a long downhill section of the road, cut into a narrow ledge of mountainside. From his position on the inside lane, Peter was conscious of the steep slope that bordered his side of the road. He was so preoccupied with his thoughts that he had not noticed the powerful vehicle that had been following him for several miles and which was now only a few feet from his rear bumper. 'Suppose his name isn't Karl Vonheim. Suppose he's somebody totally different. Who the bloody hell is he?' There was a jarring shudder as the car behind him made contact, accelerating suddenly and jolting him forward. 'Jesus Christ!'

It came at him again, this time maintaining a constant speed, so that it forced Peter's car to accelerate against his will. His automatic reaction was to put his foot on the brake, but the weight of the other vehicle was too great, and he felt himself being thrown forward at a rapidly increasing pace. He pressed hard on the accelerator and the Fiat responded, creating a small space between the vehicles. A moment later the bigger car crashed into him again. This time it had moved slightly to the centre of the road, putting pressure on the left side of the bumper and forcing Peter closer towards the edge. They were travelling at 140 kilometres an hour, and he gripped the steering-wheel, desperately trying to hold the Fiat steady as it slowly veered towards the precipitous drop at his side. The bodywork vibrated and he could hear the tyres screeching as they turned against the direction in which he was travelling. He was now only inches from the low crash-barrier. The road fell away and, for an instant, he could see a valley far below. He was not certain for how much longer he could control the car, and glanced up into the rear-view mirror. In the glare of the headlights, he could not see the other driver's face. In a final effort he let in the clutch and, accelerating to full power, threw the lever into a lower gear. The engine screamed as gears meshed, but the sudden surge made the car leap forward, breaking contact with the machine that was inexorably forcing him over the edge. It gave him the space he needed and, as he momentarily found himself freed, Peter urged the Fiat sharply to his left, moving across the centre of the road. He was vaguely aware of a heavy lorry, its lights blazing, driving straight towards him. The vehicle behind him lurched forward again but by the time it reached him it struck the right bumper violently, knocking him into a spin that threw him, careening wildly, across the middle of the road. The Fiat slithered, out of control, until it crashed heavily into the rocky ledge of the hillside and buried itself in piled snow. One of the side windows shattered, and it rocked crazily from side to side, but it did not turn over. Shaken and bruised, Peter turned in his seat to see the other car, a large Volvo, racing away at high speed down the hill. Within seconds it was out of sight. A moment later, the lorry passed, its horns blaring. It slowed to a stop thirty yards away, and the driver jumped from his cabin and ran towards him.

He was a big, red-faced man in overalls, and hammered angrily on the window, shouting unintelligibly. After a moment he dragged the door open and glared at Peter, swearing in Norwegian. His fist was clenched, and he looked as though he were about to throw a punch.

Peter held up a hand. 'English!'

The man hesitated. 'What you doing, you crazy bastard? I nearly kill you!'

'The other car.' He was panting like a sprinter. 'It tried to run me down!'

'What you say?'

'The car behind me. It tried to force me off the road. Didn't you see?'

The man reacted slowly. 'No.' He was still suspicious.

Peter gasped for breath. 'He tried to run me off the road, over the edge. I only just made it!'

'You mean he . . . ?'

'Yes!' He was shouting. 'He tried to kill me!'

'God!' He stared in disbelief and was silent. After a moment, he asked, 'Are you OK?'

'I think so.' He was shaking. 'Can you help me?'

The man nodded. 'Try your engine. I will pull you out of there.' He reached into a back pocket and produced a small bottle of spirits. Suddenly, he grinned. 'You better drink this. You look like you need it!'

They dragged Peter's car back to the road and, after checking the wheels and tyres, the Norwegian left him to make his own way back to Bergen. The Fiat was dented in several places, and shattered glass covered the back seat, but it was mobile. The lorry driver, now friendly, had wrenched back the metal of a crumpled front wing to give the wheel freedom to turn. In his large hands, the bodywork might have been made of tinfoil.

He drove cautiously, constantly on the look-out for the Volvo, but it did not reappear. After a few miles, he stopped trembling and relaxed, leaning his head against the padded rest on the driving seat. The light was fading rapidly by the time he reached the outskirts of Bergen.

He was tempted to go straight to the hotel. A drink and a hot bath would revive him, but incessant questions gnawed at his brain. Who had tried to run him down, and why? Because he had been to Fjordby? The verger had said that nobody went there any more. Yesterday, Francesca had been convinced that someone was watching them. For how long had his would-be assassin been following him? It was a frightening thought. The answers had to be connected with Fjordby.

He drove to the centre of the town, and found a parking place near the Grieghalle. Several passers-by eyed his battered car with disapproval and glanced curiously at him, but he ignored them. His mind was following a new train of thought. Cool air cleared his head as he walked briskly along Strom Gaten to the Public Library. It was a large, imposing building, across the park from his hotel.

A white-haired woman stood behind a polished wooden counter, and he approached her. 'Excuse me. I wonder whether you could help me.'

'I will try.' Thank God Norwegians spoke such good English!

'I'm doing some research on a history project. Do you keep back issues of the newspapers here?'

'Of course. How far back do you wish to go?'

'February of 1945. The eleventh. I'm investigating the massacre at Fjordby.'

Her expression was grave. 'That was a dreadful business.'

'You remember it?'

'Yes, but I was quite young at the time.' She smiled charmingly. 'I am not so very old!'

'Of course not. Would you have papers dating back to then?'

'Yes. Most of them have been transferred to microfilm, but we have a machine that you can use. Wait a minute, please.' She returned quite quickly, carrying some boxes. 'These are the daily papers from February, 1945, but I don't think they will offer you very much. Norway was still occupied, if you remember. Anything that was printed had to be approved by the occupying forces.'

'Would they have been permitted to say what happened?'

'No, I don't think so. If they did, it would have been a very cautious reference. It was in the last months of the war and the army was not anxious to draw attention to its activities. They knew the end was near. Do you speak any Norwegian?'

He shook his head. 'While you were away, I was giving silent thanks for the fact that you all speak such good English!'

'Then I will help you. What did you want to know?'

'I was interested in the names of the people who died in Fjordby. I was there today.'

341

'Oh yes? I have never been there but it is interesting that you should inquire. There was someone who asked the same question.'

'When?'

'Quite a long time ago. I believe he said he was a writer. I remember him only because it was the first time anyone had mentioned Fjordby for many years. It is something we prefer to forget. Nearly half a century has passed.' For a moment, her face was sombre. 'What monsters they were!'

'The Germans?'

'No, not all Germans. You cannot condemn a whole race. I was thinking of the SS. They were different. Monsters! The one who ordered the destruction of Fjordby, they called him the Horseman.' Seeing Peter's puzzled expression, she explained. 'He was like the fourth horseman of the Apocalypse: the one who brings death. As children we were terrified of him. We used to frighten each other, saying "The Horseman is coming to get you!" Children play such silly games. We did not like to walk past his house, in case he came out and found us there. We would creep past, after dark, listening to the music.'

'Music?'

'He played the gramophone every evening. Very loud!' She smiled, remembering. 'In those days, Beethoven and Brahms struck terror into our young hearts! Fortunately he never came out. He was rarely seen in public.'

'What happened to him?'

'He died, a few weeks after Fjordby. Our resistance caught him.'

'Did they execute him?'

'In a way. They put a bomb under his car. When he started it the next morning . . . ' She raised her eyebrows, almost comically. 'It was a very large bomb! Justice was swift and quite simple in those days!'

'Was his death reported?'

'Of course.' She smiled. 'Naturally, the newspapers were told to describe it as an act of terrorism, and made some suitable comment, but we knew, and I think the Germans realised that we were all delighted. You must understand that the Wehrmacht were just as frightened of him as we were. Everybody feared the SS!' She looked apologetic. 'Forgive me. You were asking for the names of the people who died in Fjordby. I shouldn't bore you with my reminiscences.'

342

Peter hesitated. 'No. You've been very helpful. I think I'd like to see the report of his death.' He indicated the microfilm. 'Do you have it?'

'Yes. I think I can find it. Come this way, please.'

She led him to a small room, not far from where they had been standing. In it, there was a table holding a machine not unlike a photographic enlarger. She pressed a switch, and a bright light was projected onto the white surface of the table on which it stood.

The woman searched through her rolls of film, and fed one into the machine. She turned a handle, and the film passed through a brightly illuminated slit in the metal. On the flat surface below, the front page of a newspaper appeared, and she adjusted the focus until the print was clear and legible. She examined it. 'No. This is too early. Let me see, Fjordby was February 11, and he died a couple of weeks after. I am too early.' She turned the handle, and the pictures slid past, each one depicting an individual page of the day's paper. She turned the handle quite quickly, only pausing when she reached the front page of a new edition, and checking the date. 'We're getting closer. I need something like February 26 or 27. Ah. Here we are.' On the top right corner of the page displayed, Peter saw that she was at February 26. 'No. Nothing here.' She turned the handle slowly, scanning each page as it came into view. 'Maybe we should look at the editions for March of 1945. These could still be too soon.' She looked up from the machine and smiled at Peter. 'It was a very long time ago.'

He waited silently while she moved from page to page. Inside, he felt a growing tenseness.

Her running commentary continued. 'We may as well work our way through the end of February.' The front page for February 27 came into view and she read the columns. 'Ah! This is what we want. The details are on page four. Let's have a look.' The handle turned again, moving past the first three pages. 'Here it is. Would you like me to read it for you? I can translate as I go along.'

Peter looked at the projected image of the page. There was a small photograph at the head of one column, showing a German officer, wearing the uniform of an SS Captain. It was the sort of official portrait prepared for press releases.

At his side, the woman said, 'That's him. My God! He's little more than a boy, and yet he had the authority to . . . ' She shook her

343

head sadly, then turned to Peter. 'That's the Horseman. His real name was SS-Captain Karl Heinrich von Höst.'

He stared at the handsome, arrogant face. The pale eyes, looking directly into the lens of the camera, gazed straight at him, and he recognised the high cheek-bones, the firm lines of the mouth and jaw; the narrow bridge of the nose. The features had aged over the years, but it seemed to Peter that they were unmistakable.

He was looking at the man he knew as maestro Karl Henrik Vonheim.

31

An icy wind slashed at Peter's face as he walked from his hotel on Central Park towards Lincoln Center. It had snowed earlier and, to keep their sidewalks clear, the doormen of the apartment buildings lining the street had spread chemical pellets on the ground. They crunched underfoot.

The central plaza of the Lincoln Center complex was brightly lit. A queue of yellow taxis deposited passengers, and pedestrians scurried through the bitter cold to find shelter. He turned up his coat collar and quickened his pace. Visible through the long windows of the Metropolitan opera house, the huge paintings by Chagall added a touch of warm colour and, to his right, Avery Fisher Hall, home of the New York Philharmonic, was already filling rapidly with concertgoers. He could see them behind the tinted glass, walking along the different floors of the concert hall. It was like looking at a cutaway section of a luxury ocean liner. A gust of cold wind struck him, and he joined the crowd impatiently filing through the revolving doors, eager to escape the inclement cold snap that had enveloped the city.

It was noisy inside. New Yorkers talk at a higher volume than their European counterparts, and Peter found himself buffeted in a cheerful throng of people divesting themselves of every type of outer garment, ranging from smart, velvet-collared evening coats to quilted parkas designed to withstand Arctic conditions. He felt in his pocket for his ticket, resentfully purchased by Myron Kirschbaum. Benefit galas in the Big Apple were expensive occasions, and the President of Farsight Publications remained unconvinced of the commercial potential of the Karl Vonheim biography. Peter wondered wryly what his reaction would be when he started reading it.

He worked his way through the crowd, noting that many of the men were sporting dinner jackets to accompany their mink-clad

345

companions. New Yorkers loved to dress up. For an uneasy moment it occurred to him that evening dress might be required, but he was relieved to see a wide range of casual costumes contrasted with the formal. Two young men in coloured sports shirts and jeans greeted one another effusively. The women with them were in sweaters and slacks. An elderly man wore an orange blazer that clashed violently with chequered trousers that belonged on a golf course, and Peter smiled to himself. Only in America! His attention was momentarily caught by a small middle-aged woman wearing a simple black evening coat, who walked across his path. She looked vaguely familiar, but her expression was strangely fixed, and he wondered whether she had been taking drugs. The city was the home of the eccentric and the offbeat.

His first objective was to find Francesca. In the morning, he had tried unsuccessfully to go backstage during the rehearsal. Security was rigidly enforced, and the most he had been able to achieve was a reasonable mental lay-out of the building. He made his way to a door leading to the rear, where a uniformed guard was stationed. As he approached, the man pointed towards the banks of escalators leading to the hall's main foyer.

Peter nodded pleasantly. 'It's all right. I'm with the television crew.' He pretended to search for his identification. 'Has Simon Ravenscroft been through this way?'

The guard recognised the name. 'Ravenscroft? Sure. Turn right at the end of the corridor and follow the cables round to the Control Room.' He stood aside to let Peter through.

He found Simon in a room set aside for the sound recording. The audio engineers had set up a portable control console facing two giant loudspeakers and, amid a maze of cables, junction-boxes and recording machines, were making last-minute tests. A large colour television monitor, on which he could see the empty concert stage, was placed between the speakers.

The director was involved in a heated discussion with one of the sound men. At his side, a very pretty blonde, armed with a stop-watch and a clipboard, was listening intently.

Simon's voice was raised. 'I don't give a shit what it does to your pick-up! You can't put a microphone there! It gets in the way of Camera 2.' When the man started to reply, he checked himself and smiled disarmingly. 'I'm sorry, Al, but you'll have to work it out a different way. I'm sure you'll come up with something better.' Al, who did not share his faith, shrugged and returned to his board.

'Hello, Simon. I thought I'd find you here.'

The director's smile faded when he saw Peter and his affability was rather forced. 'Hello, stranger. What brings you to the Big Apple?'

'I'm covering the concert. Francesca invited me.'

'Oh. Well, I suppose that makes it all right.' He looked uncertain. 'I didn't think you were too popular around the old homestead.'

'The maestro's getting used to the idea.'

'That's a relief.' Simon relaxed. 'I wouldn't want a re-run of our last encounter.' The blonde at his side came forward. 'Have you met my assistant, Virginia?' By way of explanation, he added, 'Rachel left, you know.' He turned to her, placing an arm round her shoulder. 'Peter's an old friend of the family.'

Virginia flashed a brilliant smile. She was wearing form-fitting shorts, and the inscription on the T-shirt stretched across her large breasts read: 'Conductors do it by waving their arms'. 'Hi! Call me Ginny.'

Simon's arm tightened round her shoulder. 'It's less of a mouthful.'

This was apparently a cue and, after sharing an intimate giggle with him, she beamed again at Peter. 'You know what they say: virgin for short, but not for long!' Her arm circled Simon's waist and, by the proprietary manner with which he drew her closer, it was clear that they were lovers. Apparently, Simon had not wasted too much time.

Peter looked at his watch. 'I won't get in your hair. You must have a thousand things to worry about.' He glanced round casually. 'Which is the quickest way to Francesca's room?'

'It's one floor up. There's a lift . . . ' He pointed across the room, 'but it's probably quicker to use the stairs.'

'Good. I'll see you later, I expect.' He walked away, leaving Simon and Ginny still locked together. The director was gazing fondly into his assistant's eyes.

There was a corridor on the next floor and Peter found the doors to the dressing-rooms. A card had been attached to the first, bearing

347

the warning: 'Maestro Karl Vonheim – Do Not Enter'. He walked slowly past it, looking for Francesca's room. As he did so, he failed to hear the gentle click of a handle being turned behind him.

Suddenly, his arms were jerked behind his back with jarring force, and he was thrown forward against the wall. His head struck the plaster painfully, leaving him momentarily dazed, and he wondered whether one of the security guards, finding him in a restricted zone, had taken him prisoner. He was about to complain, but his captor swung him bodily in the direction of the conductor's dressing-room, and frog-marched him through the open door. He was very strong and, on entering a small ante-room, threw Peter heavily to the floor. The door slammed shut, and he heard a key turn in the lock. Shaking his head to clear it, Peter looked round at his assailant. Erich, his arms folded, was standing by the door, watching him.

'What the hell do you think you're doing?' He started to rise.

Erich said nothing. Reaching into his jacket, he produced a revolver. It was a small, old-fashioned six-shooter to which a long black silencer had been attached. He pointed the gun almost casually towards Peter and motioned to him to remain on the floor.

Peter stared at the weapon. 'Are you out of your mind?'

A voice behind him spoke. 'He knows exactly what he's doing, Mr Meredith. I suggest you stay where you are. He would have no hesitation in using it.' The maestro was standing in the doorway to his changing-room. Apparently, he had just finished dressing, and was putting on the jacket of his perfectly tailored costume. He walked forward until he was standing directly above Peter. When he spoke his voice was cold. 'Perhaps you would like to explain what you're doing here.'

'I want to see Francesca.' He sat on the floor, his arms clasped around his knees. He could feel the beat of a pulse in his temple.

'Despite my warning? That's very foolish of you.' Vonheim stepped round him, and seated himself on a small settee.

'She's waiting for me. I wanted to wish her good luck.'

The conductor's voice was contemptuous. 'Luck has nothing to do with it. When Miss Noble appears with me tonight the audience will hear a great performance of the Schumann concerto. Few of them will realise how great, but that is of little consequence. I know it, and so will she and a few others. That's all that matters. As for this element of chance that you have the blind ignorance to suggest, I can tell you that her interpretation is the result of preparation, work, concentration and self-discipline: qualities you know nothing about. Furthermore, if you had the slightest conception of what she is going through at this moment, you'd understand that this next half-hour is a critical time, when she must be left alone.'

Peter stared at him. The maestro's face was devoid of expression, the blue-grey eyes unblinking. 'I think that's for her to decide.'

'No. She's a sensitive and vulnerable young woman, still discovering herself and easily influenced by dangerous and unnecessary emotions.' His voice became colder. 'I've already told you to leave her alone. You should have taken my advice more seriously. It's obviously going to be necessary to make sure that you stay away permanently.'

Peter glanced at Erich, who was leaning against the door watching the maestro, the gun resting casually in his hand. 'Your errand boy already tried that on the road into Bergen.' Erich's eyes flickered and his hand tightened round the grip of the revolver.

The maestro shrugged, not bothering to deny the accusation. 'You should have heeded the warning and considered yourself lucky to have escaped. Coming back for more suggests that you are not only ignorant but stupid, Mr Meredith. You should have gone away when you still could.'

'The way you did when you escaped from Bergen, Captain von Höst?' When he spoke the name, he saw Vonheim stiffen and become very still. Peter forced himself to speak calmly. 'That must also have taken concentration, preparation, self-discipline and a hell of a lot of luck: faking your own assassination, and disappearing into the hills!' The maestro said nothing. 'You must have taken the identity cards from the people of Fjordby when you had them destroyed. How very convenient that there was a Karl Vonheim among them, with a name so similar to your own!'

The maestro exchanged glances with Erich. When he spoke, his voice was almost a whisper, and he seemed to be talking to himself. 'After all these years! I must have overlooked something.'

'You mean, in addition to the church register? You missed the memorial.'

349

'Memorial?'

'A small wooden plaque, at the edge of the forest, to mark the communal grave where the people of Fjordby were laid to rest, on the very spot where you had them murdered. I would have missed it myself, but it was shown to me. The names are all there, clearly carved on it for everyone to see; including the one you stole.' In the back of his mind Peter was hoping that, by keeping both men occupied, the time would pass. Sooner or later, someone from the hall – the manager of the orchestra or an usher – would arrive to accompany the maestro to the concert platform. 'Had you planned the impersonation for a long time?'

The maestro hesitated before replying. The hint of a smile on his face was more frightening than his previous lack of emotion. 'No. It was a chance decision, although I'd planned something of a similar nature for some time. That particular war was lost, but there will be another time . . . ' For a moment, he was lost in thought. 'As a matter of fact, my original intention had been only to destroy the houses, but when I saw the name and the age of the man in question, it seemed that an unexpected opportunity had come my way.' He shrugged. 'There was really no alternative.'

'You were luckier than you thought. Karl Vonheim escaped that night. He crawled as far as the church . . . '

'I know.' The cold eyes stared at him. 'I'm a thorough man, Mr Meredith. When I returned to the village a few hours later, I found him there. An additional bullet, and an open door . . . ' He left the sentence unfinished. 'It was a cold night.'

Peter spoke softly. 'You bastard!'

'No, Mr Meredith. As I told you in Vienna, I am a survivor. I have always been a survivor.'

'Weren't you afraid of being discovered? Sooner or later, there was always the possibility.'

'I don't think so. Karl von Höst died at the end of February, 1945. The bomb which annihilated him left no identifiable traces of his body, and he was forgotten: a victim of the Norwegian resistance. The new Karl Vonheim travelled to a remote corner in the north, seeking refuge. Within a couple of months, the war was over and the world was preoccupied with recovery and the new menace coming from Russia. So, when a young bearded Norwegian who

350

happened to speak fluent German found his way through the chaos of Europe to begin a new life, nobody ever questioned his identity.'

'My God! You sit there, calmly discussing it, as though . . . ' He shook his head in wonder.

'What do you expect me to do: fall to my knees in a fit of remorse? It was a war, Mr Meredith, and I was on the losing side.' He paused. 'I only ever had a single ambition: to become a conductor. Circumstances prevented me from doing it sooner. It was a matter of time before I realised my objective.'

Peter hesitated. Five minutes had passed. In another ten, somebody from the orchestra . . . 'When did you remove the page from the register?'

The conductor was more sure of himself. 'A few years ago. You've been to Fjordby, Mr Meredith. Nobody goes there any more. They would prefer to forget what happened.' His voice was harsh. 'Forget! The place is an unpleasant reminder of an era that has gone. In a few years, it will be removed from the map.'

'Perhaps. It's not as easy as that. You can't erase history because it's more convenient.' He waited for a response, but the conductor did not speak. 'So you studied with Otto Thomas? At least he was sympathetic to your cause!'

'We never discussed politics.' He saw Peter's expression. 'I don't care whether you believe that or not. It happens to be true. Yes, I developed my career: dedicated my life to my work, and preferred to remain isolated from my colleagues. There were times when it would have been . . . pleasant to enjoy the notoriety that some of them relish but, as the years passed, I realised that I didn't need it. My withdrawal was, if anything, more intriguing.'

'Weren't you afraid of running into somebody who might remember you; recognise you?'

'There was nobody. My family was dead, and my . . . former associates were anxious for anonymity. Don't believe all those stories about secret societies, Mr Meredith. They make good adventures but they have little truth to them. I was a young man when the war began and, even during those years, I spent little time with my fellow officers. There was too much music to study.'

'Nevertheless, you began to travel.'

'True. Why do you think I chose South America? It was not only

351

Lancelot Gordon that drove me to divide my time between two continents.'

'And you never met . . . ?'

'Strangely enough, yes, in Argentina.' He paused for a moment, apparently lost in thought. 'Dorothea's family had problems of their own. They had . . . emigrated at the end of the war and had no desire to draw attention to themselves.' He glanced towards Erich, and Peter was puzzled by the expression which crossed his face. 'Under certain circumstances, one must make compromises – sacrifices, even – and she was a charming young woman; a very suitable companion for a successful conductor . . . ' He relapsed into silence.

'Other people have asked about Fjorby.' Peter watched him carefully.

His words seemed to interrupt the maestro's thoughts. 'Only one, as far as I know. He was another would-be biographer, and asked a few questions in Norway. I learned about him, and we reached an . . . agreement.' Once again, he exchanged glances with Erich, and Peter guessed that he was referring to the man who had visited the Public Library in Bergen. It was not difficult to guess the kind of 'agreement' they had reached. The maestro continued, 'He discussed his book with my late manager, Gregory Richmond, and decided to set aside any further work on the project.' He stared at Peter for a moment. 'Of course, Richmond over-estimated his importance to me. Now that he's no longer with us, it appears that you are the only remaining . . . obstacle. Tell me, what made you come here tonight?'

'To be with Francesca. I didn't come to see you. In fact, if you want to know the truth, I don't really give a damn about you!'

'But you know so much about me. I'm curious to learn how.'

'The evidence is sitting there, for anyone to find, and you can't do a damn thing about it! In fact, I suppose I should thank your errand boy for pointing me towards it.' He looked at Erich with contempt. 'If he hadn't tried to run me off the road, I would never have thought of looking in the Public Library.'

'There is nothing there. They did not list the names from Fjordby.'

'No.' Peter spoke softly. 'But they did print your obituary, together with a photograph.' He had the satisfaction of seeing the conductor turn pale. 'It's an excellent likeness, if you know what you're looking for. You see, I wanted to know what the butcher of Fjordby – the notorious Horseman – looked like. I should have guessed what I would find.'

The room was silent. On a table, a small television monitor, connected to the cameras downstairs, showed the first members of the orchestra taking their places on the stage. In the background, a low murmur of sound became audible as the audience entered the hall.

The maestro spoke in a low voice. 'You've known all this for three weeks. Why have you done nothing?'

'Because of Francesca. I have to get her away from you.'

'Why now? You could have called her sooner. You could have revealed what you know.'

Peter shook his head. 'I couldn't reach her and, even if I could, I know what this concert means to her. I've said nothing for her sake. This whole ugly business has waited half a century. Three additional weeks don't matter. As soon as the concerto is over, she'll leave with me.'

'No! She can't throw herself away on you! I won't permit her to . . .'

'You can't stop her.'

The maestro stood. 'But I can stop you. Erich!' He spoke sharply, and the man brought his revolver up so that it pointed directly at Peter.

The journalist stared at him in disbelief. 'You'd never get away with it. What are you going to say: that it was an accident?'

'That may not be necessary.' He turned to Erich. 'No-one is to enter this room. Understood?'

Peter watched him. 'You're mad!'

'On the contrary, I was never more lucid. By removing you, Mr Meredith, I can solve two problems. First, my little secret will remain undiscovered. The records in the Bergen library can be altered. Documents are lost, from time to time. You told me yourself that anyone searching has to know what he's looking for.' Once again, his glance slid towards Erich. 'It was easy enough to remove your pitiful little collection of memorabilia.' The maestro seemed to

353

speak to himself. 'My own obituary! What a careless thing to over-look!'

'You'll never get away with it.'

The maestro ignored him. 'Secondly, with you out of the way, Francesca will be free to continue her career. She doesn't need you, and I haven't devoted all this time and care to see it thrown away on some petty, mindless infatuation. Without you, she'll dedicate herself to her work with a greater fervour than before. I'll be there to see that she does. She trusts me.'

'I wouldn't count on that.'

'I can be very persuasive. Maybe I'll tell her that you and I talked; that I convinced you that her career was more important and, as a reward for your self-denial, that I have agreed to collaborate with you on my biography.' The smile returned. 'What a noble self-sacrifice on your part!'

'She'll never believe you. Besides, how do you know I haven't told anyone what I've learned?'

The maestro stared at him. 'Because of Francesca. You wouldn't dare, for her sake! You may be prepared to wait an extra three weeks. No-one else would.' He walked across the room. 'No, Mr Meredith, looking at you, I believe my secret is still safe.'

For the first time, Peter was afraid. He tried to keep his voice even. 'And what do you propose to do: claim you shot a burglar? This is Lincoln Center. How do you hope to bluff your way out of it?'

The maestro addressed Erich. 'No-one is to enter this room.' Then he faced Peter. 'I think my working habits are familiar enough. Nobody will come in. Later, we'll have the minor problem of . . . removing you from the building. We will find a way. Fortunately, a city like New York has a constant supply of victims of street attacks. They're so frequent that they hardly warrant a news item. It would be just another mugging!' He paused. 'On the other hand, Central Park would be an ideal location.' He shrugged. 'A visitor to the city, unaware of its dangers, might easily stray into it after dark. You may use your limited imagination!'

'You won't get away with it.'

'So you say. On the other hand, you'll never know, either way.' His voice hardened. 'Keep him here, Erich. We'll deal with him later. If he gives you any problems, kill him.' He faced Peter.

'Goodbye, Mr Meredith. I suppose I should congratulate you on your detective work. Perhaps you're a better journalist than I suspected.' He indicated the television monitor with a nod. The stage was now filled with musicians. He turned a knob on the set, and the room was filled with the sound of players tuning their instruments. 'At least you'll be able to watch the performance. It should make an appropriate finale to your career as a music critic!' The maestro passed quickly through the door and Erich locked it behind him.

Francesca sat before the mirror in her room. She found herself staring at a stranger whom she did not recognise. The face was calm and untroubled, the hair perfectly in place, the folds of the dark maroon silk dress hanging evenly. Around her neck, the little Victorian pendant gleamed against pale skin. Who was this person? That day, so long ago in Switzerland, Peter had called her serene. If only he knew . . . ! She closed her eyes, fighting back the anxiety that welled up inside.

This was the moment she had worked towards for the past year; no, for the past twenty-five years. It was as though her entire existence was now focused on one time and place. All the hours of practice and study, of listening and talking and arguing and learning from Karl, of punishing self-doubt and elated discovery, came to a halt, but all she could think was: 'Oh God, don't let me fail him now! Let it all fall into place, at last, the way it was intended!'

The concerto had become an extension of herself. She had lived with it day after day, polishing and perfecting each note of each phrase, until it seemed that all other activities were subsidiary to the moment when she would find herself at the keyboard, awaiting his opening downbeat. There had been a dream-like quality to the morning rehearsal. Her hands had moved naturally across the keys, as though directed by an unseen force, and the music had emerged from within her. It was as though she no longer controlled what was happening. At the end, she had been conscious of the orchestra applauding, the string players tapping their bows on their instruments in traditional acclaim, but she remembered little else. Karl had smiled, nodding approval, but her attention had been entirely concentrated on the music. Driving back to the hotel, she had not heard what he was saying and, as soon as she entered her room, she had fallen on the bed and slept. Waking, her first thought, as always, had been of Peter. Where was he? Why hadn't he called? Would he be there? Then, when she had washed and dressed, preferring to change at the hotel, Karl had arrived to take her to the hall. Erich had driven them. It was like being back in Lausanne, and Karl had murmured, 'Go to the dressing-room and rest. No-one will disturb you. Try to empty your mind of everything except the music.' People had greeted her in the corridor but she had not heard them. It was as though she were still sleeping.

There was a knock on the door, and she opened her eyes. Could it be Peter? He had promised to be there. The stranger in the mirror watched, and Karl appeared. She stood and, when he opened his arms, ran to him.

He felt her trembling. 'Are you nervous? That's good.' His voice was soothing. 'The adrenalin needs to flow. Once we begin, you'll forget all about it. Believe me, Francesca, you'll fly! Isn't that how you like to describe it?'

'Oh Karl!' There was such a lot to say to him: so much love and gratitude to express, but no adequate words.

He seemed to sense this, and he held her. 'Don't worry. I'm here!'

'I'm not worried. It's just that there's so much I want to say to you. I don't know where to begin.' He stood back, smiling with mock solemnity. 'No, don't laugh at me, Karl. I owe you everything. You've taught me so much, given me so much. Everything I am: everything I know has come from you! A year ago, I was just another hopeful kid with a music degree and, maybe, a couple of ounces of talent, but it was nothing! You've opened up a whole world that I never knew existed. I don't know how to thank you for that. There are millions of words going round in my head, but they won't come out the right way. I wish I could express the love, the gratitude . . . ' She shook her head. 'I don't know how to say it!'

'You'll say it with your piano, and I'll be there to share it with you.' He spoke very softly. 'We don't have to talk. I'm so proud of you, Francesca. Tonight will be very special for both of us.'

'I want it to be perfect for you!'

'It will be, but you must think of it only as another step forward: a new beginning. Tomorrow, you start the next chapter of your life.'

'Always tomorrow! Don't I ever stop for a minute?'

'One day. Not yet. There's so much to learn, and you're only beginning. I just wanted you to know that I will be there for you.' For a moment, he was thoughtful. 'I will always be there. Remember that.'

'I don't understand.'

'You will.' He glanced towards her television monitor. 'I think they're expecting me.' For a moment, he pretended to look severe. 'Please be there, ready for me, when the overture finishes. I hate to be kept waiting!'

Peter was on the settee, facing the television. At his side, but with a safe space between them, Erich let the revolver rest in the crook of his arm.

'You may as well relax. Nothing will happen until Karl tells me. Don't do anything silly.'

He glanced at the man. 'He's Karl now? What happened to "maestro"?'

Erich smiled secretively. 'We're closer than you think.' He smirked. 'Much, much closer.'

'I might have guessed. It must be handy to have a lover to do all your dirty work for you. I suppose it was you who disposed of that other writer. Presumably, Karl's arrangement involved another little walk through Central Park.'

'Something like that.'

'And Richmond.' He made it a statement more than a question. 'Nobody understood why he'd want to commit suicide.'

Erich shrugged. 'He shouldn't have tried blackmail. He was stupid enough to think it would give him control over Karl.'

'So he knew?'

'Enough to be dangerous.'

'And if anything goes wrong you're the one who'll take the blame. Karl certainly knows what he's doing!'

Erich looked at him pityingly. 'Nothing's going to go wrong so don't get your hopes up. If you have any ideas about getting away,

357

or frightening me, you can forget them. I'd quite happily put you away now. I've done it before.'

'So it was you who broke into my flat? You've been a busy little man!'

'All in the day's work.' His eyes were hooded. 'I should have hit you harder. It would have saved us both a lot of trouble.' On the monitor, the orchestra had risen to its feet, and there was a sudden burst of loud applause as the maestro appeared. 'Do you want to watch?'

'I may as well. There's not a lot else to do, is there?'

Erich let the muzzle of the silencer stroke Peter's cheek. 'Talk's cheap. Be as brave as you like, but do it quietly!'

The concert opened with Beethoven's *Leonora No. 3* Overture. It was a fine performance, and the strings of the New York Philharmonic played with spine-tingling excitement. Conscious of Erich at his side, Peter listened distractedly. In the past, he would have thrilled to the control with which the maestro led them into the climactic finale. He heard the precision of their playing, but there was a cold ruthlessness to it. Perhaps there always had been, but he had been hypnotised by Vonheim. From time to time, he glanced at Erich. The man watched the monitor, but his revolver was aimed at Peter's heart. At one point, he looked up, and their eyes met. His expression was almost bored as he gestured towards the screen, indicating that Peter should watch.

The work ended triumphantly and was greeted with loud cheers. In the sustained ovation that followed, Simon directed his cameras to roam around the auditorium, showing patrons on their feet, applauding strenuously. The conductor had now left the stage, and would not return until the next work, leaving the director with time to kill. The cheering continued. It was the sort of reception usually reserved for the end of the evening, but the maestro inspired a response bordering on mass hysteria.

At last, the sound was electronically faded to allow a television commentator to offer a few introductory comments about the Schumann piano concerto, and Erich snickered. 'Why do American announcers always sound as though they're at a funeral? They're so pretentious!'

'What do you expect: a couple of one-liners?'

'They don't have to be so bloody funereal. You can hear the man

358

trying to drop his voice an octave. I suppose he thinks it's more dignified.' For a man holding a gun, he was casually off-hand, and Peter shifted his position slightly. If he became absorbed in the music . . .

Erich must have sensed his move and was immediately alert. 'Don't get any clever ideas. I'm not afraid to use this.'

When Francesca appeared on the screen, the audience greeted her warmly. Howard Erlich and his public relations team had been heralding her arrival for several weeks, placing special emphasis on the Cinderella story of her discovery by the great conductor. New Yorkers liked a winner, and welcomed her. She stood for a moment, nervously accepting their greeting, and Simon's close-up was tightly focused on her head and shoulders. She was even more beautiful than Peter remembered, and he recognised the gold pendant at her throat. The camera moved back to show the maestro waiting on the podium behind her and, as she seated herself, the hall became silent.

It was a magnificent performance. Despite everything, Peter forgot his captor and his surroundings to listen to her playing. In the opening flourish, a descending series of dramatic chords, he wondered whether she had finally chosen a heroic approach, but as the movement unfolded, she played with warm lyricism, balancing power with poetry. The maestro complemented everything Francesca did, encouraging woodwind soloists to exchange phrases with the piano and giving the impression that each new musical idea came from a single source. It was a perfect partnership, with a maturity and depth of understanding that transcended anything she had played in Bergen. At the end of the movement, there was an audible rustle of excitement in the hall. Despite the maestro's dismissive prediction, people were aware that they were hearing something very special.

The graceful Intermezzo was thoughtful and filled with charm, and the dialogue between soloist and orchestra had an intimacy that was like eavesdropping on a lover's conversation. The delicacy with which Karl Vonheim directed the orchestra gave the music a whole spectrum of gently gradated colours. It ended almost too soon.

The second movement led directly into the finale. Woodwinds echoed a memory from earlier in the concerto, punctuated by responses from the soloist. The winds persisted, growing in volume, until

the piano suddenly swept everything aside with the joyful theme
that was to dominate the movement. Something magical happened.
It was as though a tension was released from deep within Francesca,
and the piano, borne by the orchestra, took wing. Her fingers sped
across the keyboard, creating uninhibited pleasure, and the musicians responded, carrying everything forward. Oblivious of his
predicament, Peter watched and listened as the concerto soared and
weaved, as free and joyous as a bird gliding and floating on the
wind. It was no longer Francesca and the maestro, no longer a piano
and an orchestra, no longer printed notes on paper, no longer musicians playing instruments, but the pure abstract ecstasy that only
music can convey. The sound enveloped him, transported him and
filled his consciousness until he was removed from all earthly
bonds.

Long before the final chords had died, the audience started cheering, and a massive wave of applause surged through the auditorium.
Francesca rose from the piano and, ignoring the roar that greeted
her, turned to watch Karl step from the podium. He bowed low over
her hands and, as he did so, she leaned forward to kiss his cheek.
The gesture delighted the spectators, who raised their voices in
approval as conductor and soloist turned to face them. Francesca
smiled radiantly, released from all the pressures that had weighed
upon her, and the cheering redoubled. Moments later, at a signal
from Karl, she led the way through the orchestra, who were also
applauding, to the exit on the side of the stage.

They stood together, listening to the thunderous acclamation, and
Karl inclined his head. 'You'd better go out there again.'

Her eyes shone. 'On one condition: that you come with me.'

'You know I never take a second bow.'

'Make an exception. Please Karl! Just this one time. For me!'

He laughed. 'Is it that important?'

'Yes. It will make it different from any other time.' She listened
for a moment. The applause had grown louder. 'Will you?'

'Very well.'

Together, they returned to the stage, and the audience gave a great
shout of approval. They walked to the front and stood, hand in hand,
to accept the ovation.

*

360

The small, middle-aged woman wearing a simple black evening coat walked slowly down the centre aisle of the auditorium until she was standing before the stage, a few feet from the conductor and soloist. One of the ushers noted her presence and thought of asking her to move back. She appeared harmless enough and, any-way, the house was going wild with elation. Simon, directing a long shot from the rear of the hall, considered bringing another camera into play, to take the intruder out of his picture.

The woman stared up into the maestro's face and, for a moment, their eyes met. He was about to look away, but there was something vaguely familiar about her. They must have met on a previous occasion.

Suddenly, her face was distorted with anger and hatred. 'You filthy, fucking animal! Pervert! Murderer!' The words, screamed above the roar of the applause, were audible.

The maestro stepped back, puzzled by her attack. At his side, Francesca gasped, moving closer to him. The woman was mad! His glance flicked to the side of the hall, where an usher was running forward.

The woman stood very still, watching him, then reached into a pocket. When she withdrew her hand, it was holding a revolver. She raised her arm, pointing the gun at him, and her finger tightened around the trigger.

'This is for my son! This is for Günther!'

Four shots rang out in quick succession. The maestro staggered backwards, still on his feet. He clutched at his chest, and on the starched front of his shirt, a dark patch appeared, spreading rapidly. The liquid ran through his fingers. There was a look of astonishment on his face. Someone screamed. Then he started to move forward, stumbled, and fell headlong. One of the violinists pulled Francesca clear, shielding her with his body.

'Holy Jesus Christ!' In the Control Room, Simon watched it happen. 'Somebody get a fix on her! Camera 3, can you pick her up? For God's sake, get in close!' On the panel of television screens in front of him, the images blurred as cameras were turned and focused on the woman. For an instant, every monitor in the room showed Gisela's tortured face, captured at different angles.

She stood quite still, the gun now at her side, looking at the body of the man she had just killed, unaware of the howl of sound that surrounded her. A moment later, two men hurled themselves on top of her, and she disappeared beneath a mass of bodies.

Upstairs, Erich was on his feet, watching the picture incredulously. The hand holding his revolver hung loose, and he stepped forward, peering at the screen as though hypnotised.

Peter moved quickly. Exerting all his strength, he chopped the side of his hand down on the back of Erich's neck, felling him with the blow. The man was unconscious when his body hit the floor.

He lifted the gun clear and pocketed it. Unlocking the door, he transferred the key to the outside, and locked it behind him. Then he raced the length of the corridor to the stairs that led down to the stage. He knew that Francesca would be there, waiting for him.